THE BOUND SERIES

"The complex nature of the characters, their situation, the setting and really passionate sex lead to an excellent story and I found myself hoping for more of these two in the future."
—*Rainbow Reviews* on Bound by Deception

"*Bound by Deception* is a well-written, steamy book that I gobbled up in one sitting. I would recommend it to those who like historicals, erotica, and/or have a place in their heart for some BDSM."
—*Reviews by Jessewave* on Bound by Deception

"I adored the main characters far too much—their interactions and conversations rang true, their own complex natures and inner torments kept my attention. Seized it, actually. I couldn't stop reading this one."
—*Whipped Cream Romance Reviews* on Bound to Him

"I really liked this novella because of the strong writing, the well-drawn characters and the amount of period detail that all fuses together seamlessly and in that effortless way that betrays a great writer at work."
—*Speak Its Name* on Bound to Him

"If you have not read an Ava March book you are in for a real treat with this series. *Bound Forever* is a lovely send off for Vincent and Oliver and I was very happy with the final book in this very sexy, romantic series."
—*Fiction Vixen Book Reviews* on Bound Forever

"I absolutely loved this book by Ava March. This historical romance has elements of deep love and passion that pulls at my heart for both these wonderful men."
—*The Romance Studio* on Bound Forever

Other titles by Ava March

BEYOND RECKLESS
BROOK STREET: THIEF
BROOK STREET: FORTUNE HUNTER
BROOK STREET: ROGUES
CONVINCING ARTHUR
CONVINCING LEOPOLD
FROM AFAR
HIS CLIENT
MY TRUE LOVE GAVE TO ME
OBJECT OF HIS DESIRE
PLEASURES OF SOMERVILLE PARK

The Bound Series

AVA MARCH

The Bound Series
Bound by Deception Copyright © 2008 by Ava March
Bound to Him Copyright © 2009 by Ava March
Deliberately Unbound Copyright © 2010 by Ava March
Bound Forever Copyright © 2011 by Ava March
Deliberately Bound Copyright © 2011 by Ava March

All rights are reserved. No part of this work may be sold, manipulated, or reproduced in any manner whatsoever without written permission from the author.

The Bound Series paperback edition
ISBN-13: 978-1478230755
ISBN-10: 1478230754
Cover Artist: Hot Damn Designs

Published by
Ava March
www.avamarch.com

This is a work of fiction. The names, characters, places and incidents are products of the writer's imagination or have been used fictitiously and are not construed to be real. Any resemblance to persons, living or dead, actual events, locale or organizations is entirely incidental.

Warning
This work contains sexually explicit scenes and graphic language and may be considered offensive to some readers. Intended for adult audiences only. Not intended for anyone under the age of 18. Please store your books wisely, where they cannot be accessed by under-aged readers.

* * *

DISCLAIMER: Please do not try any new sexual practice, especially those that might be found in this BDSM title without the guidance of an experienced practitioner. The author will not be responsible for any loss, harm, injury or death resulting from use of the information contained in this title.

CONTENTS

Bound by Deception	7
Bound to Him	83
Deliberately Unbound (Short Story)	177
Bound Forever	193
Deliberately Bound (Short Story)	287

Bound by Deception

Lord Oliver Marsden has a secret. He's been in love with his childhood friend for years, though Vincent's never shown an interest in him beyond friendship. Ruggedly handsome, wealthy, and successful, Vincent is everything Oliver is not. And Vincent doesn't prefer men.

Then Oliver discovers Vincent hires a man during his visits to a London brothel. Desperate to be with Vincent, Oliver orchestrates a deception, switching places with the brothel's employee. When Oliver arrives at the bedchamber, he's in for another surprise. Restraints and a leather bullwhip? Apparently Vincent isn't as conservative as he appears.

Lord Vincent Prescot has a secret of his own. One kept locked away and only indulged once a month. But this month's appointment is different. The mysterious man is so perfect, so beautiful in his submission, rousing protective instincts Vincent can't deny. Yet he refuses to believe he might truly prefer men, for it could mean the end of his hopes of earning his father's respect.

Chapter One

April 1822
London, England

"How much?"

Madame Delacroix tapped a finger to her rouged lips. "Your request is unique."

"I don't believe I'm the first man to make such a request. Certainly there is some precedent."

"Of course." The madam tucked an errant strand of auburn hair behind her ear. "But in a situation such as yours, one man is not interchangeable for another. That it is *your* request makes it unique."

Her falsely aristocratic tone held a confidence that made Lord Oliver Marsden shift uncomfortably in the crimson leather chair. He avoided this woman whenever possible, preferring to deal directly with her employees, but tonight he had no choice. After gathering his courage, he had come to this office and voiced the fantasy that haunted his dreams and most every waking moment. He would find a way to pay whatever price she named, and the madam who sat behind the satinwood desk clearly knew it. He could only hope his father, the Marquis of Campden, had a reputation that preceded him, and that she would not inflate the price overmuch for fear of going beyond Oliver's means.

But there was no reason to make it *too* easy for her. Oliver squared his shoulders. "You will receive payment from Lord Vincent as well. You will earn double, and your employee will be free to see to another client."

"That is correct." Delacroix stood. The soft swoosh of her crimson silk gown broke the silence as she walked to a console table along the wall. She glanced over her shoulder. "Would you care for a drink?"

Even a bottle of whiskey couldn't unravel the knots in his stomach. "No, thank you."

A scowl flickered across her brow. Likely the woman was unaccustomed to hearing the word no. She half filled a short, plain glass with clear liquid. The scent just made its way to his nose. Glass clinked as she replaced the stopper in the tall narrow bottle. Her choice of drink belied the contrived elegance of the room and of her appearance. She did, however, manage to take a very demure sip of the gin.

"You have requested the use of my establishment."

Oliver tipped his head then hastily pushed up his spectacles, which had slid down the bridge of his nose. "It is a necessity. He frequents your establishment on the first Thursday of every month, not another's."

Resting a hip against the console table, she swirled the contents of her glass. "You wish to deceive one of my clients. A faithful, reliable, well-paying client. Lord Vincent Prescot would not be pleased if he learns of my role in your scheme."

"He will never find out."

"He could," she said, with a casual lift of one shoulder.

"You assured me the whore will keep her silence. I will never tell him, and I will take every precaution to ensure he does not discover it is me."

She arched an eyebrow. "Lord Vincent is an astute man. He will recognize you. The stubble from a three-day-old beard will not fool him."

Oliver passed a hand over his bristly jaw. "Nor am I fool enough to believe it will. At least not by itself. The room will be dark, and Lord Vincent will have no reason to even suspect my true identity. He will believe what the whore will tell him—that I am simply a replacement for the man he usually hires."

He had known Vincent since childhood. Both second sons to marquises, they had met on the first day of boarding school, and for reasons Oliver still couldn't explain, the stiff and proper eleven-year-old boy had gravitated to him. An average student at the best of times, Oliver only kept from getting expelled on numerous occasions because Vincent tutored him. In return, Oliver congratulated Vincent first whenever he received top marks, which happened more often than not. Nearly inseparable, they even spent holidays together at Vincent's grandfather's Dorset estate. For a space of about four years, Oliver didn't return home once. Based on the lack of letters, it seemed no one had missed him. With a father who practically lived at the gambling tables and an elder brother who never bothered with him, Oliver doubted they even noticed his absence. Those holidays spent fishing, swimming, and hunting with Vincent were the most treasured of his youth. Then Vincent had gone onto Cambridge and Oliver…had not.

Though no longer as close, in their thirteen years of friendship, Vincent never once hinted at an interest in men. Apparently something he never wished to share, never wished to reveal—a reluctance he understood, as he hadn't confided his own preferences to Vincent. And if Vincent found out what he planned to do tomorrow night, he knew without a doubt Vincent would see it as a betrayal of the utmost proportions. It was one thing to indulge secret desires in the safety and obscurity of a brothel, quite another to take a friend as a lover.

After refilling her glass, Delacroix sat back down behind her desk. She was silent for a long moment. It took all of Oliver's willpower to hold her unwavering gaze.

"You have specifically asked for my discretion in this matter," she said.

They had reached the true basis for her price, and he had, in a roundabout way, told her how important it was to him that Vincent remain ignorant of his deception. He resisted the urge to shake his head in self-disgust. Christ, if Vincent were in his place, he would have convinced the madam to pay him for the night. Vincent excelled at everything he did whereas he always fell short. Fell considerably short, and tonight it may very well cost him a chance with Vincent.

He dragged a hand through his hair. "Yes. Again, it is a necessity," he said, unable to keep the defeat from his tone.

Her kohl-rimmed eyes glinted with unmistakable triumph. She had him by the ballocks and he could only hope she wouldn't twist too hard.

She pulled a square of white paper from her desk drawer, dipped her pen in the silver inkwell, and contemplated the blank paper. Pulse pounding in his ears, Oliver sat perfectly still as she tapped the nib against the inkwell. *Please, don't turn me into a eunuch.* The soft scratch of the pen seemed unnaturally loud when she finally began writing.

"Given the uniqueness of your request, you will find the price to be within reason," she said, sliding the paper across her desk.

Leaning forward, he picked up the paper. He closed his eyes, praying he had enough to compensate the madam for her discretion. He had assumed his request would cost him far more than the usual rate to hire one of her employees. The income from the small inheritance he'd received from his mother covered his expenses but left little to spare, and as such, he had been spending quite a bit of time in smoke-filled gambling hells of late. It had taken him months to win big at the gaming tables. If the sum exceeded the fold of pound notes in his pocket, it might be many more long months before he could return to this office and voice his request again.

Holding his breath, he slowly opened one eye. His shoulders sagged with relief. The two remaining paintings gracing the walls of his meager bachelor apartments would need to be sold, but combined with his winnings, he could afford one night with Vincent.

He pulled the pound notes from his coat pocket. "The remainder will be delivered later tonight."

She tipped her head, accepting his offer. The edges of her rouged lips curved in gloating satisfaction. Experienced madam that she was, she had somehow known just how far she could inflate the price. She took another sip of gin. "When Holly brings Lord Vincent to the room, she will inform him his usual man is unavailable," she said, referring to the blonde girl Vincent always selected in view of the brothel's other clients.

"What if he protests?"

"If he does, Holly will manage the situation. Hence why it's necessary she's informed of your scheme. But he won't protest. He comes here for a man. As long as the individual is passably handsome, Lord Vincent will bugger him."

Her blunt answer lanced his heart. Somehow he kept the wince from marring his brow. All Vincent sought was a man to warm a bed, when all Oliver wanted was Vincent. Tomorrow night would mean everything to him and nothing at all to the man he loved.

"There is a backdoor that leads out to the courtyard," she said. "Be there at eleven tomorrow evening. A servant will greet you and bring you to the room."

He nodded.

Her efficient tone vanished to be replaced with firm command. "This establishment is renowned for the quality of its services. All of my employees are expected to leave their clients with a very big smile on their faces. Since you will be standing in the place of one of my employees, I expect the same from you."

"Of course," he muttered. By the way she was looking at him, he wouldn't be surprised if she told him to drop his trousers to see if he measured up to her other employees. He quickly stood and gave her a short bow. "Thank you and good day."

Smiling, she leaned back in her chair, completely at ease when all he wanted to do was run from this office. "It has been a pleasure doing business with you, Lord Oliver. It is my greatest joy to fulfill my clients' desires, whatever they may be. May Lord Vincent fulfill yours tomorrow."

* * *

"You're new, aren't ye?"

"Ah…yes," Oliver said to the servant's back as he followed her up the stairs, relieved she didn't recognize him as a former client. Though he rarely saw the brothel's servants during previous visits, a house this large couldn't run efficiently without a small army's worth. And if this one assumed he was another of Delacroix's employees, then he was not about to correct her. The fewer who were aware of his identity this evening, the better.

He had arrived at the backdoor of the brothel, just as the madam had instructed him yesterday afternoon, and had been greeted by this servant. The last thirty-four hours had passed slower than he could have imagined. But he was finally here. The time had arrived. Tugging on his coat, he did his best to keep his excitement under wraps.

The narrow staircase let up into an equally narrow hall. He must be in the servants' area of the house. The girl opened a door and motioned for Oliver to enter. The room was small and bare with only a straight-back wooden chair and square spindle-legged table.

"Where'd Delacroix find you?" she asked.

He opened his mouth then promptly shut it. Where did madams find men to stock their brothels?

The girl shrugged, seeming to understand an answer would not be forthcoming. "You're different than her usual sort, that's all."

Studying his boots, he shoved his hands in his pockets. He didn't need her to remind him he fell short. Over the years, he, too, had hired his fair share of men at Madame Delacroix's. Each one had been a prime example of their gender. Yet none had come close to what he imagined Vincent to be like in bed. Their shoulders were not quite broad enough, even the few with blue eyes lacked the pure saturated hue that rivaled a clear summer sky, and not one of them possessed a deep cultured voice that swept over his skin like fine aged whiskey.

"Ye can leave yer clothes in here." The girl motioned to the pegs lining one wall. She was dressed plainly in a serviceable brown dress and had a white cap over her mousy brown hair. She couldn't have been more than eighteen years of age, yet her manner indicated she was well accustomed to the inner workings of the brothel.

Hooking her arm under one of the rungs on the back of the chair, she opened a narrow door then carried the chair into the next room.

Uncertain what to do, Oliver followed. Someone had already lit the candles and stoked the fire. The mahogany furnishings and floorboards gleamed from diligent care. Muted tan and cream paper covered the walls and a pair of comfortable black leather armchairs flanked a marble fireplace. The bedchamber would appeal to Vincent. Neat, tidy yet masculine—everything in its place, except for the straight-back chair positioned a few feet from the foot of the bed.

The clank of metal drew his attention to the dresser. Bent at the waist, the servant searched through the bottom drawer. She turned and crossed to the chair.

His eyes widened at the object in her small hands. Apprehension rushed over his skin, pricking the hairs on his nape. Standing on the chair, she reached up and hung the middle of the length of chain from a hook in the ceiling. The contraption formed a triangle—chain on top with a three-foot iron bar connecting the ends. Pursing her lips, the girl adjusted the chain until the iron bar hung horizontal to the floor.

His heart thumped against his ribs. That contraption was meant for him. He knew it without a doubt.

She went back to the dresser. Opening and closing drawers, she pulled out objects and set them on top of the dresser. Four thick leather cuffs adorned with metal rings, two smaller cuffs and two slightly larger. Another iron bar with hooks on each end. Two glass bottles filled with golden liquid he suspected was oil. A white towel. A metal ring a couple inches in diameter. Marble dildos and anal plugs in various sizes. A coiled leather bullwhip. A cat-o'-nine with braided leather tails. A wooden paddle, the type favored by the headmaster at his old boarding school. He took a step closer and pushed his spectacles higher on his nose. Was that a dog's collar?

Christ. It was all for him. He had to be in the wrong room. Discovering Vincent had a secret penchant for male partners had been shocking enough. Fortunate for Oliver, but unexpected nonetheless. But this? It absolutely did not fit the conservative man Oliver had known since childhood.

The girl hadn't asked Oliver's name. Perhaps she mistook him for someone else. He cleared his constricted throat. "Pardon, miss. I am here for a lord."

"Yes." She slipped one of the bottles of oil into her pocket and walked to the washstand next to the narrow door.

"A Lord Vincent Prescot."

She poured water from a pitcher into the basin. "Yes, his lordship should be along shortly."

His heart skipped a beat. *Holy Mother of God*. His attention snapped to the dresser, to those leather cuffs. A frisson of unexpected anticipation raced up his spine at the prospect of submitting to Vincent. Then dread dropped into his stomach like a deadweight. What if Vincent restrained him then lit the candles? He'd be powerless to prevent Vincent from discovering his identity. Rolling his shoulders, he dragged his hand through his hair.

The servant took two more white towels from the bottom shelf of the washstand and placed one next to the basin. After setting the bottle of oil from her pocket and the other towel on the bedside table, she surveyed the room, clearly checking to see if all was in place. Her gaze stopped on Oliver, who lingered by one of the armchairs. She gave a little sigh. Her brown eyes softened with compassion. "No reason to be nervous. His lordship's a good sort, and he don't 'ave heavy hands. Won't leave no permanent marks on ye. If it's any help, he's Cameron's favorite. The man's been sulkin' since Delacroix told him ye were to take his place tonight."

Oliver already knew Vincent was the blond Adonis's favorite. It had been Cameron who had dropped enough hints about the ruggedly handsome lord whom he only got to see once a month for Oliver to guess the man's identity. And hell, if anything, Oliver should be Cameron's favorite. Likely Oliver was the only male patron who paid to be bent over. "I'm not nervous," he said, fighting to keep from shifting his weight.

She shrugged. "Remove your clothes except for your breeches. If you're wearing drawers, remove them, too. His lordship will expect you to be ready when he arrives."

With that, she picked up the chair and left Oliver alone in the room.

What the hell had he gotten himself into? It would be worth it, though. This was his one chance to be with Vincent, and he wasn't turning back now. He swallowed hard. No matter what.

Forcing his gaze from the iron bar suspended from the ceiling, he began undressing.

"Damn," he muttered, struggling with the knot on his cravat. He never could tie the darn thing correctly, and now it wouldn't come undone. Using the mirror above the washstand, he was finally able to remove his cravat. Dropping the rumpled linen, he studied his reflection.

He looked more unkempt than usual. Hopefully it and a lack of light would be enough to fool Vincent. He had also purposefully avoided Vincent since the man had returned from a long visit to the country—no reason to have Oliver's image too clear in Vincent's memory. A four-day-old beard covered Oliver's jaw, and he was in sore need of a haircut. Dark waves, disheveled from his habit of running his hands through his hair, hung down to his jaw. Common brown eyes stared back at him from behind wire-rimmed spectacles. He could well understand why Vincent had never shown a hint of interest beyond friendship. Everything about Oliver was unremarkable. Average height. Average build. Average intellect.

He let out a harrumph and unbuttoned his plain brown coat. Growing up with a man who excelled at everything he did, one couldn't help but feel not quite up to snuff. Not that he'd ever been jealous of Vincent's successes. He held nothing but admiration for the man.

Well, that wasn't entirely true. Something considerably more than admiration had driven him to this room.

Using the bootjack by the fireplace, he removed his boots. After he finished undressing to the servant's specification—or rather Vincent's specification—he gathered his clothes and left them in a heap on the small table in the adjoining room. He took a step back into the bedchamber then turned around, removed his spectacles, and tucked them into his coat pocket.

Hopefully Vincent would be close enough for Oliver to see him clearly. He was quite looking forward to taking in Lord Vincent Prescot without his impeccably tailored clothes. The image would need to last a lifetime, and he didn't want to miss anything.

One by one, he doused the candles until only the soft golden glow of the fire lit the bedchamber, the light so weak it couldn't penetrate the dark corners of the room. The fabric of his breeches rubbed against his cock as he paced in front of the fireplace. It was oddly erotic to go about without drawers. The decadent sensation mixed with the anticipation and apprehension strumming his nerves.

His gaze kept straying to the chained iron bar and to the dresser. Images flashed before his mind's eye. His wrists locked to that iron bar, Vincent behind him slipping oil-slicked fingers up his arse, probing deep, preparing him. Lust shot through his body. His strides faltered. No, he wanted more than that. He wanted Vincent. He wanted the man to take him, and if that meant being restrained and collared, getting flogged until he sobbed for mercy, then he would do it.

A tinkling, feminine laugh seeped through the closed door. Oliver stopped in his tracks and strained to hear. There was a deep low rumble of a masculine voice.

He had arrived.

Oliver glanced quickly about the room, unsure what to do. Sit, stand, get on the bed? Excitement and nervousness clashed, forming a noxious mixture.

The knob clicked, and the door opened.

Chapter Two

A petite blonde walked into the bedchamber leading a man by the hand. The light from the corridor outlined a tall, broad-shouldered figure. Six feet two to be exact, four inches above Oliver's own height.

As the man turned to shut the door, a flash of green below his throat caught Oliver's attention. Without his spectacles, Oliver couldn't make out his features from this distance, but he knew it was Vincent. He was the only person Oliver was acquainted with who wore a jade cravat pin.

"Would you care for a brandy, milord," the woman said, moving toward the dark shadows along the wall.

"No, thank you."

Oliver's breaths stuttered at the deep, cultured voice. His erection twitched, straining against the placket of his breeches. He had gotten hard on more than one occasion just listening to Vincent speak. Deuced inconvenient when they were at a gambling hell, or White's, or a ball, or…anywhere.

And, *Christ*, Vincent was looking directly at him. He could feel the force of the man's stare. Oliver moved next to a nearby armchair so the firelight was behind him.

"Holly?"

"Oh, yes, milord." She stood in front of Vincent. "Cameron is unavailable tonight. Madame Delacroix personally selected another man for you. I am to give you her assurance he will not disappoint."

"Hmm." Vincent rubbed his chin.

Oliver's knees shook. He gripped the back of the leather armchair. What if Vincent rejected him? What if, with one glance across a darkened room, Vincent deemed him unworthy?

"He'll do."

Relief poured over Oliver, though Vincent didn't sound terribly pleased. If anything, he sounded bored.

"Is there anything I can do for you, Lord Vincent?" she said, an open invitation in her question. Her small pale hand caressed the sleeve of his dark evening coat.

"No."

She must be accustomed to hearing the word no, for she simply gave Vincent a short curtsey. As she walked across the room, she reached out to trail a fingertip along the edge of the dresser. When she neared Oliver, she murmured, "Try not to scream too loud. You'll disturb the other guests."

Her superior smirk said it all.

Gaping at her, he watched her leave. As the narrow door swung closed, it occurred to him. That damned madam had known all along what would be in store for him tonight. Her coy smile coupled with her parting words should have been a clue, but he'd been too eager by half for the chance to be with Vincent.

"What is your name, man?"

His head snapped back to Vincent. His mind went blank. Why hadn't he thought to select a name before now? "Jake," he blurted, giving his childhood dog's name. The one who had never learned to sit on command.

His strides long and easy, Vincent stepped further into the room. "Jake, why are the candles not lit?"

"I prefer it this way," he said, pitching his voice low and doing his best to match the servant girl's accent. "Is it acceptable to ye, milord? It's not completely dark. The fire is lit."

"I could be persuaded to accept it." Stopping at the dresser, Vincent selected one of the leather cuffs. Metal clinked as he undid the buckle. "I don't recall Delacroix ever mentioning a man named Jake."

"I'm new."

"How new?"

"You're my first client."

Vincent's hands stilled as he toyed with the buckle. His posture stiffened with obvious uncertainty.

"I want to do this. I want ye, milord," Oliver said, desperate for Vincent to accept him.

Metal clinked once again. "I like the way you call me 'milord.' Very nice. Tell me, Jake, are you good at following orders?"

"Y-yes."

"Then we shall get along very well, you and I. Come here."

Forcing his hand to unclench from the back of the chair, Oliver did as he was bid. He stopped before Vincent, close enough to take in the man's enticing scent. Not a hint of cologne, only clean male skin, the starch from his cravat and something else, something undeniably Vincent. The golden glow from the fire behind Oliver barely reached where they stood, providing just enough light for him to make out Vincent's rugged features from his shadowed face. The slightly Roman nose, the strong jaw and firm lips. Lips he wanted to feel against his own.

Though he couldn't see the details in the sparsely lit room, he knew Vincent's eyes were so startlingly blue they would have appeared feminine in a less masculine face. And those gorgeous eyes were currently sweeping up the length of his body. He quickly bowed his head, using the length of his dark hair to partially obscure his face from Vincent's probing gaze.

"You're in need of a shave."

Why hadn't it occurred to him that the days-old beard would annoy Vincent? "My apologies, milord."

"There's nothing to be done for it now." He paused. "Remove your breeches," Vincent said, as casual as could be.

Careful to keep his head bowed, Oliver tore at the placket with shaking hands, shoved his breeches down and kicked them free of his legs. His cock jutted from his body, arching toward Vincent in a silent but very obvious plea to be touched. He was completely naked, yet Vincent hadn't even removed his coat.

The man was impeccably dressed, as usual. His coat appeared to be black, though it could be navy given the yellow silk waistcoat. The crisp white cravat was tied in a perfect Gordian knot, the ends secured by the jade pin. Dark trousers hung straight down his legs, the hems brushing the tops of his polished evening shoes.

"Hold out your arm."

Oliver hesitated. His arm trembled as Vincent buckled the cuff around his wrist. Loose enough not to pinch but tight enough to be secure. The leather was pliant and warmed from Vincent's grip.

As he placed the second cuff on Oliver's other wrist, he asked, "Have you been restrained before?"

"No."

"Nervous?"

"A bit," Oliver admitted, his voice wavering. There was no point denying it. He shook like a damn leaf, from nerves, from excitement, from being naked and close to Vincent.

"There's no need." Vincent's tone softened, turned reassuring. "If you wish to stop at anytime simply give the word. I'll take care of you, Jake, and it is critical you trust me to do so."

Oliver nodded.

"Good. Now get in place."

He swallowed hard. His cock bobbing with each step, he moved directly beneath the chained iron bar.

"Lift your arms."

Oliver didn't give himself time to think on it. He raised his arms until his hands brushed the cool metal chains. Chin down, he watched under his lashes as Vincent approached. There was no hurry in his step, no impatience. The man moved as if tying up another was a common occurrence.

Vincent stopped beside him. The fabric of his coat shifted as he reached up to secure his wrists. Through sheer force of will, Oliver resisted the urge to watch. He kept his gaze on the dresser in front of him. The tail end of the leather bullwhip hung from the neat coil, grazing the side of the dresser. The firelight flickered on the oil-filled, glass bottle and cast shadows over the other objects. Would Vincent use every one of those objects on him? Or would he choose depending on his mood? Or on how well he followed orders?

Would he have to be good or bad for Vincent to paddle his arse?

His cock jumped, signaling its approval. Instinctively, he made to reach down to wrap his hand around the needy length. Chains rattled as he was stopped short. He glanced up. A metal ring on the leather cuff was fixed to the clip on the end of the iron bar. His other wrist similarly secured.

Panic chilled his nerves. Closing his eyes, he tried to push the rising anxiety aside.

"Take a deep breath," a calm voice said from behind him.

Oliver gasped but air wouldn't reach his lungs. What if Vincent lit a candle? What if he left him here?

"Do it," Vincent said, all sharp command. He grabbed a handful of Oliver's hair and tugged.

Oliver winced. The pain penetrated the stifling fog, pulling the word "stop" off his tongue. He took a deep breath, taut muscles settling on the exhale.

"Good boy." Vincent's voice flowed over his shoulder like warmed honey. A pause. "All right?"

"Yes," Oliver said, nodding. And surprisingly, he was all right. The anticipation was back—a delicious hum that occupied his senses. Vincent would take care of him, and he trusted him to do so.

Vincent crossed to the dresser and returned with the two larger cuffs and the other iron bar. He dropped to his haunches, his bowed head inches from Oliver's erection. His coat stretched across the broad width of his shoulders and the expanse of his back as he buckled the cuffs onto his ankles.

Oliver clenched and unclenched his hands. His fingers itched to tousle the neatly combed dark hair, to grip the short length, to pull

Vincent's head up and push his cock into the other man's mouth. A moan of longing shook the back of his throat.

Looking up, Vincent lifted one eyebrow. "Widen your stance."

He complied, spreading his legs to accommodate the length of the iron bar.

Vincent secured the bar between his ankles then went to the dresser, returning with the dog collar. "Lift your chin."

Straightening his spine, he did as instructed. The dark sweep of Vincent's lashes were at half-mast as he did up the buckle. As soon as his hands left Oliver's throat, Oliver tipped his chin back down, letting his hair swing forward again to partially obscure his face, thankful the two-inch-wide strip of plain leather wrapped around his neck wasn't any bigger or it would have prevented him from doing so. Hopefully it and the lack of light would be enough to continue to fool Vincent.

He took a step back. Arms crossed over his chest and head slightly tilted to one side, he appraised Oliver.

Did Vincent like what he saw? Collared and tied up tight. Arms and legs spread. Wrists and ankles secured. Absolutely helpless, yet strangely, arousal rode over every inch of his skin. And how the hell had Vincent restrained him without once touching his skin? Not even a brush of his manicured fingers against his throat.

Vincent unbuttoned his coat and shrugged it off, revealing the yellow silk waistcoat and the sleeves of his white lawn shirt. His evening shoes clicked against the floorboards as he went to the fireplace and folded his coat over the back of an armchair. Crouching, he stoked the fire, the wood popping and crackling, the flames flaring before settling back to a low even burn. When he walked back to Oliver, there was the tiniest bit of hurry in his step.

His paced slowed as he circled Oliver then stopped behind him. "Sleek yet strong." He drew his hands down Oliver's back, leaving a path of tingling skin in his wake. "Beautiful," Vincent murmured, palming his arse, thumbs tickling the crease.

Closing his eyes, he greedily soaked up Vincent's touch. He was the furthest thing from beautiful, but the reverent tone in Vincent's voice almost made Oliver believe him.

"I paid you a compliment, Jake."

Oliver bit his bottom lip. Vincent sounded annoyed. Did the man expect a response? "Ah, thank you, milord?"

"Very good and don't forget again." Vincent reached around Oliver's raised arms. Two fingertips brushed his lips. "Suck on them."

Opening his mouth, he took them inside. He swirled his tongue around the digits, reveling in the slightly salty, masculine taste of Vincent's skin. Suckling hard, he drew them further into his mouth, his cheeks hollowing, as if he were sucking on Vincent's cock and not his fingers.

A barely perceptible grunt sounded behind him. "Enough. Let go."

Cool, wet fingertips probed between his arse cheeks. Oliver trembled, wanting more than anything for those fingers to press deep inside. But Vincent toyed with him, circling the puckered flesh, tormenting him. He brought his fingers to Oliver's lips again. Oliver didn't need to be told twice. He eagerly took them inside, wetting them thoroughly.

"Good boy," Vincent said, pulling free of Oliver's mouth.

Satisfaction shot through him at Vincent's praise. He would do whatever the man wanted just to hear those two words. And he didn't mind in the slightest that Vincent called him "boy", even though Oliver was one year older than Vincent's twenty-four.

Those teasing fingers returned to his arse, tickling lightly. Then he let out a moan as Vincent pushed past the tight ring of muscle. Slick from his mouth, Vincent's two fingers slid smoothly inside him.

Slow and easy, Vincent finger-fucked his arse. Pleasure spiraled through him. Pleasure that was so much more intense than when he did it himself. Whimpering, Oliver arched, wanting more. His cock bobbed, lifting higher, the skin stretched unbelievably taut. His ballocks were drawn up so tight they tingled with the need for release.

Grabbing hold of Oliver's hip with his other hand, Vincent pressed deeper, massaging that perfect spot inside him. Sharp sensation seized his nerves. Sparks danced before his eyes. "Ah, yes!"

Vincent tightened his hold on Oliver's hip, long fingers digging into the firm flesh, and pushed even deeper. Groaning, Oliver tried to buck back, to get even more of the lush pleasure, but Vincent held him steady. On the next backward glide, Vincent pulled out completely.

"Don't stop. *Please*, milord," Oliver begged.

Vincent let out a satisfied chuckle and smacked Oliver on the arse, light and playful with just enough force for the sting to linger. Unbuttoning his waistcoat, he walked past Oliver. He shrugged off the garment, folded it and set it next to the leather bullwhip on the dresser. Dark suspenders crossed his white-shirted back. Wool trousers hugged the muscular curves of his arse.

Oliver's entire body vibrated with suspense. What object would Vincent select? Chains clanked as he leaned right trying to see around Vincent's broad shoulder.

"Stand still."

He froze at the hard command. His heart beat rapidly against his ribs as he waited for what seemed like an endless moment.

A smirk pulled one edge of Vincent's lips as he sauntered toward him. Oliver's eyes widened, his arse tightened, at the object held in Vincent's hand. A few drops of oil dripped from the tapered end of the black marble plug.

Vincent had chosen the plug Oliver would have selected if given the choice, and it was similar to one of many such toys he owned. A tremor of anticipation shook him as Vincent pulled back one cheek, exposing his entrance. Without even a preliminary nudge to ease the way, Vincent pushed the plug firmly inside him. Oliver couldn't stifle the grunt as his muscles were forced to stretch quickly to accommodate the toy. Vincent's fingers had helped prepare him, but the marble length flared to the size of a substantially endowed man before narrowing at the rectangular base. Closing his eyes, he fought to stay still, to resist the urge to jerk his hips forward and escape the burning sting.

Just when he was certain he couldn't endure anymore, when the word "stop" teased his tongue, the last of the thick width slipped beyond the protesting ring of muscle and the base settled against him.

Vincent tapped the end. The vibrations reverberated delightfully in Oliver's passage. He gasped for breath. He was stuffed full, and it felt incredible.

"You're almost ready. There's one last thing we need to see to before proceeding."

Almost ready? Oliver's eyes snapped open. Standing before him, Vincent reached toward his chest and took hold of each nipple between his thumb and forefinger. His expression intent, he pinched, steadily increasing the pressure. It should hurt, Oliver was certain of it, but oddly it didn't. It felt damn good. A flush of heat washed over his skin. He pushed out his chest, wanting more of those punishing fingers. Fluid leaked from his cock and dripped down the shaft.

Vincent twisted and all Oliver could do was moan helplessly as lust shot to his groin. His ballocks clenched, an orgasm teasing his spine. One more twist of his nipples and he'd climax.

"Your body knows how to turn pain into pleasure. Very good," Vincent said, releasing him.

Oliver shook his bowed head. "More please, milord." He flinched as Vincent brushed his knuckles over his smarting nipples. "Thank you," he said in a great rush, straining toward the other man as much as his bonds would allow.

But Vincent turned his back to him. Rolling his sleeves up to his elbows, he went to the dresser and selected—

Oliver's breath caught.

There wasn't a bit of trepidation within him, not even a hint of fear, as Vincent flicked his wrist, causing the long length of the leather bullwhip to jump and twitch as an impatient snake.

His back to Oliver, Vincent bowed his head. The broad line of his shoulders tightened. "Do you like men, Jake?"

It wasn't the question that made Oliver hesitate, but the low, almost cruel tone.

Vincent turned. A hard curl pulled his mouth, his eyes narrowed. He tugged on his cravat, yanking it from his neck. "Answer me."

Was this part of the game? It had to be, for Vincent was aroused. His erection strained against the placket of his black trousers. "Yes, I like men," Oliver said, speaking the truth. He had been with women a few times, but it never felt right. The soft curves of their bodies only made him long for the hard bulk of a man.

"Do you like *me*?"

No, I love you. "Yes, milord."

The whip cracked through the air. Oliver braced for a vicious snap. The lash grazed the head of his cock. A shudder rippled through him at the unexpectedly erotic caress, like the tongue of skillful lover.

"Do you want me?"

"*Yes.*" Oh God, how he wanted Vincent.

"Where?" The whip cracked through the air again. The lash curled around his hip, nipping his arse. "Here? Is this where you want me?"

"Yes, yes." His muscles clenched around the plug he wished was Vincent's cock.

Strides determined, Vincent advanced. "You haven't earned that right yet."

Oliver craned his neck, trying to follow Vincent as he went behind him.

"Eyes straight ahead." Then ragged puffs of warm air fanned Oliver's shoulder. "You must be very, very good to earn that reward," Vincent said into his ear, in a rich husky tone.

"I'll be good. I promise, milord."

He could hear Vincent move behind him. There was a whoosh of fabric. A white shirt was thrown toward the dresser.

"We'll see about that."

The lash came down on his back, then his arse, and then his upper thighs. Again and again, Vincent expertly wielded the bullwhip, delivering punishing kisses that were sharp and delicate at the same time. Each stinging kiss quickly flared then shifted to sublime fiery pleasure that flooded every nerve in his body. He never dreamed being whipped could feel so unbelievably good. He was so hard the head of his cock arched up to brush his lower abdomen.

Fluid leaked continuously from the tip, wetting his skin. Poised on the verge of a climax, he gasped and moaned, begging for more. The sounds of harsh breathing and leather whizzing through the air filled his ears.

"Tell me what you want," Vincent demanded, as the lash curled around Oliver's upper thigh, the thin end licking his ballocks.

He instinctively flinched but the iron bar kept his legs spread wide, kept him exposed and vulnerable. "You, milord. I—I want you."

"*What* do you want?" Vincent punctuated his question with a blow across Oliver's buttocks.

"I want your cock. I—I want you…to…fuck me. Please…m-milord," he said, fighting to form the words against the thick heavy haze of lust filling his mind.

Those amazing snaps of the whip ceased.

"No! Don't stop." He shook his arms, rattling the chains in protest.

Bare-chested and barefooted, Vincent stood before him, the whip held in one hand. A fine sheen of sweat coated his skin. Oliver couldn't stop his jaw from dropping in awe. Boarding school dormitories provided little privacy. As such, he had seen Vincent half dressed on many occasions. And that boyishly handsome, strapping adolescent had grown into—

Christ, Vincent was built like a medieval knight. Thick, bulging biceps; strong, corded forearms; and an impressively broad chest. He suspected Vincent's conservatively tailored clothes hid a well-honed body, but he hadn't expected such overwhelming brute strength.

Oliver dared to tilt his head up a bit. Had Vincent gotten taller? He seemed taller.

Vincent's gaze swept over his face then down his body.

Impatient and needy, Oliver rattled the chains again. "Please, milord."

A satisfied smile spread across his mouth. Without a word, he dropped the whip, went to the dresser, and removed his trousers. The sight of his bare backside made Oliver's mouth water with the need to pull those muscular cheeks apart, to drag his tongue down the crease, to ply Vincent with his mouth until he shattered Vincent's steely control.

Vincent reached for the oil-filled, glass bottle. When he turned back around, he was stroking his cock, spreading oil over the thick, long length. The firelight flickered over the hard contours of his powerful nude body.

"Are you ready for my cock?" Vincent demanded, all smug arrogance, without a hint of doubt of what Oliver's answer would be.

Yet Oliver gave it nonetheless. "Yes, please, *please*, milord."

Just watching Vincent stride toward him as he stroked his prick, ratcheted the lust permeating Oliver's senses even higher. That magnificent cock would be inside of him soon. He had bent over for his fair share of men, in fact he much preferred to take it than give it, but he'd never taken a man of Vincent's dimensions. Would he fit? Oliver was more than eager to try. Vincent flicked his thumb over the broad head and Oliver groaned, his passage fluttering in greedy anticipation.

Standing behind him, Vincent tapped the end of the plug still lodged firmly up Oliver's arse. Nerves drawn impossibly taut, Oliver trembled, his knees shaking. When he felt Vincent take hold of the rectangular end, he took a deep breath and exhaled, willing his muscles to relax. Vincent pulled. Oliver let out a grunt as the narrow end immediately flared to its thickest width, stretching him wide before slipping from his body and leaving him achingly empty.

Marble clattered to the floor. Whimpering, Oliver lifted up onto his toes and arched his back, presenting Vincent with his arse. "Fuck me, please."

A strong hand settled on his hip. Heavy pants singed his shoulder. Then sharp teeth nipped between his shoulder blades. Hot silken skin slid over his entrance, teasing him with the barest hint of penetration, and then Vincent pushed. Kept so long on the cusp of an orgasm, Oliver came. The climax rushed through him with amazing force, brutal in its intensity. He bit the inside of his cheek to stifle the shout as seed shot from his cock.

Determined, persistent, Vincent worked his big prick into Oliver. Stretching him, filling him, prolonging his orgasm. He howled against the onslaught of purest sensation. Rammed ballocks deep, Vincent ground his hips in a mind-shattering circle. Pleasure pulsed through him in heavy, sweet waves, fraying his overwrought and overstretched nerves. With a punishing grip, Vincent held his hips steady and began a rhythm of hard, relentless thrusts. Pounding into him, pushing him onward, driving him to rapturous new heights of pleasure he never believed were possible.

"More," he gasped, trying to buck back into Vincent and rattling the chains. He wanted to wrap his arms around Vincent, crush his mouth against those firm lips. But he could do nothing but serve as a Vincent's slave, a willing vessel for his possession.

Vincent's harsh words filled his ears. "That's it. Beg for my cock. You want it, don't you? Tell me."

"Yes, I want you. Fuck me. Harder. Please."

Vincent slammed into him. Oliver climaxed again. Fierce and swift, the orgasm rocked his senses, left him begging, pleading, sobbing for more. Hot tears leaked from Oliver's closed eyes, streamed down his cheeks. Sweat trickled down his back. His skin felt too tight, too thin. Every place Vincent had whipped him burned and throbbed. Yet he wanted more. He wanted Vincent to take him, use him, gorge himself—leave him so aching and sore he would never forget this night.

Vincent's thrusts sped up, ballocks smacking his arse. Long fingers bit harshly into Oliver's hips. Vincent let out a feral growl as he shoved somehow, incredibly deeper.

Oliver screamed against the undiluted ecstasy assaulting his senses. Then he felt Vincent's cock pulse within him, filling him with hot seed.

His strength abruptly gave out. Sagging in the chains, Oliver's head lolled forward. The leather collar dug into his jaw, keeping his chin from resting on his chest. "More," he muttered, gasping for breath. He quivered as Vincent's cock slipped from his body. "No, no, no. Don't stop."

The large hands on his hips turned gentle, caressing and soothing his bruised flesh. "That's enough for now," Vincent said, with a pant in his voice.

Fingers brushed his ankles as Vincent unbuckled the cuffs. There was the soft sound of bare feet against wooden floorboards. Knuckles scraped against his bristly jaw, lifting his chin to remove the collar. With a light touch, his tangled, sweat-damp hair was tucked behind one ear.

"Jake. Open your eyes for me."

Oliver tried to heed the gentle command, but his eyelids were so heavy he could barely open them, let alone lift his bowed head. His pulse pounded thickly through his veins, echoing in his ears. With considerable effort, he looked up into Vincent's handsome, rugged face. The dark brows were lowered with obvious concern, the firm mouth set in a grim line. The most profound adoration filled Oliver's heart. *Christ*, how he loved this man.

And he will never know how much you love him.

"My name's not Jake."

"I surmised as much. What is your name?"

Why had he admitted that to Vincent? Slow and sluggish, Oliver shook his head.

"It's all right," Vincent said, in that same gentle tone.

The moment Vincent unbuckled the cuffs on his wrists, Oliver's legs gave out, unable to hold the weight of his body. Strong arms caught him, holding him up against a hard sweat-slicked chest.

"Easy now. Let's get you to the bed."

Stumbling over his own feet, Oliver let Vincent help him onto the bed, turning him so he lay on his stomach. A fluffy pillow cushioned his cheek. The bed was so wonderfully soft, so unlike his own. *Because you're in a damn brothel.* "I can't stay," he said, trying to sit up.

The mattress dipped then shook. A kind but firm hand pressed between his shoulder blades, effortlessly keeping Oliver on the bed.

"Just for a moment. You need to rest."

Vincent's deep voice wrapped around him, lulling his senses. Just one moment, he promised himself, as he gave up the fight against the exhaustion pulling on his mind.

Chapter Three

A steady *thump-thump, thump-thump* penetrated Oliver's sleep-fogged mind. Eyes closed, he turned into the comforting sound, dragging his lips over a smattering of soft, short hair. The large hand kneading his arse felt so good—bone meltingly gentle, and possessive at the same time. It would be so easy to fall back to sleep, but his cock was twitching to life: eager, needy, and demanding attention. Yawning, he stretched against the solid body under him, bare skin rubbing enticingly against bare skin. Then he grunted as an ache seized every muscle in his body.

"Sore?"

That deep cultured voice was so familiar. It sounded just like…

Oliver bolted upright, hands pressing against a muscular chest as he pushed up onto his knees.

"Easy now. Careful or you'll cause some significant damage."

Startled, Oliver stared down into Vincent's shadowed face. He was in bed with Vincent, and he had been sleeping on top of him, sprawled over his body like a lovesick, adoring fool. And Vincent had let him.

Vincent pushed on Oliver's leg, which was lodged between his strong, hair-dusted thighs. "Careful," he repeated.

Hell. He had almost kneed Vincent in the ballocks. Embarrassment flooded him, heat rushing to his cheeks. "Sorry," he mumbled, shifting off to sit on the side of the bed. He dragged both hands through his hair. The room was near dark. The fire in the grate had burned down to glowing embers. The scents of male sweat and sex hung heavy in the air.

Why was Vincent still here? He should have left the moment Oliver fell asleep. Oliver didn't remember passing out on top of Vincent. Had he done anything else, said anything he shouldn't have? Cold fear slipped into his gut. "Why didn't you wake me?"

"You needed the rest."

"How long was I asleep?"

The mattress shifted. "Not long." When Vincent's hand cupped his hip, he flinched, startled at the light touch. "Sore?"

"A bit," he said, stifling a moan as Vincent caressed his back in slow circles, soothing his aching muscles and tender skin. It hadn't escaped his notice that Vincent had barely touched him earlier. Yet now, Vincent behaved as if they had awoken in bed together many times. He was having a hard time adjusting to this new relaxed, intimate version of Vincent, and while he knew it was beyond foolish, his heart thumped in his chest, pleading for more.

"Sore how? Good or bad?" Vincent asked.

The beginning of a chuckle teased Oliver's belly. A dull ache rode over his skin, reminding him of each punishing kiss of the bullwhip. And that wasn't the only thing that ached. He could still feel Vincent's cock buried deep in his arse. It would be days before he could sit down without thinking of Vincent. "Good," he admitted, ducking his chin, glad it was dark and Vincent couldn't see the smile on his face.

He felt the warmth of Vincent's body as he moved closer. It must be all that muscle, for the man generated more heat than a fully stoked fire. A quiver of need shook Oliver. His fists clenched into the rumpled sheets as he resisted the urge to turn and press his lips against Vincent's. He wanted to kiss him so badly, yet he held back. If Vincent rejected him, if he pulled back in disgust as he suspected he would, then Oliver's heart would shatter for certain. It was one thing to fuck a man, quite another to kiss one.

Vincent said not a word as he continued to rub Oliver's back. He was kneeling behind him, knees bracketing but not quite touching Oliver's hips. Then Vincent's touch shifted. The hairs on Oliver's forearms pricked with awareness. One strong hand reached around to glide up Oliver's chest, fingers splaying over his neck to cup his jaw. There was not a trace of resistance as he obediently heeded the pressure and turned his head.

Firm lips pressed against his. Shock seized his brain for the briefest of seconds. Then he opened his mouth. Vincent's silken tongue slipped inside, stroking his in a deep, sensual rhythm. Lush pleasure wrapped around him. Blood rushed to his groin, his cock hardening. Oliver whimpered but the sound was lost in the hot recesses of Vincent's mouth. He wanted to wrap his arms around Vincent, to crush the other man against him. But he twisted the sheets between his fingers, held perfectly still and simply experienced Vincent's slow, languid kiss.

After nipping Oliver's lower lip, Vincent pulled back, breaking the kiss.

"You need a shave." Vincent's voice was mere rasp, a low scratch from somewhere deep in his throat.

Dazed, Oliver nodded and licked his lips, savoring the taste of Vincent. Surely he was still asleep. Surely still dreaming. Lord Vincent Prescot had not just kissed him as if Oliver was a cherished lover.

Vincent stretched out on the bed, one arm bent behind his head. The long powerful length of his nude body was a lure Oliver could not resist. He twisted around, intent on joining him.

"Get me a brandy. There's a decanter on the table by the door."

That annoyed, bored tone was back. The same one from when Vincent had first stepped into the room. It stopped Oliver short. He gave his head a quick shake, and the reality of the situation came crashing down. He was in a brothel, playing the part of one of that damn madam's employees. Vincent's kiss had meant nothing.

He meant nothing to Vincent.

Oliver bolted up from the bed, stumbling a few steps before his legs started functioning properly. His eyes had adjusted to the near darkness, and he was able to locate the small table by the door. Glass rattled against glass, his hands shaking as he poured the brandy into a snifter. *He doesn't even know who you are. Nor does he care.* Avoiding Vincent's gaze he crossed the room, acutely aware of his limp cock dangling between his thighs.

"For you, milord," he said, doing his best to keep his voice from wavering.

Vincent pushed up onto his elbow. His fingers brushed Oliver's as he took the proffered glass. Sensation rushed up Oliver's arm. His breath hitched.

He turned on his heel. Where had he left his breeches? He needed to get out of this room. Now.

The dresser. He'd been standing near the dresser when Vincent told him to remove his breeches. He found them underneath Vincent's rumpled white shirt. As he grabbed his breeches, a splash of green at the base of the dresser caught his attention. He reached out, his other hand closing over the jade cravat pin.

"Wait."

Two paces from the narrow door, Oliver froze. His heart slammed high and hard against his ribs. He clenched his fist, the hard oval stone on the pin pressing into his palm

Vincent sat up and swung his legs over the side of the bed. "Bring me my coat. I need to pay you."

A wave of nausea filled Oliver's stomach. He swallowed hard, fighting it down. "Just leave it on the dresser."

"But…?"

Oliver was through the door and shut it before Vincent could finish his question. He sagged against the door, sliding down to his haunches. Uncontrollable shivers suddenly wracked his body. He dropped his head and covered his face with his breeches, trying to stifle the sobs that lodged in his throat.

How the hell was he to face Vincent again? To flash an easy smile and casually inquire about his day the next time he passed Vincent on the street? The man had branded himself on Oliver's soul and broken his heart in the process. But how could he not be with Vincent again? How was he to go the rest of his days without him?

He couldn't. He could never be with another man, not after tonight. Vincent had shown Oliver a side of himself he hadn't known existed. He had stripped him bare, exposed his soul, demanded complete submission, and Oliver had willing turned himself over. Dark and wicked, yet so right, so perfect. And so potently addictive. Even now when Vincent thought of him as nothing more than an anonymous man to bugger, Oliver still craved his touch, his attention, his praise.

How the hell had he believed he would be able to walk away from Vincent tonight unscathed? *Christ*, his chest ached so badly it hurt to breathe. He couldn't recall exactly when the longing first gripped hold. When adolescent urges had focused on Lord Vincent Prescot to the exclusion of all others. When friendship had turned into a need for so much more. Yet it had, and now, after tonight…

Clenching his jaw, he fought back a fresh surge of utter despair. He dragged his breeches down his face and tipped his head back against the door, blinking into the pitch darkness. He needed to pull himself together. In any case, he couldn't stay in this small room all night.

His mind traveled down a path it should not go. It was an open invitation for more pain, more heartache. It would be foolhardy to even contemplate, and the risk—*oh*—if Vincent ever discovered Jake was Oliver…

It had taken too long to win at the gambling tables. He needed something that required no skill, only blind luck.

The betting book at White's.

Oliver was one of those men others tended not to notice. As such, he overheard far more conversations than he should. Perhaps his ability to blend into the woodwork would help him win a few bets.

Floorboards creaked in the other room. Light flared from underneath the door. Vincent had lit a candle. He was likely getting dressed, and very soon, he'd notice what had gone missing.

Oliver scrambled up, shoved his legs into his breeches and slipped Vincent's cravat pin into his pocket. He grabbed his clothes that were heaped on the small table, his spectacles clattering to the floor. His head snapped to the door, fearing Vincent would walk through to investigate the noise. Pulse clamoring in his veins, he tugged on his shirt, waistcoat and jacket. Shoved his cravat into his pocket. Pulled on his boots. Put on his spectacles. And was out of the room with only one thought in his mind.

The first Thursday of every month. And next month, Oliver would ensure only one man was available when Vincent visited the brothel.

* * *

"Would you care for another whiskey, Lord Vincent?"

Vincent looked up from the newspaper to the footman standing at his shoulder. *I kissed a man last night.* "Yes, and be quick about it."

The footman tipped his head and left, weaving around the other patrons.

Vincent turned his attention back to the *Times*. Try as he might, he couldn't remember what he'd been reading. Shaking his head in disgust, he reached for his glass then stopped. That footman better be quick.

The drone of male voices, the clink of glasses, and the swoosh of paper as newspapers were read surrounded him. They were the sounds of a man's haven. He'd come to White's this afternoon seeking a distraction. Yet when he'd walked through the door, he had avoided the clusters of men seated in comfortable leather armchairs and taken up a spot at an out of the way table by himself.

I kissed a man.

Yes, you bloody well did, didn't you?

He gnashed his teeth. The worst of it, though? He actually looked at the calendar in his study this morning and been glad there were only thirty days in April. Then he had promptly left his town house and gone to White's.

Why the hell had he kissed that man? He never had the desire to do that before. He gave them what they begged for, what they needed. Yet Jake hadn't asked for a kiss, and still, Vincent had pressed his lips to Jake's full lips, slipped his tongue into Jake's hot, willing mouth, and *kissed a man*.

The absolute worst was he had enjoyed it. It had felt good. Beyond good. It felt right, as if kissing Jake was the most natural thing to do.

He stiffened, his spine going ramrod straight. From the corner of his eye, he quickly scanned the room. Did any of them suspect? Could they tell? It damn well felt as though it was branded on his forehead for all to see. His gaze stopped on an older man with neatly cropped silver hair seated by the fireplace in conversation with Vincent's brother, the cherished heir. The distinguished Marquis of Saye and Sele paid Vincent little notice, but if the man found out his second son was a fucking sod…any hope Vincent held of earning even a bit of his father's respect would be destroyed. Gone.

Wincing, he forced his attention back to the *Times*. He was *not* a sod. He swived women and never let another man bugger him, but the distinctions didn't matter. The threat of being hanged for sodomy aside, London society was unforgiving to those who did not meet their exacting standards. They frowned upon any deviation, no matter how slight. And one couldn't get more deviant than a desire to kiss another man.

It was all that madam's fault. She had sent him Jake—a man who had put his trust in him without question. A man who had gazed at him with such intense longing, as if he needed his touch to draw breath. And Jake had not been acting. That had not been an attempt to please a client. His every response, every desperate plea for more, every threadbare whimper from his full kissable lips had been genuine.

Vincent let out a frustrated grunt and shifted in the chair. Hell and damnation. It would not do to sport an erection at White's. He needed to stop thinking about Jake. What was wrong with him? He never had this much trouble controlling himself. Those urges were kept neatly locked away and only let out on a rigid schedule. Every appointment the same, the events carefully orchestrated so all control rested firmly in his hands.

Last night had not been the same, now had it? Scowling, he turned the page of the newspaper. Different from the moment he walked through the bedchamber door, never mind how it ended. But surely there was nothing wrong with lingering for a bit. It was the man's first appointment. His initial awkwardness, the nervousness confirmed that fact. Only a heartless bastard would have left Jake crumpled on the floor, used and wrung dry. Basic human compassion drove his behavior, and definitely not a desire to feel Jake's sleek, honed body pressed against his. Yet the absolute trust in the young man's undisturbed sleeping breaths had produced such a rush of fierce protectiveness he couldn't leave until he felt Jake would be all right.

On top of it all, he lost his cravat pin. That's what he got for not having a care with his cravat and ripping the thing from his neck. Eager to get out of the brothel, to escape the shock over that damn kiss, he hadn't stayed long looking for it. The only thing his grandfather left him was now lost forever. Some servant would probably find it when she cleaned the room and sell it for a bottle of gin. *Brilliant.*

Resting his elbows on the table, he rubbed his temples. Even better. Now he had a headache. Where the hell was that footman? He glanced up.

Head bowed and shoulders hunched, Lord Oliver Marsden was walking in the direction of Vincent's table. The sight of his old friend in the predictably rumpled coat complete with a poorly tied cravat eased the throbbing in his temples.

"Marsden," Vincent called.

Stopping in his tracks, Marsden's head snapped up. "Ah…Prescot. Afternoon."

"Yes, it is afternoon." A glass of whiskey was placed on the table. Vincent glared at the footman standing at his shoulder. "Another glass for Lord Oliver—and this time, quickly." Then he looked to Marsden and gestured to the chair across from his. "Have a seat."

Marsden hesitated then sat, a wince tightening his lips.

"Am I keeping you from something?"

"No, no. I was just," Marsden shrugged, "going to check the betting book."

"You've turned into quite the gambler of late, haven't you? I heard about your run at the tables last month. Impressive. But have a care about it. Gambling can become an addictive vice."

"I'm well aware of that," Marsden said, spearing Vincent with a knowing look from behind his slightly crooked spectacles.

Vincent fought back a cringe. "My apologies. I did not intend to infer a similarity between yourself and your father's situation."

Marsden let out a sigh. "But you're right, of course. I certainly don't want to turn into a degenerate gambler. He at least has the weight of a title to keep him out of debtor's prison." Shaking his head, he ran a hand through his dark hair. Hair that looked as though he'd recently taken a machete to it.

"Did you cut it yourself?" Vincent asked, aghast. How had the man managed to hack it to bits while leaving it too long?

"Cut...? Oh, my hair. Yes."

Vincent rolled his eyes. "Marsden, my dear fellow, are you aware there are people trained to do that for you? They're called valets. The same individuals who press one's coats and tie one's cravats."

Marsden scowled, indignation tingeing his cheekbones pink, his full lips compressing. "I don't have a valet, Prescot."

"I do. Stop by my town house and he'll see to it for you."

"Thank you, but I can see to it myself." He tucked an errant wavy strand behind his ear and snatched the whiskey from the footman before the man could place the glass on the table.

Downing half a glass of whiskey settled Marsden. He leaned back in the chair, once again the easy, unassuming man he had known since his youth. Vincent's acquaintances might look down on his association with him, but it mattered not to him that Marsden's reprobate father was considered bad *ton*, nor that he rarely had more than two shillings to rub together. Lord Oliver Marsden was his friend, and though weeks, even months could pass without them sitting down for a drink, Marsden had a way about him that made it feel as though no time had passed.

"How was your visit to the country?" Marsden asked.

"Productive." A smile curved Vincent's lips as a sense of accomplishment flowed over him. "The Rotherham property will turn a tidy profit this year and for many years to come."

"Your father finally turned it over to you?"

"No. I purchased it last fall." He had always wanted it. Always knew it could be so much more than a blight on the otherwise illustrious Saye and Sele marquisate. "Found a vein of coal, and a rather large one at that."

"Well done, Prescot. Your father should be most impressed."

The warmth spreading across his chest at Marsden's praise turned ice-cold. "He doesn't know."

"Why not?"

Vincent let out a derisive snort.

"You should tell him. He's right over there." Marsden motioned to the group of men seated by the fireplace.

"He hasn't acknowledged me since I arrived." It wasn't out of malice. His father simply forgot he had more than one son, his attention so focused on the one that mattered.

"Go pay him a call then."

"I have nothing else to discuss with him. I can't walk into his study, deliver my news, and leave. That would be absurd."

Marsden took another sip of whiskey. He was silent for a moment as he contemplated Vincent. "Is he even aware you purchased the property?"

"I don't know. My solicitor managed it, and I doubt his lordship connected the Lord Vincent Prescot who signed the bank draft with the same man who happens to be his son."

"He's aware," Marsden muttered, disgust clear in his tone. His gaze strayed to Vincent's father and older brother. His brow furrowed then he looked back to Vincent. "Your brother is not even half the man you are."

On a shaky breath, Vincent closed his eyes, avoiding Marsden's intent, deep-brown gaze. This was why Vincent sought his company.

Marsden understood. Without question. The man knew what it felt like to be a spare, to be overlooked, ignored in favor of another. All his life Vincent had strived for some sort of recognition from his father, and Marsden was the only person who gave him a "Well done, Prescot."

Vincent grabbed his glass and took a long swallow. The well-aged whiskey eased the constriction in his throat. *I'm pathetic.* Yes, indeed. No doubt about it. Yet he also knew Marsden didn't mind propping up his confidence every now and then. He understood, and the man was always simply there whenever Vincent needed him.

"Will you be returning to Rotherham soon?" Marsden asked, skimming a fingertip along the rim of his glass.

"I'll travel back next month. Lady Collarton is hosting a ball next Friday. Can't miss my aunt's seventy-fifth birthday celebration and there's other business I need to see to in Town before I leave again." Namely an appointment on the first Thursday in May. He'd request Jake, if the man still worked there. Unease leeched into his gut. Other men hadn't lasted long at the brothel. The madam was known to hire handsome young men desperate to earn a few pounds. Could Jake be one of those desperate men? Perhaps he should stop by the brothel and—

Stop!

He shoved thoughts of Jake aside and focused back on Marsden. "Are you planning to attend her ladyship's ball?"

Marsden shifted, slouching further into the chair. The man's tailor should be run out of town. The ill-fitting brown coat rode up, making Marsden's shoulders appear broader, boxier than usual. "No."

"Don't tell me you're going to let the old dragon scare you off? She might have a wickedly sharp tongue, but she's harmless. Certainly not any more frightening than your grandmother. By the way, how is your grandmother? Are you still visiting her regularly, reading her Shakespeare's works?" About five years ago, when Marsden's maternal Italian grandmother had been in a serious carriage accident that left her bedridden, the man had started acting as her companion of sorts. Paying her calls, handling errands, and reading aloud to her. According to Marsden, no one else in his family could tolerate her, and he hadn't wanted her to be left only with the company of a couple doddering servants. An act of kindness if ever there was one, as Vincent had met the cantankerous elderly woman years ago and could well understand why she had no acquaintances of whom to speak.

"She's doing quite well considering the circumstances. Still unpleasant and demanding, but I visit her a few times a week. Still her only visitor and still reading her Shakespeare." Marsden ducked his chin and dragged a self-conscious hand through his hair. "I didn't receive an invitation to the ball," he mumbled.

Vincent clenched his jaw. That haughty, pretentious old hag. He would have a word with his aunt. "My apologies, Marsden. I'm certain it was simply an oversight."

"There's no reason to be affronted on my behalf. I'm accustomed to being overlooked. Truly, it's not a bother. I don't care much for balls, in any case."

"I'll see to the invitation. Will you attend?"

Marsden hesitated. "Well, yes, if you wish it."

"I do. Now if you'll excuse me, I have a call to make this afternoon." All thoughts of Jake were gone, replaced with burning need to put his aunt in her place. How dare she deliver such a cut to his friend? He'd wrestle the invitation out of her gnarled old hands, if that was what it took to erase the humiliation Marsden had not been able to hide from him.

He stood, tipped his head to Marsden, and left White's, not sparing a glance to the old marquis still seated by the fireplace.

Chapter Four

Rolling onto his side, Oliver reached for the top drawer of the bedside table and slid it open. The early morning sunlight seeping through the slits in the threadbare brown velvet drapes provided enough illumination for Oliver to see. But he didn't need the light. His fingertips skimmed over the objects in the drawer, stopping when he encountered the distinctive ridges marking the veins on the shaft of the black marble dildo.

He set the dildo on the table beside the bottle of oil he hadn't bothered to put away last night. Flicking the blanket aside, he lay back on the bed. The fire in the grate had burned out sometime during the night, but the chill April morning air did little to cool his already heated skin. He licked his palm then reached for his hard cock. It was the way he had started and ended every day for the past week, since he had last laid eyes on Vincent at White's. His hand on his prick, stroking himself to orgasm. And after the dream he had last night…there was no way he could begin this day any differently than all the others.

That dream had been so vivid and crisp, so authentic, that when it woke him a few minutes ago, he had actually been shocked to find himself in his own bed, alone, without Vincent.

Closing his eyes, he fondled his cock as he sifted through the memories, those snippets of scenes from the dream, trying to decide where to start.

The brothel. That masculine, tidy bedchamber. Vincent, fully dressed and standing beside the large bed, arms crossed over his impressively broad chest as he appraised a naked Oliver.

Are you good at following orders? The deep cultured rumble of Vincent's voice sounded in Oliver's head.

"Yes, milord," he muttered.

I don't recall giving you permission to touch your cock.

Oliver snatched his hand to his side, left his prick resting on his lower belly. His breathing quickened. One time with Vincent and he was already addicted to the heady sense of anticipation. The added thrill of waiting, of being at another's mercy, being forced to proceed at their pace.

Good boy. Then the hard command seeped back into his voice. *Do you want me?*

"Yes."

What do you want?

"You. Your cock in my arse. Please, milord."

Ah, you must be very, very good to earn that reward. First, you must show me how much you want me. Touch yourself, Oliver.

Reaching down, Oliver cupped his ballocks, dragged his palm roughly over his sac then up to his shaft. His grip firm, he picked up the familiar rhythm. He stroked the length, flicking a finger over the needy head, spreading the leaking fluid.

He ran his other hand up and down his abdomen, sweeping over the quivering muscles, pausing every now and then to deliver a hard pinch to his nipples. Lost in the decadent sensations, his head tipped back, his lips parting. He lifted his hips, rocking into each stroke. Faster and faster, his hand flew along his cock, chasing the climax teasing the edge of his mind. The muscles in his thighs trembled. His entire body drew tight. The orgasm coiled down his spine, gripped his ballocks.

Stop.

Gritting his teeth, Oliver heeded the command. It hurt, in the most intense pleasurable way, to be left poised on the verge, teetering on the brink. Impatient and needy, his cock throbbed, sending heavy, quick pulses throughout his body in time to the rapid beat of his heart. He bit his lower lip, forced himself to remain still, to resist the almost unstoppable urge to touch his prick. Just one stroke. That was all it would take for him to climax.

Are you ready for my cock?

"Yes, yes, please, milord." The whispered words rushed out of Oliver's mouth.

Then prepare yourself.

He snatched the glass bottle from the bedside table and poured a generous amount on his palm. Bending his knees, he spread his legs, feet planted on the mattress. He reached down under his thigh and oiled his entrance. Swirled his fingertips over the puckered skin then eased two of them inside. Scissoring his fingers, he stretched himself, prepared himself. His movements quick and efficient, to hold off the eminent orgasm strumming his senses. Then he coated the dildo, his hand slipping over the cool black marble. The width so substantial his fingers barely enclosed it. He had more than a few such toys in the bedside table drawer and this one most closely matched the dimensions of the real man's cock. The crown wasn't quite as broad and the length nearly an inch short of Vincent's, but the shaft matched in thickness.

His arse tingled, eager and ready for that first amazing thrust. Holding the dildo by the flat circular base, he closed his eyes and waited for a moment. Let the anticipation build, let his nerves coil tighter and tighter. Sweat pricked his brow. A drop of fluid leaked from his cock, dripping onto his skin. His ballocks clenched, drawing up so tightly it felt as though his testicles were trying to get inside his body.

Good boy, Oliver. Vincent's voice was soaked in sin, low and luxurious. *You want me, don't you? Tell me.*

"Yes, fuck me, Vincent, please," Oliver said, the words hitching in his throat.

He positioned the dildo at his entrance then pushed. One long thrust, just as Vincent had done. Determined, persistent, demanding complete submission.

A wince tightened his brow, his mouth opening on a soundless cry of pleasure. He gasped for breath. Grabbed the blanket by his hip and gripped it tight. The intense stretch as his muscles worked to accommodate the intrusion caused a flush of raw heat to sweep over his skin. He shoved it deep, bottoming out, the base pressing hard against his flesh. It wasn't quite as long as Vincent, and he craved that extra inch, the one only Vincent could provide.

Releasing the blanket, he pinched one nipple, twisting hard. Sharp sensation radiated across his chest. He arched his back and grabbed his cock, stroking furiously as he picked up a matching rhythm of hard, relentless thrusts. With each stroke, the veins along the marble shaft teased his hole, just as Vincent's cock had done. His ballocks ached with a need to be touched. His nipples smarted, reminding him of the sweet luscious pain that was only a twist away. Damn it, he didn't have enough hands.

Beg for my cock. You want it, don't you? Tell me.

He could almost feel Vincent's broad chest pressed against his, the heavy weight of his body, the heat from his skin, the warmth of his breath as he spoke those words into Oliver's ear. He turned his head, searching for those firm lips, wanting to feel them against his own.

"Yes, I want you, Vincent. More…please," he begged in broken tones.

If the real Vincent saw him now, like this—knees drawn up to his chest and ramming a big dildo in his arse…

An orgasm rushed down his cock.

"Vincent," he bellowed, throwing back his head, hips lifting from the bed, as seed splattered across his chest.

It was several long moments before Oliver could catch his breath. He gave his head a shake to clear it, then carefully withdrew the dildo. A little jolt shot through him, shaking his limbs as the head slipped from his body.

With effort, he swung his legs over the side of the bed and bent to pick up the drawers he had discarded last night. After wiping his hands, he wrapped the linen around the dildo then dropped it to the floor. He'd clean it later. Right now, he needed to clean himself up.

He set a hand on the bedside table and made to push to his feet, then stopped. A shaft of morning sunlight streamed into the room, cutting across the table and glinting off Vincent's jade cravat pin.

The betting book at White's had proved futile. He hadn't been able to gather the courage to enter the club again after he had shared a drink with Vincent last week. The cravat pin tucked in his waistcoat pocket, directly over his aching heart. His nerves were on edge, waiting for Vincent to recognize him. But he hadn't. Oliver had thought himself relieved, yet now with the prospect of having to gamble to raise the necessary funds to be with Vincent again, the real man and not the dream...

Months of being alone. Months of avoiding Vincent.

Raw pain lanced into Oliver's chest, slicing deep. He let out a low grunt and rubbed his chest, trying to sooth the ache.

But he couldn't avoid Vincent tonight. The man had proved true to his word, as always. The invitation to the ball had arrived seven days ago, delivered by one of her ladyship's footman.

Oliver picked up the stolen pin from the dented little silver tray beside the candlestick and touched the jade stone with a reverent fingertip.

Lord Vincent is an astute man. The madam's confident words echoed in his head.

No one else would notice, but Vincent would.

Swallowing hard, he put the pin back on the tray, stood, and crossed to the washstand. He poured water in the chipped stoneware basin, wet a washcloth, swiped the sticky semen from his chest, quickly cleaned the oil from his backside, and tossed the cloth onto the floor. Then he splashed water onto his face. Dragging a short length of towel across his dripping wet jaw, he looked in the mirror. His dark hair stood at odd ends. Short yet long, but not long enough to pull back in a queue. It would need to be fixed today. He certainly didn't want to give Vincent an additional reason to scowl at him.

Vincent's valet was out of the question. He wasn't about to present himself at Vincent's door and inquire about an offer the man made a week ago.

He studied his reflection. Perhaps he could fix it himself.

* * *

"I'll be but a moment," Vincent said to his driver as he exited the carriage. He went up the stone steps, through the crimson door, and passed a footman stationed in the entrance hall, ignoring the man's offer to take his hat and gloves.

Giving his black evening coat a tug to straighten it, Vincent paused inside the open door of the brothel's elegant receiving room. His gaze skipped past the other patrons, stopping on a petite blonde who, along with a brunette, stood rather closely to a young gentleman. Two pairs of small pale hands slid over the navy coat, toying with the buttons and caressing the man's chest in a clear attempt to entice him to part with enough blunt for not one, but two girls. Judging by the young man's flushed cheeks and eager grin, the girls were succeeding.

Vincent crossed the room and tapped the blonde on the shoulder. Certainly he was violating some unwritten rule by pulling the girl away from a potential client, but he didn't much care. Marsden's invitation had come with a price, namely his word to arrive at his aunt's ball early enough to partner his entirely unpleasant cousin for the first dance. He was due there within the half hour.

"Holly," he said, when his polite tap yielded no results.

She looked over her shoulder. The reprimanding scowl shifted to a welcoming smile at the sight of him. "Ah, Lord Vincent. What a pleasure to see you. An unexpected pleasure, but a pleasure nonetheless."

After whispering in the young man's ear, she took Vincent's hand. Familiar with the routine, she didn't say a word, didn't inquire into his preferences for the evening, as she led him up to the second floor. Her hips swayed, her violet silk skirts swooshing softly with each step. Voluptuous and petite, the epitome of femininity. Holly was quite popular with the other patrons and her popularity was what initially drew him to her. No one would question what he did behind closed doors when he went upstairs with a woman like her.

She opened a door midway along the hall. Vincent went into the empty bedchamber and declined her offer of a drink.

"We are unprepared for your visit, my lord," she said, hands clasped before her, playing the part of a gracious hostess. "If you would wait here, I will alert the staff to ready a room for you."

"Unnecessary. This room will suffice. Send Jake in."

Brow furrowing, she tilted her head to one side. "Jake?"

"Yes. The young man I" —*fucked*— "saw last week."

Comprehension dawned on her face. "Oh." She pressed her lips tight together, her hazel eyes crinkling at the edges.

What about his request did she find humorous? Nerves already rubbed raw, he speared her with a hard stare for daring to make sport of him.

She quickly turned her back to him and reached for the doorknob. "Yes, of course, Lord Vincent," she said as she disappeared out the door, her voice strained, as if she held back a laugh.

Jaw clenched, Vincent let out a short, frustrated growl. He tugged off his white gloves, dropped them inside his black top hat, and set it on a dresser. Then he pulled out his pocket watch. That damn whore better be quick. If she would have deposited him in his usual room, he could have used this time to look for his lost cravat pin. Instead, she'd left him in this garish, overdone crimson bedchamber which had recently been occupied. The nauseatingly sweet scent of cheap perfume and the distinct note of female arousal lingered in the room.

Brilliant. He'd arrive at his aunt's smelling like a brothel. No one would be rude enough to mention it to him directly, but they would assume he'd stopped for a quick poke on his way to the ball.

Better they assumed that than the truth. The worry had eaten away at his stomach until he could no longer tolerate it. All he needed was a few minutes with Jake to ease the anxiety. A simple conversation—a few questions, a few answers—then he would leave.

The visit purposefully structured to prevent himself from acting on his baser urges. The first Thursday of the month was weeks away, and until then, he would continue to keep those desires locked up tight, no matter how difficult it was becoming.

His evening shoes sounded against the polished floorboards as he paced the length of the room. For the past week, worries had plagued him. One concern over whether desperation had pushed Jake into the brothel's employ had spawned another concern, then another, until they were all he could think about. Keeping him up until the wee hours of the morning and pulling his mind from his work in the afternoons. While Jake had taken to it exceedingly well, he clearly had not been accustomed to the exotic play Vincent preferred. Yet Vincent's preferences were mild compared to some of the depraved acts that were allowed in the decadent brothel. Would Jake's need for funds push him to engage in acts in which he'd be uncomfortable? Would Jake even be allowed to refuse a client? It took skill and control to wield a bullwhip without breaking the skin. What if Jake trusted the wrong man? What if some depraved bastard strung him up and abused him? Vincent's strides faltered, ice-cold dread leeching into his anxiety, at the thought of Jake left crumpled on the floor, bleeding and in pain. Who would take care of him if the brothel tossed him aside like a broken toy? What if—

The doorknob clicked. Vincent spun around.

A man clad only in a pair of breeches shut the bedchamber door. Cocksure and smug, he sauntered toward Vincent. "Good evening, Lord Vincent," he said, a sinful smirk curving his sculpted lips, as he palmed the erection visible beneath his snug-fitting black breeches. "I missed you last week."

How had Vincent ever thought this man appealing? Tall, muscular, and with deliberately tousled golden blond hair, Cameron's every glance, every gesture, every word from his lips promised untold sensual pleasures. Yet he was too slick, too obvious, too much of his kind. This arrogant creature was incapable of Jake's raw honesty and uninhibited responses. "Where's Jake?"

Cameron stopped in front of Vincent and trailed his fingertips down Vincent's arm. With heavy-lidded eyes, he gazed up at Vincent.

At six feet in height, he stood a couple inches short of Vincent's six-two.

"He's unavailable, but I *am* available. You can do with me as you please," Cameron said, his broad shoulders rounding, his chin tipping down, in a patent gesture of submission.

Unavailable? Hot, rabid jealously invaded Vincent's stomach at the thought of Jake with another man. Harsh and swift, it mixed violently with the noxious tangle of near-paralyzing worries. His hands balled into fists. "Where is he?"

Cameron leaned closer, his bare chest brushing Vincent's stark white waistcoat, his hand drifting toward the placket of Vincent's black trousers. "It matters not," he said, dismissing Vincent's sharp question.

"The hell it doesn't." Vincent shoved Cameron roughly aside and yanked open the door, prepared to drag Jake out of whatever bed he currently occupied. The muscles in his arms shook with the need to rip the man who dared touch Jake limb from limb. The sounds of his heavy breaths echoed in the empty corridor as he looked left and right. *Hell*, there were too many doors in this goddamn brothel. "Where is he?"

A hand gripped his forearm. "Lord Vincent, come back inside."

Vincent whipped his head around to look over his shoulder. Cameron went pale, true fear reflected in his wide deep blue eyes. Every trace of arrogance vanished. Taking a quick step back, he released Vincent.

"Where is he?" Vincent asked slowly through gritted teeth, as he turned to face Cameron.

"I-I don't know, my lord." Cameron's voice wavered as he spoke.

"Where?" The curt demand snapped through the air.

Swallowing hard, Cameron took another step back and shook his head.

Eyeing Cameron's neck, Vincent opened and closed his fists. His hands would fit nicely around the man's neck and he'd tighten his hold until the whore told him what he needed to know. "Where. Is. He."

"I don't know, my lord. I swear it." Cameron continued to back up as Vincent advanced. "He's not here."

The man's panic-stricken words reverberated in his head, cutting through the thick red haze of jealousy. *Jake wasn't here?* His mind blanked with shock for the briefest of moments then a thunderstorm of rage roiled up within him. "Then where the hell is he?" Vincent bellowed.

Cameron flinched, as though he'd been struck. He scrambled back, bumping into the bed and throwing out his arms to keep from landing on his arse. His gaze darted anxiously about the room, his bare golden chest working against his short, shallow pants. "I don't know. He—he left, and he hasn't been back."

Vincent threw back his head and let out a teeth-baring roar. But it did little to ease the riot of frustration and fury pervading every inch of his being. And if Cameron said "I don't know" one more time, Vincent would strangle the man.

The madam. Perhaps she could answer his question. But he'd appear a desperate pathetic fool if he stormed into her office and demanded to know the whereabouts of one of her whores. He'd already made a big enough spectacle out of himself tonight. Surely the entire brothel had heard him bellowing like an enraged bedlamite.

Reaching into his coat pocket, he yanked out a fold of pound notes and threw it at Cameron. Then he turned on his heel, left the whore on his knees and fumbling for the notes scattered on the floor.

The next moment, he was descending the brothel's front stone steps. His footman opened the carriage door. Vincent's first impulse was to direct his driver to the East End, to search the narrow alleyways and rundown boarding houses for Jake.

"Lady Collarton's. And be quick about it," Vincent said curtly as he settled on the black leather bench.

The footman closed the door with a smart snap. A whip cracked and the carriage lurched forward.

Images collided in his head. Jake vulnerable and alone. Jake destitute and huddled in a dark alley. Jake being forcibly taken by a drunk brute. Jake—

"Stop," he commanded himself. Through sheer force of will, he blocked out those god-awful images. There was no use assuming the worst, at least not yet.

As soon as his aunt's ball was over, he'd scour the streets of London until he found Jake. But he didn't know where to start looking nor did he know the man's actual name. In fact, he knew next to nothing about him. Where did the man live? How did he spend his days? Did he prefer whiskey or gin? All Vincent had was the image of a sleek, yet strong young man with dark wavy hair that fell down to a scruffy jaw and framed full, kissable lips. It had been so dark in the room he hadn't even gotten a good look at Jake's face. Where his eyes blue or brown? Or perhaps green? They definitely hadn't been gray, of that he was certain.

Resting his head against the back wall of the carriage, he took deep even breaths, trying to settle himself. Jake didn't belong to him. There was no cause to feel this possessive need to keep the man close by his side, yet try as he might, he could not make it go away. He needed to see Jake. But did he truly believe one short meeting would be enough?

No. It wouldn't be.

Oh fuck.

Wincing harshly, Vincent groaned, deep and low, the sound filled with gut-wrenching agony. *No!* The part of him that strived to be a respectable, upstanding gentleman, the type of man a father would be proud to call a son, rebelled against the realization. Yet…he wanted Jake.

Vincent let out a string of foul curses under his breath, ending with a beyond frustrated grunt. What was he to do now?

He scrubbed his bare hands over his face then scowled. Damn. He'd left his hat and gloves in that garish bedchamber. The brothel's servants already had his cravat pin, so they might as well have something else of his. He pulled out his pocket watch and held it up to the window to catch the light from the streetlamps. Ten minutes until he had to be at his aunt's. There wasn't enough time to stop at his town house. The hat he could do without but he would need to borrow a pair of gloves from his uncle.

Marsden better appreciate what his invitation had cost Vincent. One black top hat, one pair of white gloves, one dance with an unpleasant cousin, and a delay in his search for one irresistible man.

Chapter Five

Oliver yanked off the cravat and grabbed yet another. Lifting his freshly shaven chin, he placed the cravat on the back of his neck, positioning the linen so it lay flat against his shirt collar. Mouth pursed and brows lowered in concentration, he stared into the mirror above the washstand and willed his shaking fingers to cooperate.

The sun had set hours ago. Candles in pewter holders lit the bedchamber. The clean scent of shaving soap lingered in the air. And he had lingered in this room long enough. If he didn't arrive at the ball soon, he would be sure to incur Vincent's ire before the man even laid eyes on him.

After one last tug to center the knot, he studied his reflection. Not perfect, nothing close to what Vincent, or rather the man's valet, would have accomplished, but at least it somewhat resembled a Gordian knot.

He picked up the black evening coat folded over the back of a nearby chair and slipped his arms into the sleeves. After buttoning it, he ran his hands over the wool, trying to flatten the creases. Should have had it pressed properly, but there was nothing to be done for it now.

Stepping over the ruined lengths of white linen on the floor, he crossed to the bedside table. He paused, his fingertips hovering a hair's breadth above the jade stone.

He had grown quite fond of the pin. It was rarely not with him, even tucked securely in his waistcoat pocket whenever he left his apartments. Not that he'd left much this past week for fear of coming across Vincent; his only outings had been to visit his grandmother. He would miss the pin, this bit of Vincent, but he wasn't a thief. He hadn't given any thought to the ramifications when he snatched it from the brothel floor, but he couldn't keep the pin forever. Its value to Vincent went far above monetary. Oliver clearly recalled the first time he had seen Vincent wear it, and the pride in his friend's adolescent voice as he'd informed Oliver that his grandfather had chosen to leave the jade pin to him, and not his older brother.

There were other ways to return it to Vincent, but sending it anonymously via the post was a coward's way out.

And he needed Vincent to know it had been him. That Vincent had gifted that slow, languid kiss to Oliver. It went beyond his own selfish desire to be with the man he loved. Oliver could deceive his friend no longer. Even if Vincent turned his back on him, refused to acknowledge him again, Oliver had to tell him the truth.

Well, he didn't plan to actually tell him. Oliver was certainly no coward, but he couldn't fathom looking into Vincent's gorgeous, sky blue eyes and telling him, "By the way, Prescot, you buggered me last week."

Wincing, he sucked in a breath. No, no. That he could not do. But there was another way to reveal himself to Vincent. A way that did not require words.

His hand closed over the pin. A tremor shook his body. His pulse pounded in his veins with a mixture of stomach-turning nervousness and sweet resilient hope. There was no reason to be hopeful. None at all. Yet he couldn't stifle the hope; his poor heart clung to the possibility, needing it desperately.

Perhaps, just maybe, that kiss had meant something. Perhaps Vincent would allow their friendship to turn into so much more.

* * *

The statuesque brunette batted her eyelashes, moving a half step closer, deliberately positioning her bosom under Vincent's nose. "The weather has been quite mild of late, don't you agree, Lord Vincent?"

"Yes, of course." Smoothly backing up half a step to maintain the proper distance with an unmarried lady, Vincent kept the bland smile on his lips and resisted the impulse to roll his eyes in irritation. He had been at the ball for what seemed like an eternity, the impatience building with each passing minute. Forced to politely endure one dull conversation after another. And now this silly chit wanted to discuss the weather when Jake could be out on the cold, unforgiving streets alone with no one to protect him.

Gripping his champagne glass tightly, he brought it up to his lips and downed the remaining contents. He dropped the glass on a passing footman's silver tray, snatched another, and took a long swallow. The sweetly bitter, effervescent spirits did little to take the edge off the worry occupying his mind.

Apparently the young lady—he couldn't recall her name—didn't mind in the slightest if a gentleman drank to excess, for she launched into a detailed accounting of the "quite mild" weather. Nodding absently, his gaze strayed over her shoulder. Something akin to relief washed over him.

Chin tipped down and shoulders hunched, Lord Oliver Marsden lingered by himself near one of the marble columns at the foot of the grand staircase, fiddling with the buttons on his black evening coat.

"...and it's April, and it hasn't rained for—"

"Pardon, miss," Vincent said, interrupting the silly chit in midsentence. "I beg your forgiveness, but please excuse me."

The distinct look of feminine affront flashed across her face.

Not bothering to offer an excuse for his ungentlemanly behavior, he sketched a short bow and headed toward Marsden.

Certainly took him damn long enough to arrive. Vincent planned to rib Marsden for his tardiness, but not too much to annoy the man. After the evening Vincent had, Marsden's company was exactly what he needed about now.

With a determined stride, he wove around the clusters of guests, deftly avoiding any who might try to pull him into another inane conversation. Taller than most every other man in the room, Vincent had no trouble keeping his sights pinned on Marsden, lest he try to duck out the door after making a very brief appearance. He was well aware of Marsden's reluctance to attend society functions, a reluctance not purely due to having been frequently omitted from the *ton's* invitation lists. Vincent wasn't all that fond of them either, especially when his father was in attendance. But it wouldn't do Marsden permanent harm to humor him, and endure his aunt's birthday ball for an hour or so.

A genuine smile curved his mouth, the tension in his gut easing for the first time in days. Yes indeed, dancing with his unpleasant cousin had been worth the price of Marsden's invitation.

And apparently the man's tailor wasn't a complete hack. The strict black evening coat actually fit him, and highlighted the breadth of his shoulders and the sleek lines of his hard waist. He was turned out quite smartly. The state of his bank account notwithstanding, Marsden would be a good catch for a nice young lady. Perhaps tonight Vincent could introduce him to a girl with a decent dowry.

Hmm. Why was that thought so unpleasant?

Vincent put the smile back on his lips. "Marsden," he said as neared him. "How good of you to grace us with your presence."

Marsden's head snapped up. "Evening, Prescot."

"Ah, I see you didn't need my valet after all. You were able to manage it, though it took you two attempts," Vincent said, referring to the dark waves that fell in somewhat neat layers about Marsden's unusually pale face.

A strained smile pulled Marsden's mouth. He shifted, rolling one shoulder, the gesture distinctly uncomfortable. "Y-yes. Didn't take much to fix it properly."

"Marsden, my dear fellow" —Vincent clapped him good-naturedly on the shoulder— "no reason to look as though you're facing the hangman's noose. Lady Collarton's on the far side of the room. You don't have to face the old dragon if you don't want to. I can relay your heartfelt good wishes on the event of her seventy-fifth birthday for you."

"Thank you, but I'm not a coward. I can manage it myself," Marsden said, lifting his chin, steel underscoring the tension in his voice.

Vincent tipped his head and took a sip of his champagne. The stress of attending a society function had unsettled Marsden, turning him into a pale, prickly version of his usual easy self. The poor man was in need of a stiff drink. "I wasn't implying you couldn't. Merely offering to lend a hand. Very nice Gordian, by the way. Shall we go to the card room? I've had enough of this," he said, lifting his glass. "Should be able to find some whisk—"

His gaze snapped back to Marsden's cravat. Directly below the knot, affixed to the white linen of Marsden's shirt, was a green jade cravat pin. It looked just like the one he'd lost at the brothel. Brow furrowed, he studied the distinctive oval stone. "That pin. Where did you get it?"

"Off the floor, milord."

That voice. Low, rough, and with a hint of an East End accent.

Jake's voice.

The confusion vanished, replaced by mind-numbing shock. He speared Marsden with a hard stare.

There it was—that need, that longing, reflected in Jake's eyes.

Swift and ruthless, desire gripped hold of him. Startled, Vincent took a quick step back, putting distance between himself and Jake, no, *Marsden*.

Christ! They were the same goddamn man.

Why hadn't he noticed before? Same height, same build, same dark wavy hair. Except Jake's had been longer, long enough to hide behind, until Marsden cut it. And Jake's scruffy beard—Marsden had shaved it clean the following day when he had seen him at White's. The darkened room, the absence of his usual spectacles—Marsden had deliberately set out to deceive him.

He felt the flush rise up his neck, burning his cheeks. Closing his eyes, he tried to tamp down the overwhelming fury, keep it hidden from view. *You are in your aunt's ballroom.* Breathing hard, his nostrils flaring, he repeated the words in his head.

You are in your aunt's ballroom.

You fucked your friend, Marsden.

Glass shattered. Cool liquid seeped through his borrowed white gloves, wetting his skin.

"Prescot?" came Marsden's worried voice, as if from a great distance. "I—"

"Don't speak," he said, grinding his teeth together, eyes still closed, unable to look at Marsden.

Oh God. Marsden knew. He knew what Vincent did at that brothel.

Panic wrapped around his chest, tightening ever tighter, threatening to suffocate him.

"Have you told anyone?" Vincent asked in a low voice, fearing Marsden's answer, afraid he was merely the brunt of a joke, the Season's latest object of ridicule. But what sort of man played such a cruel joke on a friend?

"No, Prescot. No one else knows. Well, the madam's aware, and—and the whore, Holly, but…no one else"

Vincent could barely hear Marsden's voice through the furious rushing in his ears. No wonder that whore had laughed at him tonight. She'd known about Marsden's trick. Why had he done it? How had he known to take Cameron's place? Vincent wasn't even aware Marsden had an interest in men!

The hairs on his nape pricked. It felt as though every eye in the ballroom was fixed on him. As if they could see right through him and had already passed judgment.

His father was at his aunt's ball tonight.

Somehow he managed to keep the agonized, soul-wrenching groan inside.

Why the hell had Marsden done this to him? What had Vincent ever done to him to deserve this?

"We need to talk. But not here." But where? He had servants. Servants who knew more about what went on in his own home than he did. Any discussion with Marsden could be overheard. Then the gossip would spread to every house in Mayfair.

A ragged shudder skipped down his spine. Definitely not his town house.

"Your apartments. One hour." Perhaps by then Vincent could look at Marsden without wanting to pummel the very life out of him. It would be a sure way to ensure his silence on the whole affair, but he'd rather not resort to violence.

He took a deep breath, inhaling through his nose and exhaling out his mouth. Forcing his fists to unclench, he opened his eyes.

Biting his bottom lip, the same full lip Vincent had nipped one week ago, Marsden nodded. If he had looked pale before, it was nothing compared to now.

Good, Vincent thought with perverse satisfaction. He should be scared.

"You know the address?" Marsden asked.

Vincent turned on his heel, dismissing the man he once called friend.

Chapter Six

The end of the key skipped across the brass lock leaving a deep gouge in the wooden door. Cursing his shaking hand, Oliver shoved the key back at the lock. This time, the key slid home.

A smarter man would have taken a much longer route from Lady Collarton's. A route that wouldn't have put him at his front door until well after the appointed time. But what had Oliver done? He'd walked straight home.

Glutton for punishment, aren't I? And in more ways than one.

Shaking his head at himself, he crossed the dark front parlor of his bachelor apartment and lit a candle. The golden light illuminated the untidy room in all its glory: the brown leather couch with newspapers strewn across its lumpy but comfortable cushions; the mahogany side table with a volume of Shakespeare under one leg to keep it from wobbling; the scratched bowfront cabinet next to the old upholstered armchair, and the floorboards that hadn't been polished in ages since he couldn't afford a maid. The faded wallpaper was marred by two large rectangles where gilt-framed landscapes had once hung.

He cringed. Christ, he lived in hovel.

Well, it wasn't quite a hovel, but it was damn close especially when compared to Vincent's stately white stucco town house.

Oliver hastily gathered the newspapers he had used in an effort to fill the last week when he rarely left his apartments and tucked them under his arm, grabbed the two empty glasses on the side table, picked up the brown coat and the dusty boots from the floor, and opened the bottom drawer of the cabinet, dumping everything inside. The drawer wouldn't shut, so he took out the boots, kicked the drawer closed and tossed them into his bedchamber, not caring where they landed.

He simply shut the bedchamber door, closing off the view to the mess he had created getting prepared for the ball. No reason to attempt to tidy that room, for Vincent wouldn't want to go in there tonight or any night.

Groaning, he sat in the armchair, removed his spectacles, and rubbed his tired eyes. Resting his elbows on his knees, he dropped his head in his hands. His right leg shook uncontrollably. The rapid, unsteady tap of his heel against the floorboards echoed in the quiet room. A clammy sweat pricked his scalp. His gut clenched against the vile dread churning in his stomach.

He swallowed hard and focused on taking short, even breaths, willing his stomach to settle. He would not get sick. Could not embarrass himself like that. Not when Vincent would arrive at any moment.

The urge to drop to his knees and beg Vincent's forgiveness had been so great Oliver had not trusted himself to remain at the ball even an instant after Vincent turned his back on him. It had taken all of his courage to summon the fake accent and inform Vincent where he had found the man's cravat pin. But the hardest part of all had been standing there and watching the pain and fury distort Vincent's ruggedly handsome features. The strong jaw clenched tight. The firm lips compressed in a straight line. The gorgeous eyes clamped shut.

Oliver had not seen or heard the worst of it. Even taking the direct route home, the walk from Lady Collarton's took close to an hour. Vincent had a town carriage. Sleek, shiny, and black, pulled by four matching bays. Equipage which matched his position as second son to the obscenely wealthy Marquis of Saye and Sele. He would arrive momentarily and unleash the anger on Oliver he had contained while at his aunt's ball.

Vincent had every right to lash out at him. Oliver was not looking forward to it, but he was prepared. Nervous, sick with nerves, but prepared. On the long walk home, he had been struck by a rare moment of clarity, the realization cutting through the excruciating heartache.

He had nothing left to lose. No reason to hold anything back. In a few short minutes, Vincent would arrive, and he'd likely never speak to Oliver again once he left this shabby parlor. But while he was here, he'd receive nothing less than brutal honesty.

A sense of purpose stole over him, settling his stomach and clearing the anxiety from his mind. Standing, he unbuttoned his coat and draped it neatly over the back of the armchair. He put his spectacles back on, gave his white waistcoat a sharp tug, and removed the cravat pin in preparation for its return to Vincent.

He was checking the clock on the mantle when heavy footsteps sounded outside his door. Squaring his shoulders, he clasped his hands behind his back and gripped the jade pin tightly, the oval stone pressing into his palm.

You have nothing to lose.

The brass knob turned and the door opened.

Without bothering to knock, Vincent strode into Marsden's apartments and slammed the door. "Explain yourself, Marsden," he said, barely able to get the words past the anger and betrayal clawing at his throat. The past hour had done nothing to dim the rage, merely providing ample time for it to build to intolerable levels.

Standing across the room near the fireplace, Marsden lifted his chin. "It was the only way I could be with you. I love you. I—"

"Stop!" Vincent halted in his tracks. He wanted to clamp his hands over his ears, shut out those words. Marsden had *not* just said that to him.

"No, Prescot." Marsden's features hardened with determination. "I have loved you for so long. The feeling's so familiar, so a part of me, I can't remember when it first began. All I wanted was one night. I was *desperate* for one night with you. I understand it can never happen again, but I couldn't live the rest of my life without being with you once. If you are worried word will get out, you needn't be. I won't speak a word of it. You can trust me, Prescot."

"Trust you? You betrayed me in the worse possible manner."

"I did not reveal my identity. That was my only deception."

His only deception? Vincent gapped at Marsden. "I thought you were my friend."

"I am."

Unflinching and resolute, his steady gaze bore into Vincent's. A dark wavy chunk of his untidy hair partially obscured one eye. Jake had brown eyes. Not blue or green, but brown. So rich and dark, they almost approached black. With a start, Vincent took a step back, distancing himself from Jake. No, Marsden. Hell, his mind refused to reconcile the image of Jake's nude body, the very one that tempted him like no other, with that of his childhood friend. Yet when he looked at Marsden now, he saw Jake's broad shoulders, his lean hips, and his full mouth. How many times in the past week had Vincent stopped himself from wondering how that beautiful mouth would feel wrapped around his cock?

"You pay for a prostitute's services on the first Thursday of every month." Marsden's blunt words jolted Vincent back to the argument at hand. "It doesn't matter to you who you fuck. So what's so wrong about it being me?"

"Everything," Vincent said, throwing up his hands in exasperation, refusing to examine why it hurt that Marsden thought so little of him. "If I would have known it was you, I...I..." Teeth clenched, Vincent growled. "Goddamn it! I worried about you." He gave his head a sharp shake. "About Jake."

"You did? Why?" Marsden asked, utter bewilderment on his face.

A sneer twisting his mouth, Vincent dropped his gaze to his evening shoes. "You said you were new," he grumbled, embarrassed to admit his worry had been for naught. "That I was your first client.

Some men can be downright cruel in their pursuit of pleasure. I didn't want you to get hurt."

Vincent fought to keep from shifting his weight against the uncomfortable stretch of silence. He wanted to rub his temples, do something to ease the brutal pounding in his head. "How did you find out?" he asked, managing to infuse enough indignant anger into the demand to cover the knot of panic in his gut. He'd seen Marsden a time or two in Delacroix's receiving room, along with many other gentleman of the *ton*. If Marsden knew he didn't actually hire a woman, then there could be others. What had Vincent done to give himself away? Or had it been obvious to everyone all along?

Marsden let out a weary sigh. "You're Cameron's favorite. He never stopped going on about you. He didn't mention your name," he added quickly. "But I knew you frequented the brothel and eventually guessed the handsome, domineering lord with the sky blue eyes was you."

Marsden thought him handsome? Vincent's lips quirked then thinned. "So you fucked him, too."

"Well, not exactly." A faint blush stained Marsden's cheekbones. "It was the other way around."

The knowledge that Cameron had fucked Marsden didn't sit any better. If anything, it was worse. Much worse. The thought of another man gripping those lean hips, ramming his prick into that tight arse, kissing those full…

Oh God, he had kissed Marsden.

"Other than us both being frequently overlooked second sons to marquises, I used to believe we had very little in common," Marsden said, calm and composed when Vincent felt like the floor was tilting underneath him. "You succeed at everything you do. You're damn near perfect. Whereas I'm, well…" He waved a hand, indicating himself and the shabby room in one gesture. "You have responsibilities, property to oversee, and I have absolutely no prospects. Never even attended university. But we aren't so different after all. You know what it feels like to wonder why you're this way. Why you aren't like every other man who lusts after women and wants a wife to call his own. And you can understand the difficulty and the need to keep it hidden."

Vincent's eyes widened, cold panic gripping his spine. "I'm not like you."

"Yes, you are."

"The hell I'm not! I don't bend over and take it like a woman."

Marsden flinched, as though Vincent had punched him in the gut. "Is that what you tell yourself?" he asked, hurt and anger warring in his narrowed eyes. "That has nothing to do with it."

"Yes, it does! I'm not a…a—"

"A what?" Marsden shot back, hands fisted at his sides, advancing swiftly until he stood chest to chest with Vincent. "Go on, say it. But calling me a sod or a molly isn't going to change the fact you fucked me. Hell, you did more than that. A fuck is just a fuck. But you kissed me!" Marsden threw the truth violently at Vincent.

Bristling at the reminder, Vincent resisted the urge to take a defensive step back. "I'm well aware of that."

"So why can't you accept it? I'm not asking you to acknowledge it outside of this room. But why can't you accept yourself for who you are?" Marsden went still then, peering though his wire-rimmed spectacles into Vincent's face as though looking for something. His brows knit together. "That's it, isn't it? You're angrier at yourself than you are at me. You see it as a failure, and Lord Vincent Prescot never fails, does he?"

Vincent rolled his shoulders. It wasn't the entire ballroom that could see right through him, just Marsden. "That's not true."

"Yes, it is. Vincent, it doesn't make you less of a man, at least not in my eyes. Your father, well" —Marsden let out a condescending huff— "why should his opinion matter? He's dim enough to choose to lavish all his affection on your jackanapes brother and give you none."

Good old Marsden, always propping him up when he needed it most. Suddenly tired, Vincent trudged to the couch, sat down, dropped his head, and rubbed the back of his neck. If he was honest with himself, he had to admit he respected Marsden for standing up to him. Most of his acquaintances were too eager to garner his favor and rarely contradicted him. Yet Marsden was forcing him to examine a part of himself he had always tried to deny. It wasn't a pleasant experience, but perhaps necessary.

How long had he been going to that brothel? Years. All the while, he told himself firmly he was simply giving those men what they wanted. That if he kept his distance, didn't let them touch him, didn't kiss them, or do anything but take them, then he wasn't one of *them*. He snorted at his own stupidity. The truth was a bit frightening, but he couldn't deny it any longer. He was a goddamn sod, and he went to that brothel because he wanted a man. The proof stood but a few paces from him. If anyone else had tried to confront him, he would have vehemently denied it, even gone so far as to challenge the man to pistols at dawn. But Marsden, his old friend, understood him better than he understood himself.

He had felt lust, plain, empty lust for all those other men. But he had kissed Marsden. Worried about him. Had this instinctive need to keep him safe, close by his side. And he couldn't get the man out of his head, no matter how much he tried.

So where did this leave them? He didn't want to lose Marsden's friendship, but could they go on as they had, after all of this?

Was that what he really wanted? Or did he want more?

He didn't lift his head when he heard the sound of footsteps approaching.

"Just know there's one person who accepts you, and loves you for who you are, even if you don't feel that way about yourself." Marsden let out a heavy exhale. "Here. I know how much it means to you. I apologize for taking it and for upsetting you tonight. I just"—he sighed again, the sound tired, beyond defeated— "needed you to know it had been me."

The pure heartache in Marsden's voice tugged at Vincent's chest, and all of his questions answered themselves. He wanted more.

Standing, he closed Marsden's hand over the jade pin. "Keep it. You need it more than I. Perhaps it will keep your damn cravat straight." He gazed into Marsden's deep brown eyes. All traces of his earlier composure were gone, leaving only stark, raw vulnerability. "You said you understood it couldn't happen again."

Teeth digging into his bottom lip, Marsden nodded. Every line in his body drew taut, as if he was bracing himself for the worst.

"But it can," Vincent said. "We just need to be very discrete."

Brow furrowing, Marsden tilted his head slightly to one side. *Good*, about time Marsden got a taste of being confused. "So...your Thursday appointment. You want me to be there, at the brothel?"

"I have no reason to go back there again." Vincent snorted in derision. "To think of all the money I wasted when I could have had you all along."

Suspicion flashed across Marsden's face. He snatched his hand from Vincent's grasp. "What? You just want to use me for what? A cheap fuck? Christ, I can't believe I said that. But I can't be with you again unless I know I mean something to you. I thought I could, but I can't. I'm not asking for your heart. Just to be more than an anonymous man to bugger whenever the urge strikes you."

"Marsden, don't be ridiculous. You're more than that. How much more...I...well..." He winced, tried again then gave up. Frustrated, he scrubbed his hands over his face. The concept of being in love with a man was simply too foreign for his mind to wrap around. Yet he believed Marsden loved him. He felt it, and that affection felt right. But he wasn't at all sure he was capable of returning those feelings. Everything was much too new. Maybe with time...

But what if Marsden needed to hear the words now? Could he speak them, knowing he didn't feel them? Could he lie so blatantly to his friend, if that was what it would take to have Marsden again?

"Hell, don't strain yourself, Prescot," Marsden said, humor lacing the exasperation in his voice. He tugged Vincent's hands from his face. "Your answer will suffice. For now."

With one hand, he grabbed Vincent's head, pulled him down, and crushed his mouth against his. Bold and aggressive, a hot familiar tongue swept into Vincent's mouth.

Marsden's kissing you.

The thought passed through his mind. Then the flicker of awkwardness vanished in a flare of lust as a closed fist pressed against the small of his back, jerking him closer. Vincent grabbed Marsden's arse and kissed him back, slanting his mouth firmly over Marsden's, letting lose the forbidden desires that had been locked inside him for so very long.

Marsden broke the kiss, his fingers still tangled in Vincent's hair, holding him close. "You have no idea how long I've been waiting to do that." His hoarse whisper tickled the wet surface of Vincent's lips.

Needing to remind Marsden just who was in charge, Vincent bit Marsden's full lower lip and held it between his teeth. It took less than a second for Marsden to submit, his dark lashes sweeping down, the aggression slipping from his body, his hand dropping to rest on Vincent's shoulder. The sight so absolutely beautiful, so filled with seeped in trust, this willingness of Marsden's to turn himself over so completely. An awed smile flittered across Vincent's mouth then he flicked his tongue over that enticing lip, soothing any lingering sting. "Where's your bed?"

Marsden jerked his head to the left, indicating a closed door.

"Good. I want you on it."

Marsden blinked.

Vincent straightened and glared down at Marsden. "Now."

Marsden practically ran to the door, throwing it open. There was a *thump* followed by a muttered curse. "Damn boots."

Vincent followed at a slightly more dignified pace and glanced about the dark room. The light seeping in from the parlor illuminated the back of Marsden's white waistcoat as the man leaned down and tossed two objects, likely the damn boots, toward the wall. As Marsden scurried about the room doing God knew what, Vincent lit a candle on the dresser. Hell, Marsden needed a maid. How could the man tolerate this mess?

Stepping on the cravats littering the floor, Marsden darted from the washstand to a table beside the rumpled bed. Shoulders hunched, he shoved something into the drawer.

Four long strides took Vincent across the room. He crowded him, using his larger frame to keep the other man from turning from the table. He placed his hand over Marsden's closed fist on the drawer, holding it open. "What have we here?"

Marsden stiffened. "Ah...nothing."

He looked over Marsden's shoulder. Holy hell. Only a true devotee would amass a collection of that size, and he was certain Marsden had sampled every one at least once. The thought made Vincent's prick jump against the placket of his trousers. Somehow he kept from grinding against Marsden's firm arse, sinking his teeth into the man's shoulder, and instead managed to speak with an arrogant, unaffected drawl. "Doesn't look like nothing to me. Which one is your favorite?"

Marsden's fingertips hovered over a black marble dildo, the largest of the bunch.

"Why that one?"

"It's...it's almost the size of your cock," he whispered, his voice wavering. He touched the marble crown. "But not quite long enough."

"No, it isn't. Is it?" Vincent smirked, smug as hell that not one of the dildos in Marsden's rather vast collection could surpass his own prick. "And if you're very *very* good, you'll get the real thing tonight."

Marsden's answering whimper shot straight to Vincent's groin. Blood rushed to his cock so quickly it left him momentarily lightheaded. When he pulled his hand from the drawer, Vincent released him. The jade pin clattered as Marsden dropped it into a dented little silver tray on the table. There was that tug on his chest again as Vincent realized he had kept the pin right beside his bed, mere inches from his lumpy white pillow. Vincent would bet everything he owned that for the past week the man had never let the pin out of his sight. When he had given it to Marsden, he'd done so hoping he would wear it many times in the future. Though they would need to keep their physical relationship hidden from prying, judging eyes, he was quite fond of the idea of him wearing something of his outside this room.

Stepping closer so his chest brushed Marsden's tense shoulder blades, Vincent reached around his lean waist. "We'll need this." He took the glass bottle of oil out of the drawer and set it on the table. "The others can wait. I do want to see exactly what you do with your favorite toy, but…later." Vincent dragged his lips over his ear, the tousled dark hair tickling his nose as he inhaled the other man's scent.

Marsden gasped, a shudder gripping his body. Before Vincent gave into the impulse to throw him on the bed and pounce on him, he took a few steps back. He grabbed a nearby chair, moved it closer to the bed, and sat down.

"Take off your clothes."

At the stuttered hitch in Marsden's breaths, Vincent gripped the wooden arms of the chair.

"Now," he said, infusing a hard edge of command into his voice.

Marsden turned to face him. With shaking hands, he attacked the buttons on his white waistcoat. He tossed the garment in the general direction of the dresser then divested himself of his suspenders, cravat, spectacles, shirt, and shoes in a few seconds. He kicked his trousers and drawers free of his feet. Then the flurry of motion ceased.

Leaning back in the chair, Vincent kept his expression blank as he soaked up the sight of his naked body. He had indulged Marsden at the brothel, but never again would he allow him to hide under the cover of darkness. The faint firelight hadn't done the man's body justice. He was all lean, strong lines—compact and sleek at the same time. His golden skin, a gift from his Italian grandmother, molded smoothly over solid muscle. Vincent's fingers itched to take hold of those copper nipples, to twist the sensitive tips until he sobbed for more. Unlike Vincent, the only hair on his torso was a thin line running from his navel to the dark thatch on his groin. Vincent hadn't even touched him yet, and already his erection jutted from his body, ballocks drawn up tight.

Marsden flexed his hands by his sides, but that was the only outward sign of impatience as he waited for Vincent's next command.

Vincent let the moment draw out, tightening the suspense. Then he leaned down, picked up a cravat from the floor and stood. "Come here."

Marsden stopped before him. His bare chest was tinged pink with a flush of arousal, his breaths coming in short little pants, his gaze fixed on the white cravat held lightly in Vincent's hand.

"Turn around. Clasp your hands behind your back."

Without question, without hesitation, Marsden did as he was bid. Vincent wrapped the linen around his wrists and tied it. Marsden's biceps flexed as he shifted his arms, testing his bonds.

"All right?" Vincent asked in a low voice, as he laid a soothing hand on his forearm.

He got a single nod from Marsden. Reassured, he left the man standing there, his beautiful back to him, the ends of the cravat tickling the crack of his firm, round arse.

Was there a more appealing sight in all of England? Yes, there was, and more than one. He would get to them soon enough. First he wanted to sample Marsden's mouth.

He unbuttoned the placket, pushed aside his shirttail, and pulled out his cock, leaving his trousers hanging from his hips. "Turn around," he said, running a hand along the hard length.

Marsden's gaze went straight to Vincent's erection. His tongue darted out to lick his lips.

"Do you want to suck my cock?"

He speared Vincent with a hot stare, full of intense longing.

"Yes. *Please.*"

Vincent laid a hand on Marsden's hard shoulder and pushed. He immediately heeded the pressure and dropped to his knees.

"Then suck it, boy."

Damnation, Marsden's whimpers were almost enough to make Vincent climax. Those little sounds, the pure need in the breathy trembles of air. Vincent swallowed hard, forcing back the orgasm tickling his ballocks, and widened his stance so the head of his cock brushed those full lips.

Marsden opened his mouth, engulfing his cock in wet heat. Lashes resting on his cheekbones, he bobbed along the length, taking a bit more with each downward glide, sucking hard every time he pulled back. Vincent grabbed his nape, fingers tangled in the dark hair and thrust in counterpoint. Hell, the man was good at sucking cock. Far better than Vincent could have ever imagined. With his free hand, he tugged the knot on his cravat then whipped the linen from his neck. Pulling back, Marsden swirled his tongue over the crown, lapping up the fluid seeping from the slit and pulling a grunt from Vincent, then he sank all the way down and swallowed. Vincent gasped at the decadent sensation as Marsden used his velvet throat to massage his cock.

"Good boy." The words were almost lost in his groan. "So….ah…good."

He pulled back and did it again and again. Head falling forward, brows knitting together, Vincent held tight to Marsden's shoulder. A tremble wracked his thighs. It was so tempting to spill down that velvet throat, to let loose the orgasm burning the base of his cock.

Gritting his teeth, he let out a grunt and fought back the urge. *Not yet.* He wanted Marsden to beg for his cock. Needed to hear those desperate pleas. The ones soaked in need.

"Enough. Let go." Vincent pushed on his shoulder.

Marsden obediently released him and looked up. His eyes were glazed with lust, pupils so dilated only a thin ring of brown surrounded the black. His sharp pants seemed to fill the room. A fine sheen of sweat coated his flushed chest. The head of his prick glistened, the length so hard it was arched up, almost grazing his abdomen.

Vincent had never been with anyone who got this aroused from simply sucking cock. The experience was…humbling because he knew in his gut Marsden only reacted this way with him.

Leaning down, he planted a quick kiss on those parted lips, tasting himself and Marsden in the kiss. "On your feet, boy." With a hand on Marsden's biceps, he helped him up then turned him to face the bed. "Down," he said, pushing his upper body to the mattress.

Vincent left him there—bent over and hands still tied behind his back, his arse on display. He slowly took off his coat, waistcoat, and shirt, using the time to settle the ever rising lust and allow Marsden's to racket even higher. It had only taken a short handful of minutes with him at that brothel for Vincent to realize the man craved the anticipation, needed it. They were two halves of a whole, he and Marsden. Each feeding off the other's pleasure. The intense rush of having him pliant and writhing for more, of taking Marsden to a place where the only thing that existed in his world was Vincent. And Vincent was determined to take him there tonight.

He dragged the chair closer, grabbed the bottle of oil and sat down. "Wider," he said, tapping Marsden's bare ankle with his foot. Then he laid a firm smack on that round arse.

Marsden started then sank into the mattress, letting out a moan that sounded almost like a "yes."

Needing to hear the actual word, Vincent asked, "Did you like that?"

"*Yes.*"

"And which do you like better?" He rubbed a palm over his skin, soothing the red handprint—then smacked him again. "My hand or the stinging caress of a leather bullwhip?"

"Both," was his quick answer.

Vincent chuckled as he massaged the firm flesh, pulling the rounded halves apart. "Ah, Marsden, my dear boy, whatever am I to do with you?"

Marsden arched, pushing back into Vincent's hands. "Fuck me. Please."

"All in good time." Pulling one cheek back, he oiled Marsden's entrance, slowly swirling two fingertips over his skin. He could not explain it, but for some reason, he found a man's arse incredibly erotic. Wickedly so. Given the time, he could play with Marsden for hours, just toy with him, slide his fingers up and down the dark forbidden crease, trace the puckered hole, drive him to distraction as he waited for the penetration.

When the tight ring of muscle began to relax under his touch, he slipped both fingers inside, pressing deep. Tight heat clamped around the digits, holding him in a viselike grip. Marsden let out a low gravely groan of pleasure. Vincent shuddered, his cock hardening even further, eager to feel that tight heat. Needing to quickly take Marsden past that point of desperation, he reached between the man's spread thighs and took hold of his prick, pulling it down.

The combination of finger-fucking his arse and tugging on his cock had Marsden gasping and moaning, pleading for more. His legs shook, his hands clenched in tight fists at the small of his back. The muscles in his arms and back bunched and flexed as he twisted his head from side to side.

"Vincent, please, I'm going to climax."

Ah hell. That breathy, threadbare whimper.

"Not yet you don't," Vincent growled. He stood, shoved his trousers off, kicked the chair out of the way, grabbed hold of Marsden's lean hips, and pushed inside.

A hoarse shout rent the air. Marsden's slick, silken passage fluttered then gripped tight, clamping Vincent's cock so hard if felt as though he was being strangled. The musky scent of semen mixed with the scents of male sweat and arousal. Christ, Marsden had climaxed with nothing more than the head of his cock in his arse, just as he had done at the brothel.

Fingers digging into Marsden's skin, Vincent pushed harder, needing to be buried deep.

Gasping for breath, Marsden begged, pleaded. "More. All of it. Please."

Vincent gave it to him. Rammed his cock so deep his ballocks were pressed tightly against him. Then he rotated his hips, pulled almost all the way out, teasing the rim, and slammed back home.

Marsden arched, throwing his head back, his shoulders lifting from the mattress. His arms formed a strict V down his back, his stretched fingers brushing Vincent's groin. Vincent continued to fuck him, thrusting hard.

Marsden shook his arms, tugging hard on his bonds. Grunts of definite frustration mixed with his harsh moans. "Untie me. Please, Vincent."

He didn't hesitate. He let go of Marsden's hips long enough to tug quickly on the knot. The linen fell to the floor. But before he could grab Marsden's shoulders, hold the man steady for his hard thrusts, Marsden twisted beneath him, disengaging with a sharp grunt and scrambling onto the bed.

Disorientated from the abrupt change, Vincent gave his head a shake. Kneeling in the middle of the rumpled sheets, Marsden leaned forward and grabbed Vincent's wrist, pulling him full onto the bed and on top of him. He grasped Vincent's nape, pulling him down between his spread thighs so Vincent had to brace himself on his forearms lest he crush Marsden with his weight.

Marsden tilted his hips, his hair-dusted calves wrapping around Vincent's waist so the head of Vincent's straining erection grazed his oil-slicked entrance. "Fuck me. Like this. Please," he whispered against Vincent's lips.

Supplicant and eager, Marsden lay beneath him. The new position ignited a primitive, unstoppable need to possess. It rolled up from his belly, violently yanking hold of him. With a feral growl, Vincent lunged forward, sinking hilt deep into that exquisite tightness and pulling a groan of gratitude from Marsden. Then he picked up a rhythm of hard, demanding strokes.

"You're mine. Mine," Vincent growled, slamming into him.

"Yes, yes," Marsden panted, his hot breaths fanning Vincent's neck.

"No other man will ever touch you again."

"Only you, Vincent. I only want you."

Marsden levered up and crushed his lips to Vincent's, tongue sweeping inside, devouring his mouth. His hands were everywhere, branding Vincent's skin with his touch. His back, his biceps, his neck, his jaw, his arse, his chest. The sensations blended together, heightening the lust until it consumed him.

Marsden's hard prick was crushed between them, the satiny length rubbing against Vincent's abdomen, wetting his skin with the proof of his desire for him. By God, he wasn't going to be able to hold back, to hold off until Marsden climaxed again. The orgasm was barreling upon up him, coming ever closer with each quick jerk of his hips. And when the hell had he lost control? It had slipped through his fingers without him even being aware of it.

Desperate to wrestle it from Marsden, he twisted his head, breaking the kiss and tried to rear back. But Marsden held tight, curling his upper body into his, dragging his lips in a searing path down Vincent's neck to his chest. Wet heat latched onto Vincent's nipple, sharp teeth nipped the hardened peak.

A savage groan rumbled his chest as he drove into Marsden with all the force of his lower body. He was vaguely aware of Marsden's hand moving between them as he jerked his own cock. Liquid fire rushed down his prick, erupting from the head, his hips sputtering to a halt in time to the jolts shaking his entire body.

Exhausted and gasping for breath, Vincent flopped onto his back, pulling Marsden with him so the man lay over him. Marsden's arms were slung over his shoulders, his legs bracketing him. They were sprawled sideways on the bed, Vincent's calves hanging off the edge. Marsden must have climaxed again for there were sticky wet spots mixed with the sweat on his chest, but Vincent didn't have the strength to clean them up, at least not yet.

Turning his head, he dragged his lips over the top of Marsden's head, which was tucked against his shoulder. How had Marsden done it? Vincent had fucked him, yet he felt as though he was the one who had been taken. The thought should have been unsettling, but strangely it wasn't. No, not strange at all. Perhaps he was still in a daze from that explosive climax but it was suddenly so very clear to him. The control he believed he exerted over Marsden was simply an illusion. By willingly bending to Vincent's will, Marsden held it all, even Vincent, in the palm of his hand.

His chest rumbling with the beginnings of an amazed chuckle, he absently glanced about the room. Then he grimaced.

"You need a maid." But not a valet. No man except Vincent would be helping Marsden get dressed or undressed for that matter.

"No, I don't," Marsden grumped, sounding like a peeved, prickly adolescent.

"Yes, you damn well do. I'll see to it," he said, well aware of Marsden's precarious financial situation. "A girl will be here tomorrow. The place could use with a good dusting." He had plenty of servants. One less wouldn't be a hardship.

"I don't want a maid. Don't want any servants lurking about at an inopportune time. In any case, she'd ask about the hooks in the ceiling, and then what would I tell her? They're merely decorative?"

What was Marsden going on about? "There aren't any hooks in the ceiling."

He felt him smile against his chest. "There will be. I plan to install them tomorrow."

Vincent's spent cock surged to life, pressing against Marsden's abdomen. "No maid. I can tolerate the mess as long as you're here."

Pushing up onto his forearms, Marsden stared intently into his eyes. "I will always be here for you, Vincent. Always."

Those words echoed in his head, filled his entire being. He owed Marsden a debt he could not express. If not for the courage of his friend, he would have never stopped fighting himself. Never opened his eyes to see that everything he needed had been here all along.

He might never earn his father's respect, but he found it was no longer as important as it used to be. As long as he had Oliver, that was all that mattered.

He tucked a stray stand of hair behind Marsden's ear. "As I you, Marsden. Now about tomorrow. I'll have some errands to see to. What do you think about a paddle? A nice wooden one. Maybe covered in leather?"

Marsden's breath hitched, excitement flaring on his flushed face. "Yes, *please*, milord."

Bound to Him

Lord Vincent Prescot's life couldn't be better. Thriving investments, well-respected by his peers, and mind blowing sex with a man who submits to his every desire—what more could he want?

Lord Oliver Marsden should be more than happy with his life. He's been in love with Vincent for over a decade and six months ago the impossible happened and they became lovers. But since then, nothing has changed. More specifically, Vincent hasn't changed. Oliver has tried to be patient—it took a lot for Vincent to accept the fact he preferred men. But what felt like a tiny distance between them six months ago now feels like an ever-widening chasm. Why can't Vincent stay the night? Is it too much to ask for Vincent to call him Oliver and not Marsden? He knows Vincent cares for him, but does Vincent love him?

Then Vincent's father asks him for a favor—one that involves marriage. If Vincent agrees, he'll have the respect he's craved from his father his entire life but he could lose Oliver. Nor does Oliver make the decision easy. To keep Oliver, he'll have to do more than deny his father. He'll have to give Oliver his heart.

Chapter One

October 1822
London, England

Under normal circumstances, the sight of a gambling hell wouldn't put a smile on Lord Vincent Prescot's face. Especially not a somewhat questionable one in Cheapside.

But tonight he had a reason to smile and an even better reason to go inside that hell.

He leaned right, reaching for the brass lever on the carriage door, but stopped short as the movement caused a hard object to bump against his outer thigh. No way could he go into a hell with *that* in his pocket. He highly doubted the servants who tended to the guests' coats did so without thoroughly examining the garments as soon as their owners were out of sight. The thought of a footman finding the gift, and wondering why he would possess such an object, did not sit well. Odd, considering he'd had no such qualms purchasing the thing. Then again, he hadn't been with another man at the time. But he would most certainly leave the hell tonight with another man. And not just any man, but a man who had become so much more than his old childhood friend.

Only four-and-twenty and already Vincent possessed what most men strove their entire lives to attain: the respect of his peers, a thriving bank account, and incredible sex with someone who submitted to his every desire. Someone who loved him.

Chuckling in amazement at his good fortune, he removed his greatcoat, carefully folded it, and placed it on the leather bench. Then he got out of the carriage and gave his navy evening coat a sharp tug to straighten it.

"I'll be about an hour, but stay nearby," he instructed his driver.

The October night air was cool and thick, holding a heavy reminder of the rains that had made the roads from Rotherham to London a muddy mess. After three days of travel and more than three weeks of near constant work that should have only taken two weeks, he should be exhausted. And he had been exhausted, until he had left his town house to come here.

He sidestepped around the young bucks gesturing in drunken conversation by the streetlamp and went inside Dennett's gambling hell. The burly guard stationed inside the door barely looked at him before tipping his head, allowing Vincent to pass. As he went through the entrance hall, his upper lip curled into a sneer at the scarlet and plum-patterned rug, the equally vibrant paper covering the walls, and the worn velvet upholstery on the two armchairs in the corner. Purple and red—what a ghastly color combination. And had they gilded every piece of exposed metal? The chandelier, the candelabras on the console table, and even the hinges on the door shone bright gold. The place was a garishly overdone imitation of a West End gentlemen's gambling hell. A greedy merchant's paradise. Definitely not up to his usual standards, but Dennett's was out of the way and, most importantly, only a five-minute drive from Lord Oliver Marsden's apartments.

He stopped just inside the main hall and, using his height to his full advantage, scanned the room. The shouts of victory, the curses of defeat, and the drone of many voices pressed against his ears. The chatter of the various games rode under the din: the flick of cards being shuffled, the click of gambling chips, and the roll of dice. In less than a second, he found Marsden in the crowd. Slighter built and a good four inches shorter than Vincent's own six feet two, the man stood at one of the gaming tables near the center of the room, his back to Vincent. A smile curved Vincent's lips, the last lingering bit of exhaustion slipping from his body. Had it only been four weeks since he had seen him? Hell, it felt like four years. His sights on those hunched shoulders and the unruly mop of dark brown hair, Vincent wove around the other patrons.

One hand braced on the ledge of the roulette table, Marsden leaned forward to place a bet. The tails of his brown coat draped over his arse as he bent at the waist, his hips tilting at a most inviting angle. Vincent clenched and unclenched his hands, tamping down the impulse to rip off those poorly tailored clothes and expose the sleek, honed body. To lay a hard smack on that round arse and grab those slim hips, to hold them steady as he—

Stop it!

Gritting his teeth, he threw off the flare of lust and pacified himself with the knowledge that there would be plenty of time to fuck Marsden later tonight.

He took up a place beside him just as the man straightened. "Evening, Marsden," he said, clapping him on the shoulder.

His hand hadn't remained on his shoulder an instant longer than polite manners dictated, yet he felt Marsden's shudder. The man's responsiveness stroked Vincent's ego to no end in the bedchamber, but it wasn't such a desirable trait when they were together in public. Marsden claimed he worried overmuch, that no one would ever suspect Lord Vincent Prescot would bugger another man. Still, Vincent couldn't help but worry; sodomy was, of course, against the law, never mind that his reputation would be ruined if word got out. Hence one of the reasons Vincent had chosen to meet here instead of at White's.

Marsden shifted his weight then shoved his wire-rimmed spectacles higher on his nose before turning his attention to Vincent. His movement caused the jade pin affixed directly below his cravat to catch the light from the gaudy chandelier overhead. For the past six months, ever since Vincent had given it to him, Marsden had worn the pin whenever he left his apartments. And every time Vincent saw it, he felt that tug on his chest. No one else but the two of them knew what that pin meant, but to Vincent, it was akin to a brand on the man's forehead, declaring to whom he belonged.

Me.

Though the pin didn't do a bit of good at helping to keep the man's cravat straight. No matter Vincent's efforts, Marsden couldn't quite get the hang of tying a respectable Mathematical knot. Should have gone with a Gordian knot. He could manage a passable one of those.

"Evening, Prescot. How was Rotherham?" Marsden asked, referring to the property Vincent had purchased almost a year ago.

"Good." He pulled a fold of pound notes from his coat pocket and tossed them onto the green baize.

"Only good?"

"All right. More than good." The croupier pushed three stacks of chips to Vincent. With a couple of taps of his fingertips, he straightened the stacks. Then he took five chips and placed them at the bottom of the third column of numbers on the table. "That rather large vein of coal is actually quite significant."

Marsden's full lips curved into a genuine smile, his dark brown eyes crinkling at the edges. "Well done, Prescot."

Would he ever tire of hearing those words from Marsden?

No. Not ever.

The croupier shouted to the men gathered around the table, calling for an end to the betting.

"How have you been, Marsden? Your grandmother keeping her harassments to a minimum?"

"Don't think she's capable of that. Always has some new complaint when I visit her. Though yesterday I could have sworn she was actually pleased to see me."

"Why wouldn't she be? You're her only family member who puts up with her. If not for you, she wouldn't have any callers." Marsden's only answer was an uncomfortable shrug. The man had the patience of a saint. Vincent would have found a companion for the old woman years ago and parted with whatever sum necessary to see the task done. "And how are the tables tonight? Having any luck?" he asked, as the small marble clickety-clacked around the roulette wheel.

Marsden let out a sigh. "No." Though he need not have answered. The paltry stack of chips before him was answer enough.

"Black six!"

He didn't believe it possible, but at the croupier's shout, somehow Marsden's shoulders slumped even further.

"What bet did you place?"

"Red twenty-five."

He had bet his age? Vincent picked up the ten chips the croupier pushed toward him and placed them at the bottom of the second column of numbers on the table. "Straight-up? You didn't bet the corners or a split?"

Marsden shook his head.

"Would you prefer to play vingt-et-un or faro instead? Maybe something that relies on more than blind luck to win. I'll partner you at whist if you'd like."

"No. I don't want to be responsible for your losses. In any case, the wheel seems fond of you. Might as well play it a bit longer."

Perhaps he should not have suggested they meet at Dennett's. Marsden certainly did not have a knack for gambling, and honestly, Vincent shouldn't encourage him. The last thing he wanted was for Marsden to become a degenerate gambler like his father, the Marquis of Campden, who had recently fled Town to escape his debts.

Marsden turned his attention back to the green baize. Full bottom lip caught between his teeth and brow scrunched in concentration, he contemplated his next bet. Well aware of Marsden's precarious financial situation, he covertly nudged one of his stacks of chips, moving it next to Marsden's tiny stack. Since he had been the one to choose Dennett's, the least he could do was compensate for his losses.

Clutching a full glass of wine, a man squeezed into the space beside Vincent. Determined not to get Bordeaux spilled on his coat sleeve, he moved aside, creating enough room for the man's large frame and even larger belly, and ended up pressed against Marsden. Pure heat blazed from his upper arm to his knee, one long continual line down the side of his body. They were so close a turn of his head would have his lips brushing the dark waves of Marsden's hair. Marsden let out a low grunt. Senses perpetually attuned to the other man, Vincent could scent his arousal even at a smoke-filled gambling hell. Marsden shifted his weight, his thigh rubbing against Vincent's, his hand curling into a white-knuckled fist around the chip he held.

Please, Marsden, get yourself under control.

Vincent chanced a quick, nervous glance around the roulette table, but the other patrons appeared blissfully ignorant of the erection he was certain now tented the placket of Marsden's trousers. It wasn't as if those across from them could see it anyway—the table came up to Marsden's waist. Still, the man next to Marsden could happen to glance down, or—

"Prescot!" a voice called from behind him.

Thank heaven for a distraction. Suppressing a relieved sigh, he took a step back from Marsden and turned to face a slim young gentleman with blond hair.

"Good evening, Winters."

"Never expected to come across you here," Frank Winters said with a jovial smile. Judging by the low cut, red silk gown and the heavily applied rouge, what could only be a cheap whore clung to his arm. Likely picked her up off the street. Winters brought his glass to his lips and looked around Vincent's shoulder. "Ah, that answers it. You're with Marsden. Don't know why you bother with him. Won't be long before he follows his father to the continent."

Vincent glared at him, a muscle ticking along his jaw, a fierce rush of protectiveness tightening his throat. How dare this little whelp—by God, he was only the son of a mere baron and not a very well heeled one at that—speak so callously about Marsden when he was but two feet behind Vincent? The urge to slam his fist into the man's smug face was almost overwhelming. Through sheer force of will, Vincent kept his arm at his side and managed to speak in a cool, bored drawl. "Have a care with the gin, Winters. Wouldn't want you to follow in *your* father's footsteps."

Winters's hazel eyes widened, a flush creeping up his neck to cover his cheeks, at the blunt reminder of his drunkard of a father who had made an arse out of himself at more than one social function. When he opened his mouth to speak, Vincent turned his back to him. And bumped shoulders with Marsden as the man turned from the gaming table.

Heat flared across his biceps, momentarily distracting him. He blinked and watched Marsden's brown-coated back weaving between the patrons. Where the hell was he going?

"Red fourteen!" the croupier shouted.

Vincent snatched up his winnings and made to pick up his other chips, but stopped, hand poised above the three stacks, one not quite as neat as the others. An annoyed grumble rumbling his chest, he pocketed the chips. Marsden and his damn pride. He'd just leave a few pounds at the man's apartments. The place was always such a disorganized mess. It would take Marsden days to come across the money, and by then, he'd likely assume he had merely misplaced it and not connect it to Vincent.

He scanned the room, spotted Marsden's dark head over at the cashier's cage, and went over to him. He stopped at Marsden's shoulder, ignoring the protests from the two men in line behind him. "Ready to leave already?" He would admit to a certain eagerness to go on to Marsden's apartments. All right, more than eager. But since he'd been gone for weeks, he had rather looked forward to spending some time with him. Outside of his bedchamber.

"I've had enough gambling for one night." Marsden took the few shillings the cashier pushed under the gilded bars of the cage. Then he lowered his voice. "I've been here for two hours. Your note said eight, Prescot, not ten o'clock."

Vincent gave his chips to the cashier. "The rains delayed my travel. As it was, I only stopped home long enough for a change of clothes." *And to pick up your gift.*

Marsden said nothing, merely shoved his hands in his pockets and contemplated his scuffed evening shoes.

While the cashier meticulously counted a pile of gold sovereigns, Vincent tipped his head toward his friend. "My apologies, Marsden," he murmured. "I didn't know the roads would be such a mess when I wrote you. As it was, I was fortunate to make it to London tonight."

Marsden tucked an errant wavy strand behind his ear and studied him from the corner of his eye. It wasn't as if Vincent had purposefully dallied on his journey. Hell, he had no control over the weather. So why was he so worried Marsden would hold it against him?

Those long, dark lashes swept down. Ducking his chin, a little smile tugged on the corner of Marsden's mouth, and he lifted one shoulder. "I understand. I'm glad you made it back safely."

Vincent couldn't hold back the smile as the tension slipped out of him, and in its place settled the delicious hum of anticipation. He had spent the greater part of the afternoon staring out the window of his carriage as it slowly made its way to London and planning exactly what he would do to Marsden once he had the man alone. "Shall we be on our way then?"

Marsden nodded, a quick jerk of his head.

He pocketed the gold sovereigns, leaving one for the cashier. When they reached the entrance hall, he stopped near the footman stationed at the cloak room. "Your greatcoat?"

Marsden didn't pause but continued on. "Didn't bother with it. Did you take your carriage or hire a hackney?"

Three long strides had him at Marsden's shoulder once again. "My carriage." The burly guard opened the front door as they approached. "Marsden, it's October. You should not have left your greatcoat at home." Marsden walked most everywhere he went in Town. His apartments were close, but not so close that he wouldn't have risked catching a chill if it had rained.

"So where's yours?"

Marsden was getting an extra smack on the arse later for that cheeky comment. Then again, knowing his friend, it would only encourage him. "My coat is in the carriage. Unlike you, I only had to walk twenty feet to reach the hell." He stopped at the streetlamp and flicked his fingers, motioning to his driver waiting for him a few buildings down the road.

His team of four bays pulled up next to him. "Lord Oliver's apartments," he informed his driver as he stepped into the carriage.

Marsden's knees brushed his as he settled on the bench opposite him. The driver snapped the whip, and the carriage lurched forward. Only the soft light from the streetlamps they passed broke the darkness, the golden glow cutting across Marsden's profile; it illuminated the long curve of his lashes behind his spectacles, the high arch of his cheekbones, and the slightly parted full lips. How had Vincent managed to go four weeks without those lips wrapped around his cock?

"God, I missed you." The desperation in Marsden's whispered words sent a thrill through him.

Marsden shifted forward, as if to move to sit beside him. Aware of the open shade on the window, Vincent lifted one leg and pressed a foot over his groin, holding him down, keeping him on the opposite bench. Marsden instantly submitted, settling back, yielding to the pressure, his legs falling open. Vincent rotated his foot, rubbing the sole of his evening shoe over Marsden's rapidly hardening cock. "Were you good, boy, in my absence?" he asked, voice pitched low but with a hard edge that would have Marsden panting in no time.

Marsden's tongue darted out, a quick swipe across his lower lip. "Yes."

He pressed harder, pulling a grunt from Marsden. "Yes, what?"

"Yes, milord."

"Hmm." He passed a hand over his jaw as he continued to rub Marsden's cock through the placket of his trousers, the soft wool sliding easily over silken skin. It didn't feel as though Marsden had worn drawers. One less piece of clothing for the man to remove when they reached his apartments. "Are you certain? Did you take yourself in hand?" He knew the answer, but couldn't resist the urge to voice the question. To torment Marsden. To make the man squirm with a mixture of embarrassment and pure, stark need. To ratchet up the anticipation hanging in the air between them, so heavy he could feel it.

"Ah...I..."

"Yes or no, Marsden. Did you pleasure yourself in my absence?"

He lifted his hips, seeking even more pressure, and speared Vincent with a hot stare. "Yes."

"And what did you do, exactly?"

"Stroked my cock until I climaxed." The words rushed out of Marsden's mouth, the sharp pants of his breaths filling the closed carriage.

"That was all? Did you penetrate yourself?" At Marsden's quick nod, he asked, "With what? Your fingers or one of your toys?" Marsden possessed a collection that rivaled the quaint little shop off Bond Street that sold a nice array of paddles and leather goods, in addition to the usual erotic offerings. A collection Vincent had taken great delight in watching Marsden sample on more than one occasion.

The faint light from a passing streetlamp gave him a glimpse of the blush staining Marsden's cheeks. "Both."

"At the same time?"

His dark eyes flared. "N-no."

Vincent *tsked*. "A shame. Perhaps we shall need to try that." He dropped his voice to a low rumbling growl. "See if you can take it." Marsden's breathy whimper shot straight to his groin. The man was so wonderfully responsive, so eager to please, so absolutely beautiful. So perfect. Warmth blossomed across his chest, a lush, comforting sensation that had nothing to do with the lust spiking his senses. Vincent tamped down the grin and instead kept his features schooled in a hard mask that approached disinterest. "Would you like that, boy?"

Even with the motion of the carriage, he could feel Marsden's body vibrate as the man fought to remain still, his hands curled in tight fists on his thighs. "Y-yes, *please*, milord."

The thought of Marsden naked on the bed, his golden skin flushed with arousal, knees drawn up to his chest, working his fingers alongside a slim dildo in his tight arse… Vincent swallowed back the grunt. *Damnation.* Yes, indeed, he would definitely need to coax Marsden into giving it a try. "But not tonight. I have other plans for you." He laid a hand on the greatcoat folded at his hip, over the hard length hidden in the pocket. The man would get stuffed full, but with only one object at a time tonight. He glanced out the window. "Almost there. Best get yourself under control." He gave Marsden's prick a light tap before moving his foot back to the floorboards.

"Already?" Groaning, Marsden tipped his head back and ran his hands through his hair, further disheveling the dark waves. "Hell. Should have brought my greatcoat. Would have hidden it." He sucked in a long controlled breath, as if he were steeling himself for something unpleasant. Then he spread his legs wider, grabbed his ballocks through his trousers, and tugged, hissing sharply through his clenched teeth.

Ouch. That had to have hurt. And not in a good way. "Yes, you should have," Vincent said with a chuckle, as he put on his own coat and did up the buttons to hide his straining erection.

The carriage slowed to a stop at a familiar three-story building that looked more like a boarding house than bachelor apartments. He turned a blind eye to the bent wrought-iron rail on the stone steps leading to the front door with its peeling black paint. Instead, he focused on the two dark windows on the top floor. In just a few moments, they would be in that apartment, and he would have Marsden all to himself without having to worry about the judging eyes of others upon them.

As Marsden reached for the brass lever on the door, Vincent laid a hand on his forearm, staying him. Questioning eyes so rich and dark they almost approached black met his. He tucked that errant wavy strand back behind Marsden's ear and murmured, "I missed you, too." Then he winked. "Now get your arse inside so I can fuck you."

Chapter Two

Panting, Oliver squeezed his eyes shut tight. Vincent's "other plans" clearly involved tormenting him until he had been reduced to a quivering pile of need. Deprived of Vincent for four long weeks, his senses soaked up each sensation, savored them like the most treasured of gifts, while simultaneously frantic for more. If Vincent kept this up much longer, he'd climax before his lover worked his big prick into him.

"*Please*, milord."

Vincent chuckled, a low throaty rumble. He drew a line down the oil-slicked crease of Oliver's arse and paused once again to linger over his hole, slowly tracing the puckered flesh. His skin tingled, the ring of muscle relaxing under Vincent's touch, ready for more. Then the tip of his finger slipped inside, rewarding him with the barest hint of penetration.

Oliver let out a moan of pleasure, his body tightening greedily around that digit. After being teased for what felt like an hour, though in actuality fifteen minutes could not have passed since they had entered his bedchamber, Vincent was finally giving him the tiniest taste of what he had been promising.

Needing more, Oliver pushed back and almost lost his balance. The muscles in his thighs tensed as he fought to keep from sliding off his bed. Vincent had him naked and kneeling on the bed, his calves dangling off the edge, his chest pressed to the mattress, his arse on full display. The precarious position restrained him far more than the leather cuffs binding his wrists behind his back.

A large hand grasped his hip, steadying him. "Don't move. You will get what I give you and thank me for it."

Oliver's breaths stuttered. He loved it when Vincent spoke to him in that hard, commanding tone. "Yes, milord."

"Good boy." Vincent went back to toying with him. Up and down, a slow, luxurious caress, just the pad of his index finger sliding along the crease, driving him to distraction. The decadent sensation kept him suspended on the knife-edge of anticipation, every fiber in his being acutely aware of the man standing behind him and what he might choose to do next. The unknown, the wait—a heady thrill all its own. One he was absolutely addicted to.

He clenched his fists as Vincent skimmed past his entrance again. The ballocks hanging between his spread thighs tingled, tightened, begging for attention. As Vincent drew another line down his crease, he couldn't help but arch his lower back, lifting his arse, hoping for a touch, an accidental brush of Vincent's fingertip, anything.

He received a hard smack on his left cheek. The sting flared, radiating across his bum and down his groin to envelop his ballocks in a wash of heat. Biting his lip against the exquisite blend of pleasure and pain, he groaned.

"Did you like that?" Vincent demanded.

"Yes."

"Do you want more?"

"*Yes.*"

"Of what? This?" A long finger pushed inside him. One thrust, in then out. So quick and fleeting, it only served to sharpen his appetite for more. "Or this?" Vincent smacked him again.

A strangled gasp shook his throat. A drop of fluid leaked from his aching cock.

"Or something else? Tell me what you want."

The truth rushed out of his mouth. "You. All of you. Everything."

Vincent chuckled and smoothed a palm over his arse, soothing the smarting skin. "All in good time, boy."

Soft wool whisked past his bare foot as Vincent stepped around him, his evening shoes clicking on the floorboards. Dragging his face across the coarse woolen blanket, Oliver turned his head to the left. Through the tangled hair hanging over his eyes, he squinted, willing his eyes to focus across the room without the aid of his spectacles. Vincent stood before the straight-backed wooden chair in the corner of the bedchamber. He reached into an inside pocket of his greatcoat folded neatly over the back of the chair.

Tall, broad of shoulder, and with a powerful build, Lord Vincent Prescot defined "ruggedly handsome." Six months and Oliver still couldn't fully believe this man had chosen to be with him. Vincent had discarded his black greatcoat and navy evening coat shortly after they'd arrived at Oliver's apartments, but other than that, he was still fully dressed. He hadn't even removed his cravat yet, which meant he planned to make Oliver wait a bit longer until he fucked him.

Settling in for the wait, he shimmied slightly on the bed, pulling his knees more securely under him. The old bed creaked.

"Marsden," Vincent said, the warning clear in his tone.

Damnation. Handsome, intelligent, and wealthy. Did the man have to have excellent hearing as well?

Vincent turned from the chair and stopped beside the bed. With the lightest of touches, he combed the hair from Oliver's eyes and tucked it behind his ear. The gesture made Oliver's heart clench. The man possessed such great strength, but could touch him so gently, so tenderly, at times it almost felt like Vincent loved him.

Vincent held out his other hand. "A gift. For your collection."

The dildo appeared to be carved from a single piece of jade. It must have cost Vincent a small fortune and explained why the man had not worn his greatcoat into the gambling hell. The candlelight played over the highly polished green stone, highlighting the four graduated raised bands encircling the length, each one a bit larger than the next. It couldn't be more than seven inches in length and even at its widest point, less around than an average man. Oliver had noticed how Vincent preferred toys that were shorter and thinner than his substantial cock. He much preferred Vincent over a toy, and after weeks of nothing but dildos, plugs, and his own fingers to keep him company, he wanted the real man tonight. Still, those bands on the dildo were sure to feel divine.

His arse tightened in anticipation. "Thank you, Vincent."

A smile tugged the corners of his lover's firm mouth, but he kept it from fully curving his lips. Vincent moved back to his position behind him. "Up with you now."

With one hand on his shoulder, Vincent effortlessly pulled him up off the bed. For a moment, he swayed backward on his knees. Instinct had him tugging on his restraints, needing to catch himself. He felt the heat from Vincent's body a split second before his shoulder blades touched the smooth silk of his waistcoat.

"I have you," Vincent murmured, wrapping an arm around Oliver's waist, holding him securely against the wide expanse of his chest. The tip of his ring finger just barely touched the dark hair on his groin. Chin resting on his shoulder, Vincent's warm breath tickled his ear, sending shivers down his spine.

Before he could turn his head and press his mouth against Vincent's, give him the kiss the man had held back all evening, cool stone tapped his parted lips. He immediately opened his mouth, taking the dildo inside.

"That's it. Get it nice and wet. You know where that's going, don't you, boy?"

Oliver gave a short, eager nod. He hoped he knew where it was going. Just allowing him to suck on it would be cruel. Vincent might push Oliver to his limits, tie him up, spank him, and whip him, but cruel he was not.

"I'm going to bury it in that tight little arse of yours," Vincent growled.

Oliver whimpered, the sound so needy and desperate, but he didn't care in the slightest. He gathered as much saliva into his mouth as he could, then swirled it over the hard length with his tongue as Vincent slid the dildo in and out.

The large hand on his abdomen moved up his chest. Two fingers found one of his nipples and pinched. Hard. Sweet, luscious pain shot across his chest. Then Vincent twisted. Oliver shuddered, his cock arching up to brush his lower belly, his ballocks tightening even further against his body. Desperate to touch his lover, he stretched out his fingers and located the hard bulge of Vincent's erection pressing against the placket of his trousers. He feathered his fingers over the impressive length, wanting to wrap his mouth around it, to feel the hot satiny skin, to have the taste of Vincent on his tongue. Air hissed as Vincent sucked in a breath, proving he wasn't as unaffected as he pretended to be. He thrust his hips, pressing his prick into Oliver's hand. Oliver stroked him as best he could through his trousers, all the while sucking on the hard jade as Vincent tormented his nipple.

"Enough." Vincent pulled the dildo from his mouth. "Down," he commanded, carefully lowering Oliver's shoulders to the mattress.

Vincent passed a hand down his spine then pulled back one cheek. A slick, hard head pressed against his entrance. He relaxed into the pressure as Vincent pushed the dildo inside. *One, two, three…* Oliver squeezed his eyes shut and grunted against the burning stretch as the largest band eased past the ring of muscle…*four*. Vincent shoved the phallus deep, eliciting a moan from Oliver. Hell, it felt so good to be filled, to have that itch scratched.

"Hold onto it." Vincent tapped the base, and the vibrations teased Oliver's passage.

He obediently clenched his muscles around the hard length.

"So pretty." Vincent traced his stretched hole. "Do you have any idea how debauched you look with that dildo shoved up your arse? You love it, don't you? Tell me."

"Yes. Oh, God, yes." A spasm racked him as he focused on keeping his arse tight, on holding the jade in place. "Please, *please*. Fuck me with it." Need clawed at his throat so hard he could barely get the words out.

Vincent let out a muttered curse. He heard fabric rustle. Vincent was taking off his waistcoat and shirt; Oliver just knew it. And beneath the sounds of linen shifting and floorboards creaking as

Vincent moved behind him were the deep pants of Vincent's breaths. The erotic sound ratcheted Oliver's lust even higher.

Vincent grabbed his hip. Those pants had turned heavy, harsh, blending with Oliver's own. He let go when Vincent pulled on the dildo. He silently counted the bands as they slipped out—*four, three, two, one*—and the head slipped from his body.

His eyes flew open. "No. Don't stop. More. *Please.*"

Vincent gave him what he begged for. Long fingers digging into his arse cheek, holding him open, he picked up a steady rhythm. All the way in, then all the way out. The continual pattern of withdrawal and re-entry made each thrust feel like the first one of the night. Stretching him wide, stuffing him full, a delicious rush of sensation. Oliver pressed his forehead to the mattress, pleas for more falling from his lips as he fought to stay still, to simply take what Vincent gave him and not rock back into each long, plunging thrust.

His cock ached. He was so hard it hurt, in the most intense, pleasurable way. Sweat prickled the small of his back, dampened his hands clenched in fists. His nerve endings shimmered with the need to climax, every muscle in his body drawn tight, poised for orgasm.

"You want more?" Vincent snarled.

"Yes, yes, please."

"More than this?" He pushed the jade inside him again. In then out.

"Yes, *please*. I want your cock. I-I need it. I need you," Oliver begged, beyond desperate.

"Then take it."

"Ah!" He screamed as the impossibly broad head of Vincent's cock stretched him to his limits. In, in, in—he kept pushing deeper and deeper, the long length filling him in one determined stroke. Heat rolled through his body. Sweat tickled his scalp. The sharp mix of pleasure and stretching pain, of finally having what he wanted, made the climax he'd been fighting to keep at bay clutch the base of his cock.

With a feral growl, Vincent tugged him closer, pressing his arse to his groin, settling hilt deep, forcing Oliver to take it all. He struggled to catch his breath, the intense sensations almost too much. By God, it felt as if his prick were touching his throat. Then Vincent pulled back and pumped into him, again and again.

"Yes, yes," he gasped. "More."

Vincent smacked him on the arse, the sound cracking through the air, the sting flaring deliciously through his body. "That's it. Beg for my cock. Tell me what you want."

"More, more. *Please!*"

"I'll give you more." Grabbing his forearms, Vincent yanked his upper body from the bed and slammed hard, hitting that perfect spot inside him.

Pure molten pleasure overloaded his senses. Oliver threw back his head and howled. The orgasm raced down his spine; seed shot from his prick. The heavy pulses seized his nerves in rhythm to his lover's demanding thrusts.

"That's it. Come for me, boy. Grip my cock so fucking tight." Vincent's ballocks smacked against him, as he took what he needed, stroking hard and fast.

He hung his head, gasped for breath. Senses shimmering from that powerful orgasm, he couldn't stop himself from begging for more even though his arse throbbed under the onslaught. With each thrust, the wet tip of his still-hard cock smacked his belly, sending jagged vibrations down to his drained ballocks. Yet he took it all. Savored every bit of Vincent's undivided attention. Let the man do as he pleased with him. After four long weeks without him, he didn't want to stop. Not now. Not ever.

Vincent's pants turned into short, gravelly grunts, growing louder, harsher in time to the quick snap of his hips, until Oliver felt the shudders shake Vincent's powerful body and warmth flood his passage.

With his prick still buried deep within Oliver, Vincent hauled him fully up against his sweat-slicked chest and wrapped his arms around him. The comforting embrace calmed the frantic need pounding through his veins, enveloping him in a rich, thick languor. Oliver's eyes drifted closed, his head tipping back onto Vincent's broad shoulder. He could stay like this forever. Held close to Vincent, intimately joined with him.

For many moments, the only sounds that broke the silence were their hard, labored breaths. Then soft lips nuzzled his ear. Oliver turned his head, needing Vincent's kiss. His lover's mouth met his, and with a greedy groan, Oliver slipped his tongue past those parted lips. The sweet, hot taste of Vincent saturated his senses, made his head go light, pulling that frantic need back to the surface. Tugging on his wrists, he pressed back against Vincent's chest, trying to get closer to the man he loved, to get more of him. Damn leather cuffs. He wanted to wrap his arms around Vincent, tangle his fingers in his hair, crush the man to him, and deepen the frustratingly languid kiss.

Vincent pulled back, breaking the kiss long before Oliver had his fill. His eyes were heavy-lidded, the brilliant blue depths hazy with sated lust. A hint of a smile played on his mouth. "Let's get you untied." The low rumbling words brushed across Oliver's wet lips.

Vincent's arms tightened around him before releasing him, his softened prick slipping from his body. Oliver held back the protest and did his best to balance on weak knees as Vincent unbuckled the leather cuffs. Vincent tossed the restraints aside, the leather and metal buckles clattering to the wooden floor. Then he gently massaged Oliver's wrists and forearms, soothing the sweaty skin.

"Better?" Vincent pressed a kiss to the apple of his shoulder.

"Yes." Oliver sighed. A roll of his shoulders loosened his stiff joints. He crawled farther up the bed, past the wet spot on the woolen blanket, nudging the jade dildo Vincent had discarded to the edge of the mattress, and flopped down on his stomach. He was sweaty and sticky and should clean himself up, but he couldn't summon the effort just yet. "Come here," he mumbled with a half-hearted wave of his arm. It really was all he could muster.

The mattress dipped and shook as Vincent crawled toward him. The bed wasn't all that large, barely wide enough for the two of them. Pulling Oliver close, he lay down on his back, fitting him against his side. Letting out a contented sigh, Oliver nestled even closer, until he was draped half-over Vincent's body, his leg tangled with Vincent's, his arm slung across his broad chest. He could feel the man's heart beating against his cheek. *Thump-thump. Thump-thump.*

His world narrowed until all that existed were the strong, steady beats of his lover's heart, the intoxicating scent of his sweat and skin, and the lulling caress of the large hand kneading his backside.

I love you.

He tried to get the words out, but he was so exhausted his mouth didn't want to cooperate.

A hand gripped his wrist, the hold light but enough to bring him to full consciousness and prompt him to blink open his heavy eyelids. Vincent lifted Oliver's arm off his chest, moved out from beneath him, and sat up, swinging his legs over the side of the bed. He stood and, avoiding the clothing littering the floor, walked to the washstand.

The fire in the grate warmed the room enough to take the bite out of the air from Oliver's drafty window. Still, he felt the loss of Vincent's warm body acutely.

Water splashed as Vincent dunked a cloth in the white ceramic basin. The muscles in his back bunched and flexed as he wiped his chest. His buttocks tightened as he swiped lower, between his legs. The water was no doubt quite cold. Unlike Vincent, he didn't have a house full of servants to see to such small tasks, like heating wash water, dusting, or tidying up in his wake.

His eyes drifted closed again. He heard Vincent moving about. With each creak of the floorboards, tension seeped into him, dousing that perfectly blissful feeling of complete contentment.

Keeping his eyes closed wouldn't change the inevitable. He forced his eyelids to open.

The black suspenders attached to the waistband of Vincent's trousers stretched across his white-shirted back as he leaned down to grab his waistcoat from the floor near the foot of the bed.

Oliver's stomach tightened. "Where are you going?" Stupid question to ask. Of course he wouldn't stay the night. He never did.

"Home," Vincent replied matter-of-factly, slipping on the cream silk waistcoat.

Oliver pushed up to sit cross-legged and put on the spectacles he'd left on the bedside table. One hand draped over his limp cock, he twisted the rumpled sheet at his hip between his fingers. He hated sitting on the bed, watching Vincent prepare to leave. Made him feel like a pitiful, lovesick fool. "You could stay." *Bloody hell.* And now he sounded like one, too.

His pathetic offer didn't even make Vincent pause as he picked up his cravat. "My carriage is waiting."

"So send it home. Take a hackney in the morning. You were gone for almost a month, Vincent." *Don't leave me yet.*

"I can't leave your apartments in the morning. The other tenants in the building might notice and wonder why I stayed the night. In any case, I have an early appointment with my banker."

Yes, of course, how could he forget? Vincent was a busy man with many pressing responsibilities. Heaven forbid if Oliver dared to take precedence over any of them.

Using the mirror above the washstand, Vincent tied his cravat. A few deft flicks of his fingers and a couple of tugs, and he produced a perfect Mathematical knot. "By the way, you should let me manage your investments."

Oliver shook his head. "I can manage them myself."

"You could be earning a better return. Enough to move out of here." He motioned with the comb in his hand—indicating the shabby bedchamber with its threadbare brown velvet drapes over the drafty window and its too-small, old bed—and then went back to smoothing the short layers of his dark hair.

My apologies you have to lower your standards to fuck me. Oliver bit his tongue, holding back the surly retort. For all Vincent knew, he could be managing his accounts quite smartly. But of course, Vincent correctly assumed his investments yielded a paltry sum. Oliver wasn't comfortable putting his money into the Exchange, or other more risky ventures. Unlike Vincent, he didn't have the security of an obscenely wealthy father behind him. Yes, Vincent's father ignored him in favor of his elder brother, the precious heir to the Saye and Sele marquisate, but the man would never let his youngest son go penniless. Even with his properties and investments, Oliver was certain Vincent's father still gave him a sizable quarterly allowance. Whereas all Oliver had was the small inheritance he'd received years ago from his mother. If he lost it, he'd have nothing. The income did not yield much, but enough for him to live on if he kept a very close eye on his expenses and didn't indulge in such luxuries like hackney fare or a maid or a stately white stucco town house in Mayfair.

"It's not like I live in some flash house in the stews." He couldn't keep the defensive note from his voice.

Vincent did up the last button on his navy coat. "Don't get your hackles up, Marsden. I was only offering to help." He held up a hand to stay him when Oliver opened his mouth. "But yes, I understand. You can manage it yourself."

Good. Glad we understand each other. Oliver swiped his unruly hair behind his ear then, letting out a breath, forced aside the irritation. He didn't want to start an argument with Vincent. Not when he only had a few minutes left with him.

Vincent crossed the room and picked up his gold pocket watch from the dented little silver tray on the bedside table. From his crisp white cravat to his polished evening shoes, he was the very image of a proper aristocrat. One would never guess by looking at him that he'd just buggered another man. Oliver soaked up his strong profile—the slightly roman nose, the neatly combed hair, the dark brows furrowed the tiniest bit as Vincent attached the watch chain to his waistcoat. He must have shaved tonight before he went to the hell, for there wasn't even the hint of a shadow of a dark beard on his jaw.

"Love you," Oliver whispered.

Vincent's lips curved in a smile, his blue eyes softening with genuine affection. Oliver's heart leapt into his throat, pleading for the response he knew Vincent would not utter. He wanted to hear those words just once. One time. Even if Vincent didn't feel them. He could at least have the sound of them as a memory and play them over in head as he lay alone in his bed and pretend they had come from Vincent's heart.

Vincent cupped his jaw. Eyes drifting closed, Oliver leaned into his touch. A quiver of need shook his body. Soft lips brushed his, the lightest of touches, a mere whisper of skin against skin. Then that large hand slipped away.

"I'll bring supper tomorrow. Eight o'clock all right?"

Oliver pressed his lips together and nodded.

"Get some rest. I'll see you tomorrow."

He couldn't stop himself from watching Vincent walk from the room, his greatcoat in hand, and shut the door behind him. He heard his footsteps as he crossed the parlor. Then the front door snapped shut.

"Why don't you love me?" The words he could never make himself utter in Vincent's presence echoed in the room. Mocking him, taunting him, a harsh reminder of what he did not have.

He tossed his spectacles onto the bedside table and pressed the heels of his palms to his closed eyes, pushing back the misery, the threat of tears, and then dragged his hands down his face.

"Christ. I'm fucking pathetic." He punched his pillow and flopped down on the bed. Why did he torment himself like this? Vincent cared enough to be with him. Shouldn't that be enough? A year ago, he would have given anything for a kiss from Vincent. In love with him for too many years to count, he had subsisted on mere friendship. A chance meeting on the street. A shared drink at White's. All the while hiding his true feelings for his childhood friend.

Until he discovered Vincent had secretly hired a man and not a woman during his visits to a brothel. An establishment Vincent no longer needed to frequent since he now had Oliver at his disposal.

Hell, he had been extremely lucky Vincent hadn't turned his back on him when he learned he had hired Oliver on that fateful night at the brothel. The resulting argument had not been pleasant, but in the end, it had gained him Vincent. Or whatever it was that he had of him.

Oliver let out a heavy sigh and reminded himself forcefully that it had taken a lot for Vincent to accept the fact that he preferred men. Vincent excelled at most everything he did, and he had viewed those desires as a failure. Hadn't he told Vincent six months ago that he wasn't asking for his heart? He had known better at the time to not expect more than mere lust and affection.

But it had been *six months*. Surely enough time for Vincent to become comfortable with his sexuality. To fully acknowledge to himself that he did indeed prefer men. To completely accept that part of himself and open his heart to Oliver.

But therein lay the problem.

While Oliver loved to submit to Vincent, to give himself over to the man he adored, the tight leash Vincent kept on their sexual activities screamed loud and clear that he wasn't ready to be fully intimate with another man.

Be patient. Be patient. How many times had he told himself that? Used those words to pacify the all-encompassing need gripping his heart? But it damn well hurt that Vincent did not love him.

All he wanted was to be with Vincent. To be near the man. To be able to take in a deep breath and soak up the scent of him.

To have Vincent need him, as Oliver needed Vincent.

The pressing question was—could he?

"Enough," he told himself as he rolled over. He'd have one hell of a sleepless night if he kept this up. He tugged the woolen blanket up to his chest and did his best to clear his mind and allow sleep to overtake him. To not think about how Vincent had stayed in Rotherham one week longer than originally expected. How he had arrived at the gambling hell two hours late without even an apology until Oliver had reminded him of his tardiness. And about the tiny distance Vincent kept between them.

That distance that now felt like a damn chasm.

Chapter Three

Oliver slowly closed the leather-bound book, careful to keep the pages of Shakespeare's *Romeo and Juliet* from rustling. Holding his breath, he set the book on the pedestal tea table beside his chair and moved to stand.

"If you want to leave, say so. You do yourself a disservice trying to sneak away like some sort of inept thief."

Damnation. Oliver slumped back into the chair. "My apologies, Grandmother. I thought you had fallen asleep. I didn't want to disturb you."

"I am not asleep."

Obviously. He kept from rolling his eyes. The doctor claimed advanced age had severely diminished her eyesight, but Oliver didn't believe him. Nothing escaped the older woman's notice. He picked up the book. "Would you like me to continue reading aloud?"

She waved a small, bony hand, the intricate lace cuff of her dressing gown fluttering with the movement. "No. You clearly have had your fill of me for one day."

He sighed. "That's not true, Grandmother."

The afternoon sunlight streamed through the window, the golden rays creating a halo effect around her gray head. Propped up against a pile of white pillows, and with the ivory coverlet tucked about her waist, she looked so very tiny and frail, but her sharp tongue belied her appearance. The carriage accident almost a decade ago had left her an invalid, confining her to her massive four-poster bed. If not for him, she would be left with only the company of two servants. She might not be the most pleasant individual, but she was his grandmother and he did love her.

Frowning, she selected a scone from the box nestled at her hip and took a bite. Likely she only tolerated his visits because he brought her sweets.

"Would you care for another cup of tea?" he asked.

"You've already pushed three cups on me. I do not need another." She finished the scone and closed the baker's box.

He remained seated, waiting patiently as she struggled to retie the red ribbon around the box. If he offered his assistance, he'd only get snapped at.

When she finished, she set the box on top of one of the piles of books on her bedside table. *Othello, A Midsummer Night's Dream, MacBeth.* He knew every one of those books by heart. After readjusting the coverlet about her, she turned her attention back to him. "When are you going to take a wife?"

He squirmed in the pink floral silk chair. Where had that question come from? And how could he tell her never without revealing why? He reached up and straightened the jade pin on his cravat. He belonged to Vincent, never with another.

"Radford's married and has already produced an heir," he said, referring to his elder brother, who held the courtesy title Earl of Radford. His brother's wife had written to him from Northumberland a few weeks ago informing him of the event. The countess was as bland and aloof as his brother, but at least she remembered he existed.

"What does that have to do with your future wife?"

"There's little chance the title will come to me. So there's no need to inflict myself on some innocent woman for the sake of securing the title." A title that was little more than a name and a neglected property in Wiltshire, since his father had long since bled the estate dry.

Thin lips pursed, she stared at him, her cloudy, dark brown gaze sharp and piercing. "I never did much care for Radford or your father."

No surprise there. She didn't much care for anyone.

"But you...you should take a wife."

Oliver shook his head. The woman was definitely getting on in years. She wasn't making the least bit of sense. "But I don't have anything to offer a wife. No prospects. A pittance of an income. I can't afford to pay a lady's modiste bills, much less purchase a home for her to live in."

"Nonsense," she declared, all aristocratic condescension. "You are the son of a marquis. That alone will fetch you a chit with a decent dowry, enough for you to live comfortably. She will marry you for your name, and you will marry her for her money."

How cold and impersonal. He winced.

"That is what is done." She punctuated her words with a short, determined nod. "How marriages are made, and how your mother came to marry your father, and how I came to marry your grandfather. Sentiment has no place in marriage. Do not forget that. Expecting more will only lead to disappointment."

But of course. Why ever would he expect someone to love him? A tide of misery, so fresh it felt as if Vincent had just walked out the door, tightened his throat. He tipped his chin down, letting his overlong, jaw-length hair partially obscure his face, and studied the ornate embossed leatherwork on the book's cover in his lap, as he struggled to regain his composure. "Ah...I'll...I'll keep that in mind, Grandmother."

He should have left when she had given him the opportunity. This morning he had awoken with his patience well in hand. The doubts gone, replaced with anticipation at the prospect of seeing Vincent tonight. But now—

"Oliver."

The unexpected note of compassion in her usual whip-sharp voice brought his gaze up to hers.

Her sparse gray brows were lowered, the deep lines on her forehead in stark relief. "While I still mourn your mother's death, there was a bit of relief in it for her. Your father made her miserable. I do not want that for you."

He swallowed hard. "Yes, Grandmother. I understand." In her own odd way, she was concerned for him. But he was afraid her warning had come much too late. "If you will excuse me, I must take my leave. I have an appointment, and I don't wish to be late." He had five hours until Vincent showed up at his apartments, and it wouldn't take a fifth of that time for him to walk home. But he had no other excuse to leave at the ready. No other place he needed to be. No other responsibilities that required his attention. "Is there anything you need?" He had already checked in with her housekeeper, seen to her posts, and made arrangements to have a bank draft sent from her account to the butcher to settle the latest bill.

"No, no. Be on your way." That imperious tone was back, all traces of compassion gone.

He set the book on the tea table, stood, and took hold of her proffered hand, her skin icy cold. He pressed a kiss to her weathered cheek.

Delicate, boney fingers wrapped around his, surprising in their grip, keeping him from turning from the bed. "Old age is lonely, Oliver. Find a nice lady, if for no other reason than to eventually have a grandson who will pay you calls."

He met her solemn gaze. The cloudy dark depths held far more than mere concern. She didn't explicitly say the words, but he didn't need her to. He understood, and he could not deny that it felt good to know someone loved him.

* * *

Vincent lifted his freshly shaven chin. His slim, middle-aged valet barely reached his shoulder, and the man had to lift up onto his toes to loop the cravat about his neck. Quick and efficient, Barton molded the long length of starched white linen into crisp folds and a neat knot.

The first day back in Town after a long visit to the country was always a busy one. Yet even the continual press of appointments, calls, and correspondences had not been able to keep him from pulling out his pocket watch at least a dozen times, willing the small black hands to move faster.

"The fawn waistcoat, my lord?" His valet motioned to the garment laid out on the navy coverlet of the bed.

Vincent flicked his fingers. "Yes, yes, Barton. That will do."

At half past six and not a moment later, he had stepped away from his desk. After Barton finished with him, he could go on to White's to pick up the supper he'd sent a footman ahead to order. Marsden preferred the steak there. Oh, and the Bordeaux. Couldn't forget that. He'd grab a nice bottle from his wine cellar before he left the house.

The routine so familiar, Barton's nimble fingers were doing up the buttons on his waistcoat before Vincent realized the man had put it on him. A quick glance at the brass clock on the fireplace mantel confirmed it was not yet seven. Still plenty of time. He didn't want to risk ruffling Marsden's feathers again. Vincent slipped his arms into the sleeves when his valet held out his coat. Or had there been more to it than that? Tardiness never bothered Marsden before. Yet a little nudge prodded the back of his mind, one he couldn't quite define other than to label it disconcerting.

"Perhaps the black coat tonight, my lord?"

He blinked and focused on Barton's questioning face. "Pardon?"

"Would you prefer the black instead of the bottle green?"

"No. The green will do."

There was a soft scratch on his bedchamber door. With a tip of his head, Barton went to the door. Vincent took his pocket watch from the mahogany dresser and attached it to his waistcoat. He was buttoning his coat when Barton stopped beside him, tray in hand.

"For you, my lord."

With a quick snap, he tugged his shirt cuffs out from under the sleeves of his coat. Then he took the missive from the silver tray. His hand shook just the tiniest bit when he used the silver letter opener that had also been on the tray to break the distinctive red wax seal of the Marquis of Saye and Sele.

Prescot—

An audience is requested immediately.

—Saye and Sele

"My greatcoat. Now, man."

Barton dropped the discarded clothing he had been gathering. Vincent's sharp tone sent him scurrying into his master's dressing room, reappearing just as quickly with the requested garment.

Vincent put on the greatcoat, tucking the letter into his pocket. His father wished to see him. Had he heard about the success he had made of the Rotherham property? After his repeated requests for the property had been met with refusals, Vincent had purchased it outright. Did his father wish to congratulate him on turning what had once been a blight on the Saye and Sele Marquisate into a lucrative investment?

In less than a minute, he was down the stairs, out the front door of his town house, and in his waiting carriage.

By the time a footman clad in scarlet and gray livery was showing him to his father's study, reason had descended, replacing the surge of excitement with mere curiosity. Over six months ago, he had found that vein of coal on the property. If his father cared to acknowledge the success, he would have mentioned it well before now. Still, he couldn't help but wonder why his father wished to see him. It had been years...*years* since he had received such a missive.

The footman opened the oak door and Vincent stepped inside. With its high ceiling, dark paneled walls, somber gilt-framed portraits, and black leather wingback chairs, the room was a near duplicate of the study at the family's country estate, reminding him vividly of the times he had walked into its twin as a youth. That need for attention so strong it had clogged his throat and sent his heart pounding in his chest. He stopped before his father's massive desk and clasped his hands behind his back, reminding himself firmly that he was a man now and not a needy eleven-year-old boy.

His father didn't acknowledge his presence, merely slipped his pen into the silver penholder. Looking at his father, with his tall, broad-shouldered frame and neatly cropped silver hair, was like looking into a mirror and seeing his sixty-year-old self reflected back at him. Vincent used to wonder if their similarity in appearance had somehow caused his father to dislike him. Silly notion. But there had been a time when his father's complete lack of interest in him had left him so confused he'd been willing to grasp at any straw to explain it.

Using a silver stamp, Vincent's father pressed his seal into the red wax, sealing the letter he had been writing. He placed the letter in the center of the tray at the edge of his desk then turned his blue eyes to Vincent. Eyes which never seemed to truly see him. "I am in need of a favor."

From me? Somehow he kept his jaw from dropping.

"The Duke of Halstead paid me a call today. He wishes to form an alliance with our family."

"What sort of alliance?"

"Marriage. His only daughter is set to make her come-out in the spring," his father replied, as if Vincent were a simpleton for not deducing it himself.

Yet he couldn't stop the baffled "To me?" from falling from his lips.

His father's upper lip curled. "The duke intends to marry his daughter to the heir of the Saye and Sele marquisate. Not the spare."

Vincent rolled one shoulder, trying to throw off the hurt, but to no avail. It stuck to his spine, stiffening his back. "Then what do you need of me?"

"To free your brother from Lady Juliana. He cannot toss her aside himself. You must dance attendance on her and wed her by the end of the year, before Grafton returns from the country. Don't bother with the banns. Marry her by special license. It will be put about that it is a love match, and therefore all will be forgiven, leaving Grafton free to wed his grace's daughter at the start of the Season."

Though he rarely spoke to his elder brother, the Earl of Grafton, he had the distinct impression the man was rather fond of the girl. Grafton, however, would do whatever their father wished without question. "But what about Lady Juliana? It's been understood that Grafton would marry her."

"She's an earl's daughter and will still do well to marry you." The man's off-handed tone wiped away any shadow of a compliment.

Marriage? Vincent took a deep breath, that word bouncing about in his skull. Marriage? If a bit of tardiness had ruffled Marsden's feathers last night, then how would he react to this?

Oh, God. Marsden. His stomach dropped to his feet, his knees threatening to buckle. He gripped his clasped hands tight and kept his expression free of all emotion. "But I am only four-and-twenty. I haven't yet given much consideration to marriage." Men of his station typically did not wed until they were much closer to the age of thirty, after they had established themselves and after they had their fill of all the sins London had to offer.

His father scoffed. "You must eventually marry. Lady Juliana is as good as any other chit you could find on the marriage mart."

"What of Lady Juliana's father? Will he not take this as a slight against him?" The earl was an old friend of his father's. Hence the reason his father had originally entertained the notion of Grafton marrying the girl.

"He understands the situation. If his daughter were presented the opportunity to marry into a dukedom, he would take it."

Vincent opened his mouth, but his mind refused to conjure more excuses. He snapped his jaw shut and stared blankly at the silver inkwell on the oak desk. He had no desire to change his life. None whatsoever. He didn't need to marry now, nor did he want to.

Yet that old need to please rose up, threatening to clog his throat. His father actually needed him for something, even if it was only to use him to further his own greedy ambitions. Nor were Society's expectations so easy to push aside. Men of his standing married young ladies with aristocratic blood flowing through their veins. They made alliances for the good of their families without thought to their own selfish desires. But still…

He felt as if he were being pulled apart by opposing forces. One part of him screaming no, while the other part, the part that strove to be an upstanding and well-respected gentleman, the type of man a father would be proud to call son, wanted to bow his head in agreement.

The rustle of papers broke through the riot in his head. His father was pulling a bundle of papers from a drawer. He flipped through the stack and selected a sheet. "You will pay Lady Juliana a call tomorrow. She will be expecting you. I want you married before the New Year."

The man hadn't even bothered to ask if he agreed. His father had made his wishes known and expected nothing less than strict adherence.

Vincent took the dismissal for what it was and left the study. His footsteps echoed in the spacious entrance hall, the sound smacking his ears, unnaturally loud, as he made his way out of the stately mansion.

His footman opened the door as he approached the carriage. He stepped inside and sat on the bench.

"My lord? Where to?"

"Ah." Vincent gave his head a sharp shake. Supper. Yes, he needed to pick up supper. "White's."

The door snapped shut.

"Damn. The wine." He cursed under his breath. He had forgotten to get it before he left the house. Oh well. A bottle from White's would have to do.

The gentlemen's club wasn't that far from his father's house, and soon the carriage was winding its way to Cheapside, a wicker basket on the floor between his feet containing the supper the chef had kept warm.

Marsden would understand, he told himself over and over as he stared out the window. They were both second sons to marquises. Society and duty to one's family held certain obligations. Marsden would grasp the complexity of the situation his father had placed him in. Christ, he *had* to understand because, by God, Vincent needed his friend's advice on what the hell he should do.

Chapter Four

Head tipped down and black coat soaked through, his footman opened the carriage door. Rain dripped from the tip of the man's narrow nose, his white cravat a sodden mess around his neck.

A hackney would have to suffice for the ride home later tonight. Vincent couldn't leave his carriage waiting for him in this weather. The rain had started about ten minutes earlier, and based on the steady drum against the roof, it wasn't letting up anytime soon.

He buttoned his greatcoat, grabbed the wicker basket, and stooping to fit through the door, exited the carriage. "That will be all for the night."

The driver snapped the leather lines. Harness jangled as the team of four lurched forward, their hooves splashing in the puddles on the dirt road.

Vincent hurried inside and went up the three flights of dimly lit stairs to the top floor. Stopping at the door on the right, he let out a sigh, the tension easing from his shoulders, the knot unraveling in his stomach. Just the thought of Marsden on the other side of the door settled him like nothing else could.

He couldn't define when exactly, but at some point during the past thirteen years, ever since they had become friends on his first day at boarding school, he had come to associate Marsden with comfort. And right now, he was in sore need of that precious commodity.

"Evening, Marsden," he said, closing the door behind him. After the austere, frigid atmosphere of his father's house, with its priceless antiquities on display and everything in its proper place down to that silver inkwell perfectly centered on his father's desk, Marsden's quaint, untidy parlor was a welcome sight.

Seated on the brown leather couch, Marsden didn't lift his head from the open book in his hands. A couple of newspapers were strewn on the lumpy cushions beside him, an empty glass on the floor next to his feet. "Where have you been?"

His strides faltered as he crossed the room to set the basket on the small dining table in the corner. "I had an errand to see to."

Did Marsden just grunt?

Brilliant. He did not need this. Not now. Not tonight. He needed the easy, unassuming version of Marsden. The one who was always there for him. Not this prickly version whose feathers were ruffled. Again.

Passing a hand over the back of his neck, Vincent glanced to the clock on the mantel. For God's sake. Only thirty minutes late. It wasn't as if he'd left the man waiting for him for two hours.

He took off his greatcoat and folded it over the back of one of the two chairs at the table. "My apologies. I had not intended to keep you waiting."

That condescending snort made his stomach tightened anew. He held back a full explanation for his tardiness. There was no way he could tell Marsden about the meeting with his father, not when the man was behaving like this. Such an attitude did not encourage a confidence.

He took two glasses from the cupboard by the table. "Would you care for a glass of wine?" he asked, forcing a friendly tone.

Say yes, Marsden.

"No."

At least he got an answer that involved a word, though the man hadn't looked in his direction yet. Marsden pulled one foot up, bracing his heel on the cushion and his elbow on his knee, clearly settling in. He hadn't bothered with a coat, and Vincent could just make out his golden skin beneath the sleeves of his white shirt. His fingers itched to tuck the wavy chunk of hair hanging over one eye behind his ear.

"Marsden, come here." Perhaps a kiss would loosen those lips held in a hard, compressed line.

His friend's response was to turn a page.

Vincent gritted his teeth, suddenly frustrated beyond bearing. How dare he so blatantly ignore him?

"Now, boy." The words snapped across the distance separating them.

Marsden's fingers tightened around the book, a visible shudder racking his body. Vincent waited for what felt like an endless moment. Then Marsden finally put down that damn book.

Gaze downcast, he crossed the room and stopped before Vincent, his hands fisted at his sides, his chest rising and falling rapidly beneath the gray brocade waistcoat. The scent of his arousal poured off him, pervading Vincent's senses, until all he could think about was getting Marsden under him. Pounding him into the bed. Fucking him senseless. Dominating him completely.

"Get on your knees and suck my cock."

Without even a nudge on his shoulder, the man dropped to the wooden floor and removed his spectacles then put them in Vincent's outstretched hand. The buttons on the placket of Vincent's trousers were undone in a blink of an eye, and Marsden was pushing aside his shirttail, reaching through the opening in his drawers to pull out his semierect cock.

Those full, soft lips wrapped around the crown. Vincent had to fight to hold back the moan. Blood rushed to his groin, his cock hardening further as Marsden sank down. There was no lingering over the details. No light kisses feathered along the length, no long, luxurious sweeps of his tongue. The man sucked him with distinct purpose. One hand flat around the base, holding the placket out of the way, he bobbed up and down, his lips a hot silken drag along the length, the slightly rough texture of his tongue a delicious caress on the underside.

Reaching blindly to his left, Vincent set the spectacles on the fireplace mantel, then grabbed the edge of the table behind him and held on tight, needing something to keep from swaying on his feet against the decadent pleasure of Marsden's mouth. With his other hand, Vincent speared his fingers into those dark waves and cupped the back of his skull, urging him to take more.

Marsden didn't disappoint. He sank all the way down, until his lips touched the dark hair on Vincent's groin.

Wet heat surrounded every inch of his prick. "Oh God, Marsden," he groaned, his head tipping back. "You're damn good at sucking cock."

Hand braced on Vincent's thigh, Marsden picked up a rhythm of long plunging strokes that had an orgasm tickling the base of his spine in no time.

It would feel so good to spill down Marsden's throat, to have the man suck every last drop out of him. But...he tugged on his hair. With a crude wet popping noise, those lush lips were pulled from his prick. Marsden's long lashes rested against his flushed cheekbones, his quick pants fanning across Vincent's glistening length.

"I want you on the bed. Naked. Now."

Marsden trembled, the barest of whimpers escaping him. Then he scrambled to his feet and hurried through the open door of his bedchamber.

He heard Marsden scurrying around in the next room. Vincent removed his coat and waistcoat and draped them over the back of the old upholstered armchair near the fireplace, giving Marsden the time he needed to follow his orders. When the rustling and distinct creaks of the bed ceased, he went into the bedchamber.

Satisfaction surged through him at the sight of Marsden, naked and lying on the bed, as instructed. The man was sleek yet compact, his muscles defined beneath golden skin that looked even more inviting under the glow of the candle on the bedside table. Not a single dark hair marred his flawless chest. Legs slightly spread, he had his erection in one hand, stroking the length, and his ballocks cupped in the other. Full lower lip captured between his white teeth, his gaze tracked Vincent's every movement.

There was nothing quite like the feel of that intent dark gaze. The lust and need there. Desperate and dependent, wanting him and only him.

He stopped at the foot of the bed. "Should you be touching your prick?" he asked, as he untied his cravat.

Marsden snatched his hands to his sides. His hard cock jutted from his body, pointing straight to the ceiling.

Vincent took his time removing the rest of his clothes, allowing the anticipation to crank even higher until he couldn't keep his hands from shaking as he pushed his trousers down his legs, leaving them in a heap at his feet.

He eyed the utilitarian wooden headboard with its single plain rail spanning the width of the bed. Marsden's wrists would look quite nice tied to that rail, arms stretched overhead, his beautiful body Vincent's to do with as he pleased.

He grabbed his discarded cravat. Head lowered, he crawled onto the bed and up Marsden's body. When he reached Marsden's groin, the man lifted his hips, putting the flushed crown mere inches from his lips.

"Kiss me," Marsden murmured. Vincent watched Marsden's abdomen tighten, a tremor seizing the sleek muscles of his thighs. His prick bobbed, conveying in no uncertain terms where he wanted that kiss.

Crouched over Marsden, Vincent stared, transfixed by the drop of clear fluid beaded at the tip.

Kiss him? There? As in press his lips to another man's prick?

Gut instinct urged him to jerk back, yet the musky scent of Marsden's pretty cock was an oddly irresistible lure, begging him to discover if he tasted that sweet.

Marsden grabbed his upper arm and tugged. "Just fuck me." He twisted beneath him, his calves brushing Vincent's erection as he rolled onto his stomach. He snatched the bottle of oil from the bedside table, and reaching back, handed it to Vincent.

He gave his head a sharp shake, clearing the disorientation, and took the proffered bottle, leaving the cravat on the bed by his knee. Shoulders pressed to the mattress, Marsden arched his back and tipped his hips up. Once again on solid ground, Vincent rocked back onto his haunches and oiled his length, his gaze on that perfect round arse presented so sweetly to him. Then he quickly poured more oil onto his fingers, probed between those cheeks, searching for his entrance, and shoved two fingers inside.

Marsden sucked in a swift breath, the muscles in his back tightening and then, with a grunt, pushed back, impaling himself on Vincent's fingers. He rocked once, twice.

"Fuck me. *Now*."

Vincent pulled his fingers free. "I'll give you now," he growled, grabbing Marsden's slim hips and pushing past the tight ring of muscle.

Marsden whimpered. Not in pleasure but in pain. The sound cut through the thick haze of passion. Vincent hesitated, not wanting to hurt his friend.

But Marsden shook his head. "More. All of it, Vincent," he said, more demand than request, shimmying closer.

The hell with it. If he wanted more, he'd get it all. On his knees and straddling Marsden's thighs, Vincent tugged up the man's hips and pushed deeper, into exquisite heat, blazing hot and *oh*, so snug.

"Damn. So fucking good," he hissed, caressing the length of Marsden's back. The lust drumming through his veins eased just a bit, enough for him to take a moment to luxuriate in simply being joined with Marsden. This was what he needed. It was always so perfect with Marsden. And he didn't have to think about anything but the man beneath him.

Impatient, Marsden bucked back, working himself on Vincent's length. The lush, silken tug of his body sent lust thundering through him once again.

One hand holding Marsden steady, Vincent braced his weight on the other and slammed into him. "Is that what you want?"

"Yes. Yes." Biceps bulging, Marsden gripped the gray blanket with white-knuckled fists. His hair had fallen forward, hiding his face. Fine tendrils stuck to his sweat-slicked nape. He gasped, groaned, begged for more. Their bodies slapped together, hard smacks that made an orgasm tease Vincent's ballocks.

Marsden shifted, trying to work a hand under his belly. Vincent smacked his arm away. "No. Climax with just my cock in your arse, boy." Only him, and nothing else, would bring Marsden to orgasm tonight. He crouched lower over the man, sank his teeth into the apple of his shoulder, and thrust harder. Sharp, rough, frantic thrusts. The bed shook under the onslaught, the old wooden joints creaking, blending with the sound of Vincent's feral grunts.

He felt Marsden tighten around him, felt the tension in every line of his body as he reached for completion. Those little gasping grunts grew louder, quicker, hitching in his throat. Vincent canted his hips, changing the angle of his thrusts, needing Marsden to climax *now*.

"Ah, yes!"

Marsden's passage clutched his length so tightly Vincent couldn't hold back his own climax. It rushed upon him, a searing wave of pleasure that left him struggling to catch his breath.

Arms giving out, he slumped down, half on top of Marsden. Vincent pressed a kiss to Marsden's sweaty nape and then rested his head on his shoulder. Languor, warm and comforting and soothing, settled over him. Marsden had his head turned the other way, his tangled hair inches from Vincent's face. Vincent blindly reached around, his fingertips whispering over Marsden's brow and tucking the damp hair behind his ear.

Rain lashed the window; the once steady drops had turned into a downpour. It would be hell to find a hackney in this weather. Perhaps...he could stay with Marsden tonight. He always woke at the first light of dawn regardless of where he slept, and well, if he left early enough, then it would reduce the likelihood of coming face-to-face with one of the other inhabitants of the building.

He knew he couldn't remain here, in this shabby apartment, forever. But for some reason, he found himself loath to leave his friend.

An elbow nudged him, hard, in the ribs.

"Off. You're damn heavy."

"Sorry." Vincent reluctantly shifted off Marsden's warm body and onto the cool, coarse blanket. He was much heavier than Marsden. Should have been more considerate.

Marsden wiggled out from under the arm Vincent had slung across his back, got out of bed, and walked to the washstand. Vincent couldn't help but feel smug. He knew exactly what caused that slight hitch in Marsden's step.

My cock.

Could Marsden still feel him, buried deep in his arse? He hoped he could. That every step reminded him of Vincent. A little smile on his lips, he closed his eyes and waited for Marsden to come back to bed.

A wet lump landed on his lower back. He flinched. *Damnation.* It was icy cold, too. He reached back and plucked the cloth off his back, dropping it to the floor. "What was that for?"

"You need to be on your way, don't you?" Marsden stood at the washstand, arms crossed over his chest. His prick, hanging limp between his legs, appeared damp, as if he'd just washed away the remnants of his climax. A faint sneer twisted his full, kissable lips.

Brilliant. Sex had not cured Marsden of his prickly mood. Inhaling deeply though his nose, Vincent gathered his patience. "What's wrong? Are you still upset because I was a half hour late tonight?"

Marsden shrugged, a distinctly uncomfortable lift of his shoulder, and turned his back to him. He shook out the cloth that had been balled up next to the basin and folded it. What a perfect time for Marsden to decide to tidy up the washstand.

What had gotten into him? The man should be pliant and lax in his arms, not grumping about and throwing things at him.

Completely off balance, Vincent sat up and swung his legs over the side of the bed. Without looking at him, Marsden stalked over to the dresser and yanked out a pair of white linen drawers.

"Why won't you stay?" he asked, bending over to put on the underclothes.

Vincent let out a heavy sigh. He certainly wasn't going to stay tonight, not with Marsden behaving like a surly, malcontent adolescent. "This again? I told you why last night."

There was that condescending snort again. Vincent ground his teeth together.

"No one in the building will care or even notice, Vincent." He snatched his trousers from the floor. "When will I see you again?"

"Tomorrow if you'd like." *Bloody hell.* Lady Juliana. How could he forget? She was expecting him. "I have a call to pay, but I can stop by after. Would noon be all right?"

Vincent clenched his hand. If the man snorted one more time...

"Of course I'll be here. Where else would I be?" Marsden's hair fell over his brow, hiding his face as he buttoned the placket of his trousers. "But could you be on time for once? I hate being by myself all day, alone, just waiting for you."

For once? He was late twice, and this was the treatment he received? "Perhaps you should seek employment. Give yourself something more productive to do *all day*."

"And what should I do?" Marsden demanded, his head snapping up. "I'm not you, Vincent. I didn't attend university."

"There are many options available to you, if you choose to expend the effort to look." Therein lay Marsden's problem. He was a capable fellow, but he had yet to take the initiative to make something of himself. "You cannot hide behind your grandmother for the rest of your life. She's close to ninety years of age. Quite frankly, I'm amazed she's held on this long. Likely only did it out of spite. Eventually you will need to settle on an occupation, unless you plan to find another old woman and serve as her companion."

"Bugger off, Vincent," he snarled.

Anger surged up his throat, tightening his jaw, his patience beyond tried. "Pardon?" he asked in a low voice.

Marsden picked up his shirt from the floor and slowly straightened, the white linen balled in his fist. Hard dark brown eyes met his. "You know, the only time I see you anymore is whenever you deign to stop by and grace me with your presence. And that's only when you can find a few moments in your busy schedule. You go out of town for weeks on end, and you never invite me along. I rarely go to White's or a ball or anywhere I know you'll be because I don't want to be ignored. Christ, Vincent, no one suspects that you're buggering me. *No one.*" He tugged his shirt over his head, tucking it into the waistband of his trousers with sharp jabs. "You're goddamn Lord Vincent Prescot. You're perfect. *You* would never do such a thing and especially not with someone like me."

Vincent took a moment to try to piece together his fraying temper. "Sodomy is against the law. If word got out, we would be ruined. We could be hanged."

"I am well aware of that, Vincent. You don't have to tutor me in everything."

Unwilling to continue sitting naked while Marsden snarled at him, Vincent stood and found his trousers at the foot of the bed. This was not the way he had envisioned his evening. A pleasant meal and then sex. Not an unexpected demand to marry his brother's intended followed by a heated argument on an empty stomach five minutes after Marsden had climaxed on Vincent's cock.

He was buttoning the placket when Marsden spoke again, his voice low and unmistakably hurt.

"Contrary to what others may believe, I am not a complete idiot. I know why you insist on always being in control. On tying me up, restraining me. I will do whatever you ask of me, without question, because I want to be with you. Yet you won't even touch your precious lips to my prick."

Vincent gaped at him, alarm skittering down his spine. If he had felt off balance before, it was nothing compared to now. "Is that what this is about? I wouldn't suck you off tonight, and now you're angry with me?"

Marsden threw his hands in the air. "No." Then he shook his head and dragged his hands through his hair, a wince pulling his beautiful features. "Well, not completely. You don't understand. The way you treat me sometimes, I wonder why you even bother with me at all."

He didn't understand? That was putting it mildly. "When you behave like this, Marsden, I wonder as well."

Teeth bared, Marsden growled, his face flushed and contorted with rage, every line in his body drawn tight, poised to attack. "Stop condescending to me and stop calling me Marsden! We're not at White's. You just fucked me. You can damn well call me Oliver." He swiped something off the dresser. "And I'm not your damn whore. I don't need your money."

Vincent sidestepped, avoiding the gold sovereigns that had been aimed right at his chest. The coins hit the wall and clattered to the wooden floor.

Marsden snatched his coat and stomped from the room.

By God, the man was *not* walking away from him. Not after that fit. Vincent took up pursuit. Shoving his arms in the sleeves of his coat, Marsden was heading straight for the front door.

A strange sort of desperation leeched into his veins. Vincent quickened his pace. "If you're going to storm out the door, at least put on a coat that doesn't look like you grabbed it from a rag bin."

Marsden spun from the door. "Do you love me?"

Vincent halted in his tracks. "Pardon?" Those knots were back, twisting his stomach so tightly he was thankful they had not had that pleasant meal. His heart slammed high and hard against his ribs.

"Do you love me, Vincent?"

Stunned, he opened his mouth, but nothing would come out. All he could do was stare into his friend's eyes. Cold, hard eyes that used to look at him with such adoration and respect.

"I knew it. You still haven't fully admitted to yourself that you prefer men." A sneer pulling his lips, Marsden shook his head, all dismissive condescension. "I'm tired of waiting for you. Good-bye, Prescot."

And Vincent watched, his jaw still hanging open, as his friend walked out the door.

Chapter Five

The door snapped shut. The rapid thumps of Marsden's footsteps faded until Vincent couldn't hear anything but the sound of his heart beating, a quick harsh staccato against his ears.

He lurched forward, grabbed the brass knob, and then glanced down at himself.

"Bloody hell!"

He couldn't leave the apartments in only his trousers. But even if he were dressed, what the hell was he thinking? That he'd chase Marsden down? And then what? They'd continue their argument on the street, for all of London to see?

Letting out a growl of pure frustration, he slammed his fist into the wall. Why couldn't Marsden be content with the way things were? Why did he have to demand so much of him?

"Goddamn it, Marsden! And why tonight?" He slammed his fist into the wall again, but all he got for his effort was smarting knuckles.

Gritting his teeth, he speared his fingers into his hair, gripped his skull tight. All the words Marsden had slung at him blended together to form a brutal riot in his head, until he couldn't distinguish one word from another. Until his knees threatened to buckle under the sheer force of it.

Then Marsden's parting words rose above the tangled, noxious mass.

"*Good-bye, Prescot.*"

And all the fury and rage and frustration drained out of him, slumping his shoulders, leaving him beyond weary. His arms dropped limply to his sides.

He stood there—for how long, he didn't know—his breaths coming in great pulling gasps, the rain beating on the windows.

Then he numbly turned from the door and trudged across the small parlor. He pulled the bottle of mediocre Bordeaux from the wicker basket and poured a glass. After downing the contents in two long swallows, he refilled the glass and went to the couch.

He flicked aside the newspapers on the cushions and sat down heavily. Resting his elbows on his knees, he cradled the glass in his hands and hung his head. Never in his life had he felt so powerless. So at a complete loss for how to right a situation. In the space of a couple hours, his neat, orderly life had spun completely out of control.

First his father and now this. And here he had thought everything was perfect between himself and Marsden. That they understood each other. That Marsden was happy with him.

Apparently not.

"*I will do whatever you ask of me, without question, because I want to be with you.*"

Had Marsden only submitted to please him? Because he had been trying to mold himself into what Vincent desired and not because he wanted to?

No, no. Vincent pushed aside the anxiety and forced himself to think rationally. Over the years, he had been with enough men at that brothel to know the difference. Marsden had not been acting these past six months. No one could respond the way he did and not genuinely crave the give and take of their erotic games.

Vincent rubbed the back of his neck, trying to ease the tension there. Had it been a mistake to allow their friendship to move into the bedroom? He winced, dreading the thought of visiting a brothel again. No. Not that. Never again. The situation with Marsden had been ideal. *Had* being the operative word. Now, though... He doubted they could even go back to just being friends.

Raw pain lanced into his chest, stealing the breath from his lungs. The thought of not having Marsden in his life hurt as nothing else ever had. Not having him to turn to. Not simply being there whenever Vincent needed him. To never again hear Marsden's softly murmured "*Love you.*" He most certainly did not want to lose him, but did he even have a choice? It seemed the man had made the decision for him. But if he even had the chance, could he do what Marsden demanded?

He could not deny that there was still a small part of him that resisted his attraction to other men, that same part that strove to be an upstanding, respectable gentleman, for perfection in all things. Marsden bent himself so neatly to Vincent's whims that he had made it easy to ignore...until tonight. But that inner resistance was still there, in the pit of his stomach. And tomorrow...

Fuck. He had to pay a call on Lady Juliana. He didn't know what he should do. He only knew that Marsden had chosen the absolutely worst night to start a fight between them.

Christ, given their "conversation," he highly doubted Marsden would have taken kindly to his father's request anyway. Every inhabitant of the building had likely heard them shouting at each other. *Brilliant.* Just what he needed. For word to get out about his relationship with Marsden. Panic tightened his shoulders. Then he shook his head at himself. Judging by the state of the building, he highly doubted any of Marsden's neighbors moved about the *ton*.

He knew one thing for certain. One way or another, the night had been destined not to end well.

And here he had been looking forward to spending a nice evening with his friend. So much for that. His stomach grumbled. He eyed the wicker basket on the dining table, but food, cold or not, didn't hold any appeal.

He sighed and brought the glass to his lips, downing the wine. He got to his feet, put the empty glass on the table, grabbed his evening coat and waistcoat, and went into the bedchamber. He needed to get dressed sooner or later. Might as well do it now.

Purposefully averting his gaze from the rumpled bed, the one he had so recently shared with Marsden, he grabbed his wrinkled shirt from the floor and put it on, tucking the hem into his waistband. His cravat. Where had he left it? He glanced about the floor. *Fuck.* The bed. Closing his eyes, he reached to his right, swiping his hand over the woolen blanket, fingers closing over the linen.

Marsden would eventually return, he told himself as he finished dressing. He had to. He lived there after all. And then…they could have a discussion like civilized gentlemen. Yes. That was what they would do. Discuss the situation in an organized, objective fashion and come to a satisfactory resolution. Shouting never accomplished anything productive.

The thought offered some semblance of reassurance, and the tremor left his hands as he tied his cravat. Their friendship was not necessarily destroyed beyond repair. Marsden had been quite angry tonight, and Vincent had not helped matters. He had been a bit of a condescending arse and said some things he should have held back. Still, he would have appreciated it if the man had voiced his concerns before they had built to this point. Clearly, for some time now, Marsden had not been as blissfully content with Vincent as he had assumed.

He finished buttoning his coat and glanced about the room, looking for his shoes. A glint of green and gold caught his attention. Strides slow and reluctant, he went to the bedside table.

He stared down at the jade cravat pin in the dented little silver tray. Marsden never went anywhere without that pin. Even when Vincent happened upon him on the street, when he did not expect to see him, that pin was affixed to Marsden's cravat.

A band of sheer pain wrapped around his chest, searing a path up his throat and stinging his eyes. Jaw clenched, he looked up to the ceiling with its spiderweb of cracks in the plaster and blinked rapidly.

"*Good-bye, Prescot.*"

Oliver had meant it.

* * *

Oliver stumbled into his apartments. With a swat of his hand, he closed the door, cloaking the parlor in darkness.

He took a step to his left, and his thigh bumped hard into a wooden edge. He instinctively reached out, hands fumbling around the pewter candleholder and keeping it from tumbling off the small table. Swaying on his feet, he bent over the table, pulled open the drawer, and groped around until he found the tinderbox. It took more than a few tries, but he was finally able to get his hands to cooperate. The flare of golden light illuminated his empty parlor.

"Hell," he cursed under his breath, dropping his chin to his chest.

Of course Vincent had not waited for him. He never waited for anything or anyone. Oliver had known he'd come home to an empty room—hence why he had remained at that tavern for so long. But then, why did it hurt so much?

Damn gin. Wasn't doing its duty. He scrubbed his hands over his face and pushed his tangled, dripping wet hair out of his eyes. He was certainly foxed enough not to care that he was soaked through from the rain. But the copious amounts of gin hadn't done a bit of good to deaden the pain.

Now he wasn't just hurting like hell, but soaked to the bone, so foxed it surprised him a bit that he'd found his way home, and hurting like hell.

"You're bloody pathetic, Marsden. No wonder Vincent doesn't love you."

What felt like a blazing hot poker jammed into his heart, twisting violently.

"Ouch," he grumbled, rubbing his chest.

But he couldn't deny the truth. He was pathetic. Barely had two shillings to rub together, lived in a hovel, and did nothing with himself except wait for Vincent and tend to his grandmother a few times a week. Damn poor excuse for a man.

A poor excuse who still stood by the door, water dripping from his coat and forming a puddle on the floor.

He grabbed the candle, not wanting to try his hand at lighting another, and concentrating on each step, made his way into his bedchamber. With deliberate purpose, he set the candle on the bedside table and then fumbled with the buttons on his coat. He would most certainly wake up tomorrow with a pounding head, but he'd rather not add a head cold to the mix.

"Damn buttons. Ah, the hell with them." With a hard tug, he ripped open his coat, the buttons popping free and skidding across the floor. After peeling the garment off his shoulders and down his arms, he shook the sodden sleeves from his wrists and flung it to the floor. He didn't even bother to make an attempt at the buttons on his waistcoat. With another hard tug and a bit of a struggle, the waistcoat joined the coat.

"Should have kept Vincent's money," he grumbled, staring at the ruined garments and the buttons littering the floor. "Would have paid for the tailor."

Oh well. Not much he could do about it now. Or anything, for that matter. He had allowed his impatience and frustration to get the better of him and in the process ruined everything he had with Vincent.

Who was he fooling? He had done it deliberately. Poked and prodded Vincent until his final question had been answered with absolute shock and horror. The shock he expected—he'd never outright asked Vincent if he loved him before. The horror—now that had hurt.

It still hurt.

Hurt more, in fact, than knowing he had destroyed his friendship with Vincent.

His gaze strayed back to the bedside table, to the jade cravat pin on the silver tray. Did Vincent expect him to return it?

Not on his life. Pathetic, yes, to keep a small token of the man he loved, but he wouldn't part with the pin until Vincent showed up at his front door demanding its return.

"He told me to keep it, anyway." So what that it had been six months ago and matters were vastly different between them now. He jutted out his chin. He was keeping it.

He whispered his fingertips over the stone. His heart clenched, begging, pleading. Squeezing his eyes closed tight, he pushed back the sting of tears, refusing to allow them to fall.

"Enough," he murmured sharply. "It's over."

Then he let out a heavy sigh, his entire body slumping in resignation, and set to work removing the rest of his clothes.

He might not be able to change Vincent or replace his apartments with something more respectable, but he could change one thing. He yanked his shirt over his head. Contrary to Vincent's opinion, he wasn't a complete wastrel. He could "expend the effort" and make something of himself, or at least try. For he certainly did not want to spend his days alone in his apartments, beating himself up over how he had gone and lost Vincent. Then he might give into his broken heart and beg Vincent to take him back, even if he only wanted him as a convenient man to bugger.

No. Definitely not that. Vincent could not love him. Best he accepted it now, before he reached the point where it hurt to be with him.

He pulled back the woolen blanket and flopped down naked on his bed, the old wooden joints creaking in protest. But what to do with himself?

Not a secretary. Or a clerk. He didn't want to actually work for anyone. Elitist, but the truth. He wasn't much good at anything, either. Never attended university. Didn't know the first thing about how to manage a property. The only thing he knew was...

Books.

How many had he read to his grandmother over the years? Hell, he could open his own bookstore from the piles littering her bedchamber alone.

It could classify as an investment. Shouldn't require much of the principle from his inheritance. If he failed miserably, he wouldn't be left destitute.

He levered up onto his elbows, blew out the candle, and flopped back down again. Darkness settled over the room, the rain now a light tap against the window.

No more wallowing in his sorrows. Tomorrow he'd take a step toward making something of himself.

* * *

Bright and crisp, early afternoon sunlight filled the drawing room. Last night's heavy rain had temporarily vanquished the clouds that perpetually hung over the city. Whereas most of London's inhabitants savored rare clear days, Vincent had greeted the sunny, cheerful sky with a scowl this morning.

If the rain had continued, he might have had a valid excuse to postpone the call. But the heavens hadn't seen fit to cooperate, and therefore, he found himself in this drawing room with pale blue-and-white-striped paper covering the walls and tasteful, yet decidedly uncomfortable furniture.

He shifted in the spindly-legged armchair and resisted the impulse to rub his temple. The bright light only made his head ache more. Exhaustion pulled at his eyes, reminding him in no uncertain terms of the night he had spent tossing and turning in his bed, after that long walk home. Damn hackneys. Where had they been last night? The walk home had provided far too much time alone with his own thoughts, Oliver's words repeating over and over in his head, each pass chipping away at that inner resistance until he had been left damning himself for a stubborn, self-centered fool.

"Would you care for another cup of tea, Lord Vincent?"

He glanced to the cup in his hand, half-filled with what was now, no doubt, lukewarm tea. "No, thank you."

Seated on the adjacent ivory silk settee, Lady Juliana tipped her head and reached for the squat, white porcelain teapot on the trolley beside her. Little spirals of steam rose from the liquid as she refilled her own cup.

Vincent had only spoken to her a handful of times before today, certainly nowhere near long enough to judge her true character, but he had the impression she was polite and biddable. Would cause him absolutely no grief. Not a striking beauty but pleasant to look upon with her light brown hair pulled back in a loose knot at her nape and her welcoming, heart-shaped face. The cut of her sage green morning dress hinted at a trim figure. At least it wouldn't be a hardship to bed her.

What an absolutely maudlin thought—slipping into her bedchamber under the cover of darkness, having her lie still beneath him as he rutted between her legs. Aristocratic conjugal bliss.

He could see his future before him—married to a gently bred young lady, doing what his father and Society expected of a man of his station. They'd manage to produce a couple children—the required spares in the event his elder brother died without issue. But it would require locking away a part of himself forever. To never be with another man again. Never be with Oliver again.

Utter misery pressed heavily on his chest, threatening to tighten his brow and pull his lips into a wince. Through sheer force of will, he kept his expression schooled in a polite bland mask.

He didn't have much of a choice. If Lady Juliana had to settle for him, then the least he could do was be faithful to her. And the only man he wanted had walked out on him last night.

"Is Lord Grafton expected in Town soon?" she asked, jolting him back to the present and away from the painful memory of that door slamming shut.

He hadn't spoken to his elder brother in…months. Long before the man had returned to his estate in Devon. "I suspect he will remain in the country until after the New Year." *Until after we are wed.*

The sparkle dimmed from her hazel eyes. She brought her cup to her lips and took a small sip.

A love match? Vincent resisted the urge to shake his head. Lady Juliana possessed impeccable manners, to the point of polite distance. The two of them were little more than passing acquaintances. No matter what his father wished, no one would believe they were in love.

With a little click, she set her cup on the saucer on the low table before them and then folded her hands. "Please forgive my boldness, but if you do not have news of Lord Grafton, then what brings you here today?"

Taken aback, Vincent's spine went stiff. "Have you not spoken to your father?"

"I was told to expect your call today."

Brilliant. They had left it to him to explain the situation to her. Bloody cowards.

He set his cup on the table and glanced to the open door of the drawing room. He wanted to get up and close it, but being behind closed doors with an unmarried, unrelated gentleman could ruin a woman's reputation. Instead, he turned his attention to her and did his best to break the news as gently as possible. "The Duke of Halstead wishes to form an alliance with my family." He kept his voice low to prevent being overhead by any passing servants. Gossip spread quickly, and he'd rather spare her its wrath for as long as possible. "His grace's daughter is due out on the marriage mart next Season. Therefore, it is my fondest wish that you will come to accept me in Grafton's stead."

He held back the blunt details, but Lady Juliana proved herself an intelligent girl.

Desolation flashed across her face for the briefest of moments. Then she gathered her composure and nodded. "Of course. I understand, Lord Vincent."

Out in Society for three years, she could have had other proposals given her social standing. Yet she had held out for Grafton, waiting for him to come up to scratch. Poor thing deserved better than his dolt of a brother. And certainly better than himself.

Damn his father for putting him in this situation, but there were more than his wishes at stake. He now held a young woman's future in his hands.

"May I call on you again tomorrow? Perhaps, if the weather permits, you would like to take a drive in Hyde Park."

She tipped her head. "Certainly, Lord Vincent. I would welcome that."

He took his leave and made his way out to his waiting carriage.

"Where to next, my lord?" his footman asked, holding the door open.

Not his town house. A pile of work awaited him on his desk, but he wanted to avoid the day's post for as long as possible. He'd rather not know if Oliver had returned the jade cravat pin just yet.

"White's." He stepped into the carriage and settled on the leather bench. A glass of whisky or two or more were just the thing to help ease the adjustment to his new life as a soon-to-be-married gentleman. A new life without the man who once loved him.

Chapter Six

A knock sounded on the back door, pulling Oliver's attention from the inventory records. He dropped his pencil onto the desk and stood. Pressing his palms to his lower back, he stretched, his joints popping and cracking as he worked out the kinks from being hunched over the desk for the past hour. Thank heaven for the interruption. He adored his new bookshop, but when it came to tasks that severely dimmed his enthusiasm for his first and only investment, minding the inventory records ranked second only to balancing the account ledger.

He would have much preferred to assist the customers, but Mr. Wallace had insisted that with him being a lord and all, he might intimidate some of the customers. He doubted he had ever intimidated anyone in his life, but since he'd purchased the bookstore from Mr. Wallace, he figured he should heed the older man's advice.

That knock sounded again, harder this time. He navigated the piles of books surrounding his desk and opened the back door.

"Got a delivery." A squat, burly man indicated the cart behind him in the alley. The large draft horse hitched to the cart turned its head to Oliver, regarding him with soft, dark eyes. Rubbing his chin, the man squinted at the piece of paper in his hand. "For a Lord Oliver Marsden. Three crates. Mighty heavy, too."

New books, which meant more books to inventory, but new books nonetheless. Well, not exactly new. An old friend of his family's had passed away, and Oliver had ventured out to the estate last week to help prune the overstuffed library. The man's widow had been willing to sell off the lot of it, but the bookshop's bank account could unfortunately only afford a few crates' worth.

He signed for the delivery and had it brought into his office. The first crate was dropped to the floor with a bang loud enough to rattle the small window on the door leading to the main part of the shop. Ignoring the man's grumbles and grunts as he fetched the other two crates, Oliver grabbed a hammer and used the end to pry open the wooden crate.

The sight of the leather bound volumes, packed not so neatly inside, produced a wonderful rush of pride and excitement. His first purchase for the shop. Each volume carefully selected based on his knowledge of the shop's existing inventory. Inventory which was in sore need of replenishment. Mr. Wallace had run a decent albeit small shop, one Oliver had frequented many times over the years, but gout and old age kept him confined to Town, unable to travel the countryside to procure more stock. New books could be easily purchased in Town, but the best finds were in the country. Hence one of the reasons why the older man had been willing to sell the shop to Oliver.

A tinkling feminine laugh seeped through the office door leading to the shop. The sound of another pleased customer. Fortunately, Mr. Wallace had been willing to stay on and help with the customers and teach Oliver the business. A business his grandmother had not been pleased to hear about. Those of the aristocracy inherited their wealth or earned it from their lands. They did not—shudder to think it—engage in something as common as trade. But a promise of an unlimited supply of books had done wonders to quiet her tirade. She hadn't uttered the words blasphemous, indecent, or garish since.

He settled on his knees and started pulling out the books one by one, checking for signs of damage during shipment and pausing to read a few pages every now and then.

A couple hours later, he finished with the last crate and extinguished the lamps, closing up for the night. After bidding "good evening" to Mr. Wallace as the man trudged up the street, he locked the front door and slipped the brass key into his pocket.

He glanced up and down the lamp-lit street, the cobblestones glistening from a recent light rain. The shops across from his had already closed for the night, their windows dark. Hooves thundered past him, a team of two pulling a sleek black town carriage, merry voices spilling from the open window.

He dreaded the thought of returning to his empty apartments. The constant press of matters that required his attention at the bookstore occupied his mind during the day, but the nights were an entirely different matter. Alone in his bed, missing Vincent. A lot. How many times over the past three weeks had he told himself he should have kept his damn mouth shut? Just accepted whatever Vincent had been willing to give, even though that path would have led to an even greater heartache than the one he currently carried with him.

Didn't help that he did not have any other true friends beside Vincent. No one else to share a drink with at a tavern or meet at a gambling hell or discuss his new investment with. Acquaintances, but no one he deemed a friend.

And he was tired of going out of his way to avoid Vincent.

The hell with it.

He turned right, in the opposite direction of his apartments around the corner, and headed up the street. If Vincent was at White's, then so be it. He refused to hide in the dark and lick his wounds anymore. They lived in the same city, would eventually cross paths again. No point purposefully prolonging the inevitable.

* * *

Lord Shelburne bets Mr. Frank Winters £15 that Lord V will steal a certain lady from his elder brother, Lord G, and ask for her hand before the month is out.

Oliver forced air into his lungs and read the line again. Three weeks had passed since that fateful night, and he had not heard a word from Vincent. Nothing. He had not seen him either—not much of a surprise given Oliver had been avoiding the man's usual haunts.

Now he knew why.

Betrayal, thick and hot, filled his gut, pounded swiftly through his veins, erasing all traces of shock.

"Bloody fucking—" He clenched his teeth, cutting off the rest of the curse. The last thing he needed was to be ejected from White's because of that...that...*man*.

Mouth twisted in a sneer, he turned from the betting book and left White's, not sparing a second thought to the startled glances as he rushed down the main stairs and through the hall. As he walked out the front door, he shoved his hand in his pocket, fingers closing around the coins. Enough for cab fare.

"Number Twelve, Hill Street," he said to the driver as he got into a waiting hackney. "And be quick about it."

A whip cracked and the cab lurched forward.

"Bastard! Bloody fucking bastard!"

Oliver sat and stewed, the betrayal a physical force consuming every inch of his being.

Goddamn him. If that wager was the reason Vincent had kept him at arm's length in public, all but forcing him from attending Society functions, just so he could—

The hackney jerked to a stop outside a stately white stucco townhome. Oliver jumped from the carriage and slapped a few coins into the driver's hand. "Two more shillings if you wait here."

Driven by an unholy need to discover the truth, to look Vincent in the face and hear it from his lips, he stalked up to the black door and slammed his fist against it.

The door opened, revealing a tall, slim, older man in black attire, his spine ramrod straight and his face devoid of all expression.

Oliver took a breath, trying to settle his pulse enough so he could speak in a tone that approached calm. Such a haughty butler would never allow a raving lunatic into the house. "I am here to call on Lord Vincent."

"Lord Vincent is not at home."

Not at White's. Not at home. Where then? The brothel? *No, no, no.* Not that. Not with another man.

"Where is he?"

The butler sniffed. "Lord Vincent is not at home."

The man made to shut the door, but Oliver flattened a hand against it, holding it open. "I am Lord Oliver Marsden, an old friend of Lord Vincent's. It is imperative I speak with him tonight."

He stared hard at the butler as the man looked him up and down. He knew he must look a sight in his favorite but well-worn plain brown coat, the front dusty from unloading books from their crates, and his hair a disheveled mess from running his fingers repeatedly through it as he had struggled with the account ledger earlier that day. The last time he had been to Vincent's home was ages ago. Likely the butler didn't remember him or believe his claim that he was in fact a lord.

The butler's lips thinned. "Drury Lane." The man shut the door with a smart click, a surprising show of strength considering Oliver still leaned against it.

The theatre? Vincent didn't care for the theatre, so why…? Unless…*she* did.

Twenty minutes later, Oliver slapped the remaining coins from his pocket into the driver's hand. The doors to the theatre were closed; the space under its wide stone portico with its four sets of twin columns was vacant. A few orange sellers loitered nearby, waiting to press their wares on the patrons as they exited the building. Voices spilled from the open windows, indicating the performance had not finished for the night.

He took up a spot along the building a good ten paces from the area in front of the theatre, leaned a shoulder against the stucco wall, and crossed his arms over his chest, settling in for the wait. Absolutely foolish to be here, lying in wait for Vincent like some sort of spurned lover, but he could not have moved if his life depended on it.

The streetlamps lining Catherine Street illuminated the light mist suspended in the cool night air. He wrapped his arms tighter around himself, the cold from the theatre's wall seeping through his coat, chilling his back.

Carriages began to line up outside the theatre. The drivers called to one another, fighting with the hackneys for the spots closest to the entrance. All the while, Oliver's eyes were glued to those front doors.

They swung open and people began to stream out of the building. Breath held, he searched the crowd.

Then his heart lurched in his chest.

Dressed in strict black evening attire complete with a black top hat, his white cravat an elaborate knot beneath his strong jaw, Vincent walked out of the theatre. Taller than the other gentlemen and ladies surrounding him, he was fairly easy to spot. But Oliver could have picked him out in a crowd of thousands.

Oliver shifted his right hand up from his crossed arms and briefly pressed his palm over the cravat pin hidden in the inside pocket of his waistcoat, directly over his heart. Wearing it was out of the question. But neither could he leave it all alone in its dented little silver tray whenever he left his apartments.

Then he noticed the young lady at Vincent's side, her hand on his arm. Oliver scowled, jealousy churning in his belly. She didn't suit Vincent one bit. Her nose in the air, her light brown hair pulled back in a priggish knot, a demure pale blue gown draping her thin form. Cold, remote, a typical lady of Quality.

Then again, perhaps she did suit Vincent perfectly.

Vincent stopped at the street, his head turning left and right, obviously looking for his carriage. Others paused near him, mingling and discussing the performance.

Leave. Now. Before he sees you.

Vincent looked over his shoulder. Brilliant blue eyes met Oliver's. His brow furrowed, and then he snapped his attention back to his acquaintances.

Bitter, rancid pain stabbed into him.

He didn't even acknowledge me.

Oliver watched, feeling as insignificant as a speck of lint on Vincent's expertly tailored black evening coat, as Vincent led the young lady and an older woman, likely the lady's chaperone, to his town carriage that waited up the street a bit. Ever the gentleman, he held out his white-gloved hand, helping first the lady and then the chaperone into the carriage.

He shut the door, turned on his heel and strode through the crowd…directly toward Oliver.

That intense blue gaze struck Oliver to the spot. Unable to take a step forward and unable to turn away.

Vincent stopped before him and clasped his hands behind his back. "Good to see you, Marsden."

Jolted from his daze, Oliver called upon the betrayal, making it pound thick and hot once more in his veins. "So it's true?" Still slouched against the wall, he flicked a glance around Vincent's broad shoulder to the man's carriage waiting exactly where he'd left it, a footman standing guard at the door.

Vincent briefly closed his eyes, his face a stoic, expressionless mask.

His silence was as good as a yes.

Cruel anger built within Oliver, his breaths coming harsh and ragged. How long had Vincent been courting the girl? Had there been others? Oliver rarely attended Society functions, but Vincent did. How the hell long had he been planning to find himself a wife? Oliver flicked a glance to the carriage again. "Is she the reason punctuality eluded you?"

Vincent stiffened, quickly looking about them, but there wasn't anyone else within a few paces of them. In any case, the noise of the crowd and the carriages on the street probably drowned out their conversation.

"Marsden," Vincent admonished in a low hiss, concerned as always about appearances. "Keep your voice down. Please." He let out a heavy sigh, his lips pressed in a grim line. "It is my father's idea. The Duke of Halstead wishes to form an alliance with my family. But before Grafton can wed his grace's daughter, he must be freed of any obligation toward Lady Juliana. Therefore, my father asked me to marry her."

"When did this happen?"

"The evening you slammed the door on me."

Stunned, Oliver gave his head a sharp shake. That ambiguous errand, and the cause for his late arrival at Oliver's apartments, had been a visit to see his father? "Why didn't you mention it?"

Vincent lifted one shoulder in a mockery of a shrug.

"Your father's simply using you for his own gain. He'll forget about you again as soon as you are wed to that girl."

"Perhaps not."

Oliver snorted in derision. The Marquis of Saye and Sele cared nothing for his second son. Oliver had long accepted that he meant nothing to his own father—the man hadn't even bothered to notify him when he left Town to flee his debts—yet despite all of Vincent's successes and despite the cool, controlled facade he showed the rest of the world, he had never let go of the need for his father's respect and admiration. Never accepted that nothing he could do would ever change his father's opinion, or rather lack of opinion, of him. Now Vincent was allowing that need to lead him to the altar, tied to some woman for the rest of his life.

And hell, Oliver knew the expectations Society placed on men like himself and Vincent. As he had told his grandmother, he would never marry. But Vincent strove to be the perfect gentleman, and proper gentlemen married. Why hadn't it ever occurred to him before that Vincent would eventually choose a wife?

Fool. He rolled his eyes in self-disgust.

"You've made the betting book at White's. A wager that you will wed before the month is out. Should I bet on you or not?"

Vincent's silence hung heavy in the air between them.

Oliver nodded. "I understand. It's difficult to say no to someone when you desperately want their attention."

Vincent's jaw tightened. Tense lines bracketed his firm mouth and creased the space between his eyebrows. Dark shadows underscored his eyes. He looked so tired, so worn out. So very grim. Not even a hint of happiness on his handsome face.

The need rose up within him, so strong he almost gave in to it. To reach out, to help soothe Vincent's worries, to simply be there for him. To lend a willing ear and let the man unburden himself.

Instead, Oliver pushed from the wall and turned.

Long fingers curled around his upper arm, holding him back.

"Wait."

Staring at the cracks in the cement walkway, Oliver tugged his arm.

Vincent tightened his grip, fingers digging into his muscle. Then that strong hand slipped away.

"Miss you."

The soft, rumbling words brushed the back of his neck. A gentle caress he wasn't certain if he imagined or not. His heart threatened to shatter anew into a thousand tiny pieces. But he kept his chin up and walked away from Vincent for the last time.

Chapter Seven

Vincent set his hat on his folded greatcoat on the leather bench and stared blankly out the closed window on the carriage's door. Given the heat of the theatre, he had left the coat in the carriage. Lady Juliana and her aunt, Mrs. Caldwell, sat across from him discussing the evening's performance, their feminine voices an uninterrupted lyrical drone. He barely heard them.

Christ, he missed Oliver. It had felt so good to simply lay eyes on him, to be near him again, yet at the same time it hurt like hell. With Oliver's arms crossed over his chest and a surly twist on his full lips, Vincent had known he would not receive a warm welcome. The untidy cravat with its agonizingly bare and lopsided knot had only served as another reminder that Oliver was no longer his. Still, Vincent had to speak to him, though it had been painful to have the truth thrown in his face.

Knowing he was his father's pawn and hearing it from Oliver were two vastly different things. With only a few words from him, Oliver had understood every nuance and every detail of the situation, leaving Vincent feeling stripped bare. Vulnerable and exposed. And needing his friend more than ever.

Yet there had been no compassion in Oliver's dark gaze. Only contempt and pity. Exactly what a willing pawn deserved.

Vincent passed a hand over the back of his neck. And he called himself a man. He caught the disdain-soaked harrumph before it left his throat. Men did not allow themselves to be so neatly manipulated.

Marriage. It had once been a vague notion, a concept he gave little consideration to. But he'd had ample opportunity to familiarize himself with it recently. Definitely not something he wanted or wished for.

He wanted Oliver in his bed and no one else.

Shoving those feelings deep down where they would never see the light of day again, trying his damnedest to deny a part of himself… Three weeks of that torture had been the very definition of hell. How would he survive a lifetime of it?

He couldn't.

He needed Oliver. He was bound to him in a way he could not fully explain, yet would no longer question or deny.

The knowledge settled over him, infusing into his bones, bearing the calm, quiet weight of an undisputable fact. He belonged with Oliver, not with Lady Juliana.

He pulled his attention from the neat row of town houses lining the street and looked to the young lady who was still discussing the evening with her aunt. Head tipped toward the older woman, she absently adjusted the ivory shawl about her slim shoulders. After numerous late morning calls and afternoon rides through Hyde Park, he still knew little about her. She preferred her tea without sugar, did not mind the rain, and had a decided fondness for Grafton. Anytime he mentioned his brother, her eyes sparkled, her lips tilted up at the edges, and her polite attention turned into rapt attention.

She did not belong with him, either. Nor did she deserve to be tied to him by forces beyond their control.

But what could he do about it? Everything was settled. The outcome predetermined before his father had even voiced his "request."

His mouth thinned into a determined line.

He would do what he should have done in the first place. But first, he needed her permission. After all, it involved her future as well.

The carriage stopped outside Lady Juliana's home, a neat white town house similar to many others that lined the streets of Mayfair. Metal clanked as the footman unfolded the step and then opened the carriage door. She and her aunt politely bade Vincent good night and thanked him for a pleasant evening.

Mrs. Caldwell departed from the carriage. Lady Juliana shifted along the bench, moving closer to the door, and made to follow her aunt, but Vincent leaned forward, his shoulders partially blocking the open door.

"Wait. Please, Lady Juliana," he added at her startled glance. "Might I have a moment of your time?"

Unlike Oliver, she heeded his request. She folded her hands neatly in her lap, her expression one of polite interest.

"I wish to ask you a question." He pitched his voice low to avoid being overheard by her aunt, who lingered along the short walkway leading to the front door. "And I request nothing less than complete honesty."

The polite interest didn't falter as she nodded, bidding him to continue.

"If the choice was yours, whom would you marry? Myself or Grafton?"

* * *

Vincent shut the study door behind him.

Seated in one of the black leather wingback chairs by the fireplace, his father was reading the newspaper. Nearly nine in the evening and he appeared as though his valet had just finished dressing him. The short layers of his silver hair neatly combed, not one unwanted wrinkle in his navy coat. Yet the glass of brandy on the table beside him indicated he would retire soon.

Ten more minutes and Vincent would've had to wait until tomorrow.

Unacceptable. One way or another, he would have ensured his father heard him out. He would not allow another night to pass and have all be right in the Marquis of Saye and Sele's tidy little world where every inhabitant eagerly bent to his will.

Resolute, he crossed the room and stopped next to the other chair angled toward the fireplace. "Father. Might I have a word with you?"

His father's attention didn't stray from the *Times*. "Do you need my assistance obtaining the special license from the archbishop?"

"No. Lady Juliana and I will not be wed."

"She rejected your offer?" Eyes still on that damn newspaper, he absently reached out, fingers closing around the glass and took a sip. "I'll have a word with her father. The man assured me the girl would accept you."

"I have not asked for her hand, nor will I."

That got his father's attention. "You must."

Vincent shook his head. "Grafton cares for her, and more importantly, she is in love with him." He knew what love looked like—Oliver had taught him that—and he had seen it reflected in Lady Juliana's face when she had answered his question with a shyly whispered, "*Grafton.*"

His father waved his hand, dismissing the notion as insignificant. "It matters not. Grafton will wed the Duke's daughter and do his duty. And so must you. Lady Juliana cannot be tossed aside."

Vincent stared in detached horror at his father. The man truly did not care about his children's well-being. And to think Vincent had so desperately craved his attention. Spent years trying to mold himself into the perfect son, all for nothing.

Even if Oliver refused to ever speak to him again, Vincent still owed him his gratitude. If not for his friend, he could have become...*this*. Cold. Detached. Focused only on his business interests and Society's good opinion of him. He might physically look like his father's son, but that's where he wanted the resemblance to end.

"Lady Juliana will not be tossed aside. There will be no scandal. Nor will you create one in an effort to force my hand, for it would only reflect poorly on yourself and Grafton. As for my recent association with her, it will simply be put about that I was serving as her temporary escort in my brother's absence. She so enjoys the theatre. It would have been a shame to deprive her while Grafton is in the country."

A flush rose up from his father's neck, tingeing his ears red and coloring his cheeks. An ugly scowl contorted his features. Vincent had never witnessed the sight, but apparently his father did not react well to having his wishes ignored. How unfortunate for his father.

The man shot to his feet, flicking the newspaper to the floor with a sharp snap of his wrist. "You must marry eventually, so you will marry her. *Now*. It is your duty. You must secure an heir."

"Since I do not plan on being put in the ground any time in the near future, there is no reason for me to marry now. I am only four-and-twenty. Still plenty of years ahead of me to choose a wife." A small portion of his brain marveled at his ability to remain so calm and composed, so unaffected in the face of his father's anger. But he knew the encounter was a mere prelude, a warm-up exercise, so to speak, for what awaited him after he left this house. "If in ten years Grafton does not have an heir and a spare, then we can discuss marriage. Until that time, I am content to wait." He highly doubted it would come to that. If his suspicions about him were correct, Grafton would have a small brood before the decade was up.

"Grafton must honor the agreement I made with his grace."

"No. Grafton will honor his obligation to Lady Juliana." *And as soon as he returns to Town, I'll have a word with him to ensure he does.*

His father's nostrils flared, his blue eyes nearly bulging from his head. "Marry her or I will cut you off."

Vincent shrugged. As if it would be a change from his father's usual indifference, not that he cared one whit about the man's opinion of him anymore.

"I will cut off your quarterly allowance," his father snarled in a tone that brooked no threat of rebuttal. Hands fisted at his sides and jaw clamped tight, he was so beyond his usual stoic composure it was almost comical.

"I don't need it. Do you remember the Rotherham property? That dismal little property you refused to give me? I purchased it a year ago. You should have asked more for it." He paused and allowed the pride swelling his chest to curve his lips. "Best investment I ever made. Good evening, Father."

With that, he tipped his head and turned on his heel, leaving his father scarlet-faced and slack-jawed.

* * *

Vincent didn't recall there being so many stairs. Heart slamming against his ribs so hard and fast he was amazed it didn't burst from his chest, he rounded the landing and went up the next flight. Surely they hadn't added another floor to the building in his absence.

When the last step was finally behind him, he paused and closed his eyes, trying to will his pulse to slacken to something that approached normal levels.

Absolutely wasted effort.

Forcing his feet to move, he walked to the door on the right.

Sweat dripped down the back of his neck, a hot tickle under his stiff collar. He removed his gloves, stuffing them in his coat pocket, and tugged on his cravat. Should have left the greatcoat in the carriage, but he had not wanted to be without it in the event he had to walk home in the chill, damp late October night. After unbuttoning the coat, he held up his hands. By God, he was shaking.

He had never felt this way before. Never needed something so badly and, at the same time, been scared out of his wits. He knew what Oliver wanted from him. Had already damned himself for a fool countless times for not accepting himself for who he was ages ago. For even having brought them to this point. He knew the words he needed to speak if he stood a chance in hell of convincing the man to take him back. Yet still, opening his heart to Oliver, laying himself bare at his feet, giving up that need for control and exposing himself so completely…

A decidedly frightening prospect.

But he was determined to do it. He'd take a lesson from his friend and demand the man hear him out.

But what if he wouldn't listen?

What if Oliver walked away from him again?

What if Oliver didn't love him anymore?

His hand shot out, fingers gripping the door's frame, to keep from crumpling to his knees.

Stop it!

It was pointless to allow the worries to consume him, to batter away at him until he couldn't stay on his feet, much less form a coherent sentence. In any case, he would never know the truth unless he knocked on that door.

So do it.

He gave his evening coat a sharp tug to straighten it, reached up to check the knot on his cravat to assure it was still centered, and then knocked once on the door.

Chapter Eight

One cold hand on the wobbly rail, Oliver stopped at the top of the stairs and blinked. Yes, that really was Vincent with his back to the door of his apartments, hands clasped and legs slightly spread, as if he were standing guard. The long, dark greatcoat added width to his already broad shoulders, to the point where Oliver could barely make out the door behind him.

"Where have you been? I've been waiting for twenty-five minutes."

The accusatory tone obliterated the shock, chasing away the chill that had seeped into Oliver's bones on the walk home and making his hackles stand on end, stiff and bristly. So the man did not like to wait. Too bad. And why was Vincent there anyway? Hadn't he been clear enough already? He no longer wanted anything to do with the man.

If Vincent labored under the assumption that he could bend Oliver over, use him for nothing more than a convenient fuck, an anonymous vessel to slake his desires, then he was vastly mistaken.

Goddamn arrogant bastard.

Pulling his key from his pocket, he stalked across the distance separating them and glared up at Vincent. The man moved aside enough so Oliver could fit the brass key into the lock and open the door without brushing against him.

"Where have you been?" Vincent asked. Again.

Oliver lit the candle on the small table. The feeble golden light illuminated a not-so-empty parlor as Vincent had followed him inside. He sure as hell wouldn't answer Vincent's question. It was none of his concern, nor did he need to know that Oliver had taken a very long route home to prolong the inevitable. Three weeks and it still hurt to come home to an empty room. To know he'd have a long, lonely night ahead of him.

The door clicked shut.

Oliver ground his teeth together. By God, the man had ballocks.

Mouth twisted in a sneer, Oliver put the tinderbox back in the drawer and slammed it shut. "Have you come by to invite me to your wedding? If so, you needn't bother." Vincent was truly fit for Bedlam if he thought Oliver would happily sit in one of the benches at St. George's Church and watch as he wed that girl. And of course, Vincent would marry at St. George's, the most fashionable church in London.

Vincent slipped his greatcoat off his shoulders and draped it over his arm, fussing with it until it hung in neat folds. When the garment met with his satisfaction, he looked up and speared Oliver with a solemn stare. "No. I wanted to advise you to have a care with gambling."

Uncertain how to interrupt that statement, Oliver went to the fireplace, dropped to his haunches, and busied himself piling logs onto the grate and starting the fire. He had asked Vincent if he should bet on his impending marriage or not. Was Vincent trying to tell him that he was not going to wed the girl?

Only one way to find out.

"Are you going to marry her?" Oliver asked, using the iron poker to nudge at the burning logs. The flames flickered up, reaching toward the flue, the logs popping and cracking, offering a welcome bit of warmth. He kept the threadbare brown velvet drapes closed tight in the autumn and winter months, but they did little to keep out the chill.

The floorboards creaked once, twice, three times. Then the room went quiet.

"No."

His hand shook ever so slightly as he carefully leaned the poker against the sooty bricks of the fireplace surround. He stood and turned to find Vincent one pace from him. The dark greatcoat covered the back of the nearby armchair. "Why not? Your father wishes it." He threw the words out there, as if doing anything other than what the marquis wished was inconceivable.

Vincent shrugged, discomfort etched in every line of his powerful body. A heavy furrow marred his brow. His hands were clasped so tightly before him that his knuckles had turned white. "She prefers my brother over me. Apparently she's in love with him."

"Silly chit."

"Well, yes, but I don't blame her. I'm not the easiest man to be with, and I would have made a very poor husband." Shifting his weight, he glanced to his polished evening shoes and then back to Oliver. "And I, well...I prefer you."

Oliver's heart leapt into his throat but somehow he managed to speak with a bored drawl. "Do you now?"

"I must. I love you."

Oliver's jaw dropped. Had he heard Vincent correctly? Or were his ears playing tricks on him, letting him hear the words he had ached to hear for so long?

"I apologize for being such a condescending arse. It's rude of me to keep you waiting. To be so presumptuous. Please forgive me for behaving so abysmally toward you when we were out and about. But whenever I'm near you, I want you, and I can't help but worry it's obvious to all." Vincent dragged a hand through his hair, disheveling the neat layers. "I remember everything you said that night. Christ, I can't forget it. And I won't. I give you my word that I will never again be such a damn stubborn fool. And if you'll but give me another chance, Oliver, I'll—"

Oliver launched himself at Vincent, cutting off his words and shoving him roughly against the wall. He tangled his fingers in

Vincent's dark hair, hauled the man's mouth down to meet his, and crushed his lips over Vincent's. Absolutely devoured his mouth. Teeth nipping, tongue delving deep, tangling with Vincent's.

Unable to get enough, he pressed himself against the hard length of Vincent's body. Strong arms wrapped around his waist, holding him so tightly he couldn't draw a full breath. But he didn't care. Vincent was kissing him back with an urgency that surpassed his own.

He gave himself over to it, his fingers unwinding from Vincent's hair, hands falling to those broad shoulders, surrendering completely to the passion in Vincent's kiss. To the love so strong he could taste it.

Then the kiss softened, a slow melding of lips gliding across each other. Vincent nipped his bottom lip and broke the kiss. Warm, panting breaths brushed across his face.

"Is that a yes? Will you give me another chance?" Vincent asked, so low and reluctant Oliver more felt the words rumbling his chest than heard them.

He blinked his eyes open. "Of course. You called me Oliver," he whispered. He had been able to keep the excitement under wraps, keep it contained as it built within him as Vincent said the most unbelievable things to him, until he had heard his name. Never in their thirteen years of friendship had Vincent called him Oliver. Yet tonight, it had fallen unbidden from his lips. The clearest sign of all that Vincent had opened his heart to him.

Vincent nodded, grim and determined, not one hint of Oliver's smile echoed on his face. With gentle hands on his shoulders, he moved Oliver a step back, putting distance between them. He worked the knot on his cravat and then tugged the linen from his neck. "I do remember everything you said that night. Everything." Oliver watched his Adam's apple bob beneath the taut skin of his neck as he swallowed. "You can do with me as you please."

Oliver stared in utter disbelief at the long length of white linen in Vincent's outstretched hand.

"You can tie me up, take me, and do whatever you please with me. I am yours, Oliver. Forever."

It was almost too much to believe that Vincent was willing to put himself in Oliver's hands. To relinquish all control. "You really do love me."

"Yes."

His heart swelled near to bursting. Oliver held back the grin, but it was mighty difficult—the poor man looked absolutely terrified. Determined, but terrified at the prospect of submission. Now was not the time to grin like a damn fool and let out the bark of joyous laughter building within him.

"Don't look so frightened, Vincent. I don't want to tie you up." He took the cravat and let it flutter to the floor. "But there is something I've wanted to do since I saw you take your trousers off at Delacroix's brothel."

"And what would that be?"

Suppressing a smile, Oliver raised one eyebrow and removed his coat, taking the time to undo the buttons properly. It had taken a box of scones to convince his grandmother's housekeeper to sew the buttons back onto his coat and waistcoat. He had managed to avoid her questions the first time, but didn't want to press his luck by having to ask her to repeat the chore. With a flick of his wrist, he tossed the coat onto the armchair.

His spectacles. He should remove them, too. He wouldn't need them for what he had planned; Vincent would be plenty close enough to see him clearly.

He left Vincent standing against the wall by the open bedchamber door and placed his spectacles on the fireplace mantel. Perhaps they should move to the bedchamber? No. That terror had dissipated when the cravat fell to the floor, but the man was still clearly very nervous. If he asked Vincent to move, he might bolt for the wrong door.

Not that Oliver was all that comfortable playing the dominant, either. He could count on one hand the number of times he had taken another man, and it had been years ago. He much preferred to submit, to put his pleasure in the hands of another, but he could not deny the heady thrill that sang through his veins at having Vincent at his disposal.

His to touch. His to kiss. His to do with as he pleased.

His back to Vincent, he allowed the grin to spread across his face as he lit a candle on the mantel.

"What should I do?" Vincent asked.

"Nothing. Just stand still."

He wiped the smile from his lips and went back to Vincent. Willing the tremor of anticipation from his hands, he unbuttoned Vincent's coat and then his waistcoat, working each fabric-covered button free. Vincent could see to the task much quicker, but Oliver wanted to do it. To slowly reveal all that powerful male muscle. Vincent's body was a sublime gift, one the man had never before allowed him to thoroughly explore.

He remembered to remove Vincent's pocket watch from his waistcoat before tossing the garments behind him. After slipping the watch into his own trouser pocket, he pushed the black suspenders from Vincent's shoulders and tugged the white shirt free from his trousers.

"You'll have to remove it yourself. You're much too tall."

Vincent tipped his head. "As you wish, milord."

"No, no. Please don't call me that." The address belonged to Vincent, not to him. Then he peered up at Vincent through the chunk of unruly hair that had fallen over one eye. "Well…not unless you really want to."

Vincent furrowed his brow. "Lord Oliver?"

"How about just Oliver? I haven't heard it enough yet."

Vincent tipped his head again, the barest of smiles tugging his lips. "As you wish, Oliver." He whisked the shirt over his head, revealing the hard contours of his abdomen and his broad chest. Seizing the moment when Vincent had his arms over his head, Oliver trailed a fingertip down the underside of those powerful biceps, the skin so soft and smooth, then down his side.

Vincent twitched.

Had that been a poorly suppressed giggle?

He had no idea Vincent was ticklish. The man seemed much too hard-willed to allow such an involuntary reaction. But now he knew, for he had just found the spot. Right there, under his arm, that little spot right there—

"Oliver," Vincent protested, twisting away from his touch. He yanked the sleeves from his wrists and threw the shirt to the floor.

"You're ticklish." He stored the knowledge away, savoring it like a precious treasure. He loved to know such intimate details about the man he loved.

In answer to Vincent's stern frown, he dropped to his knees and unbuttoned Vincent's trousers, his fingers quick and efficient. Then he tugged the trousers and drawers down his long legs.

Oh. Shoes. Mustn't forget those. The evening shoes seen to, he divested Vincent of the last of his clothing.

Shifting up onto his haunches, he moved to stand. But the semierect cock at eye level proved an irresistible lure. One swipe of his tongue across the broad head pulled a groan from Vincent, an encouragement Oliver couldn't resist, either. Hands braced on those strong thighs, he crouched and tipped his chin up, captured the head with his lips and took Vincent inside, swallowing him to the root.

He looked up, caught Vincent's glittering blue gaze and pulled back, a slow hard suck, savoring the glide of his lips over silken skin, and then pressed a light kiss on the tip before shifting up to stand. Oliver coasted his hands up from Vincent's thighs, over the rippling muscles of his abdomen and to his chest, combing his fingertips through the light smattering of dark hair, reveling in the luxury of being able to touch—his tongue slipped out to tease one copper nipple—and to taste.

Pressing his nose to Vincent's chest, he took in a deep full breath of him. Clean male skin, the barest trace of cool night air, the slight hint of sweat and musky arousal. A quiver shook Oliver's body. God, he had missed this man so much.

Before the emotion clogged his throat and distracted him from his purpose, he took a step back. "Turn around."

Perhaps with time Vincent could gain the comfort to respond without the telltale hesitation. But as this was Vincent's first foray into unknown territory, Oliver forgave the lapse and waited patiently for the man to heed his command.

"Oh, and hands on the wall. And don't move them until I give you permission to do so."

He heard the shuddering breath expand Vincent's lungs. Bowing his head, he braced his hands on the wall, his legs shoulder-width apart.

That would never do. The man was pressed much too closely against the wall. With a tug on his hips, he moved Vincent into position, pulling him back so his arms were straight and his lower back curved invitingly.

He trailed his fingertips there, over the sleek sweep, and then moved down lower, just barely touching the crease of Vincent's arse. The firm globes clenched. Hell, Vincent's entire body tensed, from his taut calves to his bulging biceps. The refusal could not have been clearer.

Stepping closer, Oliver wrapped his arms around Vincent's waist, sliding one hand down to lightly stroke his now very limp cock. "Nervous?"

Vincent cleared his throat. "A bit."

"There's no reason to be." He dragged his lips over Vincent's shoulder blade and gave into the urge to rub his trouser-covered erection along the cleft of Vincent's arse. Vincent tensed once again. Ah, hell. He couldn't keep the man in suspense any longer. "Relax, Vincent." Nipping at his lover's skin, he smoothed his hands down his sides, slow and patient. "I'm not going to bugger you. That's not what I want. Not tonight. But maybe in the future and only if you really want it. In fact, maybe I should only fuck you if you beg for it."

What a scandalous and utterly delicious thought—one day hearing the words *Fuck me, Oliver. Please* from Vincent's lips. And if he applied himself sufficiently, he was certain he would hear them. But not tonight. This was all much too new to Vincent. While his lover had verbally given him leave to take him, Oliver couldn't help but feel that neither of them was quite ready to stray so far beyond their usual roles.

"Then...what do you want?"

"Umm," Oliver murmured, kissing a path down the strong line of Vincent's spine. "This."

Chapter Nine

Wet heat probed between his arse cheeks. Vincent's eyes flew open. Shock swamping his brain, he went up onto his toes, but with a firm tug on his spread cheeks, Oliver pulled him back down. Oh…God…the man was licking his arse. Long strokes, dragging the flat of his tongue from just above his ballocks and over his entrance, painting a line along the entire crease.

A hot, wet, thoroughly indecent line.

Oliver had wanted to do…*this*—Christ, he didn't even know the name for it—since he had removed his trousers at that brothel?

Holy hell.

His muscles were tensed, poised to jerk away, to escape the intimate intrusion. Yet he clenched his teeth and held still, determined to prove true to his word, to let the man do as he pleased with him, even though he never felt so vulnerable, so exposed in all his life.

But it was damn hard. That wet tongue swirled over his flesh, tracing his entrance, and then…

"*Oliver.*" The name came out on a strangled yelp as the man sucked hard. His spine locked, jolts of sensation seizing his nerves. His brain screamed that such a thing was beyond the pale, but his cock didn't mind in the slightest.

Arousal licked at his groin in time to the rapid flicks of Oliver's tongue. Sweet and lush, forbidden to its core, and so very different from anything he had ever experienced. It spread up over his ballocks, engulfing his prick in a wash of pure heat, suspending him between acute self-consciousness and blinding pleasure.

Humming a low, entirely too erotic purr, Oliver intensified his efforts, licking, nipping, and sucking, until Vincent couldn't hold back the groans clogging his throat.

When that amazingly skilled tongue swept up the crease to his lower back, Vincent almost, almost, *almost* begged him not to stop. The words were right there, on the tip of his tongue. But he kept his jaw clamped tight as Oliver licked a path up his spine.

Soft wool brushed his legs as Oliver moved to stand behind him. Hot, sticky pants bathed his shoulder blade. The musky scent of his arousal poured off him, so thick Vincent could taste it.

"I know you've never let another man bugger you, so I won't even ask. You already told me so once before. But…" The hand kneading his arse shifted, fingers drifting into the crease, sliding over the moisture there. "Have you ever penetrated yourself?"

"No." The word popped out of his mouth before it even formed in his head.

"Haven't you ever wondered how it would feel? Ever been curious?"

Vincent fought to drag air into his lungs as Oliver swirled the tip of his finger over his entrance. Slow and decadent, a slippery wet caress that obliterated any attempt to hold back the truth.

He squeezed his eyes closed tight. "Yes," he admitted on a low, ragged breath. God, *yes*, he had thought about it. His mind had wandered down that forbidden path more than once before he'd yanked it back. But even under the cover of darkness, when he was alone in bed, stroking his prick to orgasm, he had never given in to the impulse.

"Well, wonder no more," Oliver replied, the grin clear in his far-too-smug voice.

A finger pushed, sliding easily inside and lighting up nerve endings Vincent didn't know he possessed. His eyes flew open, his cock jerking its approval, fluid beading at the tip.

"You're so tight. So hot, Vincent," Oliver moaned, wrapping his other arm around his waist, the linen of his shirtsleeve almost too rough against Vincent's highly sensitized skin. Oliver straddled one of his legs, grinding the hard arch of his arousal against his thigh, as he kept up those agonizingly sweet thrusts.

Another finger joined the first, filling him, stretching him wide enough to cause a slight burn, probing deep, until…

"Fuck!" Vincent slammed his fist against the wall, fighting off the white-hot surge of a sudden, impending orgasm. His ballocks lurched up closer to his body.

With each stroke, Oliver rubbed that spot inside him, pumping more pleasure into his already overloaded senses. All traces of modesty gone, he hung his head and rocked his hips, fucking himself on Oliver's fingers. No wonder Oliver begged for him to fuck him. It felt goddamn unbelievable to have his arse filled.

The notion ticked the edge of his mind, encouraged by the hard, demanding rub of Oliver's erection against his thigh. But could he throw aside his pride and beg to be taken? Bend over and plead for Oliver to ram that pretty prick of his deep in his arse—

Lust slammed into him, a startling undiluted wave, so potent he would have crumbled to his knees if not for the support of the wall before him.

He pushed back, impaling himself on Oliver's fingers. But it wasn't enough. "More." Christ, Oliver had reduced him to begging, but he no longer cared in the slightest.

Oliver let out a whimper, threadbare and breathy, and then worked another digit alongside the other two.

"Yes, yes," Vincent panted, flames licking his arse as he was stuffed full. So wonderfully, blissfully full. He rocked back, his erection bobbing between his legs with each thrust. Their heavy pants blended together until he couldn't distinguish the sounds above the pulse hammering in his ears.

Oliver abruptly yanked his fingers free; a slick, wicked rush of sensation that pulled a grunt from Vincent's throat.

"Don't stop!" he protested, glancing over his shoulder.

"I won't. But I have to taste you again," Oliver gasped, sliding down his body. "Turn around."

Vincent didn't hesitate. Kneeling at his feet, Oliver grabbed his cock and sucked it down to the root. Those nimble fingers tickled his ballocks, tugged hard, and stopped just before crossing that line into pain, and then snuck behind. One hand braced on the wall behind him, Vincent widened his stance and tilted his hips, granting Oliver access to slip his fingers back up his arse. The lush drag of Oliver's soft lips, the hard insistent penetration... The combined sensations were too much. The climax coiled down his spine, winding tighter and tighter. Then Oliver swallowed, the velvety muscles of his throat massaging the head of his cock. At the same moment, Oliver rubbed that sweet spot, and Vincent couldn't hold back the orgasm any longer.

Letting out a mighty roar, Vincent spilled himself down his lover's throat, his muscles clenching around the digits buried in his arse in rhythm to the spasms racking his entire body.

Oliver gently pulled his fingers free and then released his prick. With a swipe of his forearm, he used his shirtsleeve to wipe the trickle of creamy semen from his swollen, wet lips.

He gazed up at Vincent, the most profound adoration reflected in his dark eyes. His cheeks were flushed, his forehead glistening with sweat, his chest rising and falling rapidly beneath the gray brocade waistcoat. Still on his knees, Oliver clasped his hands behind his back and bowed his head, dark waves tumbling over his face. His body went lax, the line of his shoulders visibly relaxing.

"I am yours, milord."

Still reeling from the orgasm, Vincent could do nothing but marvel at how easily his friend gave up control. His trust was an awesome responsibility, and Vincent would never take it for granted again.

"Love you," Vincent murmured, reaching down to tuck Oliver's tangled hair behind his ear. He glanced down Oliver's body. The erection that had rubbed so insistently against his thigh tented the placket of his trousers.

He would need to see to that, and he knew just how to do it.

"Don't move." The edge taken off his lust, Vincent left Oliver kneeling on the ground and went into the bedchamber.

Ignoring the rumpled bed and the clothing littering the floor, he lit a couple of candles and gathered the necessary supplies. With each step he took, his arse throbbed a bit. Nothing painful or uncomfortable. Rather, a pleasing burn that served to get the blood coursing through his veins once again. Hell, being the object of Oliver's undivided attention had been quite the experience. One he would definitely need to repeat.

From the top drawer of the dresser, he selected the leather cuffs that had an attached length of chain and a black leather flogger. Then he went to the bedside table. He'd forgo the plug but did need the oil. He made to pick up the glass bottle then stopped at the sight of the empty silver tray.

"Where is it?" he demanded, stalking across the bedchamber, the flogger and cuffs clutched in one hand.

Oliver snapped his head up. "Pardon?"

"The pin. Did you sell it?" He shouldn't be such an arse about it, but he couldn't help it. If Oliver had sold the pin, then that meant he had given up on Vincent. Completely. And the possibility hurt more than he could have imagined.

Oliver ducked his chin and reached inside his waistcoat. "Never, Vincent. I would never sell it," he whispered, holding out his hand.

He had carried it with him, directly over his heart.

Grabbing his chin, he tilted Oliver's face up and leaned down to give him a quick kiss. "Good," he grumbled, snatching the pin from Oliver's outstretched hand. He turned on his heel and returned to the bedchamber. "Take off your clothes and get your arse in here, Oliver."

The last lingering bit of panic left him as he placed the jade cravat pin back in its place in the dented little silver tray. He heard the sound of bare feet against floorboards and looked up. Hell, the man could get his own clothes off in a trice, but it had felt like forever when he had removed Vincent's.

"Shut the door," he instructed as he took the oil and moved it to the washstand so it would be within easy reach. He set the flogger on the foot of the bed and held out the cuffs, the chain dangling from his grip. "You know where I want you, boy."

Erect cock bobbing with each step, Oliver moved directly beneath the iron hook in the ceiling positioned one pace from the foot of the bed and two paces from the washstand. Hands fisted at his sides and a flush tingeing his bare golden chest, he bowed his head and waited patiently for Vincent's next command.

He belonged to Oliver. There was no doubt about it, but in this moment, Oliver belonged to him. A fierce surge of possessiveness gripped hold of him.

Mine.

He would take Oliver to dizzying heights of pleasure. Push the man to his limits, but never take him one step beyond. For Oliver trusted him to do nothing less.

"Hold out your arms."

Once Vincent had both cuffs buckled about his wrists, he lifted Oliver's arms. As he reached up to slip the end link of the chain onto the hook, sharp teeth nipped at his chest.

Vincent took a quick step back and stared at Oliver, whose head was bowed once again, the perfect image of submission with his wrists bound and arms stretched over his head.

Impudent whelp.

He kept the chuckle inside and instead spoke in a hard tone. "It appears you have forgotten your place, boy."

"My apologies, milord."

Was he smiling beneath that curtain of dark hair?

"We'll see how sorry you are." Vincent stepped behind him, grabbed the flogger, and smacked the flat end against his own hand.

Oliver started then let out a low moan. "*Yes.*" His hips rocked back, presenting Vincent with his round arse, the perfect canvas for a few strikes of the flogger.

Arousal seeped anew into his blood, ratcheting higher and higher. His cock hardened, lifting from his body at the prospect of what was to come. But before the lust grabbed hold of him completely, he took a deep breath, settling his pulse. He needed to keep his control firmly in hand else risk actually hurting Oliver. A flogger wasn't a child's toy. It could cause serious harm if not wielded with an eye toward inciting pleasure and not true pain.

Oliver shifted his weight, rattling the chain. "Vincent, *please*."

Starting slowly, he slapped the leather against first one round cheek then the other.

"Harder, please, milord."

"Harder than this?" He drew back his arm and let the leather strike that now pink cheek again.

Oliver arched, shuddered, gasped. "Yes, yes. Harder."

And Vincent gave him what he begged for. The leather whipped through the air. Satisfying smacks filled the room as that round arse turned a most becoming shade of scarlet. He alternated the rhythm, not wanting Oliver to tense in anticipation of the blows. And his lover took it all, pleading for more, his sleek, honed body writhing in ecstasy under the onslaught. The most beautiful sight to behold.

When Oliver's gasps turned ragged, when his head tipped forward and the pleas stumbled over each other, Vincent stopped.

Sucking in great pulling breaths, he dropped the flogger and moved to stand before him. Sweat trickled down the center of Oliver's chest. His cock was arched up, the damp head brushing his flat lower belly that glistened with the proof of his arousal.

"Don't stop. More...please, Vincent. *Please*." He shimmied, rattling the chains and thrusting his chest out.

Vincent grabbed hold of one of those flat copper nipples and twisted. "Is that what you want?"

"Ah, yes!" Oliver threw back his head, his body arching in a bow of undeniable pleasure.

Unwilling to give up his grip on that nipple, he grabbed the back of Oliver's head with his other hand and crushed his mouth over his. Kissed him fiercely, thrusting his tongue boldly inside, sweeping the hot depths of his lover's mouth, drinking in his gasping moans.

After delivering a sharp nip to his full bottom lip, he pulled back and met his lust-filled gaze. "Or perhaps you want something else?"

Before Vincent could think twice, he dropped to his knees and took hold of that pretty cock. Not pausing to even flick his tongue over the head, Vincent opened his mouth and took Oliver inside.

Oliver bucked forward, and Vincent jerked back a bit, fighting the impulse to gag. Closing his eyes, he swallowed down the gag reflex and bobbed along Oliver's length. Salt and sweat and hot silken skin blended together to form the sweetest thing Vincent had ever tasted. It lit up his tongue, urging him to take more, to suck harder, to pull every last drop from his lover's prick.

"Stop, stop, stop!"

He pulled back and glared up at Oliver. He might have never sucked a cock before, but he knew what it felt like to be on the receiving end, and that damn well should have felt good to him. "My precious lips finally touch your prick and you tell me to stop?"

"Yes," Oliver whined. There was no other word for it. The man actually whined. "You were going to make me climax."

Vincent arched one eyebrow. "That's the point."

"But I want you to fuck me. Please, Vincent. I need you."

"Do you now?" he asked, fighting to keep the smug smile from his lips as he got to his feet.

"Yes, yes. *Now*. I need you. I need to feel you inside me. *Please*."

His threadbare whimper did more than crank up the lust pounding through his veins, it tugged on Vincent's heart, reminding him anew of how perfect they were together. Two halves of a whole, he had once described them. How the hell could he have been so foolish as to even consider his father's request? He wouldn't give up Oliver for the world.

The impatient rattle of chain snapped him to his senses. Vincent slicked his cock with oil then poured a generous amount in his palm and swiped it between those still red cheeks, the skin hot to the touch. He pushed one finger inside, then another.

Oliver went up onto his toes, breath hitching in his throat. "I need you. *Now. Now. Now.*"

Grabbing hold of his slim hips, Vincent pushed past the tight ring of muscle and into hot, clinging, welcoming heat.

As Oliver shuddered beneath him, he wrapped his arms around him, pressed a kiss to his shoulder and growled, "And now you have me. Forever."

* * * * *

Oliver snuggled closer to Vincent. The man generated a remarkable amount of heat, but it only warmed one side as he sprawled on top of him. He blinked open his tired eyes and turned his head, looking for the blanket.

Shafts of sunlight seeped through the gaps in the drapes. Morning? But...

He bolted upright, straddling Vincent's hips, and stared down at him. Alert and bemused brilliant blue eyes met his.

"You stayed."

Vincent's lips twisted in a grimace, all aristocratic affront. "Of course. Did you honestly believe I wouldn't?"

"Well, you never have before."

A deep sigh expanded Vincent's chest. "And I apologize for that. I should have stayed, many times. And I will stay more often than not in the future. But not every night. You do understand, don't you?" He took hold of Oliver's hand and gave it a squeeze. The amusement left his eyes, replaced with solemn gravity. "Just know that when I do return home at night, it's not because I don't want to stay with you. I do. But we still need to be very discreet, Oliver."

He feathered his fingertips over Vincent's mouth, drawn in a grim line. "It's all right. I understand." The reality of their relationship was sometimes hard to bear. It seemed wrong to have to hide his love for this man, but it was something he had learned to accept long ago.

Twisting around, Oliver snagged the edge of the blanket from the foot of the bed. He should start a fire, but he didn't want to get out of bed just yet. With the blanket draped over him, he dropped down and snuggled back up to Vincent again.

His eyes drifted closed. The soft hair on Vincent's chest lightly tickled his nose. The strong beat of Vincent's heart lulled his senses, tempting him to fall back into a blissful sleep.

"Oliver."

"Yes?" he muttered.

"I need to go to Rotherham next week, and I want you to come with me. The house is small, and therefore the staff is small. They only come up from the village when I'm in residence, and only for the day. We can get a nurse to watch over your grandmother in your absence."

He smiled against Vincent's chest. "For how long?"

"A fortnight, maybe longer."

"No longer than a fortnight. Can't leave the shop unattended for an extended period. Just purchased the thing. Don't want to be perceived as a negligent investor." He tried for an off-handed tone, but he couldn't keep the pride completely from his voice.

"You've made an investment?"

He shifted up onto his forearms. "Yes, I bought Wallace's bookshop. It's just around the corner. Not much of a shop, but I've grown quite fond of it."

"And when did this happen?"

"Two weeks, five days ago. No, make that six days. Decided to expend a bit of effort."

Vincent frowned once again. "I do apologize for that. Uncalled for and in bad form to say such a thing."

"But necessary."

"I wouldn't—"

Oliver cut off his words with a kiss. "I would." If not for Vincent, he would have never taken that step toward making something of himself.

"Well then, congratulations are in order. Well done, Oliver."

"Why thank you, Vincent," he said, flopping back down and hiding his grin against Vincent's chest.

This man was his. Forever.

What an amazing concept.

Or was he?

Oliver levered up onto his forearms again. "I most certainly am not going to marry. Not ever. But are you ever going to marry?"

Vincent raised his eyebrows, clearly taken aback by the blunt question. "Um... I-I don't want to. I truly would make a very poor husband. You're the only person who will tolerate me and who will keep me in my place. But, Oliver, I won't lie to you. I might need to someday. I sure as hell don't want to, and I honestly don't believe it will come to that, but if Grafton doesn't produce an heir within a decade or so..." He turned his head, avoiding Oliver's gaze. The truth was not pleasant to hear, but the strong arms holding him tight kept away any trace of despair. "I can't let the estate go to Adams. He's my father's brother's son. Next in line and more of a dolt than Grafton. Completely useless fellow. You understand, don't you?" He sneaked a peek at Oliver from the corner of his eye. "Please say you do."

Sharing Vincent was not a concept he was willing to explore. The man was his. No one else's. And certainly not some woman's. But he couldn't demand Vincent turn his back on his responsibilities. He loved every inch of the man's noble, honorable soul. The future might hold an unpleasant reality, but he had Vincent now and would savor every moment with him. "Yes, of course I understand." He felt the tension ease from the powerful body under him.

Nodding solemnly, Vincent cupped his jaw in both hands and brushed the pad of his thumb over his bottom lip. "I do love you," he murmured. "No matter what, I will always be yours."

"Forever?"

"Yes, Oliver. I am bound to you, forever."

Deliberately Unbound
Short Story

After spending long days behind his desk negotiating the purchase of a new property, Lord Vincent Prescot is more than ready for a night of pleasure with his lover, and he has a definite plan in mind for Oliver—one that involves making good on a wicked suggestion Vincent made months ago.

Lord Oliver Marsden is well aware of his lover's dominant tendencies, and he's quite fond of them. Nothing rivals the sensation of being bound for Vincent's pleasure...or so he thought.

Deliberately Unbound

June 1823
London, England

No. Not that one. Much too thick for what he had in mind.

Vincent let the lid drop. The faint *click* as the box closed echoed in the quiet shop. It had been a couple of months since he had visited the quaint little shop off Bond Street. Nestled between a tailor and a solicitor's office, with a nondescript storefront void of windows, only the words *For the Discriminating Gentleman* painted neatly above the door gave a hint Mr. Harton's merchandise was not for the faint of heart. If it had anything to do with the erotic arts, it could be found within these walls or the elderly gentleman behind the counter knew how to procure it. Therefore Vincent was not at all disheartened when the contents of the next two boxes weren't quite what he was looking for.

Nor was he at all disconcerted to even be there, carefully perusing objects of an erotic nature. It wasn't as if the proprietor had any reason to suspect the intended recipient of his purchase was not of the female gender. Most everything in the shop could be for a man or a woman. And there was just something about Mr. Harton's calm, efficient manner which put Vincent at his ease. The man treated the purchase of a leather bullwhip as though it was perfectly normal to want such a thing, never mind use it to bring another to dizzying heights of pleasure.

Vincent moved to the mahogany box at the end of the shelf and lifted the lid, revealing a sleek length nestled on the black velvet interior. He trailed a fingertip over the surface, the silver smooth and cool to the touch.

Perfect.

There was one more thing he needed…

On the way to the counter, he paused at another shelf and selected a small bottle. He gave it a little swirl and watched as the viscous oil within clung to the glass walls. Thicker than his usual variety and ideal for tonight.

As Mr. Harton packed his purchases in a plain brown sack, Vincent pulled out his pocket watch. Plenty of time remained to make it to White's to meet Oliver by seven o'clock. After a nice dinner, they would go to Oliver's bachelor apartments. A foregone conclusion. What they did when they reached his lover's apartments varied. Sometimes Vincent only stayed for a couple of hours as they shared a drink. On other occasions, drained and sated from the pleasures of Oliver's body, he stayed the night. Sometimes they did nothing at all except crawl into bed and go to sleep. In fact, they had been doing a lot of that recently, since Vincent had been spending long days behind his desk, planning and negotiating the purchase of the property adjoining his in Rotherham. Tonight though, he had definite plans for Oliver.

Over six months ago he had asked Oliver the question which had sparked the idea for today's purchase. *"Y-yes,* please, *milord."* Oliver's reply, soaked in eager desperation, sounded in his head. He couldn't say why it had taken him so long to make good on his suggestion, but the notion had snagged hold of him the moment he had signed the contract that morning, making the property his, and it refused to be denied. Arousal curled down his spine, thick and lush and spiked with the heady, wicked sensation that came at the mere thought of dominating Oliver, of having the man gasping for breath, sleek body strung tight and needing him and only him.

With effort, he tamped the lust down. No matter the contents of the shop, it wouldn't do to sport an erection.

A tip of his head and he bid Mr. Harton good evening. A warm, summer evening's breeze brushed his cheeks as he exited the shop. His town carriage stood along the street at the ready, the four bays in the traces waiting patiently. After giving the direction to his driver, he went inside and set the bag on the leather bench next to his hip. A couple of hours and he would be able to present Oliver with his newest gift.

A smile curved his lips as a low grunt rumbled his chest. The wait would most definitely be worth it.

* * *

"Hold out your arm."

There wasn't a trace of hesitation as Oliver did as he was bid. The moment smooth leather touched his wrist, a decadent shiver raced over his bare skin. He fought the urge to shift his weight and instead stood quietly as Vincent buckled the cuff, tight enough to be secure but loose enough not to pinch, and then repeated the procedure on his other wrist and both ankles.

He could always tell when Vincent was in the mood to play. It was in his eyes, in the wicked spark lurking in the brilliant blue depths. No one at White's would have noticed—Vincent had been his usual aloof self—but Oliver had seen it the instant the man had settled across from him at the small dining table. All traces of the stress that had lingered over Vincent for the past fortnight had been gone. In its place had been that thoroughly wicked spark announcing his intentions to Oliver clearer than if he had shouted.

The knowledge had made it difficult for him to focus on their conversation, yet alone keep his prick from hardening. His mind wandering to floggers and paddles and bullwhips, his wrists bound over his head or behind his back or to the bed, Vincent looming above him, behind him, covering him. The anticipation building with each passing second. The unknown, the wait, a delicious torture.

They didn't play as many erotic games as they once had. Not quite a rarity now, but it was as if Vincent had realized he did not need chains or restraints to gain his complete submission. The man wore command like a cloak, ever present. One look was all it took for Oliver to want to bow his head, to give himself completely to the man he loved.

The buckles on Oliver's ankles seen to, Vincent stood and took a step back. Navy-coated arms crossed over his broad chest and features schooled in a bland mask, he appraised Oliver. If not for the blatant erection tenting the placket of his trousers, one might think him unaffected. The man's iron-willed control an aphrodisiac all its own.

Oliver curled one hand into a fist to resist the impulse to reach out and tug on that placket. To free his lover's cock. To have the weight of him heavy in his palm. To feel the silken skin slide past his lips. To taste the proof of Vincent's desire for him.

A wave of need washed over him. *Please, tell me to suck your cock.* Somehow he kept the plea inside. It was all he could do not to grab his own prick, clutch it tightly at the base and push back the orgasm teasing his ballocks. Hell, Vincent had barely touched him. Just being cuffed by Vincent had the most profound effect on him. Breaths quickening, his gaze swept over his lover's body. He knew exactly what those strictly tailored clothes hid. Six feet two inches of pure muscle and power. Enough power to easily force Oliver to do his bidding, not that force was ever needed.

Then his gaze slid up the broad chest to Vincent's handsome face. The strong jaw, the firm mouth drawn in the straight line of consideration, the slightly roman nose. The absolute command, the rock-solid control in the man's eyes…

Oliver's shoulders went lax. His chin tipped down, the dark waves of his untidy hair falling forward as he dropped his attention to Vincent's polished evening shoes. He wanted to drop to his knees, pledge his undying devotion, but he kept his legs under him and his mouth shut, focusing only on Vincent, on following each and every order for each one would take him one step closer to complete and utter bliss.

"Good boy."

Those two words, spoken in that deep, rumbling voice, never failed to make Oliver feel damn good.

"Get on the bed."

Oliver's gaze flickered up to the iron hook in the ceiling directly overhead. He had thought…but perhaps Vincent planned to make good use of the headboard. Wouldn't be the first time. Turning, he stepped over the clothes he had earlier discarded and crawled onto the bed, the old frame creaking in protest.

"On your back. Legs spread."

Positioning himself in the middle of the gray woolen blanket, he rested his head on one of the pillows and did as he was bid, knees slightly bent and legs spread. A quick swipe of his hand, and he pushed his hair from his eyes. His hard cock rested on his abdomen, ballocks kissing the base.

As casual as could be, Vincent removed his coat and waistcoat then dragged a straight back wooden chair from the corner of the room to the foot of the bed, close enough for Oliver to be able to see him clearly without his spectacles. Oliver kept his hands at his sides, knowing better than to touch himself without Vincent's permission.

Vincent's gaze swept like a hot caress over every inch of Oliver's body, making his nipples tighten and a drop of fluid seep from the tip of his prick.

"Perfect." A hint of a smile dared to tug the edges of Vincent's mouth. "Don't move." Turning on his heel, he left the room, returning a moment later with the brown paper sack he had brought with him to his apartments. *"Nothing of any importance. For an errand tomorrow,"* Vincent had replied earlier, waving off Oliver's inquiry. He should have known…

Rather than be upset with himself for failing to see past Vincent's ruse, every bit of his attention was fixed on that paper sack as Vincent withdrew a narrow mahogany box and a bottle of oil and set them on the washstand. And he had a fair idea what was in that box. He possessed over a dozen dildos and anal plugs, and each one had come in its own little box.

Vincent was going to make him beg. Bind him to the bed and fuck him with a dildo or plug him and torment him until he was pleading and beyond desperate for the man's cock. A thin whimper slid past his lips. Swallowing hard, he watched as Vincent crossed to the bedside table and dropped the towel he'd grabbed from the washstand onto the surface.

"And you will need this," Vincent murmured, setting the bottle of oil down with a faint *click* and removing the stopper.

A full body tremor shook him. He watched as Vincent turned from the bed. Waited for that command to lift his arms over his head. The lines would be next. Attached to the iron ring adorning each cuff and secured to the bed to hold him immobile. To put him completely at the mercy of Vincent's every whim.

But instead of crossing to the dresser, Vincent settled in the chair. Legs casually spread, he briefly palmed the erection tenting the placket of his trousers before resting his elbows on the arms of the chair. A man completely at his ease.

"Stroke your cock, boy."

His hand went immediately to his prick, fingers closing around the rigid width. The only sounds that broke the silence were the soft *swoosh* of his hand working his length and the hard pants of his breaths. He flicked his thumb over the crown, gathering the moisture there, his pace quickening with each stroke, building toward the climax.

"Stop."

Oliver kept the groan inside and forced his arm to his side. Christ, he could feel each rapid beat of his heart in his prick. Each one begging for just one more touch.

"Suck on your fingers. Get them nice and wet."

Again, Vincent received nothing less than complete obedience.

"Now lift your legs and touch your arse hole."

A jolt of embarrassment shot through him. A flush that had nothing to do with the lust drumming through his veins heated his cheeks. Pulling his knees to his chest and fully exposing himself to Vincent's watchful gaze, he pushed the modesty aside, reached under his thigh and swirled his fingertips over the puckered skin. So tempting to push inside, to scratch that itch for more, yet he held back. Waited. And was soon rewarded.

"Slip one finger inside."

But one wasn't even close to enough. A tease and nothing more. The frustration built as he shoved deep, his body clamping greedily around the digit, and started stroking.

"Do you want more?" Vincent asked, as though he was merely inquiring if Oliver wanted another glass of brandy.

Oliver's tongue darted out to swipe across his bottom lip. "Yes, milord. Please."

"Then do it. Shove another finger in your tight arse." The determined calm vanished as if it had never been there. The last words barely above a low, gravelly growl that rolled through the room.

On the next stroke, he pushed a second inside. No burn, barely a hint of a stretch. His body long accustomed to his lover's thick prick, he could take two fingers easily. He looked between his knees drawn up to his chest, to Vincent at the foot of the bed. Read the desire, the need, clear as day in the heat of his gaze. In the heavily lidded blue eyes and the slight flush staining his cheeks. He adored Oliver's arse. Took great pleasure in toying with him, slicking him with oil and preparing him. Lingering over each caress until Oliver would do anything to feel the man inside him. And tonight Vincent wanted to watch Oliver do it for him.

Holy Hell. Lust spiked his senses, mixed with the thrill of wickedness. Of putting himself on display for Vincent's pleasure.

"Very good, Oliver. Can you take another?"

"Yes. *Please.*" Damnation, he wanted more. Wanted Vincent. Needed that sweet, wonderful stretch, that blissful fullness only Vincent could provide.

"Then do it," he growled.

A moan shook his chest as he pushed a third finger inside. His eyes drifted closed as he finger-fucked his own arse. The leather cuff smacked the back of his thigh with each stroke. He kept his other arm locked to his side, resisting the almost unbearable urge to grab his prick. To drag a palm roughly over his ballocks. To capture one nipple and twist hard. To keep himself from doing anything other than what Vincent demanded.

At the sound of footsteps on floorboards, he opened his eyes to find Vincent's imposing figure standing beside the bed.

He trailed his fingers over the leather cuff on Oliver's ankle, up his shin to his knee, his touch light, almost reverent. At the tap on the cuff on his wrist, Oliver immediately pulled free, fingers slipping from his body and leaving him achingly empty.

Bracing a hand on the back of his thigh, Vincent pushed, canting his hips upward. Then he leaned down to spit on his hole. "Beautiful," he murmured, his breath fanning Oliver's ballocks, making his prick jump. With his other hand, Vincent traced the perimeter of his entrance with one fingertip, spreading the fluid. The lightest of touches. A slippery wet caress that had Oliver arching up, needing more. But Vincent pulled back. "Very nice. However I do believe you'll need a bit more." He grabbed the towel from the bedside table and placed it beneath his hips.

Oliver gasped as Vincent dribbled a slow, thin stream of oil onto his ballocks. Tipping the bottle further, he poured a generous amount onto the smooth expanse of skin directly above his hole. The viscous oil slid down, tickling his skin, coating his hole, then it followed the crack of his arse. Explained why Vincent had grabbed the towel. Would not be comfortable to sleep on oil-slicked sheets.

"Hold out your hand." Vincent dribbled oil onto his fingertips. "You know where to put them."

"How many?"

One corner of Vincent's firm mouth lifted in a hint of a smug smile. "As before."

He eagerly shoved three oiled fingers back up his arse. Clutched the blanket with his left hand and rocked his hips into each thrust. Drops of oil slid around to the underside of his ballocks. Tickling and teasing.

His gaze never leaving Oliver, Vincent reached for his own throat. A few deft flicks of his fingers and the meticulously tied Mathematical knot was undone. Slow and deliberate, he dragged the long length of white linen through a closed fist. Was Vincent going to tie him up? But he received his answer as the cravat fluttered from Vincent's fingertips, dropping to the floor. Vincent pulled his shirt over his head, baring his chest, the muscles bunching and flexing with his movements.

Turning on his heel, Vincent went to the washstand and removed his trousers, baring his gloriously nude body. He didn't return empty handed.

He crossed to the foot of the bed, his heavy cock bobbing between his thighs with each slow step. Watched Oliver for a moment and then crawled onto the bed to settle on his knees between Oliver's spread legs. Bracing one hand on the mattress, he leaned between Oliver's knees, crouching over him. The hot silken skin of his gorgeous cock brushed his inner thigh. The pure, unadulterated scent of an aroused man, of Vincent, filled Oliver's senses.

"When I saw this, I thought immediately of you," Vincent said, dragging the tip of the sleek, silver dildo across Oliver's parted lips. "Does it meet with your satisfaction?"

"Yes, milord."

Oliver opened to allow Vincent to slip it inside his mouth. Cool, smooth metal slid over his tongue. Oliver shoved his fingers deeper, a groan rumbled his throat.

Vincent pulled the dildo free. "Do you think you can take both?"

Oliver's breaths stuttered, his hand stilling. His cock hardened to the point of pain. That moment in Vincent's carriage—hell, it must have been almost eight months ago—crystallized in his mind. *"Perhaps we shall need to try that. See if you can take it."* He glanced to the dildo in Vincent's hand, tried to calculate the effect of the added width. It would be more than Vincent's thick cock. Not much more, but definitely more.

"Yes or no, boy. Can you fit this pretty dildo and three fingers in your tight arse?"

In the dark confines of the carriage, impatient after having gone weeks without his lover, it had sounded like a tempting notion. But now when presented with the actual opportunity…

The frantic lust and need pounding through his veins stumbled. "I-I…" He swallowed back the uncertainty, called upon his trust in Vincent. The man pushed him to his limits, but never beyond. He met Vincent's beautiful brilliant blue eyes. "*Yes.*"

Vincent arched one dark brow. "We shall see about that." He cupped the back of Oliver's thigh with his free hand, thumb grazing his hole, and spread him wider. Slid the dildo over his ballocks, gathering the oil there.

Oliver shifted his hips, pulled his wrist down so Vincent could slide in above. His lover's gaze flickered between his arse and his face, as he inched the dildo inside. Slow. Careful. Unlike when he fucked him and rammed hilt deep on the first stroke.

Fire lashed at his arse, his body shouting its protests. He forced a deep a breath, and on the exhale tried to will the tension from his muscles. Damn difficult, when he was strung between the cusp of an orgasm and the threat of completely losing his erection.

The slick silver moved along his fingers as Vincent pushed deeper, slow inch by slow inch. Then Vincent's fingers, wrapped around the end of the dildo, meet the back of his own knuckles.

Head tipping back, Oliver groaned. By *God*, the stretch… He lost the fight to keep his eyes open.

"So pretty," Vincent said, thick and heavy with his satisfaction.

The soft touch of Vincent's fingertip tracing his obscenely wide hole proved to be too much. He trembled, shook. "Vincent, please," he begged in broken tones.

"Out?" Vincent asked, true concern reflected in the question.

"No. Just…just…move it. *Fuck me.*"

Vincent growled, a low feral sound that rumbled over his sweat-slicked skin. Then he felt the soft press of his lips on his shin. "Gladly."

Vincent started with short little nudges, working up to long plunging thrusts. With the dildo positioned above his fingers, the crown rubbed over his gland with each stroke. Sensation swamped his senses. The sharp sting of almost unbearable stretch, the heavy pleasure of being filled, the smooth slick glide of the dildo working his arse. It was too much. *Damnation*, too much, yet…yet *perfect*. Far beyond the point of coherent speech, indecipherable moans tumbled past his lips. He was vaguely aware Vincent was speaking, but he couldn't make out the words. The climax so close, yet so far away. Every muscle in his body drawn tight, reaching for it, needing it. His cock ached so damn much. He needed…needed…

A strong hand wrapped around his prick. He felt the brush of a ragged breath across the crown the instant before wet heat slid down his length. And it shoved him right over the edge.

The orgasm rocked through his body. He heard the echo of his own shout as he poured down Vincent's throat. Then that perfect mouth left his prick. Vincent pulled the dildo free, swatted at Oliver's hand. "Out." The word came out on a grunt, hoarse with unbridled need.

With the last tremors of that powerful release still racking his body, Vincent shoved his cock inside him.

"God, yes!" he shouted, back arching as he blindly reached up with his left hand to grasp the hard bulk of Vincent's biceps. The combined width of the dildo and his fingers had been wider, but Vincent had length. Thick and long. Filling him completely until it felt like the man's prick was tickling the back of his throat. Vincent crushed his mouth over his, thrust his tongue inside. Oliver tasted his own release in that thoroughly wicked kiss, and it ratcheted the lust consuming him even higher.

Vincent's hard thrusts shook the bed. Quick, fast and rough, hips slamming against Oliver, pumping pure pleasure into his already overloaded senses. Then he stiffened above him, his soul-deep groan lost in their kiss as he climaxed, buried deep inside him.

The next thing Oliver knew, something cold and wet was being dragged over his ballocks. "Cold," he grumbled.

Warm lips pressed lightly to his abdomen. "My apologies."

He let out a little grunt as Vincent reached lower to carefully swipe the cloth between his arse cheeks. Hell, he was going to be sore for at least a couple of days. Definitely worth it, though.

He heard the slap as the cloth was dropped to the floor. Fingers brushed his wrist. With effort, he blinked open his tired eyes and watched as Vincent, standing beside the bed, removed the leather cuff. Only the candle on the bedside table remained lit, the rest of the room shrouded in shadows. "Why?"

"Pardon?" Vincent asked. The cuff joined the cloth on the floor.

Vincent held out his hand and Oliver lifted his arm from his side, holding it out so Vincent could see to the other cuff. Damn, his arm was heavy.

"The cuffs. Why? You didn't use them to restrain me." He dropped his bare arm to his side.

Vincent moved to the foot of the bed. A faint breeze drifted over Oliver's bare skin, warm yet with a hint of coolness and quite refreshing. Vincent must have opened the window, allowing the night air into the room.

"Restraints didn't quite fit my plan for tonight." Vincent traced the outline of the leather wrapped around his ankle before flicking the buckle open. "But I couldn't resist putting them on you." He looked up, caught Oliver's gaze. A sinful smile curved his mouth. "You wear them so well."

The beginnings of a tired chuckle shook his chest. "Why thank you, Vincent."

He could add it to the very short list of things he could do with any success. If just wearing them pleased Vincent, he'd don them every night, if that was what his lover desired.

His ankles now bare, Oliver held out his arms. "Come here."

Vincent crawled onto the bed, blew out the candle and settled beside him, pulling Oliver close. He rested his head on Vincent's broad chest and wrapped his arms about him. Sleep was just beginning to overtake him again when Vincent spoke.

"By the way, I signed the contract. As of this morning, the property is officially mine."

Ah, the explanation for Vincent's more than playful mood this evening. Oliver should have known, but he'd been too fixated on the evening ahead. Vincent had been working himself to the bone of late to finalize the details of the purchase. He smiled as pride for the man he loved rushed through him. He pushed up onto his elbows and pressed his lips to Vincent's. "Congratulations, Vincent. Well done."

"Thank you, Oliver." The large hand resting on Oliver's back drifted up and around to palm his jaw, pulling him back down for another kiss, this one deeper, longer. "Love you," Vincent whispered against his lips.

"Love you, too." He snuggled back up to Vincent's side. The heat rolling off Vincent's body was the perfect complement to the light breeze drifting into the room, and within no time at all, sleep overtook him.

Bound Forever

Lord Oliver Marsden's life is perfect...well, almost perfect. His bookshop is doing well, his bank account isn't empty, and his nights are filled with a deliciously dominant man...who tends to be a bit too domineering outside of the bedchamber. But Vincent loves him and that's all that should matter. Right? And of course, Vincent still firmly holds the reins of control. Yet while Oliver feels Vincent is finally ready to give himself fully to him, to make good on the offer Oliver refused a year ago, the looming threat his lover could someday be forced to marry keeps him from tugging the reins from Vincent's grasp.

Then Vincent receives a letter that changes everything. Oliver seizes the moment and pushes Vincent toward a night neither of them will ever forget. Yet come dawn, Oliver awakens to an empty bed.

Lord Vincent Prescot knows he loves Oliver. The man's his best friend and he trusts him. So why does submitting to Oliver leave him so shaken? It doesn't take him long to find the answer, yet his solution could drive his lover away for good.

Chapter One

December 1823
Rotherham, England

The familiar press of hot, silken skin against his thigh roused Vincent from sleep. For a moment, he kept his eyes closed and soaked up the feel of the soft breaths tickling the hair on his chest, the weight of the sleek yet honed body sprawled half over him, and the arm slung across his waist. A combined sensation that had not gone the least bit stale after a year and a half with this man, and one he knew for certain he would never grow tired of.

With the barely audible grunt of one in a deep sleep, his lover shifted, pressing closer. A smile stole across Vincent's mouth. That was most definitely an erection, hard and insistent, the heat of it practically branding his thigh.

Desire flared under his skin, rousing his sleep-fogged senses. Blood rushed to his groin. What had once been the beginnings of a pleasant morning erection now pushed against the blankets covering him and Oliver. He blinked his eyes open. Light cut through the breaks in the forest green drapes but didn't fully penetrate the night shadows clinging to the corners of the bedchamber. Judging by the crisp yet weak golden quality of the sunlight, dawn had just arrived.

Plenty of time before his housekeeper arrived to cook breakfast and tidy the bedchambers.

A gentle nudge to Oliver's shoulder and, taking the coverlet and sheet with him, Oliver rolled onto his back. Beautifully compliant, even in sleep. The chill December air hit Vincent's skin, but he didn't bother getting out of bed to light the fire in the hearth. Within a handful of minutes, the heat quickly building within him would make the warmth of a fire feel like a hot summer day.

Shifting onto his side, he levered up onto a bent elbow. Oliver's chest rose and fell in a relaxed, rhythmic pattern. A whisper-light flick of Vincent's fingers pushed the tousled waves of his overlong hair from his eyes. At the sight of Oliver's hard cock jutting from the dark thatch of hair on his groin, Vincent smiled. They hadn't played last night, merely crawled into bed together. One of the benefits of visits to his Rotherham estate—with so many nights at their disposal where they had the luxury of sharing a bed, they could take one or two or more to simply sleep together. But judging from the state of his pretty cock, Oliver definitely appeared up for some play.

Far be it from Vincent not to indulge him.

His gaze traced the length of Oliver's body, as various options flittered through his head. He wasn't of a mind to fetch anything from the locked trunk beside the dresser. That would require getting out of bed. However…

Leaning over the side of the mattress, he snatched the wrinkled white cravat from the floorboards. Carefully and slowly, he moved Oliver's arms over his head. The long, black fan of his lashes resting against his high cheekbones did not even flutter at the change in position. The man slept as soundly as he had as an adolescent. Back when they had shared a dormitory at Eton, even a full-blown thunderstorm wouldn't wake him.

A few deft flicks of the cravat and Oliver's wrists were secured to the mahogany headboard, the knot loose enough so one quick tug would release it. When Vincent had purchased the estate from his father over two years ago, he hadn't given much thought to the furnishings. His only interest had been the unwavering belief that he could turn the property into a thriving investment. The bed, though, with its four sturdy posts and intricately turned spindles spanning the width of the headboard and footboard, had proved as valuable to him as the vein of coal he had found in the northwest end of the property. And Oliver's reaction when Vincent restrained him between those four posts indicated the man had far more fondness for the bed than anything that generated income.

Sitting back on his heels at his lover's side, he took in the results of his handiwork. A corner of the sheet had tangled around one of Oliver's calves, the rest of him bared to Vincent's view. His legs were casually spread, one knee slightly bent. His arms stretched over his head put his flawless chest on full display. The white linen around his wrists presented an enticing contrast to his golden skin. Vincent let out a low grunt of satisfaction. The man had a body made to be bound and a soul that craved it almost as much as he craved Vincent himself.

He reached out, slowly whispered a hand down Oliver's sleep-warmed chest, the skin soft and smooth beneath his palm. With effort, he resisted the impulse to pinch those copper nipples. To twist a hardened tip. To make Oliver shudder and gasp with pleasure. To make him beg for more. But it wouldn't do to wake him just yet.

His attention slid back up to Oliver's face. On anyone else, his features would almost approach average, but somehow he simultaneously embodied both beautiful *and* handsome. A hint of a morning beard darkened his jaw, his full lips slightly parted…

Vincent leaned down, brushed his lips across Oliver's in the barest brush of a kiss, their breaths mingling ever so briefly. Then he moved along the bed to settle on his knees between Oliver's legs. With one hand braced on the mattress, he bent down, wrapped a gentle hand around the base of that pretty prick, and lowered his head. Light and soft, he dragged his tongue across the crown, waiting, every sense attuned to his lover.

Oliver let out a breathy moan, more sigh than sound, and lifted his hips slightly. Vincent opened, let the slick head slide past his lips. The short, little, lazy nudges of Oliver's hips as he fucked Vincent's mouth indicated the man hadn't awoken yet. Vincent kept his mouth languid and yielding, only occasionally sucking on a downstroke, allowing the flames of desire to build within Oliver, within himself.

It didn't take long for a salty tang to tease his tongue. Vincent's cock, hanging hard and heavy between his thighs, jerked in response. Another moan, this one more sound than sigh, and Oliver spread his legs wider. Vincent released his hold on the base of Oliver's prick, cupped his ballocks, drawn up tight to his body, and rolled the weight of them in his palm. Then he drifted his fingertips down, past the smooth expanse of skin to his entrance. Pressed but didn't penetrate.

Oliver's thrusts stuttered. Glancing up, Vincent caught his gaze. His eyes were heavily-lidded, mere slits, the dark depths glittering with lust. Hollowing his cheeks, Vincent sucked hard as he dragged his lips up the length. Oliver arched with a moan, tugged at his bonds, and moaned again. His cock hardened even further in Vincent's mouth. Vincent kept sucking as he began bobbing along the length. Increasing the pace, urging him onward.

Oliver had the edge of his full bottom lip captured between his teeth, desperate need pulling his beautiful features. Vincent swiped his fingers at the base of Oliver's cock, gathering the moisture that had slid down the length. The moment Vincent brushed his entrance, Oliver pulled his knees to his chest, hips canting up, the request clearer than if he shouted.

"Please, Vincent." Thick with need, his whispered words trembled on the air.

Lust slammed into Vincent. His muscles coiled, ready to spring forward to cover the man, to shove his hard cock into Oliver and give him exactly what he begged for, but Vincent held back and instead lifted his head, letting the crown slip from his lips with a crude *pop*.

"Good morning," he said, smiling, as he pushed a finger inside.

Oliver's body greedily clamped around the digit and made Vincent's cock ache with jealousy. Dropping his head once more, he dragged his tongue up and down the underside of Oliver's length as he slowly stretched him with first one finger and then a second, forcing Oliver to wait. Letting the anticipation continue to build, needing to take him past the point of sheer desperate want to where the only thing that existed in his world was Vincent.

Pleas for more tumbled from Oliver's mouth, mixing with his gasping breaths. A heady thrill sang through Vincent's veins, briefly rising above the lust saturating his senses. It felt incredibly good to give Oliver pleasure. To know those pleas were because of *him*.

When the tight ring of muscle began to relax, Vincent crawled up Oliver's body. Oliver's legs wrapped around his waist in welcome as Vincent captured those full lips with his own. With a muffled grunt, Oliver dove into the kiss. Urgent and greedy. His tongue tangling with Vincent's, heavy breaths scorching his cheek. His need so strong Vincent could taste it.

So tempting to lose himself in the blistering heat and need of Oliver's kiss, to let it completely overwhelm him.

But he pulled back, broke the kiss before the force of it wiped away all semblance of control.

Those heavily-lidded dark eyes, the ones that could see into his very soul, stared up at him. "Fuck me." Oliver's whisper held no trace of command, only pure unadulterated desperation.

All thoughts of resisting, of keeping his lover poised on the knife-edge of anticipation, flew out of Vincent's head.

Leaning right, he quickly reached into the bedside table and grabbed the glass bottle of oil. His hand shook the slightest bit as he slicked his cock. Gaze locked with Oliver's, he positioned the head at his entrance and pushed inside. Hot, clinging heat engulfed his prick, almost pulling the orgasm out of him, as he sank to the hilt. Clenching his teeth, he fought off the climax. He planted his hands on either side of Oliver's raised arms and picked up a rhythm of slow, purposeful strokes, his ballocks pressing against the smooth skin of Oliver's arse with each downward thrust.

Oliver's head tipped back, his eyes drifting closed. Indecipherable moans of pleasure escaped his lips, wet from their kisses. The man was so goddamn beautiful, all flushed with desire, his body still relaxed from sleep, compliant and lax beneath him as he gave himself up to Vincent.

Crouching over his lover, he rubbed his jaw against Oliver's, against the stubble of his morning beard, then dropped his head to Oliver's neck. He sucked hard enough on the hot, delicate skin of his throat to leave a mark, one easily hidden by a cravat. Then he dragged his mouth over Oliver's chest, captured one hard nipple, and sucked.

"Ah yes, *please*." Oliver gasped, arched, pushing his chest upward, wanting more.

Vincent gave it to him. Rolled the tip between his teeth, tugged, and then released it to blow across the wet surface before shifting to the other nipple.

With each thrust of Vincent's hips, Oliver's erect prick bumped his lower belly, leaving a smear of wetness on his skin. The urge to taste him once again rose up—an urge too strong to deny. Abruptly he pulled out. Broke free of Oliver's legs wrapped around his waist, scooted down, and took Oliver's cock in his mouth, turning the man's groan of protest into one of absolute gratitude.

Sucking hard, he brought Oliver right to the cusp of release. To the point where he was squirming beneath him, tugging on his bonds, breaths hitching sharp and fast. Then he quickly shifted up to slide back into his arse.

Oliver shuddered, moaned. His bound hands were clenched in white-knuckled fists, every line in his body drawn tight, sleek muscles pronounced beneath golden skin dampened with sweat. Vincent pulled all the way out simply to hear that moan rip from his lover's throat again, and couldn't help but watch his cock disappear as he glided back in. A damn erotic sight—the glistening crown stretching Oliver obscenely wide, his body yielding so sweetly against the intrusion as Vincent sank to the hilt, the oil-slicked hole constricting in greedy need when he pulled free. He repeated the motion. Once, twice, the tension visibly coiling within Oliver, and on the third plunging stroke, a hoarse shout shook Oliver's chest. Pearly white seed shot from his cock, painting his abdomen. His muscles gripped Vincent's prick so tightly it took considerable effort to thrust through the man's climax. The heat, the tightness, the slick tug of Oliver's body along his length…

The orgasm ripped through him. He pounded into Oliver, the sound of flesh slapping flesh filling the room as he poured deep within his lover.

With the last tremor from the release shaking his body, he slumped down to rest his forehead against Oliver's chest, which rose and fell as quickly as his own.

Panting for breath, he gathered his sated muscles, levered up, and tugged on the end of the cravat, releasing Oliver. His lover let out a low, lazy purr as Vincent gently massaged his sweaty wrists. The cravat hadn't left any marks—he hadn't tied him too tightly. Just secure enough so he would not slip free when he tugged on his bonds. Something Oliver had a fondness for. Each tug akin to a shout for more.

The moment he flopped down next to Oliver, the man rolled into him, nestling against his side, arms wrapping around him and holding him close. They were both slightly sticky with sweat and needed to clean up—with Oliver plastered to his side, the remnants of the climax on his abdomen was now smeared on Vincent's skin as well—but it mattered not to him. He pressed a kiss to the top of Oliver's head and let out a sigh of complete and utter contentment.

What a bloody fantastic way to start the day. A chuckle tickled in his throat, but he felt too sated to give it voice.

By the time his breathing returned to normal, the chill morning air had begun to nip against his rapidly cooling skin, a reminder he shouldn't dally overlong.

"I should get dressed."

"Already?" Oliver asked, his voice a low, slow rumble that vibrated Vincent's chest.

"Yes. It's getting late."

With effort, he pulled himself away from Oliver and swung his legs over the side of the bed. He crossed to the washstand, stepping over the clothing Oliver had discarded before climbing into bed last night. He had long given up hope his tidy habits would have any influence on Oliver. His lover was distinctly his own man, and Vincent preferred him just that way—clothing littering the floor and all.

After pouring water from the pitcher into the basin, he grabbed a couple of cloths from the shelf below, dropped both into the water, and wrung one out. Stealing himself against the cold, he swiped the cloth over his face, down his side, and between his legs. Quick and hasty, but it would suffice for now.

He tossed the cloth into the bin beside the washstand and grabbed the other from the basin. The wrung-out cloth clutched in one hand, he returned to the bed. Oliver was sprawled on his belly, arms holding the white pillow beneath his head, one leg drawn slightly up toward his side, exposing delicate skin that still faintly glistened with the sheen of oil.

With a light touch, he brushed the stray strands of Oliver's hair from his closed eyes. "This will be cold," he murmured before reaching down to wipe the oil from his backside.

The man twitched, the muscles of his back contracting, as he let out a grunt in protest.

"My apologies." Not much to be done for it. He didn't have a live-in servant to deliver warm wash water in the morning. A small price to pay to awaken in bed with Oliver.

The task seen to, he dropped the cloth into the bin. He had just finished lighting the fire when the faint sound of a door shutting reached his ears, announcing they no longer had the house to themselves. Vincent grabbed the clothes he had left folded on the chair last night, but before leaving the room, he stopped by the bed again to nudge Oliver. "Mrs. Hollister has arrived. Breakfast will soon be waiting."

Oliver's response was a sleepy grumble.

Likely the man would sleep a bit longer. Vincent coasted his hand down the sleek lines of Oliver's back and pressed a kiss to his shoulder. "Love you."

"Love you too." Oliver's mouth barely moved, the words a mere thin, raspy whisper, but Vincent heard them nonetheless.

A smile on his lips, he snagged the rumpled coverlet from the other side of Oliver and draped it over his back, and then crossed to the narrow door next to the washstand. As he passed through the small dressing room, he dropped the clothes into another bin so his housekeeper, Mrs. Hollister, would see to them. He selected a fresh shirt and a pair of trousers from a shelf, grabbed a waistcoat and coat from the hooks on the wall, and went through the other door and into his bedchamber.

He tugged open the draperies, letting the full force of the morning sun stream into the room. A beautiful day, but judging by the chill seeping through the windowpanes, a decidedly cold one. Fortunately he had no plans to leave the house. The stack of paperwork on his desk needed his attention.

The water in the basin on the washstand proved just as cold as in Oliver's room, but he used it nonetheless to wash up and shave and did not bother Mrs. Hollister with a request for warm water. As he dressed, he paused to pull back the navy coverlet and rumple the white pillows on his bed. A simple enough task, and all it took to keep his housekeeper unaware of the fact ages had passed since he'd laid his head on one of those pillows. Leaving his valet behind when he traveled helped as well. Vincent found keeping the full extent of his relationship with Oliver hidden surprisingly easy while at the country estate. They rarely went into the nearby village and did not mix with the local society, preferring to keep to the house. The last thing he needed was for any marriage-minded young misses in the area to brand him an eligible bachelor. London posed a bit more of a challenge, so much so the worry of discovery still resided, lurking in the back of his mind. Still, he had to admit Oliver had been correct. He was *"goddamn Lord Vincent Prescot."* A man no one would ever suspect would bugger another man.

A self-deprecating chuckle rumbled his chest as he lifted his chin to form the long length of white linen into a neat Mathematical knot. God forbid if anyone knew just how…unique his preferences ran.

The cravat seen to, he slipped his arms into the sleeves of his bottle green coat. A few nights had passed since he and Oliver had indulged in more exotic play, and Oliver needed to return to London soon. Though the companion they had hired for his grandmother would not protest if they remained in Rotherham for an additional week, as a business owner, Oliver should not be absent from his bookshop for much longer than a fortnight. And in Rotherham, under the cover of darkness and surrounded by acres of grassy fields, he needn't worry Oliver's shouts of pleasure would rouse the suspicions of any neighbors.

With that tantalizing thought fresh in his head, he made his way downstairs. First breakfast and a hot cup of coffee, followed by the post and the stack of paperwork on his desk, and then perhaps later he'd have the pleasure of hearing the full force of Oliver's need.

Chapter Two

Eyes closed, Lord Oliver Marsden reached out a hand, palm coasting over rumpled sheets. Cool, without a trace of warmth from Vincent's body. It seemed like just a second ago when he heard the faint creaks of the floorboards as Vincent left the room, but he must have fallen back to sleep.

He should get up. Not laze away any more of the morning. But his bed at Vincent's country house felt so much more comfortable than his old bed at his bachelor apartments in Town. Even the sheets were softer, and though no longer as warm, they still carried Vincent's scent.

He took a deep, full breath, letting the air slowly fill his lungs. The distinct scents of Vincent's skin and male sweat and…sex. He let out a low grunt. By God, Vincent excelled at sucking cock. Not a surprise—Vincent excelled at everything he put his mind to. And he had clearly put his mind to mastering all the options he could have at his disposal to render Oliver senseless. Unbelievable to think a time had existed when Vincent refused to even consider touching his lips to Oliver's prick. The once hard, remote man, the one who insisted on keeping Oliver at arm's length the moment they stepped into the bedchamber, was long gone. Vincent still held the reins of control—never let them slip completely through his fingers—though Oliver had yet to attempt to tug them free. Even when he was sucking

Oliver off, the man held him in the palm of his hand. But now, even when they played their more extreme games, an undeniable current of true intimacy rode behind every touch, every command, every kiss from Vincent's whip. An intimacy that said louder than words that Vincent loved him.

Hearing the words felt quite nice as well.

Smiling, he tugged the coverlet higher to cover his shoulders, seeking its warmth. Perhaps if he drifted back to sleep, he'd awaken again with Vincent's mouth on his prick. Lovely thought, though highly improbable. Unless he remained in bed until nightfall, after the housekeeper left.

Still, a very nice thought. Sleep began to tug heavily at his mind. Vincent would be tucked behind his desk until at least midafternoon. And today was… He scrunched his brow, trying to orient his sleep-fogged brain to the correct day of the week…Wednesday. Nowhere he needed to be—

Hell.

He flung off the covers and forced himself to sit up and swing his legs over the side of the bed. Hanging his head, he scrubbed his hands over his face, rubbing the sleep from his eyes.

The Widow Middleton. He was due at her home that afternoon. He should get up now to avoid running the risk of falling back to sleep and missing the appointment altogether.

Shielding his eyes as he passed through the rays of sunlight cutting through the breaks in the drapes, he padded over to the washstand. He splashed water on his face and grabbed his straight razor. Chin tilted up, razor poised over his jaw, he paused. Leaned closer to the mirror. Brushed a fingertip over the bruise on his throat, over Vincent's mark.

Chuckling to himself, he set the razor to his jaw. After seeing to the shave, he dragged his fingers though his hair, doing his best to tame the unruly waves.

He pulled trousers, drawers, cravat, and a white shirt from the dresser drawers, tugged them on, and then went into the small dressing room. He snagged a cream waistcoat from a hook along the wall and slipped it on. The brown coat? Definitely his favorite but, well, a bit worn about the edges. His gaze fell on the black coat hanging on a peg beside the brown one. For an appointment, the black would be the better choice. Better fit and never worn, so no chance of frayed cuffs. It would make him appear more creditable. Like he actually had cause to own a bookshop.

He reached out, then paused, hand hovering an inch from the fine black wool. A frown pulled his lips. Vincent had purchased the coat for him two months ago. What was to have been a simple outing on St. James Street to pick up Vincent's repaired pocket watch had ended at a tailor's shop. Caught unaware, he had allowed Vincent to herd him into that shop, and once there, he could only silently relent to Vincent's whims lest he give the tailor reason to wonder about the source of his protests.

But however much Oliver did not agree with it, the deed was done. Past time he got over his reluctance to wear the thing. He had brought the coat with him, hadn't he? Yet he could not forget that uncomfortable feeling as he had stood for Vincent's tailor, never mind the fact that Vincent had never once asked if he even wanted a new coat. The man had simply taken the matter into his own hands and expected Oliver to bow his head and do as he bid. Expectations Oliver relished behind closed doors. Outside of a bedchamber though…

With a shake of his head, he pushed the mix of bruised pride and impotent frustration aside and grabbed the brown coat. The day had started wonderfully. No need to ruin it for himself.

The coat buttoned, he picked up the jade pin from the bedside table and went back over to the washstand. Lifting his chin, he affixed the pin to the simple knot on his cravat. Then he studied his reflection in the oval mirror above the washstand. *Not straight.* He removed the pin, tugged the knot, and reaffixed the pin. Not perfect, but better.

On his way out of the room, he grabbed his wire-rimmed spectacles from the top of the dresser and slipped them on.

The runner in the short corridor muffled his footsteps as he made his way downstairs. It wasn't a plush Aubusson rug like those in Vincent's stately white stucco town house. Rather it was simple and functional, fitting the quaint country house. Oliver spent a fair amount of time at both of Vincent's homes, and he felt much more at his ease in Rotherham, where a footman didn't lurk about every corner.

And he knew for certain Vincent felt more comfortable being with him here. Vincent even shared a bed with him in the country. In London, that only happened at Oliver's bachelor apartments. But at least more often than not he stayed until dawn.

"Good morning, Lord Oliver." Mrs. Hollister turned from the sideboard, an ivory coffeepot in hand, as Oliver entered the dining room. Short and plump, with a ready smile crinkling the edges of her hazel eyes, the housekeeper was the most pleasant servant Oliver had ever encountered. The cleaning, the laundry, the cooking… She saw to it all and never appeared the least put out by even the most mundane of requests. A stark contrast to the formal versions at the town house or the surly ones that had inhabited his childhood home.

"Good morning to you, Mrs. Hollister. And a wonderfully fine morning it is." He indicated the windows lining one wall, the drapes open, revealing the expanse of sun-warmed grass on the side of the house.

"Mighty fine indeed." She lifted the ivory pot. "The coffee's gone cold. If you'd like, I will deliver your cup to the study."

"Thank you." He picked up a small plate from the sideboard, ignored the two silver covered dishes, and selected a tart from the neat pile of pastries on the oval platter.

She bobbed a short curtsy before turning on her heel and disappearing through the narrow door that led to the kitchen, her dark brown skirts swooshing about her ankles.

Oliver found Vincent tucked behind his large desk in the study, dark head tipped down and silver pen in hand. The simple yet elegantly tailored bottle green coat accentuated the broad width of his shoulders; the stark white cravat framed his strong jaw. Vincent fit perfectly in the room with its heavy, masculine furniture and rich, mahogany wood, as if it had been made for him.

"Good morning, Oliver." Vincent made a notation on the paper before him, then looked up. A trace of disapproval flickered across his face. "You are aware Mrs. Hollister is quite adept at cooking a proper breakfast?"

Oliver took an unabashed bite of the raspberry tart. "Indeed, but her skill with pastries knows no rival."

Ignoring Vincent's arched brow, he set the plate on the small table beside the leather couch and, taking another bite of the tart, crossed to the mahogany shelves flanking the gray marble fireplace. Though not a large room, every inch of available space along the walls of the study was given over to books. All lined up like neat little soldiers, as if they knew their master would not tolerate otherwise.

Oliver finished the tart, wiped his hands on his trousers, and, unable to resist the lure, reached out. "Are you certain you don't want to part with any of your books?" He pulled a volume from a shelf, traced a finger lovingly over the embossed leather-bound cover. It would make a perfect addition to his bookshop.

"Yes, I'm certain." Another scratch of pen on paper.

Oliver frowned. "I'll pay you a fair price."

"I don't need the money."

He carefully opened the cover. An attempt to flip the first page revealed the pages had not been cut. Physical proof no one, least of all Vincent, had yet to read this particular book. A shame, really, to allow it to linger on the shelf for no other purpose than appearance's sake. "But you don't read them."

"You do."

His fingertip paused on the edges of the uncut pages. The man kept all those books for *him*. It shouldn't mean so much. Vincent certainly did not need the funds a sale could bring; still... He slipped the book back into its place on the shelf and looked to Vincent. As if sensing his stare, Vincent glanced up.

"Thank you, Vincent."

A crisp tip of his head and Vincent turned his attention back to his work, but he couldn't hide the faint hint of a blush tingeing his cheeks.

Aware he had left the study door open, Oliver kept from voicing the *love you* on the tip of his tongue and instead grabbed

Shakespeare's *Othello* from the mantle and settled on the couch to pick up where he had left off yesterday evening.

The patter of slippers on floorboards announced the housekeeper's arrival. "The post has arrived, Lord Vincent." She handed Oliver his cup of coffee, then placed the small silver tray on the corner of Vincent's desk. She received the same crisp tip of the head for her efforts. "Is there anything I can get for you, my lord?"

"No, thank you." Vincent took a letter from the top of the stack and, using the silver letter opener he had pulled from a desk drawer, broke the wax seal.

At her questioning glance, Oliver shook his head. He had everything he needed at the moment in the study with him—coffee, a book, and Vincent. After taking his empty plate, she left the room.

Oliver brought his cup to his lips and took a sip, savoring the hot, rich liquid as it flowed down his throat. With a little *clink*, he set down the cup and flipped to the appropriate page in *Othello*. Within no time at all, the book pulled him in. Even the crinkle of paper as Vincent went through the pile of letters seemed to fade to nothingness.

"Oliver."

The hint of a reprimand behind Vincent's voice had Oliver's head snapping up. "Yes?" Vincent's stare indicated he expected a response other than a yes. Clearly Oliver had missed something. "My apologies. I was not"—he lifted the book from his lap, showing Vincent his excuse—"listening."

Fortunately Vincent didn't appear at all put out. Rather than an imperiously raised eyebrow, Oliver found a smile lurking on his mouth.

"Congratulations are in order. I am now an uncle."

"Lady Grafton already had the baby?" Oliver asked, referring to Vincent's older brother's wife. To his knowledge, the doctor had not anticipated the arrival for another fortnight.

"Yes. Four days ago, and Grafton reports the child is in good health."

His pulse sped up. His grip tightened on the book. It was Grafton's first child, he told himself in an effort to prepare for the very real possibility of disappointment. The man had married less than a year ago—it had not taken Vincent long at all to convince his elder brother to honor his unspoken commitment to Lady Juliana and to follow Vincent's lead. However, unlike Vincent, the treasured heir had not been cut off for refusing to serve as a pawn to further their father's greedy ambitions by marrying a duke's daughter. Fortunately Vincent's bank account was large enough so the loss of his quarterly allowance had not proved a hardship. The loss of his father's notice…rather hard to miss something one never had to begin with.

It was much too early to worry overmuch about the gender of the baby. Juliana, Lady Grafton, was a young woman, and with Grafton only a few years older than Vincent's twenty-six, plenty of years lay ahead of them. But if the baby was a boy…

Oliver briefly closed his eyes, took a deep breath, and asked as casually as he could, "Do you have a new niece or nephew?"

A smile that held a distinct note of relief spread across Vincent's mouth. "A nephew. The honorable Christopher David Prescot, the new second in line to the Saye and Sele marquisate."

A tremor of excitement racked his body. It was all he could do not to jump to his feet and let out a shout of pure joy. He did, however, grin like a damn fool. "Congratulations, Vincent."

"Thank you for the congratulations, Oliver. Though in this instance, I believe Grafton deserves them more than I." Vincent reached across his desk to grab the silver pen in the holder beside the inkwell. "In fact, I should pen him a note this moment."

As Vincent took out a sheet of paper from a desk drawer and began writing, Oliver tried to turn his attention back to his book, but *Othello* no longer held his interest.

His attention was drawn back to Vincent. The end of his pen caught the sunlight streaming through the windows as he wrote the note. His dark head was tipped down, a hint of a smile still tugging at the edges of his mouth. His broad shoulders square and straight, as always.

He's now truly mine.

Warmth filled Oliver's chest. Hell, it filled his entire being as a sense of—he could only describe it as *calm*—settled over him. It wasn't as if he had worried about losing Vincent on a daily basis. But that lingering threat, the one that hung in the distance with more menace than the most ominous of thunderclouds, had vanished.

Grafton had produced the next heir to secure the future of the marquisate. No more worries his lover would feel compelled to do his duty and take a wife, or that Oliver would be forced to someday walk away from the man he loved.

Vincent was his.

Forever.

"Love you," he said, barely a whisper, unable to keep it inside.

The pen stilled. Vincent didn't lift his head, didn't pull his gaze from the letter. His lashes still kissed his cheekbones, but his mouth moved. Oliver couldn't hear the words, but he didn't need to. He'd watched Vincent's lips form those words enough times to know exactly what he had said.

Smiling, he adjusted the book on his lap and gave Shakespeare another chance to draw him in. The familiar sounds of Vincent working drifted around him. The faint creak of leather as he shifted his weight in his chair. The scratch of a pen on paper. The shuffle of paper. The little noises did not annoy him, did not scrub across his nerves. Rather they kept his focus firmly on the man he loved.

He closed the book, giving it up as a lost cause, at least for today. "Do you mind if I borrow your carriage this afternoon?"

"Not at all. It's at your disposal. Any particular reason?"

"I have an early afternoon appointment with the Widow Middleton. Going to have a look at her library. Unlike you, she is willing to part with her books."

Vincent looked up from his desk. His gaze traced Oliver's chest. "Are you going to wear that coat to a business appointment?"

"Yes."

Vincent's lips briefly thinned. Oliver's grip tightened on the book as he waited for Vincent to question his response, but the man instead asked, "Will you be back for supper?"

"Of course. The widow resides outside of Maltby, not even an hour's ride east." An easy enough distance. Hence why he had scheduled the appointment during one of his Rotherham visits.

Vincent set down his pen and pulled his pocket watch from his waistcoat pocket. "Then you need to ring for the carriage now."

"But it's only ten. I needn't leave until noon."

Vincent arched a brow. "You will be in that library for hours, Oliver, and you are well aware of it."

All right, the man had a point. Oliver lifted a shoulder in a half shrug of agreement. In any case, he couldn't work up the effort to take issue with Vincent's attitude, which bordered much too close to domineering. Not today. Not when Vincent was finally his forever.

"I'd rather not dine alone tonight. The earlier you leave, the greater the probability I will not be the only individual seated at the table."

"You will miss me if I dally overlong at the widow's?" He didn't know why, but he wanted Vincent to admit it. Vincent would miss him, even if only for a handful of hours.

His face a stoic mask, Vincent tipped his head.

With effort, Oliver kept the smile from curving his mouth. "But she's not expecting me until early this afternoon."

"If she's a widow, then she likely lives alone. She will welcome your charming company, no matter the hour."

Oliver let out a snort. As if his company could truly be classified as charming. "All right then. I'll find Mrs. Hollister, ask her to alert the stables that I have need of the carriage."

"And have her warm a couple of bricks for the carriage. It's downright chilly today."

Setting the book on the couch cushion, Oliver got to his feet and crossed to stand before Vincent's desk. "*You* could always keep me warm." He spoke for Vincent's ears only.

His lover's gaze darted around his shoulder, likely to the open study door, then met his. For a brief moment, desire banked the brilliant blue depths. "I'll warm you plenty…later tonight, after you return home."

The low, intimate rumble wrapped around him, a potent temptation to send the widow his regrets and stay right here, with Vincent.

Knowing Vincent would resist any efforts to indulge now, much less in the study, Oliver tamped down the lust that had started to wind its way into his veins. He grabbed the letter on the silver tray. "If you'd like, I can drop this at the post office as I pass through the village."

A nod of thanks from Vincent and Oliver turned on his heel. Mrs. Hollister would likely be in the kitchen about now. The sooner the groom readied the carriage, the sooner he could leave, and the sooner he could return so Vincent could make good on his promise.

Chapter Three

A slightly stale, musty scent hit Oliver's nose as he walked through the door. He stopped in his tracks. A few books? Good Lord, they were everywhere. Not just the random discarded book, but stacks upon stacks of them. The side table next to the wingback chair before the hearth, the large oak desk, and the short cabinet by the windows. The bookshelves lining the walls from floor to ceiling were crammed full near to bursting. Books turned on their sides and nestled in the small spaces between the tops of rows and the shelves above, with stacks on the floor blocking the bottommost shelves. An open volume lay on the cushion of the chair, as though someone had merely set down the book to return any moment.

A twinge of melancholy pulled at his heart. The book's owner would never return.

Light streamed into the library as Mrs. Middleton tugged back the partially open curtains on one of the two windows. "My apologies for the state of the room, Lord Oliver. I had to let the maid go, and the study was Mr. Middleton's..." The uncomfortable, restrained lift of her slim shoulders spoke volumes. With her light brown head bowed in concentration, she made a little project of tying back the heavy damask curtains.

Oliver waited patiently. He was not well acquainted with the young widow. Had only met her on one other occasion months ago when he and Vincent had stopped at the inn's restaurant in Rotherham for a bite to eat. The Middletons had sat at the table next to theirs. But he had heard she recently lost her husband, and quite unexpectedly at that. A misfired gun while shooting in the surrounding woods. Clearly the loss still weighed heavily on her, a blanket of grief surrounding her like a cloak.

He had assumed she merely intended to thin the library. A common enough desire of a widow. Rather morbid of him to follow behind death so closely, but it was the primary means by which he procured new stock for his bookstore. Usually the widow's request was not driven by an urgent need for funds, but more as a method to tidy a library. Given she had let her maid go, he had a strong suspicion the young widow needed more than a bit of extra pin money. Judging by the state of the room, Mr. Middleton had spent every shilling on his collection.

She moved to the other window and repeated the procedure, tugging open the curtains and tying them back. Her slight frame strongly lent the impression of youth. At first glance, one might easily mistake her for an adolescent. Yet her refined manners, the rich timbre of her voice, and that air about her that she had seen and experienced far more than a mere girl indicated she was many years older. Likely just below his own seven and twenty. Still, a young woman. If he recalled correctly, Mr. Middleton had been a young man as well. The thought of saving to provide for his wife had likely been far from his mind. With death came tragedy, but it was especially hard when it took someone so young, snatching a loved one well before his or her time.

It made him acutely aware of how fortunate he was. He could leave this house and return to Vincent. Hold the man close, feel the strong beats of his heart, the warmth of his breath. Sensations that were now mere treasured memories for Mrs. Middleton. Hopefully he and Vincent would have the long years together that had been denied the young widow. And now that the threat of marriage was gone, the hope was solidly within his grasp.

Another little tug on the ties and then she turned from the window. The polite hint of a smile could not hide the sadness lurking in the depths of her brown eyes. She flicked her wrist, the motion encompassing the entire room. "You needn't stand by the door. Please, have a look around. There aren't any I particularly wish to keep, so the entire lot is available if you so desire."

If the bookshop's account could manage it, and if the shop had the space, he would readily buy them all, if for no other reason than to help her. "Thank you." He tipped his head. "The collection is quite impressive, to the point where the shop could not hold it all. A few crates will likely need to be the limit, though it will require some self-restraint to narrow the selection."

She nodded in understanding. The skirts of her somber black day dress rustled softly as she crossed the room. When she made to drop down before the fireplace, he held up a hand and stepped from the door.

"You needn't bother with that. I can see to it."

Crouched before the dark hearth, she looked up at him askance, her eyes wide with uncertainty. He might be the son of a marquis, but that did not mean he'd ever had the opportunity to grow accustomed to others waiting on him.

"Truly. I'm well versed in starting a fire. Please, leave it to me." He shifted his leather bag to his left hand and held out his right to help her to her feet.

A brief hesitation and then with a barely audible murmur of thanks, she laid her small, pale hand in his and stood. "Would you care for a cup of tea?"

"Thank you for the offer but no. I would not want to risk an accidental spill. Tea does not rub along well with Shakespeare."

The edges of her lips lifted, this time in a hint of a genuine smile. She clasped her hands before her. "Well then, I shall leave you to it. If you have need of anything, please do not hesitate to ask." With that, she left the room.

Shrugging out of his greatcoat, Oliver glanced about. Where to start? He could spend days perusing so many books. A part of him did not want to miss even one, for the one he missed could be the ultimate treasure. But he had been on such appointments enough times to know he needed to push aside the urge to set up a pallet in the corner and not leave until he'd laid his hands on every volume. In any case, he would much rather spend his nights with Vincent than alone on the floor.

Especially tonight.

"*I'll warm you plenty...*" Vincent's voice sounded in his head. The low, intimate rumble pushed Oliver into action.

Another glance about the room. Best to start where he stood. Turning, he moved the book on the wingback chair to the side table and set his leather bag on the cushion. He pulled a pencil and a ledger from the bag and flipped to a blank page. Then he set to work going through the stack of books on the side table.

* * *

Oliver looked out the carriage window. The sun must have just dipped out of sight, for a last lingering wash of deep honey gold light warmed the edge of the horizon. Plenty of time remained for him to make it back to Vincent's. No worries the man would be left to his own company for supper. Still, Oliver's foot tapped against the floorboards in rhythm to the team of four's brisk trot. It was all he could do not to push the driver for more speed. A handy gallop would cover the distance in no time, but since the team was not his own, he left the pace to the driver.

In any case, a few hours stretched ahead of him before he would have Vincent all to himself.

He curled his gloved hand into a fist at his side, his body fairly vibrating with eagerness, effectively keeping the chill in the air from seeping into his bones. He knew he should not allow himself to get overexcited. Not yet. He needed to judge Vincent's mood first. Gauge his frame of mind. But if his lover did not appear as if he would shove aside the possibility...

A jolt of heady anticipation shot through him. His cock twitched, bumping against the placket of his trousers. The brief, wicked flare of desire in Vincent's blue eyes had spoken loud and clear the man had his own plans for the evening ahead. Plans that would leave Oliver panting for breath and begging for more. Plans he certainly would thoroughly enjoy and wholeheartedly approve…on any other night. But at some point during the past few hours, as he cataloged selected titles into his ledger, a different idea for their evening seized hold.

Not that he had been perusing books of an erotic nature. Mr. Middleton's library focused on philosophy, poetry, history, and animal husbandry. Perhaps he could lay the blame on the books piled on the floor. Every time he stooped to grab one had made him acutely aware of the faint lingering ache in his arse…and how he got that pleasurable ache.

Nor could he identify the moment when the image from that morning of Vincent looming above him had changed. The moment when he no longer looked up at Vincent but down into his face, absolute bliss pulling his rugged features, the gasping pleas tumbling from Vincent's lips and not his own.

That image had stayed with him all afternoon. Hell, it had grabbed hold and refused to be pushed aside. And for the first time, he wanted it. Absolutely and completely, with every fiber of his being.

Briefly closing his eyes, he took a moment to savor that image. Of Vincent laid out on the bed and desperate with need for *him*. A grunt issued from his throat. Shifting on the bench, he reached down, moved aside the length of his greatcoat, and adjusted his hard cock, trying to find what room could be had in the confines of his trousers.

It wasn't as if he had never entertained the notion. But it had been a fleeting thought. Erotic and wickedly tempting, but a fleeting one nonetheless. Yet now…

All the worries had gone and with them that last bit of restraint. Of course, Grafton had yet to produce the required spare to go with the heir. But the probability that the chore of producing the next Marquis of Saye and Sele would fall onto Vincent's broad shoulders had diminished to almost nothingness. So insignificant Oliver would not even bother to worry about it.

He understood now why he had never attempted to tug the reins of control from Vincent. At first he had told himself Vincent was not ready. Regardless of the fact Vincent once gave him verbal leave to do with him as Oliver pleased, the man's unease at the time had been more than obvious—breaths short and shallow and muscles drawn tight in trepidation, never mind the limp cock dangling between his legs. Neither had Oliver felt comfortable with such a sudden reversal of their usual roles. Sometimes one needed time to acclimate oneself to a new idea, and it had definitely been one of those circumstances. But many months had passed since Vincent even flinched in hesitation when Oliver trailed his fingertips along the crease of his arse. Hell, the man now had no qualms at all bending over and ordering Oliver to lick his arse.

And it wasn't that Oliver did not believe himself capable of taking Vincent to the necessary point. He held no illusions Vincent would ever walk into the bedchamber and surprise him with another offer to put himself in Oliver's hands—the notion was too foreign, too new for him to feel comfortable voicing on his own with no prompt at all. But if Oliver sufficiently applied himself, he felt confident he could strip away every one of Vincent's inhibitions and pull those four words from his lips. The words he had once promised himself he would wait for.

The opportunity had presented itself many times. He adored lavishing Vincent with pleasure, trailing his lips over every inch of his body, feeling those powerful muscles tighten to the point of trembling with need, hearing those deep, low groans of pure lust. Yet he always held back, just enough, and had long ago stopped questioning his reasons. But now he knew the true cause. He could not ask it of Vincent, could not accept that gift from him when the possibility of being forced to part still hung over them.

But with the direct threat now gone…

A broad smile curved his lips, one he knew had to appear downright wicked. Anticipation nipped at every nerve in his body. Tonight, if Vincent was amenable, the man would be well and truly his, in every sense of the word.

The carriage turned right, onto the road that led to Vincent's estate. A few large oak trees lined the long dirt road. All hints of the day's sun were gone from the sky. The light from the full moon cast the trees' bare branches in spidery shadows across the sparse winter grass. Oliver settled back against the black leather bench and turned his mind to how best to get Vincent to abandon his own plan for the evening and put himself in Oliver's hands.

An outright request was out of the question. A shrewd businessman, Vincent tended to analyze a situation. Best if he did not have time to think on it, else his nerves would seize hold and destroy any hope for an enjoyable evening, regardless of the man's willingness. He would need a strategic assault. Slow and careful yet deliberate. Building the tension, the want. Nurturing the need he knew lay buried deep within Vincent. Until his lover could not stop those words from tumbling past his lips.

Please, Oliver. Fuck me.

Chapter Four

Vincent reached for the silver bowl of carrots and spooned more onto his plate. "Was the appointment a success?" Oliver had returned to the house before Vincent even started to worry he had been left to his own company for supper, prompting Vincent to wonder if the appointment had been worth the effort. Present Oliver with a stack of books and the man tended to lose track of all sense of time.

"Oh yes." Oliver took another bite of the pork. "Middleton's library…" He let out a blissful little sigh that Vincent knew had nothing to do with the quality of the pork tenderloin. "Books everywhere and most were in pristine condition. Well, at least those I was able to sort through. Mr. Wallace will certainly be pleased when the books I selected arrive," he said, referring to the shop's prior owner who had remained on to assist Oliver with the day-to-day running of the small bookshop. Oliver paused, his fork suspended a couple of inches from his open mouth. He looked to Vincent, who sat at his left at the head of the table. "I need to arrange for someone to crate them and deliver them to the shop."

Likely that detail had just occurred to him. Oliver was not the most organized of individuals. Vincent reached for his glass of wine and took a sip. "Inquire with the blacksmith, Mr. Young. You can find him at the inn's livery, and his son should be able to transport the crates to London."

The line of Oliver's shoulders went lax with relief. He popped the piece of pork into his mouth. His jaw worked as he chewed, and then he swallowed the food down with a sip of wine. A sheen of Bordeaux clung to his full lips, reminding Vincent of how those lips looked slicked with spit after sucking him off. A memory he could verify just as soon as they finished supper and Mrs. Hollister left the house. And after Oliver put his beautiful mouth to good use, then Vincent would strip him of his clothes, restrain him, and redden his arse with the flogger. Or perhaps the bullwhip? It had been some time since he'd heard the erotic snap of leather cracking through the air, followed by Oliver's shuddered moan of pleasure. An entirely different moan than when he applied the flogger. One breathy and broken, thin and delicate, like the sleek, long length of a bullwhip. The other low and guttural, thicker and more substantial, like the smack of a flogger.

His hand curled around his fork. He could almost feel the leather handle warming in his palm, could almost hear those thin, breathy moans slipping past Oliver's lips.

"I'll call on him tomorrow," Oliver said, jolting Vincent's thoughts away from the bedchamber and back to the dining room. "It will cost considerably less to hire someone in Rotherham than to have someone travel from London to see to the task. As it is, I wish the shop's bank account could afford more. Had to limit it to four crates, and it definitely took some doing to narrow the selection. That library was a true find, though I had the distinct impression Mr. Middleton did not leave his wife well provided for."

"What led you to believe that?"

"She mentioned how she had to let her maid go. I don't believe she has any servants helping her at the house. Didn't spot a one while I was there. And she offered up the entire contents of the library. I'd hazard a guess Middleton spent the majority of his income building that library. The books did not appear old or well used, as if they had been inherited from another. Most were newer editions."

Vincent frowned. Completely irresponsible of Middleton to leave his wife beggared. The first concern upon his marriage should have been to ensure her security. A young woman from a good family would have no means of providing for herself in the event of her husband's death. "Surely she has family who can assist her."

Oliver shrugged. "Haven't a clue. I would like to hope so, but Middleton passed away almost a month ago. If she had family, one would think they would have offered their assistance by now."

Vincent took the last bite of his supper and set his fork down. "How substantial is the library?"

Brow furrowed, Oliver pursed his lips. "I'd say at least another dozen crates worth, likely more."

He made a mental note to send a letter to the widow on the morrow and a note to Mr. Young. His son was a strapping young man, well able to pack and transport more than four crates to London.

"Prime stock," Oliver added. "Really wish I could have purchased the lot of them, but at the very least, she should have no trouble finding a buyer for the remainder."

No, she would have no trouble at all.

With a soft tap of footsteps, Mrs. Hollister entered the dining room. "There's more pork in the kitchen if you'd like, Lord Vincent."

"No, thank you." He pushed from the table and stood, giving his bottle green coat a tug to straighten it.

She looked to Oliver, who shook his head. "I could not eat another bite. You have outdone yourself yet again, Mrs. Hollister. The tenderloin was perfectly cooked."

"You are too kind, Lord Oliver." She beamed at Oliver, as if the man had just presented her with a trunk full of jewels. She never bestowed that look on Vincent, and he employed her.

With an easy smile, Oliver got to his feet. "It's not kindness, but the truth."

"There's brandy in the study, if you gentlemen would care for it. And a plate of raspberry tarts as well."

Nor were those tarts intended for him. She clearly adored his lover. Well...he couldn't much blame her.

Oliver's smile widened. "Ah, now that *is* kindness."

Mrs. Hollister giggled. The older woman actually giggled as she began clearing the table of the remnants of their supper.

Somehow Vincent kept from rolling his eyes. He walked to Oliver's side and clasped a hand on his shoulder. "Shall we retire to the study?" If he allowed it, Oliver would remain in the dining room and chat with the housekeeper, keeping the woman at the house precious minutes longer than needed.

Oliver must have picked up on the hint, for he didn't glance at Vincent in question when he nudged him—all right, the nudge bordered on a shove—toward the door. When they reached the study, he found Mrs. Hollister had already stoked the fire in the hearth. The strong flames warmed the room.

Rather than head straight for the small plate of tarts, Oliver stopped before the console table situated in front of one of the windows. With the candles lighting the room and the dark sky backing the window, Oliver's reflection was visible in the glass as he picked up the crystal decanter from the silver tray. He bowed his head, a chunk of his wavy hair falling forward, and focused on pouring brandy into first one tumbler and then another.

Vincent settled in the armchair angled toward the couch. Glass clinked faintly as Oliver set the decanter back on the tray.

"For you," Oliver murmured, offering a tumbler to Vincent.

"Thank you." He brought the glass to his lips. The well-aged brandy flowed smoothly down his throat.

Oliver sat down in his usual spot on the couch, conveniently enough within arm's reach of the tarts on the side table. After taking a sip of brandy, he reached for a tart. "Care for one?"

"No, thank you."

"Are you certain? They're delicious."

"I'm certain they are. However, I'll leave them to you." Unlike his lover, he had never had a taste for sweets. After a satisfying meal, a nice glass of brandy and good company were all he needed.

A little smile played on Oliver's lips as he chewed. Then he popped the last bit of the tart into his mouth, swallowing it down with a long sip of brandy. He brushed a fingertip to the edge of his mouth, swiping up a droplet of liquor. The motion quick and without thought, unlike when he wiped the trickle of pearly white seed from the corners of his mouth.

The decadent image played in Vincent's mind—of Oliver, his heavily-lidded gaze locked with Vincent's as he slipped his fingers back into his mouth to suck on the tips as if savoring every drop.

Vincent shifted, stretching out his legs and settling more comfortably in the chair. Oliver was damn brilliant at sucking cock. But a good half hour remained before the housekeeper finished tidying the kitchen and left for the night. A good half hour before he could give Oliver the order to drop to his knees. Rather than let impatience build, he simply savored the low hum of anticipation and the smooth glide of the brandy down his throat.

Heat rolled off the fire in the hearth behind him, warming him from the outside while the brandy heated him from within. Resting his head on the back of the armchair, he let his eyes drift shut.

The only sounds that broke the companionable silence were the very faint clinks of china and glassware as the housekeeper worked in the kitchen, the crackle of the logs in the hearth, and the creak of leather whenever Oliver shifted on the couch.

He sensed Oliver's presence a second before he heard the splash of liquid. He opened his eyes to find Oliver refilling the tumbler resting on the arm of the chair, Vincent's loose grip just enough to keep the glass from falling to the floor. Lashes at half-mast, Oliver looked down at him, that little smile playing once again on his mouth.

"Thank you." Though one more splash and Oliver would have been in danger of overfilling the glass. Vincent carefully brought the tumbler to his lips and took a long sip. No reason to allow perfectly good brandy to go to waste.

After replacing the decanter on the tray, Oliver settled back on the couch. "Did you enjoy supper?"

"Most assuredly, and especially the company."

Oliver tipped his head in acknowledgment. "Mrs. Hollister should be finished soon."

"Indeed."

Vincent's gaze swept over his lover. He had one leg drawn up, elbow resting on his bent knee and his heel braced on the edge of the couch cushion. At first glance, he appeared fully at his ease. Yet the little smile that seemed fixed to his full lips, the faint glint lurking in the depths of his dark eyes...

He swore he could detect a new layer of...confidence radiating from his lover. Not blatant but subtle and definitely there.

Interesting. Perhaps it was merely a by-product of his afternoon appointment. Oliver adored books, and the purchase of a few new crates' worth surely pleased him.

"Is there anything else you gentlemen need before I leave?"

Vincent pulled his attention from Oliver. The housekeeper stood in the open doorway of the study, her brown woolen coat buttoned to her chin and her gloved hands clasped before her.

He opened his mouth, but before he could reply, Oliver spoke.

"No, thank you, Mrs. Hollister. I hope you have a good evening."

She tipped her head and turned. Vincent gathered his wits just in time to bid her good evening before she disappeared down the corridor.

His attention snapped back to Oliver, who regarded him with that same little smile. The *click* as the back door shut seemed to fill the study, fairly echoing off the walls. His lover's gaze remained locked with his over the rim of his glass as the man drained the last splash of brandy. Oliver set the empty tumbler on the side table and, in one fluid motion, stood from the couch.

He did not know what to make of this new version of Oliver. Not that he held any qualms with it, yet he could do nothing but stare at Oliver as he crossed the distance separating them. Of their own accord, his legs opened wider, just enough for Oliver to step between them. Bracing a hand on the back of the chair, he leaned down. Vincent expected a light brush of his lips. Instead Oliver's mouth slanted over his. Hot and quick, his agile tongue sweeping into Vincent's mouth.

Lust washed over him. A startlingly thick, heavy wave that clung to his senses.

Oliver pulled back just enough to break the kiss. "Are you ready to retire to my bedchamber?"

Struck mute by the combination of anticipation and need and determination blazing in the dark brown depths of his lover's eyes, Vincent could only nod.

Chapter Five

Oliver set the single candle he'd brought up from the study on the mahogany dresser. The soft golden glow provided enough light for him to see clearly, while leaving the corners of the bedchamber darkened with shadows. The fire in the hearth was already lit and the drapes closed tight courtesy of the housekeeper. The room felt warm and comfortable and was very familiar to Vincent. The perfect setting for tonight.

The door snapped shut. A tremor of anticipation rocked through him. Oliver took a deep breath and focused on keeping the exhale smooth and even. When he felt he could proceed without pouncing on Vincent, he turned from the dresser.

Unbuttoning his coat, Vincent stepped farther into the room. "You seem rather pleased with yourself this evening."

"I am," he admitted, somehow keeping the predatory grin from his mouth. The second glass of brandy appeared to have done its duty, lulling Vincent's senses just enough so the tiniest bit of languid ease lurked behind his movements. He did not want the man foxed. He wanted Vincent to remember every detail from tonight. But the large glass of spirits would hopefully aid him in stripping away every one of Vincent's inhibitions.

Vincent folded his coat and put it on the chair by the narrow door to the dressing room. "Any particular reason?"

Oliver shrugged in an attempt at nonchalance. At the slight narrowing of Vincent's eyes, he added, "I had a productive day and shared a wonderful meal with you."

To his relief, the hint of suspicion left Vincent's eyes, yet his gaze lingered on Oliver's face, as though searching for something. He was giving his lover too much time to think. That wouldn't do at all.

Oliver crossed to the bedside table, removed his spectacles and the jade cravat pin, and placed them in the small silver dish. He unbuttoned his coat and flung it toward the washstand. Then he turned to face Vincent. "I missed you today." Letting every bit of desire and need rush to the surface, he gazed at his lover.

As if drawn by an invisible cord, Vincent breeched the distance between them. "As I you." Vincent cupped his jaw, brushed the pad of his thumb across Oliver's bottom lip. "Now why don't you put that beautiful mouth to good use?"

"It would be my pleasure." Not wanting Vincent to settle into the role of dominant, he deliberately left off the *milord* address. He wanted the man focused on him and on the pleasures he offered, not on the locked trunk beside the dresser that his gaze had already found once since entering the room.

No restraints and no floggers. No crossbars or toys. Tonight it would be just him and Vincent. His breath hitched in his chest. He took a moment, a very short moment, to calm his pulse. Then he dropped to his knees.

Slow and deliberate, he unbuttoned the placket of Vincent's trousers. A light tug and the string of his drawers released. Reaching inside, he carefully pulled Vincent's semierect cock free. The sight alone of that gorgeous prick, the length thick and heavy in his hand, made his arse tighten in anticipation. As he flicked his tongue over the crown, he could almost feel the flared head breach his entrance, stretch him wide. A low moan shook his throat. But he ignored the demands of his own body and focused on Vincent—on slowly building the tension, on nurturing the want, the need he knew was within him.

Leisurely glides of his mouth along the rapidly hardening shaft. Teasing swirls of his tongue across the head. Soft presses of his lips to the satiny smooth skin. He adored the man's cock. Could worship it for hours. Had done so on more than one occasion, the resulting ache in his jaw nothing compared to the pure pleasure of pleasing Vincent.

A large hand threaded into his hair to cup the back of his skull. Oliver yielded to the pressure as Vincent guided him up his length to the crown.

"Take me inside."

The tiniest bit of impatience behind Vincent's words threatened to bring a smile to Oliver's lips. Instead, he opened his mouth and eagerly followed Vincent's command.

He suckled the head, flicked his tongue to the sensitive spot beneath, and slowly slid down the length until Vincent's cock nudged the back of his throat. Then he picked up a rhythm of long strokes, keeping the suction more gentle than hard, not wanting the lust to build too swiftly.

Vincent's grip flexed against his skull like a cat kneading a blanket. His groans even resembled the purrs of a content lion, low and gravelly, the sounds rumbling around Oliver.

If the man had even an ounce of tension in his body when he walked into the room, it had now gone. Oliver glanced up. Vincent's head was tipped back, lips slightly parted. From his vantage point, he could not make out Vincent's features, but he'd bet his shop the man's eyes were closed, every sense fully focused on what Oliver did to his prick.

He took a moment to luxuriate in the taste of Vincent and on the decadent feel of his lover's cock sliding in and out of his mouth, gliding over his tongue, nudging his throat. But only a moment lest he get lost in those sensations. Ignoring the twinge of regret, he pulled back. A soft kiss to the crown and he got to his feet.

Vincent's lashes slowly swept up as Oliver began to unbutton the other man's waistcoat. To Oliver's delight, Vincent let Oliver undress him, his large hands roving up and down Oliver's back, pausing to grip his arse, but not making a move to stop him or to take back control of the evening. He dragged his lips along Vincent's jaw, nipped lightly against the skin, occasionally brushed his trouser-covered erection against Vincent's, keeping the man focused on him. Yet as he worked his way down the tan waistcoat, awareness seeped into his veins. His fingers began to shake just the slightest bit, just enough so the small fabric-covered buttons would not slide easily from their moorings.

The confidence that had seized hold in the carriage on the drive to Vincent's country house began to slip away. What if he did something wrong? What if Vincent didn't enjoy it? Oliver pushed the waistcoat off Vincent's shoulders and reached for the stark white cravat. It had been ages since Oliver had taken a man, and to his knowledge, never a virgin. It wasn't as if he didn't know how it was done. But…

Another tug on Vincent's cravat. He did his best to hide the sigh of relief when the elaborate knot finally gave way to his struggles. He stepped back just enough to pull the white shirt up Vincent's chest.

His lover finished the task for him, whisking the shirt over his head. By God the man was gorgeous, bared to the waist with his erection jutting stiff and hard from the open placket of his trousers. A thin moan slid past Oliver's lips.

Unwilling and unable to resist the lure, Oliver reached out to touch his bare skin. The heat radiating from Vincent's body almost scorched his palms as he swept his hands up to those impossibly broad shoulders. This man was his and only his. Forever.

"Love you," he whispered against Vincent's neck.

"Love you too."

A tremble shook Oliver's body, breath catching in his chest.

The hell with it.

Oliver grabbed the back of Vincent's neck and pulled him down for a kiss—slanted his lips harshly over Vincent's. With his hands on Oliver's arse, Vincent jerked him closer, pressing their bodies tightly together, and thrust his tongue into Oliver's mouth. Oliver let go and gave in to Vincent's kiss, to the power and the strength of the man in his arms. No more trying to gauge Vincent's reactions. No more trying to keep the man on a predetermined path for the evening. If it happened, it happened. If not, it wasn't meant to be.

Threading his fingers into Vincent's hair, he dived into the kiss. He rubbed against Vincent, reveling in the complete lack of give in the man's hard, strong body. The scent of his lover filled his every breath—clean male skin, not a hint of cologne, and undeniably Vincent. His head went light under the onslaught of sensations. The last drop of the tension he hadn't even realized existed slid out of his body, and his senses focused absolutely and completely on pleasuring Vincent.

The lust built within him with each brush of Vincent's tongue. With each groan that rumbled his broad chest. More. He wanted more.

He kissed his way down Vincent's chest, pausing to flick his tongue over one copper nipple, then over the hard abdomen, following the thin line of dark hair to that beautiful cock. But before he wrapped his lips around it again, he pulled Vincent's dark trousers down his legs.

Vincent nudged his hips forward so his erection brushed Oliver's parted lips. But the silent request wasn't necessary.

Bracing his hands on Vincent's thighs, Oliver opened his mouth and worshipped Vincent's cock in earnest. Long, plunging strokes coupled with hard suction. Relaxing his throat, he took him all the way down and swallowed, massaging the sensitive head. When the powerful muscles beneath his palms began to draw tight, he shifted down, ducked beneath, and pressed openmouthed kisses on his ballocks. Vincent widened his stance, granting him greater access. Oliver took it and more. He drew one testicle into his mouth, sucking and tugging lightly before moving to the other. All the while, he pumped Vincent's length, his grip firm, his hand sliding easily over the spit-slicked skin.

Vincent's hard pants filled the air around him, mixing with the distinct scent of male sweat. They pushed him onward, demanding more.

"Turn." He nudged Vincent hip. "Let me lick your arse."

A low growl rumbled from Vincent's chest.

Oliver shifted back, giving Vincent room to comply, and glanced down. Damnation. His clothes. He tugged at his waistcoat, not caring in the slightest when a few buttons popped loose and skidded across the floorboards. He yanked on his cravat and whipped his shirt over his head. Very briefly got to his feet to push off his trousers. His erection sprang free, so rigid it slapped against his belly. Need drumming through his veins, he drew his hands down the strong lines of Vincent's back to his hips and nudged him to better face the bed.

Vincent bent at the waist and braced his hands on the mattress. Oliver dropped to his knees and parted those muscular cheeks, baring Vincent fully to his view. He painted a line down that forbidden crease with his tongue and pressed a kiss to his entrance.

"Ah hell." Vincent pushed back, pushing against Oliver's mouth.

He eagerly gave Vincent what he needed. Licked and kissed the perimeter until the tight ring of muscle began to relax. Pulled his cheeks more firmly apart and slipped his tongue inside, teasing the highly sensitive nerves. Then he slid a finger alongside his tongue, gently stretching him.

He heard a muffled *thump*—likely Vincent punching the mattress—accompanied by another curse.

A wave of lust washed over him. Thick and potent, soaking his senses. His cock jerked, demanding attention. His ballocks were drawn up so tightly they ached. Rather than give in, he savored the heady thrum of anticipation, savored the need so strong a twinge of pain rode hard and heavy behind it.

Finger thrusting and mouth working, he lavished Vincent with pleasure until Vincent's curses filled his ears. Gasping for breath, he pulled back.

Vincent growled. "Damnation, don't stop."

"I'm not." Hell no, he wouldn't stop. He pushed on Vincent's arse. "Get on the bed."

Vincent didn't pause, didn't hesitate, didn't even glance back at Oliver in question. His muscles bunched and flexed beneath pale golden skin as he shifted onto the bed to lie on his side. Oliver quickly joined him, pausing only to snatch the bottle of oil from the bedside table drawer before nestling behind him.

He poured a generous amount onto his fingers, pressed a kiss to Vincent's shoulder, and pushed two digits inside. Tight muscles clamped around his fingers. Slick and hot and soft as the finest silk. His cock jerked again, bumping against Vincent's thigh. Careful and slow, he pushed deeper to rub Vincent's gland and was rewarded with another muffled *thump* of Vincent's fist against the mattress.

Of their own accord, his hips thrust in short compact nudges in rhythm to the strokes of his fingers fucking Vincent's arse. His hard cock rubbed against Vincent's thigh, greedy for any sort of friction. The heat pouring off Vincent's back scorched his chest. Sweat pricked Oliver's skin, slicked the hollows behind his knees, and threatened to drip down his temples. Every fiber of his body screamed for release. He could feel the frustration seep into Vincent, hear it in the hard pants of his breaths and the grunts reverberating through his back.

The pleas started tumbling from Vincent's mouth. "More, Oliver. Need…*hell*, harder."

With each thrust, he grazed Vincent's gland, yet he stayed right on the edge of complete satisfaction. That need grabbed hold, the same one that had seized him in the carriage. His own release suddenly lost all importance.

He wanted Vincent. Wanted to mark the man as his own. Needed to bring him to climax while buried deep within him. Wanted to feel the orgasm rack his lover's body. Wanted to be the one to make him scream from the sheer force of it.

He intensified his efforts. Slid another digit inside Vincent, stretching him wider, boldly pushing the pleasure past the point where he normally would stop and beg Vincent to fuck him.

They moved together yet in counterpoint, bodies straining, indecipherable moans mixing together. And then Vincent spoke the words Oliver had waited over a year to hear.

"Oliver…*please*." Vincent groaned, pushed back against him. "Fuck me."

He didn't stop to ask if Vincent was certain, though he did pull free to grab the oil. The touch of his own oil-slicked palm to his prick almost triggered an orgasm. He bit the inside of his cheek, hard enough to taste the metallic tang of blood, then took a deep breath and rode the surge of pure need until it ebbed to a manageable level. Then he poured more oil on his fingers. Vincent was already quite slick, but he wanted nothing left to chance. Reaching down, he swiped his fingers over Vincent's entrance.

Vincent shifted his leg forward and tipped back his hips, granting Oliver access.

For a moment, the sight of Vincent laid out on the bed struck Oliver mute. The golden glow of the candle caressed every line of his powerful body, his most intimate flesh slick and ready, chest heaving with each heavy breath, and wanting *him*.

Emotion clogged his throat. Somehow he was able to give voice to the "love you" that filled his entire being.

Then he positioned his cock at Vincent's entrance and, slowly pushing forward, made Vincent his in the most intimate way possible.

Vincent's broken gasp cut through the silence. His body clamped around the head of Oliver's prick. So damn tight and hot and perfect. Unwilling to break the spell, Oliver resisted the urge to ask if he was all right. Instead, he cupped Vincent's hip, pressed his mouth to the apple of Vincent's shoulder, and began to gently rock his hips.

Pressure filled him as Oliver nudged inside. A pressure that satisfied the overwhelming need that had built to unprecedented proportions. Oliver's cock certainly did not rival his own in size, but hell if he didn't feel goddamn huge. Stretching Vincent wide, pushing in so damn deep, stuffing him wonderfully, blissfully full. A tiny bit of pain threaded under the pleasure. But strangely, he welcomed it. Wanted more.

Even as the word "more" tumbled from his lips, a portion of his brain reeled in shock. Stunned that Oliver's prick was in his arse. And doubly stunned it felt so unbelievably amazing.

Completely drunk on the all-encompassing sensations, Vincent slung his leg up, shifting so that he was partially on his back, and draped his arm around Oliver's neck. Oliver palmed Vincent's thigh, pushing his leg up higher, and dropped his head to brush his lips across Vincent's nipple. Pulling the tip into his mouth, he thrust even deeper—slow, plunging strokes that had Vincent's head lolling back.

Oliver's grip on his thigh tightened, but he kept his thrusts lusciously slow. A chunk of his untidy hair had fallen forward to obscure one eye. Vincent's fingers itched with the need to tuck it behind his ear, to fully expose those beautiful features he knew so well. Yet every muscle in his body felt completely lax, so consumed by pleasure he could not have lifted his other arm if he tried.

And then Oliver shifted behind him, and on the next downward thrust, he hit that spot inside him. The one that made a white-hot surge of lust shoot through him.

Again and again, the head of Oliver's prick massaged that spot. Ratcheting the ecstasy drenching his senses. Building it stronger and stronger. Coiling tighter and tighter, past anything he had ever experienced before.

Vincent struggled to catch his breath, but the effort was in vain. His breaths hitched, high and sharp, in his chest. His cock ached. Goddamn it, it hurt. He wanted to grab his prick, but he was…afraid to move. To even shift enough to bring his hand to his groin. One move and he could lose that absolutely perfect angle of Oliver's prick. The one that brought the orgasm so close he could taste it.

As if reading Vincent's mind, Oliver's hand slid down his thigh to close around Vincent's cock.

"*Yes.*" The word ripped from Vincent's throat.

Oliver's grip was almost too rough but at the same time exactly what he needed. His thrusts turned harder, longer, more demanding. The strokes so deep his ballocks slapped against him.

Shameless and needing even more, Vincent bumped back. He was right there, on the very edge, senses poised on the brink, but… *Damnation!*

Beyond desperate for the climax that frustratingly eluded him, Vincent gazed up at Oliver.

"Come for me, Vincent," Oliver whispered, those dark eyes boring straight into his soul.

The orgasm slammed into him, harder and more powerful than a runaway stagecoach. His hoarse shout echoed in his ears. Seed shot from his cock, splattering his stomach, as Oliver continued to drive into him, prolonging the climax until Vincent could only gasp in awe.

As the remnants of that powerful release still thrummed through Vincent's body, Oliver's hips snapped forward. It felt as though his cock somehow grew thicker, longer, harder, stretching Vincent's body to its limit. Teeth bared, Oliver let out a growl, deep and low and unlike anything Vincent had ever heard from him. Then warmth filled Vincent's passage.

Oliver slumped, his forehead dropping to Vincent's chest. Hot, sticky pants fanned Vincent's chest, clinging to his sweat-slicked skin. Lazy and slow, and almost unconsciously, Oliver slid his hand, still wrapped around Vincent's cock, up to massage the crown. A spasm racked his entire body, abrading his overwrought nerves, muscles clenching around Oliver's prick, still buried deep.

"Hell!" The curse burst from his throat, though the word sounded embarrassingly much closer to a yelp.

"Sorry," Oliver murmured as he released his hold. He didn't sound the least bit apologetic. If anything, he sounded smug. Oliver was a man. He damn well knew how sensitive one was after an orgasm.

For a long moment, the only sounds that broke the silence were their heavy breaths. He could feel Oliver softening within him, and then the man's spent prick slipped from his body. The protest, the need to keep Oliver with him, rose within. So strong it took all his willpower to keep the plea inside.

The strength of it jolted him harshly to the present. His arse burned, throbbed, yet it was strangely pleasurable. Hell, his entire body felt sore. He was suddenly aware he was practically lying in Oliver's arms. And it felt good. So good, he never wanted to leave.

His gut tightened.

Oliver levered up to lean over Vincent. His dark hair stuck to his temples, damped with sweat. His cheeks were flushed, his heavily-lidded eyes reduced to mere slits. The most content smile curved his mouth. "Love you."

The words were whispered against his lips an instant before Oliver's mouth found his. But the kiss did nothing to vanquish the leaden feeling building in the pit of his stomach.

Chapter Six

Sprawled on his belly, Oliver kept his eyes closed as the sensations from last night drifted from his dreams to fill his sleep-logged, barely conscious mind. The press of Vincent's hard body along his. The sounds of Vincent's hoarse, desperate moans for more. The urgent thrusts of Vincent's arse against his pelvis as the orgasm built within his lover. He flexed his hand tucked under his pillow, the memory of his grip on Vincent's thigh still fresh on his palm.

He had watched Vincent climax countless times, but never like that. Every line in his powerful body lax yet thrumming with undeniable need. And the look on Vincent's face when the man's release claimed him—absolute bliss, undeniable awe, and unwavering trust. A look Oliver would never forget. Vincent had completely given himself over to him, placed his pleasure fully in Oliver's hands. And judging by the pearly white seed that had coated the man's rock-hard abdomen, Vincent thoroughly enjoyed the experience.

The smile teasing the edges of Oliver's lips broadened into a sleepy, triumphant grin.

He felt like a damn god.

He shifted his hips, pulling one knee up toward his side, in an effort to relieve some of the pressure on his erection trapped between his belly and the mattress. An erection that just last night had been buried hilt-deep in Vincent's no-longer-virgin arse.

His own arse tingled with awareness. Need threaded under his skin, seeped into his veins, building stronger with each passing second. Perhaps he could convince Vincent to repay the favor.

He reached out his senses, searching for the heat radiating from Vincent's body, yet...

Oliver opened his eyes and found the place next to him empty. He levered up onto his forearms. The white pillow still held the impression from Vincent's head, and the coverlet was rumpled as though someone—Vincent—had hastily flung it back into place after vacating the bed.

He could not recall Vincent getting up. Granted, Oliver had a tendency to sleep soundly, but Vincent always at least nudged him before he left the room, be it this room or his bedchamber at his bachelor apartments.

Perhaps the man had simply gone to relieve himself. But... He passed a hand over the sheets under the coverlet. Not a trace of warmth from Vincent's body. A glance over his shoulder toward the marble fireplace confirmed his suspicions.

Vincent had been gone for some time—so long, the fire he usually lit before leaving the bedchamber had burned down to faintly glowing embers.

Brow furrowed, he looked to the forest green drapes covering the window beside his bed. The gray daylight seeping through the breaks in the heavy damask made it virtually impossible to discern the time of day. He snatched his spectacles from the bedside table, slipped them on, and focused on the brass clock on the fireplace mantle.

A few minutes before nine.

He had not significantly overslept, which meant Vincent had left before dawn.

Unease nipped at his stomach. Flinging back the coverlet, he threw his legs over the side of the mattress. He grabbed his clothes from the floor and dressed. He did not bother to shave. He could see to the task later, after he located Vincent.

A check in Vincent's bedchamber and in the study did not turn up the man.

"Good morning, Lord Oliver."

Oliver turned from the open study door to find the housekeeper walking down the corridor toward him. "A good morning to you as well. Have you seen Lord Vincent this morning?"

"No, I have not." As she usually arrived at the house around eight, that meant Vincent had left well over an hour ago. "There's breakfast in the dining room. Kippers and eggs. And I just put out a fresh pot of coffee." She smiled as though nothing made her happier than to prepare breakfast for him and Vincent.

But breakfast was the farthest thing from his mind at the moment. "Thank you, Mrs. Hollister. Would you be so kind as to keep it warm? Lord Vincent and I will be taking a late breakfast this morning."

After grabbing his greatcoat from the closet off the entrance hall, he stepped out of the house. The morning air felt brisk and cold and held the threat of snow. Thick clouds hung heavy in the sky, blocking any attempts by the sun to provide even a hint of warmth. He buttoned his coat and tugged on his black leather gloves as he made his way around the side of the house toward the stables.

He found the stall belonging to Vincent's preferred mount—a big-boned black hunter—empty except for about half an armload of hay in the corner. The tall stallion had not even had a chance to finish his breakfast. The grooms who tended to the horses arrived quite early from the village, usually around dawn, if he remembered correctly.

Oliver wracked his brain, but he could not recall Vincent mentioning an errand or any obligation that would require him to leave the house so early. To his knowledge, he did not have any plans for the day save working in his study.

The unease nipping at his belly turned into a tight fist of worry. On any other morning, Vincent's absence would not rouse much more than mere curiosity. But last night had not been any other night.

"Good morning, Lord Oliver."

Oliver turned from the empty stall. One of the grooms, a wiry young man with an unruly shock of pale blond hair, stood in the partially open door of a stall on the other side of the aisle. He had a pitchfork in one hand, as though he had been tidying the horse's stall.

"Morning," Oliver said, with a tip of his head. He resisted the impulse to ask the groom if he had seen Vincent that morning, and if so, if he knew in what direction the man had gone. He had already asked Mrs. Hollister with no success. If he inquired with any more of the staff, he'd only end up inciting their curiosity as to why Oliver was so concerned about their master's whereabouts so early in the day. In any case, it wasn't as if Vincent was in the habit of keeping his servants abreast of his comings and goings.

"Do you have need of the carriage, my lord?"

"No, but could you saddle a horse for me?"

In no time at all, Vincent's efficient groom saw to the task and brought the horse out into the stable yard. Oliver swung his leg over the chestnut gelding's back, and with a nudge of his heels, the horse obediently slipped into an easy canter.

He took the dirt lane leading from the stables. The cold wind bit at his cheeks, yet Oliver did not tuck his chin into the collar of his greatcoat. He sat tall, his gaze sweeping the surrounding grounds, looking for any sign of the black hunter.

At the fork in the lane, he pulled the horse to a stop. Should he turn left or right? Where would Vincent have gone? About six months ago, Vincent had purchased the property adjoining his, making the Rotherham estate more than sizeable. The man could be anywhere. Perhaps he had been called to the coal mine? No, too early in the morning for that. Vincent would have nudged him awake if someone had called at the house before dawn.

The forest on the east side of the property? Hadn't Vincent once mentioned a gamekeeper's cottage? But as neither of them hunted, he hadn't given the comment much notice. Perhaps the pond?

He turned the horse left and headed across the expanse of grass toward the west end of the property. During the summer months, he and Vincent occasionally indulged in a swim on hot afternoons. Highly doubtful he'd find Vincent swimming laps in the ice-cold pond, but he would check along the bank before going across to the forest and then on to the village.

When he had awoken that morning, nothing but the pleasures of the prior night had filled his mind. Yet now he could not forget that look in Vincent's eyes when Oliver had leaned over him to kiss him. That moment after his spent cock had slipped from Vincent's body. The dark brows furrowed the tiniest bit, a trace of hesitation in the brilliant blue depths of his eyes. His senses drenched with the heady sensation of having had Vincent, he had not given it any thought. Had simply snuggled up to Vincent's side and promptly fallen asleep. Now though…

Did Vincent harbor regrets? For all Vincent's physical strength and for all his successes in his business dealings, the man had a fragile sense of self. He did not have Oliver's rock-solid acceptance of who and what he was. He could have sworn Vincent seemed ready to fully relinquish control and take their relationship to the next step. But had Oliver pushed him too soon? Should he have continued to hold back? Should he have waited until Vincent broached the subject of his own accord?

His lover had a tendency to analyze every situation. To turn a matter over and over in his mind. But intimacy wasn't a business deal. He truly feared if he allowed Vincent to overthink last night, Vincent would quickly turn even the tiniest smidge of a doubt into a full-blown regret. Given what hour Oliver could discern Vincent had left the house, the man already had far too much time with nothing but his thoughts.

He nudged the horse for more speed. The chestnut's easy stride lengthened to a ground-covering gallop. The worries tumbled about in his head, growing stronger and stronger as he traveled across the property, every sense attuned for any sign of Vincent.

A sigh of relief expanded his chest at the sight of the black horse tied to a low branch of a tall tree near the pond. The stallion turned his head to look over his hip as Oliver slowed his horse to a walk. Ears pricked in attention, the animal nickered softly.

Oliver dismounted and tied his horse's reins to a branch on the other side of the tree. Sitting on the bank of the pond, Vincent did not look over his shoulder as Oliver approached. A breeze ruffled a few strands of his neatly cropped, dark hair. Even with the greatcoat broadening his frame, Oliver could detect the slump hunching his usually straight shoulders.

All traces of the relief at finding Vincent vanished.

Hell, he *had* pushed Vincent for more than he'd been ready to give.

But he couldn't take back last night. It had happened, and he could not change it. The best he could do was help Vincent to accept it. Hopefully—damnation, he hoped with all his heart—Vincent loved him enough not to allow his insecurities to come between them again. He could not go back to how it had once been—Vincent keeping him at arm's distance, holding his heart back, far from Oliver. Vincent giving his body but not his love. He could not survive that sense of…isolation again.

Without a word, Oliver settled next to him. Vincent's gaze was fixed straight ahead on the pale blue surface of the pond, yet Oliver had no doubt the man knew exactly who sat beside him.

His heart heavy in his chest, he waited a long moment. Waited patiently for Vincent to speak or at least acknowledge him in some fashion.

Vincent dropped his attention to his bent knee, which was drawn up, the other leg stretched out before him. The furrow pulling his brows deepened. Still though, not a word passed the tight line of his lips.

Dark smudges underscored his eyes, and stubble darkened his usually clean-shaven jaw. Instead of a crisp, neat Mathematical, he had tied his cravat in a simple knot. If Oliver wasn't mistaken, Vincent had donned the same deep brown trousers Oliver had pulled down his strong legs less than twelve hours ago. He'd hazard a guess the coat, waistcoat, and shirt hidden beneath the black greatcoat were also the same ones the man had worn yesterday evening.

"Did you get much sleep last night?" he asked.

A long pause, and then Vincent shook his head, slow and reluctant. "Don't believe I got any."

The knot clutching his stomach tightened to a viselike hold. "You do know I love you?" At Vincent's single nod, he asked, doing his best to keep the all-consuming worry from showing itself, "Did you at least enjoy last night?"

Vincent looked up from his study of his knee. "You doubt it? I climaxed with your cock in my arse." And his arse was still a bit sore, the ache a constant reminder of exactly where Oliver's pretty cock had been.

Intent and probing, Oliver swept his dark gaze over Vincent's face. "So why does that bother you?"

He focused on a spot over Oliver's shoulder and dragged a hand across the back of his neck. Trust Oliver to go directly to the heart of the matter. "It shouldn't." He heaved a sigh. "But it does for some reason."

How could he explain that sense of utter vulnerability? Giving responsibility for his pleasure so completely to another was definitely a new experience. Last night he had felt connected to Oliver in a whole new way. And it frightened him.

"I will not deny I had a very good evening." The long black fan of Oliver's lashes drifted down. A smile pulled the edges of his lips. But when he looked back to Vincent, his gaze was once again somber, begging Vincent to confide in him. "But if you weren't comfortable with it, then we don't have to do it again. Honestly, Vincent. My love for you is not contingent on you bending over for me." He laid a comforting hand over Vincent's, which was braced at his side in the grass. "I know you love me. You don't need to prove it that way."

Vincent's lips curved in a weary half smile. "I know." Ridiculous to even have this discussion. Oliver gave himself up to him on a regular basis—his lover's more than obvious enjoyment shouted loud and clear he had no issues with it. So why did Vincent?

Not because he was still in denial. Over a year ago, he had finally stopped fighting himself and fully accepted that he preferred men. And above all, that he loved Oliver. He trusted the man implicitly. So much so he had given himself over to his lover, let the man have his way with him. Something, not that long ago, he would have never allowed. Yet just last night, he had done so without a second thought.

It wasn't that the experience totally put him off the idea. Not something he wanted to become a habit or even a somewhat frequent activity. He enjoyed dominating Oliver far too much. Nor did he worry Oliver now wanted to completely flip their dynamic in the bedchamber. The man's soul truly craved submitting to him. But every once in a long while, he could now see himself wanting more than Oliver's eager submission. Yet…

His gaze dropped to the jade cravat pin affixed to the untidy knot of Oliver's cravat, and the answer that had eluded him since Oliver had fallen asleep beside him last night hit him.

Last night had made him realize how much he truly loved Oliver. How much he needed him, and not just for evenings together to share a supper or as a more than eager bed partner willing to submit to Vincent's every whim.

He needed Oliver in his life. Needed the man at his side, and not only as he was now, but until the end of his days.

Now that the marquisate had a new heir, the threat of having to marry had disappeared. His lover could remain at his side forever, yet the knowledge did not offer the comfort it should. In fact, it had become the source of the fear that had settled in the pit of his stomach, building stronger as the night had given way to the dawn. It made him acutely aware of how lucky they were Grafton had a son. What if it had been a daughter? What if his brother's wife could not have children? What if some unknown force tore them apart? Their relationship was against the law, after all. What if something happened to Oliver? Would he end up like the Widow Middleton, the man he loved ripped from his life far too soon? Accidents did happen. For all he knew, today could be their last day together.

The fear flared from his belly, an ice-cold, prickly rush that encompassed his entire being. His heartbeat stumbled, his breath hitching in his chest.

"What would you have done if I had been forced to find a wife?" The question tumbled from his lips before it formed in his head.

Oliver frowned. "What does it matter now? Grafton has his heir."

"Please, Oliver. Answer me. Would you have stayed with me?" He needed to know. Needed the comfort of the knowledge that Oliver would have stayed with him, though he had a very strong suspicion Oliver's answer would offer no comfort.

His lover's gaze, heavy with regret, remained locked with his. "No. I could not have shared you. I could not have welcomed you with open arms when you came to me smelling of her."

"But I would have married out of duty and nothing more. I would not have loved her. I love you." *My heart belongs to you.*

Oliver shook his head. "I know. Still, I could not have been the secret you kept from your wife."

"But we already are each other's secrets."

"Yes. Though it would have been different, and you know that. You would have gone to balls with her, went to the theater, discussed your day with her, gone home to her, laid between her legs. Had children with her. I could never share you like that, Vincent. It would have destroyed me."

And it would have destroyed Vincent in the process. He looked down, avoiding Oliver's gaze, and adjusted the length of his greatcoat, draped over his leg. "I don't know what I would have done if I had lost you," he admitted. He had a brief taste of it once before, and it had been *agony* not to have Oliver in his life.

With a gloved hand, Oliver cupped his cheek and brought his chin up, refusing to allow him to hide. He cursed the chill temperature, needing to feel the comforting warmth of Oliver's palm.

"You would have been all right, Vincent. You would have succeeded in marriage, just as you succeed in everything you do."

Oliver's confidence in him was staggering at times but, in this instance, entirely misplaced. Vincent made to shake his head, but Oliver held him still. "Would you have been all right?"

That gloved hand slipped off his jaw. "No. You are the only man I have ever loved. I could never love another. But as you no longer need to marry, we do not need to discuss this. So let's not speak of it."

"If you insist." Vincent let out a heavy sigh. "But I would not have been 'all right,' not if I didn't have you," he grumbled.

A little indulgent smile tipped the edges of Oliver's lips. A smile that indicated Oliver's confidence was still misplaced. But he knew he would not convince the man otherwise right now.

Oliver's gloved hand came back up to cup his jaw. Leaning close, he pulled Vincent down for a kiss. Just one brush of his lips provided the comfort Vincent sorely needed, vanquishing almost every trace of the fear, but not all of it. A tiny tendril remained, but he pushed it aside, focused on kissing the man beside him.

He reached up and threaded his fingers in the wind-tousled waves of Oliver's hair. With a firm tug on the strands, he slanted his lips over Oliver's and pushed his tongue inside, demanding entry. Oliver moaned into his mouth and shifted closer, pressing full against Vincent's side.

Lust shot straight to his groin. His cock hardened, pushing at the falls of his trousers. But before the lust grabbed hold of all his senses, he pulled back just enough to whisper against Oliver's lips, "I never said never again."

Oliver's eyes flared, and a moan, this one thin and threadbare yet thick with excitement, shook his throat.

Lest the man misunderstood his intentions, Vincent gave Oliver's hair another tug. "But not now, boy," he said, as firm as that tug.

His lover instantly yielded. The dark fan of his lashes fluttered behind his spectacles, brushing the curve of his high cheekbones. A whimper slid past his parted lips.

The man was so beautiful. So perfect. The other half of his soul.

His heart clenched, the fear flaring to grip him anew. Needing the lust to mask it again, he slanted his lips harshly over Oliver's. Let the silken depths of his mouth, the sweet sounds of his sighs, and the hot pants of his breaths clinging to Vincent's cheek command all his attention.

Rubbing against Vincent's side, Oliver shifted closer. He let out a little grunt of frustration, then pushed up onto his knees. Vincent felt the man's hands move between them.

A shrug of his shoulders and Oliver's greatcoat slipped from his arms. He dragged his lips along Vincent's jaw. "Now, Vincent. I need you now." Desperation soaked his plea.

Vincent glanced down. The waistband of Oliver's trousers was bunched just above his knees, exposing the golden skin of his compact yet sleek thighs. The flushed head of his cock poked out from under the hem of his white shirt. No doubt at all what Oliver wanted, and Vincent was more than willing to give it to him. Hell, he *needed* to give it to him. Needed to have the man beneath him, compliant and desperate, wanting only him. Yet…

Vincent pulled his gaze from Oliver to scan the surrounding grounds. Nothing but grassy fields and the two horses tied to the tree. The pond's slight downward sloping bank offered some measure of concealment, but he could still see if someone approached. Not that anyone was apt to. They were on his property, and the servants had no cause to travel so far as the pond, especially on such a cold day.

Reassured, Vincent nodded. "Get down on your stomach, but don't remove any more clothes." The lust and need drumming through his veins provided its own brand of warmth, but doubtful enough to ward off the frigid morning air. The last thing he wanted was for Oliver to catch a chill.

Oliver quickly moved onto his belly, his discarded greatcoat a rumpled heap beneath him. Upper body braced on a bent elbow, he reached back with his other hand and tugged at Vincent's wrist. "Now. *Please*, Vincent."

"You want me? Then prepare yourself."

Without a trace of hesitation, Oliver bit the end of one fingertip and hastily pulled his hand free of the black leather glove. He stuck his fingers into his mouth, sucking on them. Canting his hips up, he reached back to push two digits between his cheeks. A wince flickered across his brow. Then he let out a sigh of undeniable pleasure.

Vincent pushed the tails of Oliver's coat to his waist and tucked the end of his shirt under the hem of his waistcoat, baring the man more fully to his view. He shifted onto his knees, his gaze never leaving the sight of Oliver working another finger beside the other two and thrusting between the round globes of his arse. He flicked the length of his greatcoat behind him, unbuttoned the placket of his trousers, and pulled out his erection. After removing his gloves, he flung them aside and spit on his palm. He slicked his prick, then spit once more onto his palm and took care to liberally coat the head of his cock. Oil would serve them better, but he had none with him. The thought of fucking Oliver had not entered his mind when he left the house, but it sure as hell did fill it at the moment.

He straddled Oliver's thighs, tugged his hips up to the necessary angle, and swatted at Oliver's hand. On the next thrust, Oliver slipped his fingers free to pull back his cheek, exposing that perfect, tight hole, the skin glistening with moisture.

Vincent positioned the spit-slicked head of his cock at his entrance and pushed inside on one long stroke, settling hilt-deep.

"Ah, *yes*." Oliver arched beneath him, pushing his arse back against Vincent, wanting more.

Vincent gave it to him. Not even allowing a moment for Oliver's body to adjust to the invasion, he pulled back and snapped his hips forward, slamming hard and fast into Oliver. Tight muscles gripped his length in the most decadent of caresses, pulling the climax down his spine with surprising speed.

Head bowed, Oliver clutched at the grass, fingers digging into the soil. Braced over his lover, Vincent pounded into him—rough, hard, and frantic. He could feel the tension building within Oliver, hear it in his gasping pleas for more.

The orgasm clutched his ballocks in a fist. "Stroke your cock. Come for me," he urged, needing Oliver to climax *now*.

With a nod of his bowed head, Oliver worked a hand beneath his belly to stroke his prick in rhythm to Vincent's thrusts. Those pleas hitched in his throat. "More, Vincent. *Please*. I...I—"

Oliver let out a shout. The climax gripping him sparked Vincent's. On a low growl, he slammed his cock into Oliver with all the force of his lower body, spilling deep within him.

Panting for breath, he dropped his forehead to Oliver's shoulder. His pulse pounded through his veins, echoed in his ears. He took a moment to simply bask in the bliss drenching his senses, his muscles finally lax from the tension that had gripped him for seemingly endless hours. Then he gathered his tired muscles and shifted off Oliver to tuck his spent prick back into his trousers.

Oliver rolled onto his back and gifted him with the most beautiful smile, happy and content and full of love for him. Vincent could not have stopped the smile from curving his own lips even if he tried.

"Love you," Oliver said, voice scratchy, as though he'd just woken from a deep slumber.

"Love you too. Now up with you. It's damn cold, and I don't want you to catch a chill."

Oliver rolled his eyes but did as Vincent bid. As they made their way back to the horses, Oliver asked, "Any other plans for the day?"

After the last few hours alone by the pond and a sleepless night, it felt as though it was midevening and not midmorning. The thought of crawling into bed with Oliver, holding the man close, and sleeping the day away held much appeal. But he could not ignore the press of obligations. In any case, lazing the day away in bed with Oliver would certainly draw Mrs. Hollister's attention. He wished he did not have to hide his love for the man. It just didn't seem…right.

Pushing aside the flare of irritation, he said, "I need to see to the post."

Oliver swung up onto his horse. Gathering the reins, he speared Vincent with a frown. "Can't it wait until tomorrow? You should relax, get some rest. Perhaps read one of the books lining your study walls."

The mention of books reminded him he had a couple of letters to write as well. "I won't be at my desk all day. And yes, I need to see to the post today, as we need to depart for London tomorrow."

Oliver's frown deepened.

"You need to get back to your shop."

"Well, yes," he conceded. "It's just...I like being with you here."

Vincent swung up into the saddle and turned his horse from the tree. "As I you." He didn't relish the thought of returning to London, to early mornings spent slipping out of Oliver's bachelor apartments versus simply walking a few steps to his own bedchamber. But given Oliver's bookshop and his grandmother, and Vincent's business obligations, spending all their time in Rotherham wasn't an option.

He held back the sigh and nudged his black hunter into a canter. As they traveled back to the house, he could not help but think about those two letters he needed to write and why they were even necessary.

His gaze went to Oliver riding beside him. Even at their pace, Vincent could make out the frayed cuffs of his sleeves and the tattered hem of his greatcoat resting on the chestnut's back. To Vincent's knowledge, Oliver had owned that same coat since he was seventeen.

Unwilling to endure another round of questions from Oliver, he kept the frown from his lips and turned his attention back to the grassy field in front of him. But Oliver's tattered coat did not leave his mind.

Chapter Seven

"Are you certain, Lord Vincent? This is a significant change and one which should not be taken lightly."

"Yes, I am quite certain." Vincent glared at his solicitor. He had given the matter more than considerable thought over the past week, since he and Oliver had left Rotherham. Nor was he a simpleton who did not understand the ramifications of the changes he had requested.

Efficient and trustworthy, Mr. Barrington had proven himself more than competent at managing the various legal matters that arose from Vincent's investments. The man usually did exactly as Vincent asked. But if the solicitor questioned him again, he would have no qualm taking his business elsewhere. The solicitor had no place concerning himself with why Vincent wished the changes made. The man need only to see them done.

Mr. Barrington's attention dropped to the instructions Vincent had provided. A notched V pulled his brows. Then he looked back up at him. His eyes flared the tiniest bit before he tipped his head. "As you wish, my lord." He reached for his pen and dipped the tip in the pewter inkwell on the edge of his desk. "The main Rotherham property was purchased from and not gifted from your father. I need to review the deed, but there should not be any issue with a transfer of the property."

"I'll have a footman deliver the deed later today."

Another crisp nod. With a quick scratch of his pen, Barrington made a notation on Vincent's instructions. "Then I'll have everything I need to make the changes." His gaze swept over the paper once more. "No, I do have a question. Would you like a one shilling clause added for Lord Grafton?"

"Why ever would I add that? Seems rather rude and deliberate."

"Exactly the reason to add it. One shilling clauses are commonly used to ensure a family member is aware they were not forgotten but deliberately omitted, thus removing grounds that the writer was not of sound mind and simply forgot the individual."

"Then yes, add the clause, but make it one thousand pounds." He wanted no slight against Grafton. Though not close to him, the man *was* his brother. "If there are any other possible grounds for contention, please make me aware of them. I want them all removed."

Another scratch of Barrington's pen. "If anything else arises, I will send one of my secretaries with a note. But please understand that while I will do my best, the only way to remove all possible grounds for contention is to have a blank document. A disgruntled party may go so far as to fabricate claims. The grounds may ultimately be judged without merit, but they could prove costly to defend against, never mind the resulting delay in the execution of your wishes."

Vincent frowned. Highly doubtful Grafton would go to such lengths, especially when Vincent had made a point to include an annuity for the man's son, but the unknown held far more risk than he was willing to blindly accept. He might be comfortable with risk when it came to investments, but definitely not when it involved the well-being of the man he loved. He pulled out his pocket watch. Not yet eleven o'clock. If he left Barrington's office shortly, he would have time to stop at the bank before his next appointment.

"Understood. I simply ask you do your best," he said, slipping his watch back into his waistcoat pocket.

"Of course, my lord." Barrington tipped his head. Vincent knew the man would do no less, yet he wanted nothing left to chance. "When do you need this completed?"

"By tomorrow afternoon." He wanted it done and in hand before Oliver arrived for supper tomorrow.

"Then you can expect it by three in the afternoon."

A tiny bit of the tension that had gripped him for days eased. Satisfied Barrington would complete the task to his satisfaction, Vincent stood from the chair, gave his coat a tug to straighten it, and bid his solicitor good day.

* * *

Oliver crossed out the figure at the bottom of the account ledger. After studying the column of numbers for a moment, he identified the cause of his error. He'd forgotten to carry the one. He had just squeezed the correct sum in the small space beside the incorrect one when a knock sounded on the back door.

Setting down his pencil, he rolled his shoulders, the joints popping and cracking. He was sorely in need of an interruption, but he'd nearly finished with the pile of the prior day's receipts. If he did not record them all that evening, then they would be waiting for him tomorrow, along with a new pile from today. Not something to look forward to. So the sooner he could get through them, the sooner he could meet Vincent for supper.

He pushed from his desk and made his way across the small back office of his bookshop. A chill gust of evening air blew in as he opened the door, revealing the blacksmith's son.

"Good evening, Lord Oliver," Joseph Young said, with a deferential tug on the brim of his hat. Oliver had briefly met the strapping young man when he had gone to the Rotherham inn's livery to arrange for the books he'd purchased from Mrs. Middleton to be delivered to London. "I've got your crates. Where would you like them?"

"Over there will do." Oliver motioned in the direction of a barren spot along the wall. "Any trouble on the journey?"

"No. None at all. Took a bit of time, though. Couldn't push the horses too fast, considering the weight and all. But the weather was decent, so the roads were in as good of shape as can be expected this time of year." He shifted his weight and shoved his gloved hands in the pockets of his overcoat. "I'll see to those crates then." With another tip of his head, he turned on his heel.

Oliver left the door open and settled at the desk once again. Picking up his pencil, he went back to work as Joseph Young trudged back into the office, setting a crate down with a *thump*. In the four days Oliver and Vincent had been back in London, he had only seen Vincent on one occasion. His lover had shown up at his apartments late in the evening. Had not stayed long. Barely made it onto his bed. Well, Oliver made it onto the bed; Vincent had not. But no bother. He'd take a quick tumble from Vincent over none at all. And before Vincent departed, he had extended an invitation to supper at his town house for that evening.

After a long absence from Town, it wasn't uncommon for business affairs to occupy Vincent. But four days had passed, and Oliver was quite looking forward to spending some time with him tonight. Time that included conversations and good food, and not merely a few moments—albeit scorching hot and very pleasurable moments—in the bedchamber. Though if the evening ended with both of them on Oliver's old wooden bed, then all the better.

A little smile of anticipation flittered on his lips as he recorded the receipts into the ledger. The shuffle of footsteps behind him was broken by a *thump* as Joseph deposited each crate on the floor. A draft of cold air slid around him, slowly seeping through his coat and negating the effects of the meager fire in the small hearth. With a scratch of his pencil, Oliver made another correction and then flipped to the last receipt. He had just recorded the sum when another *thump* caused his pencil to pause.

He glanced over his shoulder to the crates along the wall. Five? Hadn't Joseph only packed four? Had he selected more books than he realized?

With a shuffle of footsteps, Joseph reappeared. He had discarded his overcoat at some point, and his muscles bulged beneath the sleeves of his white shirt as he carried another crate into the office.

Six?

No, that wasn't correct. He pushed from the desk. Cold air snapped against his cheeks as he went outside. Twilight was full upon the city, casting the narrow alley in dark, heavy shadows. The golden light streaming from the open door illuminated the team of two large draft horses hitched to a wagon. Crossing his arms over his chest to ward off the cold, Oliver went around to the back of the wagon and counted the crates as Joseph grabbed another to haul into the office.

Twelve crates. Nineteen total? No possible way he had accidently selected that many books. Oliver dragged a hand through his hair. Clearly Joseph had made a mistake. Damnation. He had been very specific with Mr. Young, even left him with written instructions.

What must Mrs. Middleton think? Joseph had cleared out her library, and Oliver had not even paid for a quarter of it. Now he would have to sort through it all, find the books he did purchase, and have the remainder returned. And he could not leave them crated. They needed to be returned to the library's shelves. Oliver shook his head. He'd have to take the books back himself and try to explain the mishap. Another long journey to Rotherham lay ahead of him. He let out a heavy sigh. Highly doubtful Vincent would go with him. They had just come back to Town.

What a bloody mess.

A now familiar shuffle sounded behind him. Oliver tamped down the frustration and turned from the wagon. "Joseph, there has been a misunderstanding. You were only to deliver the books I left stacked on Mr. Middleton's desk."

A look of puzzlement twisted Joseph's face, flushed with exertion. "I was to deliver them all here." He reached for his overcoat on the side rail of the wagon, pulled a fold of crumpled papers from a pocket, and handed it to Oliver.

He smoothed the papers flat and angled them toward the light streaming from the back door. The first contained his own instructions. The second... He recognized the tidy yet masculine script before he reached the signature.

Dear Mr. Young—

In addition to the crates arranged by Lord Oliver Marsden, please have the balance of the books in Mrs. Middleton's library crated and delivered to the same address. A sum has been enclosed to cover the additional expense.

—Lord Vincent Prescot

Annoyance surged within him. Paper crinkled as he balled the letters in his fist. Significantly more than presumptuous of Vincent to make such arrangements and not inform him. It wasn't as if Vincent did not know where to find him, and they had seen each other a couple of days ago, never mind the fact they had traveled together in the same carriage for three days on the journey from Rotherham to London. Many opportunities for Vincent to discuss the books with him. Yet he chose not to.

Typical of Vincent. Arranging things as *he* saw fit, without bothering to consult others. Hell, it likely did not even occur to Vincent that he should consult Oliver. And where the hell would Oliver store all these books? They all could not fit in the shop.

Letting out a frustrated grunt, he dragged his hand through his hair.

"Lord Oliver, did I read the instructions incorrectly? Father said to simply deliver the lot of them here," Joseph said, and not without a good measure of hesitation.

Briefly closing his eyes, Oliver took a moment to gather his composure. Wouldn't do to vent his frustration on the wrong target. Joseph had done nothing wrong, save follow Vincent's instructions. Instructions the man had no right to give.

"No, the fault does not lie with you. It is I who misunderstood." Never should have even mentioned the library to Vincent. With another shake of his head, he motioned to the crates stacked in the back of the wagon. "You can bring the rest inside."

As Joseph hauled the crates from the wagon, Oliver went through the office to the front section of the shop to help Mr. Wallace close for the evening. After he bid good night to the elderly man, he returned to the office to find it near overrun with crates. At the sight of Joseph standing by the door with more than a hint of worry pulling his brow, Oliver kept the curse from making its way past his lips.

"That's all of them. Is there anything else you need, my lord?"

"No. That will be all." Oliver reached behind a stack of crates and grabbed his greatcoat from the hook on the wall. "Thank you, Joseph. And my apologies for the misunderstanding."

He followed the young man out the back door and bid him good night. Joseph settled on the driver's bench, and with a soft click to the horses, he guided the team down the alley, the rattle of the empty wagon echoing off the brick walls of the surrounding buildings.

"Damn you, Vincent," Oliver muttered as he locked the door. In the back of his mind, behind the ever-mounting frustration, resided the knowledge he should not feel so annoyed with Vincent. The man was simply being generous. Those fifteen unexpected crates had not come from a desire to shove his wealth in Oliver's face or to make him feel inadequate because his little bookshop could not afford more. But…

Bloody hell. Why couldn't Vincent at least mention such matters to him?

Tugging on his gloves, he went down the alley. Those not-so-subtle pieces of advice that screamed Vincent's doubts in his abilities, the condescending arched brow of silent disagreement, the way Vincent assumed more often than he asked, the damn black coat Vincent had felt compelled to purchase for him, and now the books…

Enough.

This time Vincent had gone too far.

* * *

"His lordship is in the study."

Oliver handed his greatcoat to Vincent's butler.

The butler's thin lips curled just the tiniest bit as he took Oliver's coat. Tall and slim and with his spine ramrod straight, the older man appeared as though he only reluctantly allowed Oliver and his old coat, the hem frayed and mud flecked, into his master's stately town house. After countless visits over the past year, Oliver had decided it was simply the man's way.

Yet tonight it rankled. The cold, haughty stare abraded the nerves already bristling with affront. So much so that Oliver turned on his heel, dismissing the butler without a word.

His footsteps clicked, quick and determined, on the pristine gray marble floor as he made his way across the entrance hall. Taking a familiar path, he went up the stairs to Vincent's study. Without bothering to knock, he opened the first door on the right and flicked it shut behind him.

"Good evening, Oliver." Tucked behind his massive desk, Vincent made a notation on the paper before him.

"It would have been much appreciated if you had informed me you purchased the remainder of Middleton's library before the crates arrived."

"They arrived. Good," Vincent said, looking up from the paper.

Oliver stopped before Vincent's desk. "Good? That is all you have to say?"

A furrow of confusion briefly pulled Vincent's brow. A furrow that only served as fodder for the frustration churning in Oliver's belly.

"Did the shipment arrive intact?"

Oliver ignored Vincent's question. "How much did you pay for them?" Vincent likely would not have known the true value of the books. The man had not even laid eyes on them—Oliver knew it as fact, for after that morning by the pond, Vincent had not left the country house until they had departed for London. Hopefully he had not underpaid, though more than likely he overpaid in a blatant show of the size of his bank account.

"A more than generous price."

He clenched his hands at his sides. "How generous, Vincent?" It should not irritate him so much. Not as if the money had gone to him. Still…

"The price matters not, Oliver," Vincent replied, crisp and succinct, as if they discussed some business transaction.

"Yes. It does."

Vincent held up a hand. "Please, don't protest. While it was obvious you wanted the books, I purchased them to assist Mrs. Middleton."

Completely altruistic reason, Oliver couldn't help but concede. He himself had wished he had the means to offer the poor widow assistance. Yet it did not excuse Vincent for completely neglecting to mention the purchase to him, let alone ask if he wanted the books for the shop.

"My lack of funds wasn't the only reason I limited the purchase." Leave it to Vincent to assume money was his only impediment. "The shop could not hold all the books even if I had the means. Hell, I have so many crates stacked in the office I can barely make my way to my desk."

"Then keep them here if you are in need of space. My garret is more than sufficient to accommodate them."

Oliver scowled. The man had a bloody answer for everything. "Should not have to keep them in crates. They deserve to be shelved."

Vincent arched a brow, displaying a hint of incredulous exasperation and making Oliver feel like an irrational, demanding child, grasping at anything to sustain his protests. But damnation, he wasn't a child, and he would damn well tell Vincent where he could take his condescending attitude if he did not put a stop to it very soon.

"If that is your primary concern, then I suggest you invest in enlarging the shop."

"I wouldn't need to enlarge the shop if you hadn't purchased the books without my consent." He slammed his hands on the desk. "It's *my* shop, Vincent. Not yours!"

Flicking his pen down, Vincent got to his feet. "Enough, Oliver." The words snapped between them.

Enough? A growl rumbled his throat. "Don't you bloody condescend to me."

Briefly closing his eyes, Vincent took a deep breath, his broad chest expanding and contracting. A clear attempt to gather his temper. "I am doing nothing of the sort," he said with forced calm. "My apologies if it appears as such. Now please, stop your protests. The books are yours to do with as you see fit. Sell them, store them, give them away. It matters not to me. They are simply the by-product of my desire to help a widowed young woman who, for all appearances, had no one else able to offer her assistance."

Oliver's hands clenched at his sides again. Obviously Vincent didn't understand the source of his anger. And in typical Vincent fashion, he felt himself justified in his actions, and that was enough for him. Discussion over.

Hell no. Not tonight. But before Oliver could press his point again, Vincent continued.

"However there is something I do need to discuss with you. Likely should discuss it later, since you are not pleased with me at the moment, but I will not have it delayed."

Vincent picked up a neat fold of papers from his desk and speared Oliver with a stare, so pensive and solemn, so very grave, it took him aback. The ever-mounting frustration stuttered to a halt.

"Mrs. Middleton's situation has been weighing heavily on my mind," Vincent said, his gaze boring into Oliver's. "It was inexcusably irresponsible of Middleton to have not made arrangements for his wife. While he certainly did not expect to meet with an accident at such a young age, accidents do happen. They are beyond our control. But by making her his wife, he made a lifetime commitment to her. If he had cared for her in the least bit, he should have chosen her security over something as frivolous as books."

Frivolous? His livelihood was now frivolous? Oliver opened his mouth, the protest on his tongue, but Vincent held up a hand to stay him.

"They were not the man's business. They were an indulgence. Not as irresponsible as gambling one's fortune away—he at least left her with assets—but a selfish indulgence nonetheless." Vincent dropped his attention to the papers in his hand. He ran a contemplative fingertip along the crease. "I have been busier than usual these past few days, but with good cause. When I returned to Town, I met with my solicitor and banker. I have revised my will." He held out the fold of papers to Oliver. "Copies for you. Do you have a safe?"

Stunned by Vincent's gravity and not quite certain how the man's will related to him, Oliver shook his head and took the proffered papers.

"Then have the bank keep them for you. You should read them before you lock them up. If you have any questions, simply ask, but it is relatively straightforward. There's an annuity for Grafton's son once he reaches his majority, a bit for Grafton as well, and pensions for my staff, but the bulk of my estate will go to you. I have also set up an account in your name. The papers are there, as well."

Oliver's mind seized with shock. He flipped through the papers, found the ones from the bank. His eyes flared. "Thirty thousand pounds?" The sheer enormity of the sum left him reeling.

"You can do with it as you please. Enlarge the shop, if you so desire, or purchase an apartment in a better area of town. But I would hope you don't spend it all in a great rush. In the event something would happen to me, I want you at the very least to have the account. I want to make certain you are provided for. I would have done nothing less for a wife, and therefore I will see to it and more for you."

Oliver's bruised pride reared its head, demanding to be heard. "I'm *not* your wife, Vincent." The size of his bank account might be beyond paltry in comparison to Vincent's, but he wasn't some helpless woman, unable to fend for herself. Hell, if nothing else, Oliver had shoved the proof up Vincent's no-longer-virgin arse a week ago. If the man needed a reminder, he was more than happy to bend him over the desk and oblige him.

"I'm aware of that, Oliver." His gaze darted over Oliver's shoulder. "And please, keep your voice down," he admonished.

Paper crinkled harshly as his fist closed around Vincent's will and the damn papers from the bank. He'd bloody well shout if that was what it would take to get through Vincent's thick skull. The will was one thing, but the account?

Impotent frustration pounded through his veins, but when he next spoke, his voice was low, determined, backed by iron. "I have told you before, I don't want your money. I don't want new apartments, and I prefer my shop just the way it is. I don't need you to take care of me. I'm quite capable of doing it on my own."

"I'm aware of that as well," Vincent replied, resolute and unbending. "But I want you to have the account."

Oliver shook his head. "No, I refuse to accept it."

"Please, don't argue with me. It's done. Just accept it. You needn't even thank me."

"Exactly! It's done. You made the decision for me. Yet again."

There was that flicker of confusion across Vincent's brow again.

"You don't understand, do you? Just because I submit to you in the bedchamber does not mean I submit to you outside of it. You have no right to make decisions that impact me without discussing them with me beforehand. I saw you two nights ago, and you mentioned not a word of your meetings with your solicitor or banker or the damn books." He lifted the papers in his hand. "Yet another glaring example of the fact you don't see me as an equal."

There it was—the crux of the problem.

He had thought Vincent had finally abandoned his attempts to push money on him. It had been a year since he last found not-so-random coins on his dresser or stray pound notes in a coat pocket. Vincent no longer outright offered to manage Oliver's investments or made comments about the state of his lodgings. The man had grown more subtle, making it easy for Oliver to brush the instances aside as minor annoyances that came part and parcel with a strong man like Vincent. Yet behind all those condescending arched brows and Vincent's penchant for assumption lurked the hard truth of their relationship.

Vincent did not see him as an equal.

Tonight's events illustrated the fact so loud and clear, Oliver could no longer turn a blind eye.

To be faced with the truth, to actually hold proof of it in his hand, hurt more than he could have imagined.

And he'd actually rendered Vincent mute and slack-jawed from confusion. *Bloody hell*. Not a good sign at all.

Oliver dragged a hand through his hair, then shook his head. "I truly wonder if you can ever understand." He tossed the papers onto Vincent's desk and turned on his heel. He needed to leave before he said something he would truly regret. And he needed time to think, to answer the question that now filled his head.

Knowing the truth of how his lover viewed him, could he stay with Vincent?

Chapter Eight

Heart heavy with pain and crushing disappointment and more than a lingering trace of frustration, Oliver reached for the brass doorknob of Vincent's study. A large hand closed around his upper arm. The grip hard and harsh, long fingers digging into his muscles.

"*No.*"

The hoarse, desperate urgency stopped Oliver short. He looked over his shoulder.

All the color had drained from Vincent's face, his eyes wide with absolute shock and horror. For a long moment, he moved not a muscle. Oliver swore even his chest had gone still.

"Vincent?"

The man's gaze dropped to his hold on Oliver's arm. He blinked, then released him. Vincent brought his arm slowly to his side and flexed his shaking hand. His lashes swept down. "Please don't leave me again."

Oliver turned from the door. "I'm not leaving you. Just leaving your house for a bit. I'm frustrated and hurt and…" That look of utter fear had not lessened one bit, so he reiterated, "I'm *not* leaving you, Vincent." He hoped to God he had not just lied. With all his heart, he prayed it would not come to that, but he had a sinking feeling it just might. He let out a weary sigh. "You truly don't understand why I'm upset, do you?"

"Of course I do," Vincent grumbled. "The books. The account. You don't like it when I help you."

"But do you understand why?" Perhaps he could explain it a different way. "Success comes easy to you. You always earned the best marks in school. Anything you touch turns to gold or coal. You have always been well respected with a strong family name behind you. Whereas I'm…I'm the opposite of you. I had to work hard just so I wouldn't get sent down from school. Nothing has ever come easy for me."

"You let me help you at school. Why won't you allow me to help you now?"

"Because I'm a man now, and I want to do things on my own. Because I need to do things on my own."

"But you accept help from Mr. Wallace," Vincent countered. "You've had the bookshop a year and never once expressed anything but appreciation for the fact he's remained on to assist you."

"He's not you, Vincent. You're the man I love. Your opinion means a great deal to me, and I need to feel you believe I'll succeed. I can't help but feel every time you offer assistance that it's your way of telling me I'm failing. That I'm not capable. That you *believe* I'm not capable."

Vincent scowled. "I have never said you were not capable."

"You have not said it explicitly, but it's how you make me feel." Hell, did he want too much? Vincent loved him. Spent time with him outside of a bedchamber. Didn't make him feel as though mere association with him was a dirty secret he needed to hide. Shouldn't that be enough?

There had been a time when it would have been more than enough. But that time had long passed. Deep down, he knew it would eventually ruin their relationship. And damnation, after all they had been through together, he deserved Vincent's respect. He needed the man he loved to see him as an equal, yet could he?

Above all, above the differences in their bank accounts and their status in society, Oliver truly feared the sheer fact he submitted to him in the bedchamber made it impossible for Vincent to see him as anything but someone who needed a strong, steady hand to guide him."

Oliver sagged against the door and shook his head.

"Don't do that."

He looked askance at Vincent looming above him.

"Don't shake your head. It makes me worry you're going to leave me."

Oliver let out another weary sigh. "Do you respect me, Vincent?"

"Of course I do. I love you," he added in barely a whisper.

He nodded. Vincent was not the type of man who could give his heart to someone he did not at least marginally respect. "But do you respect me as an equal? Because the way you treat me sometimes makes me truly doubt it."

Suddenly aware he leaned against a door servants were apt to pass by on the other side, he pushed up and crossed the room. Vincent followed on his heels, so close his breaths practically scorched Oliver's neck.

Stopping at the chair facing Vincent's desk, he turned to Vincent. The man's concerned gaze tracked his every movement, as though fearing he'd run from the room at any moment.

"How would you feel if I told you how to manage your properties?"

Vincent's lips twisted in affront. "I don't believe you consider yourself an expert in property management."

"I wasn't aware you had ever owned a bookshop."

"But it's a business."

"And therefore it is something you excel at, whereas I do not? I will grant you are more astute with business matters than I am, but I don't meddle in your affairs. I don't prod you to buy more properties or offer an opinion beyond encouragement and support."

"You cannot claim I am not supportive of your endeavors."

"That's not what I'm saying, Vincent. You are supportive. But it's so much more than how you show your support." He briefly closed his eyes, struggling to find the right words. "By not consulting me on matters that affect me, you are making decisions for me. I doubt it even occurred to you that maybe you should have consulted me in regard to Middleton's books, the changes to your will, or the account. Can you see how that would make me feel like you look on me as someone who isn't as capable as you? I don't need your guidance, Vincent. Just because I put myself in your hands in the bedchamber does not mean I want nor need that outside of the bedchamber."

Brow furrowed, Vincent's gaze swept over his face, then drifted somewhere over Oliver's shoulder. Vincent possessed an agile mind. Hopefully he understood, because Oliver did not know how else he could explain it.

For a long moment, the man remained silent and still. Just when all hope began to drain from Oliver's heart, when that horrible, numbing sense that this was truly the end began to settle over him, those brilliant blue eyes met his.

"I do respect you as an equal, Oliver," he said, voice low yet filled with conviction. "Please don't doubt it. If anything, I envy you."

"You envy me?" Vincent, who succeeded at everything he put his mind to, envied *him*?

"You have a strength, a confidence in yourself I wish I possessed. Regardless of others' opinions, you remain true to yourself. You have been, and I hope will always remain, the one person in my life I can rely upon. And contrary to what you may believe I think, your willingness to submit so completely to me in the bedchamber, to put your trust in my hands, holds me in awe."

Oliver took a breath, a counterargument on his tongue, but snapped his jaw shut as Vincent's words turned about in his head. He considered himself an average individual. A hard fact he had long ago accepted. The proof lay before him every time he walked into his shabby apartments. Yet it was becoming clear to him that Vincent judged him on an entirely different scale. One that had nothing at all to do with Oliver's bank account or the marks he had received at school—physical evidence he had long believed Vincent held in the utmost regard. But a scale where everything had to do with the intangible.

Definitely a major shift to wrap his mind around, but he couldn't dispute the strength of Vincent's sincerity.

His lover truly did respect him as an equal and even envied him a bit.

Amazing.

"I apologize for making you feel otherwise, Oliver. It was not my intention." Vincent squared his shoulders. "But I also won't deny I feel protective of you. Feel a need to help you and take care of you. I know you don't want my assistance, and it's not that I believe you necessarily need my assistance, but I want to help you in any way I can. It's because I love you and I don't want anything bad to come to you. I want you to be happy. I wish you could understand that and not see it as a slight against you."

When put that way, it made Oliver feel like an ungrateful brat for even questioning his lover's motives. The man's hurt was unmistakable. The thought of willingly accepting help from Vincent still caused his hackles to rise, but his shortcomings weren't Vincent's fault. He couldn't continue to punish the man for them.

"I do understand, Vincent. At least now I do." He had thrown Vincent's penchant for assumption in his face, and here Oliver had been just as guilty. Not a comfortable feeling at all.

A bit of the tension gripping his broad shoulders eased from Vincent's frame. "I know I can be overbearing at times, and for that I apologize. I should have consulted you, and I did not. It will not happen again. You have my word. But know I did not neglect to consult you out of some belief you were unworthy of such consideration. Based on your own information, Mrs. Middleton clearly needed assistance. Purchasing the remainder of the library and giving it to you seemed the logical solution. I certainly have no use for so many books, yet you own a bookshop. I never predicted it would upset you. You love books. You're always after me for mine. I thought the delivery would make you happy."

"I can see how you would believe that, and I never did mention the lack of space in the shop," Oliver conceded. "I don't doubt the goodness of your intentions, but I still can't accept the books. Fifteen crates are just too…much." Vincent opened his mouth, but before he could get a word out, Oliver said, "I will sell them for you though, and I'll charge you a fee for the service." He'd have to work with Mr. Wallace to shuffle some inventory and take Vincent up on his offer to utilize his garret for storage, but the arrangement would not leave his pride bruised.

Vincent pursed his mouth, then gave a crisp nod. "We can negotiate the fee later."

"No more than thirty percent."

That earned him a frown. Likely Vincent had hoped to negotiate a heftier fee. "Thirty it is, then."

Oliver tipped his head in agreement.

Vincent's gaze dropped to his polished evening shoes, then met Oliver's again. Worry weighed heavily on his face. Dark brows lowered and mouth drawn in a straight line. "I thought you were happy with me, but obviously you have not been blissfully content for some time. I wish you would have voiced your concerns before they built to this point. The last thing I want is to risk losing you again."

"I have been happy with you, Vincent. I just don't like fighting with you."

"Nor I you. But it doesn't have to be an argument. I simply ask that you not burden me with the worry at the end of the day that I might have said something to ruffle your feathers. You may have the ability to see right through me, but it's one I have yet to fully acquire when it comes to you."

Vincent made him sound so complicated and…prickly. All he wanted was the man's love and for him to respect him. Two things he now felt certain he possessed. "All right. I will let you know whenever my *feathers get ruffled*." Least he could do, considering Vincent had more than met him halfway.

"Thank you." Vincent stepped around him and picked up the papers on his desk, the once-neat folds now crumpled. "I need you to accept this." That grave, solemn stare had returned. Tension once again gripped every line of Vincent's strong body. "Please, it's important to me. Since there's no longer a need for me to take a wife, I will never take one. I only want you. Hell, if I could take you to wife, I would—"

"I'm not a woman, Vincent." His stomach sank, as that perfect sense of complete and absolute happiness began to drain out of him.

Letting out a sigh, Vincent rubbed the back of his neck. "I am quite aware of your masculinity. That's not the point I am trying to make. While I accept as fact that our relationship is against the law, it can be more than frustrating at times and not only because of the constant need for discretion. If I took a wife tomorrow, pledged myself to her, no one would bat an eye or question my commitment to her. Yet because you are a man, the law and the church have decreed what I feel for you is somehow wrong. It doesn't seem at all…*fair*," Vincent said with a threatening scowl that would have sent any clergyman scurrying toward the closest door. "But I will not allow the law or the church to completely tie my hands. I cannot predict what the future holds. If something were to happen to me, I want to ensure you are provided for. You are…the only person in my life who has ever truly cared about me. I want my estate to go to you. But if for some reason the will is contested, then at least you have the account."

"Why would anyone contest it?"

"Because I have changed my will so the bulk of my fortune will no longer go to Grafton or to any family member. He could contest it, either on his behalf or the behalf of his son. He has the means to engage in a lengthy legal battle, if he so desires. I don't believe he would go to such extremes, but it is not a risk I am willing to take. Hence the account. It is in your name and your name only. No one can take it from you."

Well, that explained the thirty thousand pounds, but it seemed all so complex. He appreciated Vincent's sentiment far more than he could ever express, and quite strangely Vincent's desire to take him to wife made perfect sense. A connection he'd have never made on his own. The whole point of marriage was to produce children, a desire Oliver did not have in the slightest. Yet to Vincent, a man who valued his standing in society and needed the esteem of his peers, above all marriage stood for the physical proof of commitment. Though if Vincent started calling him wife, he'd definitely have issues with it. But...

His attention was drawn to the papers in Vincent's hand. The weight of the fortune they held more than intimidated him, never mind the possibility of engaging in a lengthy legal battle with Grafton, the current heir to the powerful Saye and Sele marquisate.

No, Vincent did not need to go to such lengths for him. It wasn't necessary. "Vincent, you don't need—"

"Oliver, please. I know you can't depend on your father or your brother. Your grandmother is not a wealthy woman, either. While I am alive, it is not a concern. I am here if ever you have need. I don't know what would become of me if you were taken from me. If I didn't have you in my life. I certainly would not be anywhere near all right. But if something ever happened to me, I...I just need to know you would want for nothing. Please say you understand."

The same fragile vulnerability he had glimpsed a week ago now filled Vincent's gaze.

The pieces clicked together.

The way Vincent had left him after their night together in Rotherham. Their resulting conversation by the pond. He had thought he had eased Vincent's mind—the man hadn't seemed out of sorts since then. But he now saw the true source of Vincent's unease. It had not been the act of giving up control that left Vincent shaken, but the fact Vincent had done so with *him*. Vincent loved him, and he certainly told Oliver enough for him to believe it. But giving himself over to Oliver must have somehow driven it home to him. Combine that with their conversations about the Widow Middleton's situation... Vincent had not been merely shaken. He had been scared.

Financial security was something Vincent knew well. Something solid and tangible. Something he could control. And changing his will and creating the account for Oliver was his solution. It had nothing at all to do with Vincent trying to find a new way to give Oliver money he had not earned on his own. And everything to do with how much Vincent needed him.

"Yes." Oliver nodded, more than a bit awed at the depth of Vincent's love. "I understand."

"Then don't argue with me over this matter. Take it and ease my mind."

"All right." He took the papers from Vincent's outstretched hand. "But you are all that matters to me. You're all I want." All the money in the world could not take Vincent's place in his heart. He wanted to wrap his arms around him, hold him close, but they were at Vincent's town house. Even behind the closed door of his study, Vincent had never allowed such an intimacy. The servants were a continual presence his lover could not ignore.

"You're all I want as well, Oliver." Slow and tentative, Vincent reached out, took hold of Oliver's other hand, and gave it a squeeze. A shuddering breath expanded his broad chest. "Forever."

Oliver's heart clenched. The hell with the servants. The damn door was shut.

Tugging Vincent by the hand, he pulled him close and wrapped his arms around him. Buried his face in his chest. It took not even a moment for those familiar, strong arms to wrap around him. Vincent held him so tightly it made it hard to breathe, but Oliver did not mind in the slightest. Vincent's breaths fanned the top of his head, and then warm lips pressed against his temple in the lightest of kisses. Chaste and pure. Oliver tipped his face up, seeking more. Vincent's mouth found his, the deep kiss sealing forever more solidly than a mere fold of papers.

Vincent pulled back just enough to break the kiss. "I want you to stay with me tonight."

"Of course. We'll go to my apartments after supper."

"No. Not there. Here."

He looked up at Vincent in question. "Are you giving your staff the night off?"

Vincent shook his head. "But you can still stay the night. I have plenty of guest rooms. One's next to mine, though they're not connected like at the country house." His hands drifted down to palm Oliver's arse. "I want you in *my* bed."

Oliver blinked in shock. They had spent countless hours in the old bed at his apartments, and always shared the bed in what had become his room at Vincent's country house. But never had Oliver so much as laid his head on Vincent's own bed. Hadn't even stepped foot in Vincent's bedchamber at the town house. Sex anywhere there had never been an option.

Yet it was now.

A smile curved his lips. "I would like that very much." He would need to leave before dawn, steal into the guest room without gaining the servants' notice. Play Vincent's role. But it meant more than he could express that Vincent wanted him to stay.

"It won't be every night, but tonight I want…"

"Of course. I understand. A change of scenery every now and then doesn't do any harm. Though…what type of bed do you have? Four posters? Sturdy headboard? Do you believe it's up to the task?" He tipped his hips forward and rubbed against Vincent.

Vincent went stiff. "Oliver." Dear Lord, the man looked positively scandalized. "I don't intend to…" His gaze darted to the closed door. "I am not going to tie you up *here*."

Oliver could not help it. He chuckled. One would think he had asked Vincent to bugger him under his father's roof. "You do intend for us to do more than sleep, correct?"

"Most assuredly, but you'll need to be quiet." He dropped his voice to a low, commanding rumble. "Think you can do that, boy? Can you hold back your shouts when I finally allow you to have your release?"

Oliver's lashes fluttered. His spine went lax even as anticipation began to wind its way into his veins. "Yes, milord. I can be quiet. I promise." He would do anything for Vincent, and staying quiet was a small price to pay to share his lover's bed.

Vincent's eyes darkened to a lust-banked deep blue. One edge of his mouth curled in distinct challenge. "We shall see about that."

Chapter Nine

After prodding the fire in the hearth, Vincent leaned the iron poker against the marble surround and stood. He took the small brass clock from the mantle and angled the face so it caught the light from the fire. Ten minutes until midnight.

He scowled at the black hands. Perhaps he should have told Oliver eleven o'clock. His valet always retired shortly after himself. The servant would have been abed by eleven tonight. His other staff as well, at least those who would have cause to be on the second floor of the house.

Were the hands even moving at all? He stared hard at the clock, and after what felt like an exceedingly long moment, the larger black hand moved forward.

Letting out a short, frustrated grunt, he replaced the clock on the mantle.

Next time, definitely eleven. Well, perhaps half past eleven. The kitchen staff had a tendency to linger overlong in their duties. And the footman stationed in the entrance hall would not retire until midnight.

No, no. Midnight was the most prudent time.

He glanced over his shoulder to his bed, the coverlet already turned back courtesy of his valet. Only the fire lit the room. He had extinguished the bedside candle a good half hour ago lest any servants travel by his door and wonder if he'd fallen asleep with it lit. Everything was at the ready, down to the bottle of oil he had stowed in the bedside table drawer.

Nothing at all for him to do but wait.

He grabbed the glass of brandy from the mantle and downed the last splash within. Did he really need a footman to watch the front door after his butler retired for the night? He couldn't recall the last time he'd had a late-night caller.

Nope, no need for the footman to remain on duty so late. Tomorrow he'd have a word with his housekeeper and have the man's schedule adjusted.

He shifted his weight. The floorboards creaked faintly beneath his bare feet, the sound filling the quiet surrounding him. He reached for the decanter of brandy on the mantle, but stopped before his hand closed around the bottle. The last instance he had partaken more than he should before bed, the night had ended with Oliver's prick in his arse. Not that there was any worry of a repeat tonight. Definitely not. He needed the man under him.

An ice-cold prickly sensation tightened his gut, threatened to flare up his chest. With effort, he tamped it down. *Oliver didn't leave me.* The knowledge offered considerable comfort, but if his lover scared him like that again, Vincent would not be responsible for his actions. He swore his heart had stopped when Oliver had made to leave the study. A trace of that all-encompassing panic still lingered in his veins.

Yes, that was it. Not nervous at all. He just still hadn't fully recovered from watching Oliver walk away from him in an eerily similar manner as he had done a good year ago…when his lover had actually left him. He tugged on the fabric belt of his navy dressing gown, righting the tie at his waist. In any case, there was no logical reason to be on edge. He had shared a bed with Oliver countless nights.

Tonight was just one more night to add to a long list of many, many more to come. No need to worry Oliver would keep his concerns bottled up until they exploded in a repeat of their argument in the study. And above all, the man had accepted the will and the account.

Vincent nodded. Yes, indeed. Everything was in order. Or would be, if the clock would just hurry the hell up.

A hand settled on his lower back. Vincent started, then relaxed as the heat from that hand seeped through his dressing gown. He knew who he would find behind him before he turned around.

Oliver gave him a sheepish smile. "Didn't mean to startle you, but you did say to be quiet," he said in an undertone. "Four times, I might add."

He tipped his head in acknowledgment. No use denying the truth. Once in the study before supper, and by the time they had departed the study after their meal, he had managed to work three more reminders into their conversation.

Oliver's lips quirked. "I like your bedchamber."

"I like you in it." He swept his gaze over Oliver's body. He had come to Vincent's bedchamber dressed in only brown trousers and a white shirt, the collar open and exposing his throat. No shoes, no waistcoat, not even his spectacles. The untidy waves of his dark hair framed his face. An erection tented the placket of his trousers. Oliver flexed his hands at his sides but otherwise stood perfectly still, his full attention fixed on Vincent and his eyes filled with undeniable love.

The most beautiful sight Vincent had ever beheld.

He took a moment to savor it; then the impatience that had built over the past hour got the better of him.

His arms shot out to tug the shirt from Oliver's trousers and whisk it over his head, not caring in the slightest where it landed. A quick tug on the placket and he shoved the man's trousers down his slim hips. His erection sprung free, jutting from his body.

A shiver racked Oliver. A shiver that Vincent knew had nothing to do with the temperature of the room.

Oliver's agile tongue darted out to swipe across his full bottom lip. Unable to resist, Vincent gripped the back of Oliver's skull and drew him in for a kiss. Slanted his lips over Oliver's, swept his tongue into his mouth, drank up his sigh. Oliver sagged against him, his body pliant and willing in his arms.

He pulled back, breaking the kiss. With his fingers still gripping Oliver's hair, he stared down at his lover. The quick pants of the man's breaths fanned Vincent's lips. "But I would like you better in my bed."

A moan shook Oliver's throat. "Yes. *Please.*"

Need shot through him. Without giving it a moment's thought, Vincent grabbed Oliver by the waist and tossed him on the bed. With a faint little sound of surprise, Oliver landed in the center of the mattress, his prick slapping his stomach, the ropes beneath creaking in protest of the abrupt movement. Oliver pushed his hair from his eyes, then went still, his dark, fathomless gaze pinned on Vincent.

Vincent unclenched his hands at his sides and took a moment to rein in the almost unstoppable impulse to leap onto the bed. To cover Oliver. To have the man beneath him.

But that wouldn't do at all. At least not yet.

He had, in essence, issued a challenge to Oliver in the study. Far be it for him to not see it through, and he was quite looking forward to testing the limits of Oliver's ability to remain quiet.

When he felt somewhat in control, he crossed to the side of the bed. The fire from the hearth just reached the mattress. The soft golden light played happily across Oliver's bare skin, highlighting sleek, compact muscles and the glistening drop of fluid beaded on the head of his hard cock.

His lover was exactly where he belonged. In his bed.

The last lingering thread of fear finally vanished, leaving only lust and need and pure, true love.

Oliver was his. Would remain his always. Just as Vincent would always remain Oliver's.

"Love you," he whispered, forcing the words past his suddenly constricted throat.

"Love you too."

His heart swelled, nearly filling his entire chest. He couldn't stop a mirror of Oliver's content smile from curving his lips. Then he let the haughty mask fall over his features. "Now be a good boy and raise your arms over your head."

A full-body tremor shook Oliver. Another swipe of his tongue over his bottom lip, then he did as Vincent bid, lifting his arms over his head without a trace of hesitation. With one hand clasped around his other wrist, he laid his body out for Vincent in a silent offering.

Intent on giving Oliver everything he desired, Vincent remained where he stood. Let the anticipation build. The fire behind him warmed his back, but it had nothing on the lust drumming through his veins, heating his skin. Oliver's nipples had hardened into tight buds that seemed to scream for Vincent's attention. He watched as a bead of fluid dropped from the tip of Oliver's prick, landing on his flat abdomen. He would get to that soon enough, but first…

He tugged on the belt of his dressing gown, shrugged his shoulders, and let the garment slip from his arms. Leaving the dressing gown pooled on the floorboards, he placed a knee on the bed.

The creak of the ropes beneath the mattress cut through the silence, unnaturally loud. He fought to keep the wince from crossing his features. He swore his bed wasn't normally so noisy, but it wasn't as if he had ever shared it with another or had reason before to be concerned about the creak of ropes. So much for any plans to pound Oliver into the bed tonight. Fortunately he didn't need brute strength to keep Oliver on the cusp of a climax for hours.

Moving slowly, he made his way up Oliver's body. The man immediately spread his legs, knees coming up to bracket Vincent's hips in undeniable welcome. His eyes drifted shut as his chin tipped up, exposing the lines of his throat and the rapid beat of his pulse, in a glorious display of willing submission.

Crouched over Oliver, Vincent bent his head and pressed a reverent kiss to his lover's throat. Then worked his way down: the delicate hollow at the base of his throat, the curve of his collar bone, and directly over his heart. Each press of lips to skin light and delicate, containing not a trace of the desire clamoring within him to be set free.

"Remember. Quiet," he whispered against Oliver's flawless chest. Head bowed, he felt Oliver's nod in the trace movement of the mattress. "And don't move. Nor are you allowed to climax until my cock's buried in your arse."

The absolute lack of movement of the man beneath him, down to the chest that had gone momentarily still, was akin to a sweetly sighed *yes, milord.*

Reassured Oliver would try his best to do exactly as Vincent bid, he captured one nipple between his teeth and began to torment Oliver. He tugged on the sensitive tip, sucked hard, plied it with his tongue, then shifted to the other and lavished it with attention.

Oliver's quickening pants filled his ears, the slight hiss behind each breath a telltale sign his lover had clenched his teeth in his fight to hold back his pleas for more. Vincent pushed harder, determined to take him right to the edge and hold him there. To make it a night the man would never forget.

He dragged his lips down Oliver's chest. Deftly avoiding the man's prick, he lapped up the proof of Oliver's desire from his lower abdomen, felt the taut muscles quiver beneath his tongue. Then Vincent rocked back onto his knees, splayed his hands over Oliver's inner thighs, and pushed.

Oliver instantly yielded, bringing his knees up to his chest and putting his ballocks on display. An invitation Vincent could not refuse.

He dropped down, drew one testicle into his mouth, and gently sucked. Oliver's breaths hitched, the muscles beneath Vincent's hands tight as an archer's bow. The musky scent of Oliver's arousal poured off him. Yet still, not one threadbare whimper passed his lover's obedient lips.

Pulling free with a crude, wet sound that seemed to smack against Vincent's aching erection, he cupped the round globes of Oliver's arse and lifted his hips from the bed, fully exposing that tight, perfect hole. The muscles there briefly contracted, as if Oliver could feel the force of Vincent's gaze. Vincent's cock instinctively jumped at the memory of his lover's body wrapped around his length, eager and needy to experience it again. Yet he held back and stayed focused on Oliver. On cranking the pleasure to unbelievable heights. He knew just how amazingly good it felt to have a man lick his arse—Oliver had introduced him to that particular pleasure. Beyond time he repaid the favor.

He bowed his head. A jolt shot through Oliver, briefly shaking his limbs, at the first touch of the tip of Vincent's tongue to the smooth expanse of skin behind his lover's ballocks. Vincent fought back the smug grin and traced a path down to Oliver's entrance.

With each flick of his tongue over the puckered skin, he could hear the force of his lover's need. Each pant hitching sharper. Each hiss of air between his teeth harsher, louder.

The moment Oliver's body opened for him, he stabbed his tongue inside.

Absolute silence suddenly pressed against his ears. He lifted his head.

Oliver's eyes were clamped shut, bottom lip held tight between his teeth. Pure, unadulterated need was written all over his face. Obvious proof Oliver was doing his damnedest to hold back a climax.

While behind closed doors, his lover would do anything for him, expend every bit of effort within himself to follow Vincent's orders. Oliver's willingness to please him humbled him like nothing else could.

He shifted up his lover's body. Pressed a light kiss to that poor abused lower lip.

"So good. So perfect." Consumed with awe, it was all Vincent could do to give voice to the praise, the admiration, filling his entire being.

The sweat-slicked chest beneath his own expanded on a greedy gasp of air. Oliver blinked his eyes open.

The plea, the shout for more, the sheer desperation in the man's gaze, struck Vincent square in the chest, the force more potent than a prizefighter's blow. It radiated throughout his body, ratcheting the lust to a fever pitch.

He leaned back, broke the contact of their bodies, and reaching into the bedside table drawer, grabbed the bottle of oil.

Oliver's desperate gaze tracked his movements, the weight of his need a physical force prodding Vincent to quickly slick his cock. Urgency pressed against him. He could feel the man teetering on the brink—one touch, one kiss could push him over the edge. And by God, he did not want Oliver going over that edge without him. He needed to be there with him, joined with him. Needed to experience that exact moment when the ecstasy claimed him.

He closed the bottle, let it drop to the rumpled sheet, and shifted back between Oliver's still-spread legs. Holding his prick steady in one hand, he braced his weight on the other and crouched over Oliver.

"It's yours," he murmured as he pushed inside his lover. "All of it, all of me, is yours."

Oliver's arms shot out, fingers tangling in Vincent's hair and hauling him down for a passionate kiss that threatened to pull the orgasm out of Vincent.

Buried only halfway inside Oliver, he stilled his hips. Instinct screamed to break out of Oliver's hold, to pull back from Oliver's delicious mouth, to give himself a moment to regain control so he could keep each thrust slow and quiet.

But the heat and exquisite tightness gripping his cock, the feel of the man beneath him, the blistering need in Oliver's kiss…

He met Oliver's kiss and then some as he slammed deep within his lover. Oliver arched beneath him, taking everything Vincent gave him and greedy for more. The lines between them blurred. He swore he could feel everything Oliver felt. The desire saturating his lover's senses, the way the lust coiled tighter and tighter, stringing his nerves taut, the fight to hold off and savor, the silent pleas for even more, the all-encompassing depth of his love.

That blistering kiss still unbroken, Vincent thrust harder, faster, desperate to get even closer to him. Deep, demanding strokes that soon had him drinking up Oliver's shout of completion and following his lover over the edge.

* * *

The last flicker of flame from the fire in the hearth joined the glowing embers. Oliver did not need his spectacles to see the clock on the mantle to know dawn soon approached. He took a few more moments to simply soak up being with Vincent: the man's strong arms wrapped around him, the rhythmic rise and fall of the broad chest beneath his cheek.

Sleep tugged heavily on his eyes, yet he refused to bow to it. Before Vincent had—well, passed out described it best—what had to have been a good couple of hours ago, Oliver had given him his word he would depart before dawn, before any servants started their day. If he followed his lover and succumbed to sleep, he highly doubted his ability to hold true to his word. No bother, though. He could sleep the morning away in his bed in the guest bedchamber.

A smile curved his mouth. A year and a half ago, he would have never dared to dream of being here with Vincent, in the man's bed. Never even allowed himself to hope for a night like tonight where Vincent's every touch, his every kiss, the way he had looked at Oliver had made him feel...*worshiped*. Yet tonight was the first of many to come with a man who loved him as deeply and truly as Oliver loved him in return. A man who would love him forever.

A man who would have his hide, and rightly so, if his valet found his master's guest snuggled up close to the man's side.

He pressed a kiss to Vincent's chest and reluctantly began to ease out of Vincent's hold. The man's arms tightened, stopping Oliver's progress.

"It's all right, Vincent," Oliver whispered, braced above him. He couldn't make out his features in the darkness, but he would bet the man's eyes were open. "It will be dawn soon. I need to return to the guest bedchamber."

Vincent let out a sleepy sigh. "All right." He coasted his large hands down Oliver's bare back, leaving a path of tingling skin in his wake, and briefly palmed Oliver's arse before dropping his hands to the mattress.

Halfway across the room, Oliver remembered his clothes. Wouldn't do at all to leave them behind. Shaking his head at himself, he turned back, snagged his trousers and shirt from the floor, and quickly tugged them on. The guest bedchamber was but a few paces from Vincent's door; still, prudence and all.

Keeping his steps light and quiet, he crossed to the door and reached for the knob.

"Love you." The murmured words brushed the back of his neck.

"I'm yours too." With a smile on his lips, Oliver slipped out of the room.

Deliberately Bound

Short Story

Lord Oliver Marsden loves books, but what he loves even more is submitting to Vincent. A large purchase for his bookshop, however, puts Oliver in the mood to push Vincent's boundaries in bed farther than ever before.

Lord Vincent Prescot is more than happy to have his lover home. Two days without Oliver were far too long in Vincent's opinion. But before he can toss his lover onto the bed, he realizes Oliver has his own plans for the evening…

Deliberately Bound

July 1824
Rotherham, England

Vincent followed Oliver inside the man's bedchamber and shut the door. As he turned the lock, a sense of peace settled over him.

Two days without his lover. One would think it had been a month given how long last night had felt. It wasn't as if he and Oliver spent every night together when they were in London. But at Rotherham... The country house had felt downright empty without him.

As Oliver crossed the room, he shrugged his black coat from his shoulders and flung it in the general direction of the narrow door leading to the dressing room. "It's good to be home."

"It's good to have you home." Vincent's gaze tracked his lover as the man stopped at the bedside table.

Oliver glanced over his shoulder, fingers poised over the jade cravat pin at his throat. "Did you miss me?" A smile that said he had no doubt of Vincent's answer played on his full lips.

Yet Vincent answered nonetheless. "Yes."

That smile broadened. "Well, I certainly missed you." Oliver turned his attention back to the bedside table. With a faint *clink*, he dropped the cravat pin into the silver dish. "But the appointment was well worth the trouble." He let out a little sigh. The same little blissful sigh that had accompanied a detailed account over supper of the books he'd purchased on his visit to Wakefield.

As easy and unassuming as Oliver was, his dedication and attention to detail—when it involved the acquisition of books—was earning his shop a reputation as the place to go among the booklovers in London. Vincent had overheard more than one individual at White's recently recommend Wallace's Bookshop—the best selection of prime stock in the city. Certainly by now the shop warranted an expansion. Oliver couldn't argue he did not have the funds at his disposal, yet he preferred to keep the shop small. He claimed he liked the intimacy, the quaint atmosphere, and didn't want it to become so large that it occupied all his time. Unlike Vincent, the acquisition of wealth had never been one of his priorities. Not that it showed a lack of ambition, but rather Oliver being true to himself. And Vincent wasn't about to argue with Oliver over his decision. He very much preferred having more of Oliver's time devoted to him.

"When do you need to return to Town?" Vincent asked, as he began to unbutton his navy coat. Since the post ensured business matters reached him in Rotherham, he could remain for a good month or more. Unfortunately, Oliver's obligations and not Vincent's tended to dictate the length of their stays in the country.

Oliver let his waistcoat slip from his arms, the garment falling to the floorboards, and shrugged. "Not for a few days. Perhaps Saturday."

Four days from now? That wouldn't put them back in London for a week, making their absence from Town push three weeks in total. But Vincent held back the urge to question him with a firm reminder that it was Oliver's business and not his own. The man would know when he was needed back at his shop.

Vincent folded his coat and set it on the chair next to the dressing room door. "I'll have word sent to the stables tomorrow to have the carriage prepared to depart on Saturday." In any case, who was he to complain about having more nights than anticipated with

Oliver in Rotherham, where not a single servant spent the night under their roof?

Where there were absolutely no worries anyone else would hear the full force of Oliver's desire.

Lust spiked his senses, wound its way into his veins, settling in his groin. The candles on the mantel provided enough light so he could just make out the faint outline of the sleek lines of Oliver's back beneath his white shirt. His fingers twitched with the need to rip the trousers from his lover's body, to expose the firm round globes of his arse. To toss the man onto the mattress, bind him to the bed, and fuck every last "more" from his lips.

But he stopped himself before he took even one step closer to Oliver.

Patience. He repeated the word in his head.

The entire night awaited them. Many, many hours until his housekeeper arrived at dawn. No reason to rush at all.

Desire firmly in check, he set to work on the buttons of his waistcoat. A warm, summer night's breeze drifted into the room, fluttering the drapes covering the window near the bed. Fabric swooshed softly as Oliver tugged his cravat from his neck, the sound amplified in the quiet room.

Oliver turned from the bedside table. A little smile curved the edges of his lips as he regarded Vincent. "Will you put yourself in my hands tonight?"

Vincent's fingers stilled over the last button on his waistcoat. Apprehension pinched his stomach. He knew exactly when he'd last seen that confident little smile. And the way Oliver had phrased the question—never mind the cravat he had yet to drop to the floorboards—led Vincent to believe he wanted something more than taking him. Not that merely being taken by Oliver held no cause for at least some concern. Oliver had only buggered him twice. Once seven months ago, and second time in early spring. Oliver hadn't asked then, and neither had Vincent. The man had somehow sensed though, exactly what Vincent had wanted on that particular night.

Tonight though...

"Is that a no?" Oliver asked, the smile diming a fraction.

"I'm not certain." There was no point in trying to dissemble with Oliver. His lover had an uncanny ability to see right through him. "Care to enlighten me as to your plan for the evening?"

"I'd rather not. You'll think on what's to come, and it would take some of the…enjoyment out of it. And I believe you will enjoy it. We both will," he added with an all too eager spark in the dark depths of his eyes.

Oliver indulged his whims most every night, submitting so beautifully he never failed to hold Vincent in awe. He *should* let his lover do as he pleased with him on occasion. And it wasn't that he was completely against the idea. He could still remember the strength of his climax from four months ago, an intense slam of sensation that had left him utterly boneless. Not something one tended to forget. The mere memory made his cock jump against the placket of his trousers. Yet…

His gaze was drawn once again to the rumpled cravat in Oliver's hand, the long length dangling from his closed fist.

"If you want to stop at any time, you can simply give the word, Vincent."

He took a deep breath and nodded. He trusted Oliver, and if the man pushed him beyond his comfort, he'd call a stop to whatever Oliver had planned for the evening. The thought calmed the knot in his stomach.

"Is that a yes?"

"Yes," Vincent said, doing his best to appear perfectly composed.

Oliver's smile broadened into a damn grin. "Thank you, Vincent. You can take off your clothes while I gather a few things."

A few things? Vincent's brows drew together as he watched that cravat flutter to the floorboards. His gaze snapped to Oliver as the man opened the top drawer of the dresser and reached inside. He knew exactly what Oliver was after.

The key.

Oliver dropped to his knees before the small trunk beside the dresser. He fit the key into the brass lock. The *click* as the lock opened echoed in the room.

"I thought about nothing but you on the drive back from Wakefield." Oliver lifted the lid and reached into the trunk.

The journey would have taken a good six hours. Vincent suddenly wished the village wasn't such a long distance away, for Oliver obviously had too much time with nothing but his own thoughts. Thoughts which had taken a decidedly wicked turn if his lover's plans involved something from that trunk.

And Vincent knew exactly what that trunk contained, as he had selected each item for their holiday in Rotherham from Oliver's bottom dresser drawer.

Oliver stood, holding a pair of leather cuffs in each hand that answered the question pressing heavily on Vincent's mind and spawned a good dozen more. Cuffs were typically used to restrain. To keep one immobile. The buckles and metal rings on the cuffs clanked as Oliver set the items on the dresser, and then he dropped back down before the trunk. Vincent shifted his weight. The floorboards creaked.

Oliver glanced over his shoulder. "Aren't you going to undress?" He righted his wire-rimmed spectacles, pushing them higher on his nose. "Or have you changed your mind?"

"No, no. Well, yes, I'll undress. No, I haven't changed my mind."

"You'll enjoy it. I'm certain of it."

While Vincent thoroughly enjoyed seeing those cuffs adorn Oliver's wrists and ankles, he wasn't so sure he'd enjoy them on his own. His prick, however, didn't completely object. It pressed, semi-erect, against his trousers.

"And it will be good for you," Oliver added, turning his attention back to that damn trunk. The dark waves of his untidy hair fell forward, obscuring his face, as he rummaged around for whatever the hell he was after.

"In what way will it be good for me?" Chain clinked. Vincent's breaths stuttered.

"You don't always need to be in control. At least not with me." His lover got to his feet. "I love you."

"I love you, too." The words fell from his lips without conscious thought.

Oliver set a familiar length of leather line on the dresser beside the cuffs, then turned back to Vincent and arched a brow.

"Yes?" Vincent asked, meeting Oliver's expectant stare.

"Your clothes?"

He fought down the surge of frustration at himself and instead focused on untying the knot of his cravat. "Yes, of course."

Oliver merely stood there as Vincent removed his clothes, the weight of his gaze a physical force branding every inch of Vincent's skin as it was exposed. Vincent pushed down his drawers and pulled them from his feet, then he set his clothes on the chair with his coat.

He had stood bare before Oliver countless times, yet how was it possible to feel even more naked now?

"Do you plan to remain dressed?" Vincent asked.

Oliver smirked. "No. I'll see to that in a moment. First…come here."

Vincent forced his feet to take him the short distance to stand before his lover.

"Hold out your arm."

The request jarred an old memory. Vincent hesitated before complying. Had it been really only a little more than two years ago when their positions had been reversed, and he had been placing the cuffs on Oliver's wrists for the first time?

Was this how Oliver had felt? Nervous as all hell yet determined to see the evening through? Using the last available notch for the buckle, one that had never seen use before as Oliver's wrists were smaller than his own, Oliver secured a cuff to Vincent's wrist. The leather felt strange against his skin. Thick and foreign. Was Oliver planning a repeat of their first night together? The memory of leather cracking through the air echoed in his head.

He stiffened.

Oliver secured the second cuff. "Relax, Vincent. I'm not going to whip you."

Letting out a huff of self-disgust, he rolled his eyes. *I'm as transparent as damn glass.*

After grabbing the other two cuffs from the dresser, Oliver dropped to his knees. The position was so familiar Vincent's hand had started to reach out to palm the back of the man's head before he recalled himself and pulled his arm back to his side.

"What *do* you plan to do?"

Oliver merely shook his bowed head and secured the cuffs to his ankles. Vincent would bet the Rotherham estate that the man had a smirk affixed to his lips.

"You are enjoying this immensely, aren't you?" Vincent muttered.

"Indeed." Oliver stood. Crossing his arms over his chest, he took a step back. The remnants of that smirk turned into stark appreciation.

It was rather difficult to feel ridiculous when his lover looked at him with such unabashed hunger. Oliver's cock tented the placket of his trousers. A faint flush tinged his cheeks, his breaths quickening. Vincent's own prick began to harden once again; an instinctive response to his lover's arousal.

After what felt like a never-ending moment, Oliver reached for the leather line. "I won't keep you in suspense on every detail. After I tie you to the bed"—his gaze dropped to Vincent's groin—"I'm going to suck your cock."

Vincent's attention was drawn to Oliver's mouth, to those soft, full lips that felt like heaven sliding up and down his prick.

"First though, the bed." Oliver tipped his head in the direction of the four-poster bed.

Fully focused on getting that beautiful mouth on his prick, Vincent complied. He knew exactly where Oliver would want him on the bed, as he'd put Oliver in the position many times. He lay on his back, shifted slightly to the right, putting himself directly in the middle of deep green coverlet, and then lifted his arms over his head so his knuckles grazed the spindles spanning the width of the headboard.

The mattress dipped as Oliver kneeled beside him. With the leather line in his hand, he reached toward the headboard. Through sheer force of will, Vincent resisted the urge to tip his head back and watch.

Fingertips brushed his wrist.

"Stop." The words burst from Vincent's throat.

A heavy furrow on his brow, Oliver rocked back onto his heels. Oliver opened his mouth, but before he could give voice to a single word, Vincent spoke.

"No. You don't need to stop. I just wanted to…check."

"You doubted I would stop if you asked?"

"No, of course not. I just…" Ah, hell. Now he felt ridiculous. He let out a breath. "I'm not very good at this," he admitted.

Oliver smiled, indulgent and understanding. "It's only your first time, Vincent. You should not expect perfection of yourself." He leaned down and brushed his lips against Vincent's. A fleeting ghost of a kiss that still somehow managed to calm Vincent's racing pulse. "If you promise not to move, we can make do without the line."

"No, I want you to tie me." He could do this. Was determined to prove to Oliver that he *could* do it. He had asked it of Oliver enough times that it only seemed fitting that he allowed his lover the same liberty.

Oliver was silent for a moment, then he nodded. "All right." Rather than reach for the headboard again, he scooted off the mattress and bent down. When he returned to Vincent's side, he held not the leather line but his wrinkled white cravat.

This time when fingers brushed his wrist he didn't even flinch.

"Hold this," Oliver whispered.

Vincent opened his hand, then closed it around what had to be the end of the cravat. Tipping his head back, he looked to the headboard. Oliver had tied the cravat to one cuff, passed the length through a ring on the other, and secured him to one of the spindles with a simple loop knot, the end of which now rested in Vincent's palm. His lover had put the means to untie himself in his own hand.

No doubt at all. Oliver could see right through him.

"Now that you're tied to the bed, what comes next?" Oliver asked, trying but failing to keep the pleased smile from his lips.

Vincent narrowed his eyes. "Suck my cock, boy."

A visible shudder went through his lover. That agile tongue darted out to sweep across his full bottom lip. "Well, I do believe you're correct," he said without even a hint of a tease.

After setting his spectacles on the bedside table, Oliver moved to kneel between Vincent's spread legs. He wrapped a hand around Vincent's length and lowered his head.

It took no time at all for Oliver to coax his cock to full attention. Soft lips slid up and down his length, fluid and effortless, as if the man had been born to suck his cock. The crown bumped the back of Oliver's throat with each stroke as the man worked his fist in counterpoint. The heavy, wet suction of his lover's mouth had the hint of an orgasm teasing Vincent's ballocks. Rather than pull back, Oliver pressed onward. Sucking harder. Stroking faster.

Was this all Oliver wanted? To tie him up and suck him off? He ignored the twinge of disappointment and reveled in the heady rush of sensation as a climax barreled closer and closer. His body drew tight. His panting breaths echoed in his ears. His hand flexed around the end of the cravat as he resisted the almost overpowering urge to free himself, to grab the back of Oliver's head and urge him to take even more.

With a crude popping noise, Oliver abruptly pulled free. Air brushed across Vincent's wet, aching erection.

"More," Vincent demanded, lifting his hips.

Oliver's eyes were heavily-lidded, glazed with desire, with stark, undeniable need. Yet the man shook his head. He dragged his forearm across his mouth, using his shirtsleeve to wipe his very wet and very red lips. "No more of that." He spoke as though he was more trying to convince himself than give an order.

The man shifted off the bed. He closed his eyes for a moment, hands fisted at his sides. A deep breath expanded his chest, the air shuddering on the exhale. When his lashes swept up, the stark, unbridled need in the dark depths of his eyes had dimmed just a fraction.

"Oliver," Vincent growled. "What do you plan to do next?" Obviously, Oliver wasn't done with him yet. At least he better not be. If the man intended to leave him like this, skin beaded with sweat and poised on the brink of a climax…

A little furrow creased his brow. "It really bothers you that you don't know what comes next."

It hadn't been a question, but still, Vincent answered. "Yes," he bit out through clenched teeth. He lifted his shoulders from the bed and watched as Oliver went back to the trunk.

He should have known. The man had left it open.

Oliver leaned down. His trousers stretched across his firm, round arse. Vincent flexed his bound hands.

"All right then. I'll tell you. I'm going to fuck you." Straightening, Oliver turned to face him. "With one of these first."

Vincent's eyes flared. He recognized each object. An elegant jade dildo with raised bands along the length. A short, fat steel plug. And a long, thick black marble dildo—Oliver's favorite toy.

How could he have forgotten he had packed that one?

Vincent's gaze didn't leave Oliver as the man put the three toys on the bedside table.

Oliver pulled a bottle of oil from the bedside table drawer. "Legs up," he murmured, as he got back onto the bed.

Taking a deep breath, Vincent did as he was bid, drawing his bent knees up toward his chest. He made a mental note to be on his guard the next time Oliver made a large purchase for his bookshop. He was sensing a pattern…that involved him getting buggered.

Oliver opened the bottle, then went still. He frowned. "Stop thinking, Vincent. The only thing you need to do is enjoy. No responsibilities whatsoever."

Easy for you to say. Well, it *was* easy for Oliver. The man gave up control so easily, so effortlessly, it was like drawing breath for him.

"All right. I shall try."

"Thank you." Oliver pressed a kiss to his shin. "That's all I ask."

Oliver poured oil onto his fingertips. His touch light and teasing and *oh*, so damn luscious, he coated Vincent's entrance. Tracing the perimeter. Swirling over the sensitive flesh. And then he slipped one finger inside.

Vincent's eyes drifted shut. He let out a groan, his body clamping around that digit, eager for more. The thought of getting buggered never held much appeal for him. The actual act though...

Shifting his hips, he bore down on Oliver's finger, desperate for the full length. Desperate to be filled. Oliver pushed a second finger inside. Another groan rumbled Vincent's chest. Then Oliver pulled free.

Vincent's eyes flew open. He would have never guessed it of his lover, but the man was a damn tease.

Oliver reached for the bedside table again. "Which one should I choose?" A rhetorical question if ever Vincent heard one, so he kept his opinion to himself. Oliver's hand hovered over the black marble dildo. "This one's my favorite, but you already know that." His voice dropped to a dreamy murmur, as if lost in a decadent memory. "Almost rivals your cock, but it's not quite long enough."

His fingers tightened around the end of the cravat in his hand. While Oliver's prick certainly did not rival his own in size, it damn well felt huge when it was in his arse. He was suddenly acutely aware of his own hard prick resting on his abdomen. The weight of it, the length and the width. How did it feel to Oliver when Vincent buggered him? How would it feel to be stretched that wide, stuffed that full?

A heavy jolt of lust shot straight to his groin.

"But not tonight." Oliver's hand closed around the plug.

As the man liberally coated the steel with oil, a thread of nervousness seeped into Vincent's gut. Oliver had barely prepared him. At its widest point, the plug appeared almost as thick as Vincent's own cock. "Oliver..."

He must have heard the warning, for Oliver said, "Trust me, Vincent." A little smile playing on his lips, Oliver pressed another kiss to Vincent's shin. "I'm not about to just shove it inside of you. I'll go slow."

True to his word, Oliver went slow, pushing the blunt, narrow tip of the plug inside him. Just that bit of penetration. Teasing Vincent's hole. Slowing pushing in just a fraction of an inch more then pulling back out. Oliver caressed the back of his thigh with his other hand. The long, slow sweeps of his palm were the perfect accompaniment to the luscious strokes. But rather than lull his senses, each thrust made him hungry for another. Another longer thrust. For more stretch. But Oliver kept to his frustratingly slow pace.

Arching, Vincent lifted his hips into the next stroke. "Oliver," he said, coming dangerously close to a plea.

The man shook his head. "Not yet."

"Oliver," he growled, with a tug against his bonds.

"I want this to feel good for you. And it will, if you'll let me do it my way. Trust me. I know how big this plug is."

Vincent's brow furrowed. He had shoved that plug inside Oliver on more occasions than he cared to count, with little more than a couple of hasty fingers worth of preparation. "Do you not like it when I—"

"*Oh*, I like it." Oliver pushed the plug a bit deeper on the next downstroke. A wicked grin tipped his lips. "But I've also had considerably more *practice* at this than you. And well..." Another fraction of an inch deeper, but nothing near to what Vincent needed. "I've discovered why you're so fond of playing with my arse."

Vincent clamped his eyes shut. Dear Lord, Oliver was staring at his hole. But shutting his eyes only made him more aware of the slow, slick glide of the steel in and out of his well-oiled arse.

"You're gorgeous, Vincent."

Thick and heavy with wonder, the compliment washed over him, ratcheting the lust soaking his senses even higher.

Oliver kept slowly deepening the strokes. Vincent let out a grunt at the hint of stretching pain. He lifted his head, trying to see how much more he needed to take, but his erection, jutting stiff and hard between his legs, obscured the view. A drop of fluid dripped from the crown, falling to his abdomen. He gasped as that hint became true stretch.

"Relax, Vincent," Oliver whispered. His harsh panting breaths matched Vincent's own. "Let it in. It will feel good."

In and then out. More and more with each stroke, pushing him beyond anything he'd ever felt before. Vincent's head fell back onto the pillow. He clenched his jaw against the pain swamping his senses. His nerves screamed in protest, but *damnation*, it felt good.

A groan ripped from his throat as he was stretched unbelievably wide. Then the sharp lance of pain eased as the thick width slipped past the tight ring of muscle and the metal base settled against him.

Oliver gently jostled the base.

"Fuck!" Vincent shouted, as he fought back the climax suddenly gripping his ballocks.

"Feel good?"

He struggled to catch his breath. "You needn't sound so smug."

His lover let out a little chuckle and pressed on his knee. "You can lower your legs but keep them spread." He shifted off the bed.

"What are you going to get now?"

"Nothing." He pulled his shirt from his waistband, and then whisked the garment over his head, revealing the sleek lines of his flawless chest and the flush warming his golden skin. Vincent didn't miss the way Oliver's hands shook the barest amount as he tugged on the placket. The man pushed down his trousers and drawers in one hasty shove, freeing his beautiful prick. The tip was damp with moisture, the length so rigid it jutted from his body.

As he got back onto the bed, he grabbed the bottle of oil once again and poured a generous amount into his palm.

Unable to stay still, Vincent shifted. "What are you going to do?"

Oliver's hand closed around Vincent's cock, quickly slicking the length. Then he straddled Vincent's hips and leaned forward, bracing a hand beside one of Vincent's raised arms. With his other hand, he reached behind to grab Vincent's prick, to hold it steady.

"*...you will enjoy it. We both will.*" Oliver's earlier promise echoed in his head. Anticipation rushed through Vincent, stinging his nerves with the force of it.

"What am I going to do?" Oliver slanted his lips over Vincent's in a quick, searing hot kiss. "This," he whispered.

Oliver pressed down. He fought back the grunt and instead carefully sank lower onto Vincent's cock. His lashes fluttered as he savored that initial thrust. The heavy thread of pain riding behind the pleasure, nearly overpowering it but not quite. The wonderful, all-encompassing feeling of being filled. Playing with Vincent had been divine, but this? Nothing could surpass this.

And knowing the plug was lodged firmly in Vincent's arse? A groan slipped passed Oliver's lips.

When his arse met Vincent's thighs, when he had taken every inch of his lover, he paused. Planting his hands on Vincent's broad chest, he hung his head, let the sensations completely overwhelm him. Having Vincent restrained somehow lessened the urgency, the desperate need for more he felt every other time he'd been with Vincent. When Vincent was in control, Oliver never knew how long the man would gift him with pleasure. A few precious minutes or hours of intense sensation. Each thrust could be the last of the night. The unknown a heady pleasure all its own. Yet with Vincent his to do with as he pleased...

He slowly lifted his hips and picked up a rhythm of leisurely thrusts. Pulling up until the flared head teased his rim then sinking back down. Lingering over each stroke. He adored Vincent's rough fucks. The absolute power and command behind every slam of his lover's hips. Yet this...this was more than nice as well.

Leaning back, he braced his hands on Vincent's thighs and tilted his hips, searching for...

There, there! An added jolt of pleasure coursed through his veins. A moan tumbled past his lips.

A low growl rumbled around him. "Fuck me harder, Oliver."

He shook his head.

"Do it."

For the first time...ever, he ignored a direct order from Vincent in bed. "Not yet," he gasped, as he continued to ride his lover's cock. Up and down. Long, slow, perfect thrusts that had the head of the man's prick pegging his gland with each downstroke.

Stronger and stronger, the pleasure built. He couldn't stop himself from slamming down harder, his prick slapping against Vincent's abdomen. Seeking more. Needing more. Yet, yet...

His breaths hitched in his chest. "*Vincent.*" The name was a plea, soaked in desperation.

Another growl, this one sharper, harsher. The muscles in the strong body beneath him bunched and flexed. Opening his eyes, Oliver lifted his head.

Pure lust blazed in the brilliant blue depths of Vincent's eyes as the man sat up. The length of the cravat dangled from one cuff as he wrapped his arms around Oliver's waist. In one fluid motion, he effortlessly flipped Oliver beneath him, the contact of the bodies unbroken. Oliver pulled his knees fully up to his chest, opening for Vincent as much as he could.

"Is this what you want?" Vincent demanded, as he slammed into him.

"Yes, yes. *Please.*" The words tumbled in a desperate rush from his mouth.

Hard and relentless and so wonderfully deep, Vincent pounded into him. Unable to do anything but serve as a willing vessel for Vincent's lust, Oliver clung to his shoulders. His gasping grunts blended with Vincent's. The bed creaked under the onslaught. Every muscle in his body drew unbearably tight, then pleasure exploded across his senses. He climaxed, spilling onto his stomach. With an all-mighty howl, Vincent rammed hilt deep, filling Oliver with hot seed. Then he collapsed half on top of Oliver, his broad, sweat-slicked chest heaving under the force of his heavy breaths.

Oliver slung his arm over Vincent's back and let his eyes drift closed. A smile curved his lips. Good thing they weren't at his bachelor's apartment. That howl would have woken the entire building.

It was many moments later when Vincent lifted his head. "Next time you need to travel on business, I'm going with you."

Oliver forced his sated brain to process his lover's words. He chuckled. "If you insist."

His lover shifted onto his elbows, then he let out a grunt. Oliver was about to ask if he had pulled something—the evening's activities had definitely approached strenuous—when the source of that grunt occurred to him. He did his best to keep the lascivious smile off his lips. "Do you want me to help you with that?"

The question earned him a scowl. Vincent pushed up onto his knees and reached behind him. "I can manage it on my own." He took a deep breath. A harsh wince pulled his brows, compressing his lips into a straight line. "I'm going to feel that for a week," he muttered, dropping the plug onto the floor.

Oliver couldn't stop the possessive growl from rumbling his throat. "Love you."

"I love you, too. Now up with you." He swatted at Oliver's hip. "Unless you plan to sleep with your head at the foot of the bed."

It took some effort to coordinate his muscles and limbs enough to turn around, crawl to the pillows, and tug back the coverlet. He should play Vincent's role, remove the cuffs from his wrists and ankles and offer him a wet towel to clean up, but, well…Vincent seemed content to handle that part on his own. So he merely laid there and waited for his lover to douse the candles and return to bed.

The mattress shook, jostling him back from the edge of sleep. Strong arms wrapped around him and pulled him close to a wonderfully warm body.

He rubbed his cheek against Vincent's chest. "You should know that wasn't how I had intended the evening to end."

"You didn't plan to splatter us both with seed?"

"Well, yes, but I wanted to make you climax first. You never do when you're buggering me. And I wanted to toy with the plug a bit more. To give you the best of both sides, at the same time."

The beginnings of a chuckle shook Vincent's chest. "You are welcome to try again. But not now and not too soon. Those cuffs won't be available for a few weeks…as they'll be on you."

A fission of anticipation skipped through him. He never would have guessed he'd enjoy dominating Vincent so much. Definitely an enjoyable experience. But being cuffed and bound for Vincent's pleasure? His lashes fluttered. "Promise?"

"Most assuredly."

About the Author

Ava March is an author of smoking hot M/M historical erotic romance. She loves writing in the Regency time period, where proper decorum is of the utmost importance, but where anything can happen behind closed doors.

www.AvaMarch.com
www.avamarch.blogspot.com
twitter.com/Ava_March
www.facebook.com/AvaMarchBooks
www.goodreads.com/Ava_March

Made in the USA
Charleston, SC
06 August 2012